MW00780341

A Daring Pursuit

Other Books by Stephenia H. McGee

Ironwood Plantation
The Whistle Walk
Heir of Hope
Missing Mercy
*Ironwood Series Set
*Get the entire series at a discounted price

The Accidental Spy Series
*Previously published as The Liberator Series
An Accidental Spy
A Dangerous Performance
A Daring Pursuit
*Accidental Spy Series Set
*Get the entire series at a discounted price

Stand Alone Titles
In His Eyes
Eternity Between Us

Time Travel
Her Place in Time
(Stand alone, but ties to Rosswood from The Accidental Spy Series)
The Hope of Christmas Past
(Stand alone, but ties to Belmont from In His Eyes)

Novellas
The Heart of Home
The Hope of Christmas Past

www.StepheniaMcGee.com
Sign up for my newsletter to be the first to see new cover reveals
and be notified of release dates
New newsletter subscribers receive a free book!
Get yours here
bookhip.com/QCZVKZ

A Daring Pursuit

THE ACCIDENTAL SPY

SERIES

Book Three

Stephenia H. McGee

A Daring Pursuit
Copyright © 2020 by Stephenia H. McGee

An updated and revised rewrite of the previously published title
Labeling Lincoln

Copyright © 2016 Stephenia H. McGee. All rights reserved.

www.StepheniaMcGee.com

This novel is a work of fiction. Though some locations and certain events may be historically accurate, names, characters, incidents and dialogue are either products of the author's imagination or are used fictitiously. Any resemblance to actual events, organizations, or persons, living or dead, is entirely coincidental and beyond the author's intent.

All rights reserved. This book is copyrighted work and no part of it may be reproduced, stored, or transmitted in any form or by any means (electronic, mechanical, photographic, audio recording, or any information storage and retrieval system) without the author's written permission. The scanning, uploading and distribution of this book via the Internet or any other means without the author's permission is illegal and punishable by law. Thank you for supporting the author's rights by purchasing only the authorized editions.

Cover art: By The Vine Press, Photography by Melissa Harper
Cover Models: Katie Beth Simmons
Cover Design: Carpe Librum Book Design

Library Cataloging Data
McGee, Stephenia H. (Stephenia H. McGee) 1983 –
Labeling Lincoln: The Liberator Series Book Three/ Stephenia H. McGee
376p. 5.5 in. × 8.5 in. (13.97 cm × 21.59 cm)
By The Vine Press digital eBook edition | By The Vine Press Trade paperback edition | Mississippi: By The Vine Press, 2020
Summary: A Southern Belle struggles to keep her plantation and regain the man she loves.
Identifiers: Library of Congress Control Number: 2020933999 | ISBN-13: 978-1-63564-051-9 (trade) | 978-1-63564-050-2 (ebk.)
1. Historical Christian 2. Clean romance 3. American Historical 4. Mystery and adventure 5. Redemptive healing 6. Overcoming racism 7. Spies and espionage

For Katie Beth,
A young lady who is as beautiful on the inside
As she is on the outside.

One

"To sin by silence, when they should protest, makes
cowards out of men."
Abraham Lincoln

Washington, D.C.
April 15, 1865
8:00 a.m.

*E*verything hurt. Annabelle's feet throbbed from walking,
her raw eyes burned from crying, and her shoulders
refused to relax after the harrowing night she'd endured. The
physical discomfort brought a leaden weariness to her bones,
but the exhaustion of feeling—the terror in the theatre, the
momentary joy of Matthew's declaration, and then the crushing
weight of despair at knowing the North would seek retribution
for Lincoln's blood—made her truly ache.

She pinched the bridge of her nose and tried to remain
calm. Surely they wouldn't make her wait much longer. Didn't
they know she held information that could bring this all to an
end?

Annabelle tapped her foot nervously underneath the table as
she waited for the lawman to return. Her head pounded with the

pulse of unanswered questions, lurking fears, and the lack of sleep. She closed her eyes and attempted to push aside her doubts. Soul weary or not, this had been the right thing to do.

Then she could finally return to Rosswood. If she had a home to return to.

She could hear the others, even this far down the hall—agitated voices and the hum of pent-up frustration and excitement. How many people were out there now? Fifty? A hundred? She suppressed a shiver and shifted her weight on the hard chair. Why were they detaining so many? It seemed as though every person in Ford's had either come—or been dragged—into the Washington police station.

The door opened with a bang and Annabelle jumped, her hand flying to her thudding heart. The officer, who'd introduced himself as Mr. Fitch, strode into the cramped office. He twitched his mustache as he flipped through a stack of papers in his hand. He looked even more displeased than when he'd first escorted her to this office. He circled around his plain desk and sat behind it, not meeting her eyes.

The exhausted man's oiled hair hung limp across his forehead as he squinted at the pages in his hand, and he kept angrily flipping the locks away from his eyes. The more he did so, the more disheveled he appeared.

Finally, he leveled his deep brown eyes on her. "You say you have new information?"

"Yes, sir. Very important." She'd known O'Malley had plotted an abduction, but she hadn't known Mr. Booth sought murder. She glanced to the door, the noises of the people growing louder, and clasped her hands tightly.

He gave a sniff. "Already interviewed eight young ladies that were in the theatre last night. All claimed their particular story was important."

Had someone listened to her a week ago, perhaps neither of them would be regarding one another with thinly veiled distaste now. "I don't suppose any of *them* knows the identities of the conspirators nor foiled the original abduction plot on the road to the Soldier's Home a month past."

Surprise widened the officer's eyes, and she felt a momentary swell of satisfaction. A short-lived triumph, however, because now his face reddened. "How would you know about *that?*"

She ran her trembling fingers along the embroidered edge of her sleeve. "I warned Mr. Lincoln's driver about their plans." She met his assessing gaze. "Do you know how the president fares?"

He gave her a sour look. "He's dead. Passed about half an hour ago."

A single tear rolled down her cheek and she whisked it away. The tolls of the melancholy bells had long since told her what she'd not wished to know, and Mr. Fitch's clipped words only provided the confirmation she didn't truly need.

Mr. Fitch regarded her for a long time, and Annabelle held his gaze, unsure if she should speak further until he made his intentions clear. She flicked another nervous glance to the door.

Finally, Mr. Fitch pushed his chair away from his desk and the sudden movement made Annabelle startle. She offered a fabricated smile as he propped his ankle on his knee.

"Perhaps you should start from the beginning."

Her mind scurried back across the last weeks and her swirling tumult of emotions. Deciding succinct words might best appease the stern face across from her, Annabelle settled on firing out only the most pertinent details. "I first discovered the plot while here in Washington about a month ago. I overheard men talking in the boarding house parlor. They disclosed their intentions to abduct Mr. Lincoln later that afternoon and take him away to Richmond. They said they planned to ransom him for the release of Confederate soldiers."

Mr. Fitch nodded along, writing in his little book.

Remembering the disaster she'd almost caused when she'd told the major at Elmira prison that George was her brother, she'd decided to be forthcoming with everything she knew. "While looking for a hired coach to take me to my mother's family in New York, I happened upon a young man by the name of Thomas Clark, who claimed to be Mr. Lincoln's personal driver. I told him some men were planning on overrunning the carriage on the way to the Soldier's Home. It's my understanding that he warned Mr. Lincoln of this, and the president changed his plans, going to the National Hotel instead."

Mr. Fitch stroked the pointed beard on the tip of his chin. "And where were you when you learned of this plot?"

"At the Surratt Boarding House."

He scribbled quickly with a nub of pencil. "Which men had this discussion?"

"Mr. David O'Malley and Mr. Harry Thompson. There were other men involved, but the only one I recognized was John Wilkes Booth."

Forgive me, Father. I can't say Matthew's name. I cannot condemn him.

Mr. Fitch frowned at the remark and made another notation. "And you're certain you saw Booth?"

Annabelle ran her tongue over her lips, trying to get them moist again. "I followed the men—there were seven of them, I believe—to the road and watched the entire thing. I recognized Mr. Booth from a likeness I'd seen in town. A playbill, or some such, I believe."

"And you didn't think to inform the law?"

Annabelle offered an apologetic smile that Mr. Fitch didn't return. "I thought the matter settled, and since I had urgent business in New York, I left later that day."

"To see the family you mentioned."

Her heart thudded, but she'd promised herself to tell everything. "Yes, but not only that. I also went to Elmira prison."

"What for?"

"To find my…." *Friend's? Beau's?* "To find Mr. Daniels's brother. I'd learned from the Commissary General's Office here in Washington that he'd been imprisoned at Elmira."

"And this was your reason for being in Washington a month past?"

"Yes, sir." True enough. Finding George *had* been their reason to go to Washington. When she reached the part about Matthew finding George on the riverbank, she paused.

Mr. Fitch leaned forward in his chair.

"Matthew found George freezing and took him back to our room to warm him."

Mr. Fitch stared hard at her. "He helped a prisoner escape?"

"George would have died otherwise." She tugged on her pearl earring, but her hand shook so badly she quickly dropped her fingers to her lap. "It wasn't an escape. He'd already signed allegiance papers."

Mr. Fitch scribbled again. "Mr. George Daniels?"

"Yes, sir."

Heat crept up her neck. When George had come back to the hotel during the wee hours this morning, he'd found her and Matthew locked in an embrace.

"So why did you return to Washington after you took Mr. Daniels from Elmira?" Mr. Fitch asked without looking up from his writing.

"One of the men I mentioned, Harry, followed us. When Matthew questioned him, he found out that Mr. O'Malley was working on another abduction plot. He came straight to Washington to try to stop Mr. O'Malley."

"And when was this?"

Annabelle thought back. "I'm not sure exactly—but around the time when Richmond fell."

"And you came with him?"

She shook her head. "George, my grandmother, my maid, and I came separately."

He set his pencil aside. "And *none* of you thought to report this to the law?"

She straightened her shoulders, wishing she could rub the aching muscles. "Of course we did. My grandmother informed Mr. William Crook about the abduction plans. He said that the president received many such threats and that we shouldn't worry. They would see to his safety." Her tone held a touch of bitterness she couldn't contain.

Mr. Fitch scowled. "Indeed." He sat back in his chair and propped his ankle on his knee once more, regarding her. "And why, then, were you at the theatre last eve?"

"My grandmother purchased tickets. I knew that Mr. Booth had been on the road the day that O'Malley had first planned to abduct Mr. Lincoln. So when we learned Mr. Lincoln would be going to the theatre, we assumed Mr. Booth knew the building well and concluded it would be a good opportunity for the men to attempt another abduction." Her voice hitched. "But we never expected…." She squeezed her eyes shut.

"There, there, miss. It's all right." Mr. Fitch pulled a handkerchief out of his coat pocket, surprising her with a dose of sympathy. "We're all distraught over this tragedy."

She accepted the offered cloth and dabbed her eyes, then handed it back with a tired smile. "Thank you."

Mr. Fitch placed the handkerchief into a drawer in his desk. "Did you inform anyone of your suspicions about Mr. O'Malley and the possibility of an abduction at the theatre?"

"Mr. Crook knew. He promised Mr. O'Malley would be arrested immediately, should he be seen in the theatre."

Mr. Fitch's frown deepened, and he made another note in his little book before snapping it closed.

The policeman rose and rounded the desk, and Annabelle stood as he approached. Feeling relieved, she turned toward the door. "I do hope this information has helped you some, Mr. Fitch. I'll be in my room at the National Hotel, should you wish to ask me anything further."

Mr. Fitch's fingers clamped down on her elbow. His eyes looked sad, but hard lines firmed his mouth. "I'm sorry, Miss Ross, but I'm afraid you cannot leave our custody just yet."

"I…what?"

"I'm going to have to detain you until we can look deeper into your claims."

Annabelle couldn't come up with a response as Mr. Fitch gently led her out the door.

Matthew paced the floor, his boots thudding against the wood in a steady rhythm. The holding area of the Metropolitan Police building overflowed with people of various degrees of unrest. Some seemed eager to be in the midst of the commotion while others fidgeted and paced nervously. Men, women, and even a few youths crammed into the small holding space and waited their turn at questioning. Had the policemen detained everyone on the street outside of Ford's?

He tightened his fists and tried to remind himself he hadn't been brought in for questioning. He'd come on his own volition to offer information. Flashes of the conditions at Elmira flitted through his mind, and he had to shake his head in a futile effort to dislodge them.

A strangled noise off to his left made him twist. His elbow clipped a disgruntled gentleman in a fine suit. The other opened his mouth to protest, then seemed to think better of it and ducked away. Matthew frowned at him, wondering what had sent the man scurrying like a mouse. People shifted and the space around him widened.

Heat swirled up from his chest and pulsed through the vein in his neck. He must look half-mad. Struggling to gain control of his emotions, Matthew forced his features to relax and lowered his eyes.

A door to his right opened and a young man of about eighteen or twenty years entered the lobby. He scanned the room with a determined gaze, his shoulders straight in his pressed suit. A policeman's polished silver badge shone brightly against his blue double-breasted jacket.

"Mr. Daniels?" the man called out over the hum of a dozen private conversations.

"Here!"

The younger man tilted his chin back to regard Matthew as he stepped near. "You're the brother of a Mr. George Daniels. Correct?"

"I am."

"This way, sir." The policeman gestured toward a hallway behind him.

Matthew tugged on the knot of his blue cravat in an attempt to keep the foul thing from choking him. George had been called back first, and it'd been hours since Matthew had last seen him. Then they'd taken Annabelle, and his composure had begun to slide as soon as her delicate fingers had slipped free of his grasp.

How long had he been waiting? At least what he'd shouted to a passing officer about the Surratt house seemed to gain their attention. As far as he knew, they'd since sent men to investigate. If they'd found anything, though, it hadn't made much difference. They still left Matthew waiting with the other people they'd collected off the streets without thought to who might know something important and who might be here only for a bit of the excitement.

He followed the young policeman down a hallway lined with closed doors. Where were George and Annabelle? When George had returned to the hotel hours earlier, it had been to tell them he'd caught a glimpse of Booth galloping away but hadn't been able to stop him.

Matthew knew where Booth might be headed, but every

person who'd been in the theatre or had joined the crowd outside in the streets thought they had something important to say.

Fools.

"Here we are, sir." The officer opened a heavy door at the end of the hall. Without waiting for a response, he turned and strode back toward the crowded waiting area.

Inside, a man with dark hair and a trimmed mustache stared at him expectantly. The man motioned toward a chair in front of his plain desk. "Take a seat, Mr. Daniels." He flipped open a small writing book.

Matthew pulled the door closed behind him and positioned himself in the chair without taking his eyes off the man across from him. Likely another officer, but he didn't sport a polished badge on his rumpled jacket.

The man rolled a short pencil between his fingers. "State your name please, sir."

"You already know my name."

The man looked up from his paper with a sniff. "I've been told your identity. I wish to hear it in your own words."

"Matthew Gregory Daniels of Westerly Plantation, Mississippi. Former captain, Mississippi Infantry, Confederate Army under the command of—"

The man held up his hand to slow Matthew's words and scribbled in his little book. "You served in the Rebel Army, is this correct?"

"I just said—"

"Brother to a George Daniels, also of Westerly Plantation, Mississippi?"

Matthew clamped the rounded edges of the armrests and

refused to answer until the man lifted his eyes from his writing. "Who are you?"

"Mr. Fitch."

They regarded one another for some time before Fitch turned his attention back to his scribbling. "Are you brother to a George Daniels of West—"

"Yes," Matthew said, cutting the man's repetition short. "What does that have to do with Booth?"

The man's eyebrows dipped for only an instant before an indifferent look smoothed his forehead again. "You do understand, of course, that knowing the purpose and identity of everyone giving a statement is imperative to our search?"

"And you, *of course*, understand that you've already wasted valuable time and let your quarry escape. I told your men hours ago I knew where he was going. Not one seemed interested."

Fitch stroked his mustache. "How well do you know Mr. Booth?"

"Not well."

"On how many occasions have you met with him?"

"Only one."

"And this was…?"

Annabelle and George had both insisted that each of them give a full accounting. He'd even planned on coming here himself before O'Malley had followed the Grants. But now, sitting in this chair with a Yankee regarding him with thinly disguised suspicion, the words stuck in his mouth.

The man started writing again.

Matthew scowled. "What are you doing? I didn't say any-thing."

"Precisely."

Matthew made a low noise in his throat and Fitch looked up expectantly. "I met Booth on only one occasion, when he was introduced to me by David O'Malley. After that introduction I was in his presence only once more, on the day when they planned to abduct Lincoln and take him to Richmond."

"And you were a part of this ploy?"

"I was." The words felt like needles as they passed his tongue. They pierced and stung with the promise of painful repercussions.

"And were you aware that Mr. Booth planned an assassination of President Lincoln?"

"I was not."

"But you did tell one of my fellow officers—" he flipped through his pages, "—that you 'knew who the assassin was.'" He tapped his pencil on the page. "Is that correct?"

"It is." How much did this man already know? Judging by the look in his eyes, probably enough to decide Matthew's fate. Everything within him rebelled against this pretentious Yank and his foul little notebook, but he stretched his neck and tried to release some of the tension from his shoulders.

He'd promised Annabelle he'd give a truthful account.

Fitch looked at him curiously, then slowly closed his book and sat back. "Is there something you wish to disclose?"

Hoping he wasn't about to lose all he'd only so recently gained, Matthew nodded. "I was involved in a plot to abduct, but never to murder, your president. After the failed attempt to take his carriage, I left Washington. You can arrest me for that if you wish. But first, I can help you catch the men responsible."

Fitch snatched up his pen eagerly. "Men?"

"One was sent to kill General Grant. I can tell you everything you need to know about him. Booth would have gone to Surrattsville, where these same men stashed weapons and supplies at the tavern."

Fitch narrowed his eyes and stared at him for a moment, a myriad of emotions scurrying over his face. Finally, settling on determination, he gave a single nod. "Mr. Daniels, I have a proposition for you."

Two

"Lincoln is gone at last. Booth has carried out his oft-repeated threat, and has, so it is said, really taken the life of the tyrant."
John H. Surratt

George struggled to keep his composure as they led him deeper into the bowels of the prison. Sweat beaded on his forehead fell into his eyes. He squinted and wiped at his face with the sleeve of the fine jacket Mrs. Smith had given him.

Old Capitol Prison.

Only weeks out of Elmira, and already they were bringing him back! George tried to remain calm as the thought swirled around within him, stoking fires of both fear and anger. His breath quickened, heaving his chest rapidly. He still couldn't find enough air to breathe freely. His stomach roiled.

Inside. At least it's inside. Won't freeze.

George shook his head vigorously in an attempt to clear his thoughts, and the policeman at his side took a small step closer. George swallowed the bile rising in his throat.

Held for questioning. Short time. Just a short time.

His teeth chattered, his body reliving the horrors of Elmira.

No. He wasn't being arrested. They only wanted to question him. Just questions. No overcrowded tents, no coffin duty. No men wallowing in their own filth…or the Hopeless on the wall staring at him with empty eyes….

Can't go back! Won't go back.

George spun on the uneven stone floor and lurched forward. His guard let out a cry and lunged for him, but George sidestepped the move and broke into a sprint. His vision narrowed, blocking out his view of the other cells he passed. His mind strained for the only hope of salvation—the lone doorway at the end of this impossibly long corridor.

His feet pounded on the floor, his hands reaching out in an effort to grasp the door. It was there, heavy wood banded in iron, close enough to promise escape. He could make it. Leaping over a broom handle that had fallen across the way, George ignored the startled expression of a boy who'd been sweeping a moment earlier.

"You! Halt!"

The guard shouted behind him, but he couldn't stop now. He should have run from Elmira. Should have tried at least. They'd taken his pride, his honor, and nearly his life. And he'd let them. Not again.

Three more strides. Five at the most. How can it be so far away?

Liars. All of them. He'd signed their papers. Pledged himself to them—in treason to his own country!—and still they sought to lock him away! George's hand closed around the cool metal of the door handle.

Victory!

The Yanks wouldn't take him again. They would not get the chance to—

His breath left him in a whoosh as he hit the floor, jarring all the thoughts of escape from his head. Someone shouted, and a heavy weight pressed down between his shoulders. His captor wrenched his arms behind him, tying George's hands with a coarse rope before rolling George over.

"Now what'd you have to go and do that for?"

George blinked at him rapidly, and the sneer of an Elmira guard, the one they'd dubbed Corporal Carnage, faded away. In its place loomed the curious expression of a man in his forties with sandy hair and bushy mutton chops.

"I...uh...." George licked his lips. What had happened to him? His heart still thudded wildly, but his mind cleared. "I wasn't...myself."

The man grunted and pulled George to his feet. "I know it's not the best, but orders are we've got to hold you all, at least until they catch him."

The guard...*policeman*... seemed agreeable enough, even though he now kept a firm hand on George's elbow as they started down the hallway once again. He kept glancing at George's profile, and George couldn't say he blamed the man.

"You have nightmares?" the man asked softly.

George looked over at him. "Nightmares?"

The man nodded, speaking low. "I've seen lads like you. All tore up in the head about what they've seen on the battlefield. Gets to some more than others. Some, you wouldn't even know unless something sets them off."

He knew this wasn't Elmira, but his body responded as though it was. "No, no nightmares." He gave the boy with the broom a sheepish shrug as they passed.

"Hmm." The man didn't sound convinced. Not that George

faulted him there either.

They came to a stop in front of a cell with thick bars and nothing but a cot and chamber pot inside. "That's good though, right?"

The policeman opened the door and guided George inside. Then he flicked open a knife and cut through the short length of rope, freeing George's hands. "Most of the boys, they get nightmares. You had one of those attacks, best I can figure, which means you probably have the nightmares, too."

"Attacks?" George rubbed his wrists.

The pity in the policeman's eyes made George uncomfortable. "Makes a fellow do funny things."

George straightened himself in an effort to regain a little of his dignity. "Thank you. For telling me." He tugged on the hem of his jacket. "And for not making it worse on me."

"Don't worry, lad. Soon as they find that actor fellow, then this'll all be over and you'll be free to go."

George nodded and sat down on his cot. *Free to go....*

A moment later the door clanged, jarring his senses. He fell back on the hard bed, panic rising. Closing his eyes helped some, as did focusing on each breath as he pulled it in and released it. Perhaps in a moment this strange sensation would pass.

Images flashed through his mind unbidden. Broken bodies. The gut-churning smell. And the boxes. So many boxes to make.

No!

He had to think about something, *anything* else, or he might find himself in a fit of madness. He'd spent weeks at the Smith house in New York without suffering any effects from his time at Elmira.

A lovely face filled his mind. Smooth, delicate features. Shimmering waves of ebony hair that begged his fingers to touch its softness. *Lilly Rose.* A mystery he'd yet to solve. He thought about the way her eyes glimmered and the smile that bloomed on her lips for little Frankie.

As George thought about playing with the boy, his heartbeat slowed. He pictured himself tossing the tot in the air and the joyful sound of childish giggles. Finally, his sweat dried and his breathing turned even. Keeping his eyes closed against the reality of the prison, George thought back on his time with Lilly and Frankie.

Lilly Rose, the strikingly beautiful woman who worked in the Smith house. Not a lady of family means, but what did that matter to him? Father could no longer dictate he must marry a woman of wealth. He could court whomever he wished.

A warm sensation filled him at the thought, pushing away the lingering chill reluctant to leave his veins. He embraced the feeling and let his mind conjure images of evening strolls, afternoon teas, and morning rides. They'd bring the boy along, and George would teach him to cast a line while Lilly set out a picnic lunch in the meadow.

George began to drift off and smiled as the little Frankie in his mind struggled to pierce the worm on his hook while his momma made a face. After they ate, they watched the boy play with butterflies in the field. George took Lilly's hand in his. Her brown eyes grew wide as he slipped a ruby ring onto her finger. A marriage in the spring and, with any luck, a sibling for Frankie come Christmas. She smiled at him, her lips beckoning him to come closer.

The wind picked up and bits of her hair slipped free from under her bonnet. So beautiful, so peaceful. Sighing with contentment, George reached up to tuck one of the freed strands away, but the sudden terror in Lilly's eyes stilled him.

Silently, she pointed behind him. Her fingers trembled and tears welled in her eyes. George turned, only to see the creek where they'd fished now filled with fallen soldiers, their lifeblood draining away and turning the water red. He reached out to pull Lilly to him, but in her place now stood a sneering guard with his rifle pointed right at George's chest.

"In the water you go, Johnny Reb."

George shook his head, but his feet moved involuntarily. He trudged down into the thick mud. It reached up and pulled on his trousers, trying to bring him down. He pulled one foot free, losing his boot to the mud's maw. His toes plunged into the icy water beyond.

His teeth chattered. *Cold. So cold.* Lifeless bodies floated by, bobbing on the current. All the eyes looked at him, accusing.

Where are our boxes? You didn't make us enough boxes. Then you let us drown!

"No!" George lunged into the water. "I tried to save you!" He grabbed the hand of the nearest man. His pock-marked face twisted in a snarl as his lifeless eyes stared at George. The corpse opened his mouth. *"No coffin. No coffin. Only the bottom of the river for me."*

George screamed and released the bony hand. He plunged into the icy depths. Down farther and farther until—

George bolted upright, panting. His clothes soaked in sweat, he shivered violently. He pulled his feet up under him and pressed his back against the wall.

The cold would come for him. Take him in the vulnerable time of his dreams. His failures would haunt him. Where the prison walls robbed him of his waking freedom, the memories would steal his rest. He'd signed allegiance to the enemy in order to save himself. He'd left his brothers in arms to die in shoddy boxes or watery graves.

He'd betrayed them.

Lilly's face rose up in his mind again, but this time he pushed it away. He couldn't bear to see what would happen to her if the nightmare returned.

Despite his exhaustion, George rose and stood in the center of his cell. Standing, he couldn't sleep. And without sleep, he wouldn't see their faces.

Outside, mournful bells tolled their sorrow. George ignored them. He was the mighty oak. Firm, still, and silent. He didn't know how long he stood there. His eyes dried from being forced wide. Eventually, they began to droop. George fought the battle for as long as he could. But soon his body betrayed him and he sank to the floor.

Then the darkness came again.

Three

"Dear Madam, No one can better appreciate than I can, who am myself utterly broken-hearted by the loss of my own beloved husband, who was the light of my life – my stay – my all – what your sufferings must be; and I earnestly pray that you may be supported by Him to whom alone the sorely stricken can look for comfort, in this hour of heavy affliction."
Queen Victoria, in a letter to Mary Lincoln

"I demand to speak to Mr. Crook!" Annabelle wrapped her arms around her waist and pressed her trembling fingers into her sides.

The policeman shook his head. "Sorry, miss. We've been instructed to hold all persons associated with the murder of the president until things can be sorted out."

She'd never seen the inside of a prison before. The older man guided her past several tiny rooms covered with iron bars. Several people filled the cells, all of them seeming just as confused as Annabelle. Presently, they came to a cell about halfway down the corridor. The policeman pulled a heavy ring of keys from his belt and stuck one in the lock. It grated as it turned, and the haunting sound of rubbing metal sent a shiver down her back.

A young woman not much older than herself stood in the far corner.

Annabelle stepped inside and faced her captor. "I've already given my account, which I brought to you of my own free will. I don't see how this is necessary."

The man pushed the bar door closed and the lock slid into place.

She wrapped her fingers around the cold bars. "Sir? Did you hear what I said? There must be a mistake."

"I heard you, miss. But all of Washington City is in turmoil, and until the assassin is caught, all suspected parties will be held."

Before she could form another plea, he strode away down the unusually quiet hall. Did none of the others think to cry out at injustice? Maybe they were too stunned by their imprisonment. Or afraid outcry would make things worse.

Annabelle straightened a slipping pin in her hair and faced the woman behind her. "Hello. I'm Annabelle Ross."

The woman dipped into a shallow curtsy. "G'day, mistress. I'm Alice Taylor."

Annabelle motioned toward the single cot in the room. "Why don't we sit? Since we might be here for a while, we should get to know one another."

The woman drew her lips into a disapproving pucker but did as Annabelle asked. She sat as close to the foot of the cot as she could manage and tucked the sides of her plaid skirt underneath her. Dressed plainly, Miss Taylor wore her auburn hair pulled away from her face in a simple fashion. She watched Annabelle with chestnut eyes.

As Annabelle turned slightly so as to better regard her companion, she noticed the smeared blood still on the sleeve of her white jacket. Was this why they were holding her? Did they think she'd lied about her involvement? She'd told them about the injured man in the president's booth, whom she'd since discovered was a man by the name of Mr. Rathbone.

Miss Taylor stared at the copper-colored stain.

"I tried to help him, but the doctor sent me out," Annabelle said softly.

"Mr. Lincoln?"

"No, though I tried to help him as well. There was another man in the box who'd been badly cut with a knife." Annabelle gestured toward her sleeve. "When he took my arm to ask me to remain outside, he must have had blood on his hand."

Miss Taylor leaned closer. "Did you see it then?"

"It was…horrible. Poor Mrs. Lincoln." The woman's distressed cries had been so wretched. Annabelle forced the sound from her mind. "What about you, Miss Taylor?"

The woman lifted her chin. "Missus."

"Mrs. Taylor," Annabelle corrected. "Did you see anything?" The woman must know something, or she wouldn't be here.

Mrs. Taylor clamped her hands in her lap. "All I know is what they're saying on the streets."

Annabelle frowned. "You weren't in the theatre?"

"No, miss. I was just on my way to the kitchens at the boarding house where I work when I heard this big commotion. People were out in the streets shouting about a great tragedy. I was much distressed about it, but I had to get to work, so I hurried on. But just as I got there, some lawmen were knocking on the door to question the matron, and they saw me trying to go around the back way, like I always do." She twisted her hands together. "They made me come here."

"Where do you work?" How odd the woman would head to work in the middle of the night.

"The Surratt Boarding House." Mrs. Taylor hurried on, apparently guessing Annabelle's thoughts. "I make the bread. That's why I have to be there so early, to get the dough ready for the breakfast. The matron doesn't tolerate anyone coming late." She started to wring her hands again. "I've lost my employment now for certain."

Annabelle chose her words carefully. "So at this place— where you work in the kitchen—there were already policemen there when you arrived?"

"Yes."

"What time was that?"

The other woman answered slowly. "Around four."

Four o'clock this morning. That'd been about the time they'd made plans to go to the Washington police, so the lawmen had already gone to the boarding house before hearing her, Matthew, and George's story. Who else had tipped them off about the Surratt house? "I wonder what they were doing there, so far away from the theatre?"

Mrs. Taylor shook her head. "I sure don't know." She looked back at the door. "But we need the money I make from that job, times being what they are and all."

Annabelle reached over and patted the woman's arm. "Surely your employer will understand, knowing what must have occurred."

The other woman looked doubtful. "Hope so, miss."

"Do you know why policemen would have been around at such an odd hour?"

"Maybe it had something to do with one of the matron's boarders, but I wouldn't know. I only work in the kitchen for the morning and noon meals. I never go into the main house, and I don't know anything about who stays there."

"I stayed there once."

"Did you now?" The woman's eyes widened. "That why you're here?"

Annabelle offered a half-hearted smile. "I was at the theatre, remember?"

"Oh, yes." Alice Taylor's face fell, the curiosity in her eyes replaced by a cool indifference. "Apologies, miss."

"None needed." Annabelle plucked at a loose thread on the embroidery of her skirt. "I believe being in the theatre is what led to my current detainment, but I did stay for a short while at that very boarding house about a month past. On my way through to visit my family in New York."

Mrs. Taylor nodded and fell silent.

Why would they detain the kitchen cook from the boarding house? Were there others from the house here as well? Was her talking about her time in the Surratt house the true reason they detained her?

Annabelle rubbed her temples and tried to push the thoughts aside. Regardless, she'd be here until they caught Booth.

What about Matthew and George? Were they being held as well? The answer beat in her head, in rhythm with her fluttering heart. Of course.

At least her grandmother hadn't come with them to the

police station. Hopefully, that meant she'd remain free.

Trying not to become overly anxious, Annabelle took a ragged breath and reminded herself her best option would be to pray for help. She'd told herself to stop doing everything her own way. So far, that approach had done little more than drop her into quite a bit of trouble.

Annabelle turned back to Mrs. Taylor and offered a timid smile. "Are you a praying woman?"

Matthew crossed his arms. "What sort of proposition?"

Mr. Fitch stroked his mustache. "Are you familiar with the law, Mr. Daniels?"

"As much as any man, I suppose." Had he broken some unknown Yankee ordinance? His foot twitched.

"The law states that an accused cannot bear witness."

Matthew stiffened.

Mr. Fitch watched him a moment longer, then gave a curt nod as though making up his mind on some internal debate. "My recommendation will be you'd be more useful as a witness than as an accused."

And George and Annabelle? Would they—

"Of course, you do understand that the words of a known Rebel will naturally be regarded with suspicion."

Matthew glared at the man. "I've already told you I had nothing to do with the murder and have offered information to aid in your search. The war is finished. You've won. What does it matter if I fought for Mississippi? I came here to *help* you."

The policeman didn't seem at all disturbed by the frustration seething in Matthew's tone. "Perhaps that was a mistake."

"Of course," Mr. Fitch replied, "if you were to sign allegiance papers...." He gave Matthew a meaningful look as he twisted his mustache.

"War's over. What would you need that for?"

"Over, perhaps, but not entirely finished." Mr. Fitch drummed his fingers on the desk, then gave a shrug. "Besides, the words of a loyal Unionist certainly would be more...acceptable...to a military court, wouldn't you say?"

Military court? The implications swirled in Matthew's gut, though he tried to keep any emotions from leaping onto his face.

Mr. Fitch watched Matthew closely.

"Perhaps."

"Your sincerity would be more solid with proven loyalty." Fitch spread his fingers.

"Proven?" Matthew forced his voice to lower. "How much more proof do you need, man? I've already given you the information to catch the murderer and have told you where another would-be murderer is located. For heaven's sake, I put my own life at risk to save a Yankee general! What more proof could you possibly want?"

"Indeed you have." He tapped a finger on his desk. "But these are all claims that have yet to be proven, unfortunately."

Matthew clamped his mouth shut. He was already at the mercy of the Yanks. He spoke slowly, keeping his tone even. "How else, then, might I *prove* my intentions, sir?"

Mr. Fitch reached into a drawer in his desk and pulled out a slip of paper with the words *Oath of Allegiance* printed in large letters across the top. "First, you'd need to sign the proper paperwork. Then, as a loyal patriot, you'd want to aid your country in the search and capture of the conspirators, would you not?"

"What about my brother and my…Miss Ross?"

Mr. Fitch smiled. "We'd keep them safe until you return."

"And after I return?"

"Then as would be the duty of any patriot, they'd wish to give their testimony to the military court." His words were light, but their meaning fell heavy in the room.

Matthew leaned forward. "As witnesses, not as accused?"

"Most likely," Fitch agreed. Then hastily added, "If they've shown they're not involved with the assassination."

Matthew's stomach soured. Annabelle and George had both been at the theatre last night. George, thankfully, hadn't been present for anything else, but Annabelle had been involved in the abduction plot. Thanks to him.

"Once the assassin's been caught," Mr. Fitch said, "then we'll release people who won't stand trial." He tapped the paper. "And Union citizens will be allowed to return to normal life while they wait to testify."

Matthew eyed the paper sitting between them on the desk and withheld a snort. Normal life. Such a thing no longer existed. He set his jaw. What did the formality of allegiance papers matter now anyway? The South had already lost the war and would be subject to Union law again. He picked up Mr. Fitch's pen, twisting it in his fingers. "In what way would I aid in the capture of Booth?"

The man smiled, sensing his victory. "Seeing as you claim to know where the murderer might be going, after you aid the detectives with a few things here in Washington, I'd like for you to go with one of my detectives on the pursuit. You can join up with one of the dispatches, the Sixteenth New York Cavalry."

Join the Yankee Army? Never! Mathew leaned back, away from the traitor's papers.

"A mob tried to burn the Old Capitol Prison. Did you know that?" Mr. Fitch toyed with the edge of the paper.

Matthew narrowed his eyes. "And?"

"It seems the longer the assassin remains free, the more the people try to take out their anger on the Rebels. With all of our men trying to calm the fighting in the streets, who knows how long we will be able to keep things…under control." Mr. Fitch lifted his shoulders. "Seems to me like the best way to keep everyone in holding safe would be to bring the man to justice as quickly as possible."

The words were simple, delivered without the first trace of malice. Even still, the underlying threat caused Matthew's lip to curl. Sign and aid the Yanks or leave his brother and Annabelle to even more dangers than they already faced.

Matthew clutched the pen so tightly it cracked, then he dipped it in the inkwell and scrawled his name on the line.

Four

"I firmly believe that if he had remained at the White
House on that night of darkness, when the fiends
prevailed, he would have been horribly cut to pieces.
Those fiends had too long contemplated this inhuman
murder to have allowed him to escape."
Mary Lincoln

What an odd way to spend Resurrection Sunday. Matthew
followed men in blue uniforms and a small number of
inquisitors down the streets of Washington. It'd taken some
time, but Mr. Fitch had placed Matthew under the suspicious
eyes of the Yankee procession that walked somberly around
him. The fact that it was now eleven o'clock at night seemed to
have no bearing on their mission.

He'd spent Easter in encampments and had listened to
Army preachers give the same story each time. Not much
different from his Easters at Westerly in that regard. But in all of
his twenty-five years, he never expected to spend Resurrection
Sunday in the company of enemy troops on his way to question
a boarding house matron. One who, he felt quite certain, would
loathe to lay eyes on him.

Even at this hour, the church bells continued to toll their lament. Some of the men had commented that the bells rang throughout church services this morning. Services where the preachers compared the loss of Lincoln to the loss of Christ.

They called Lincoln the Great Liberator—the one who would bring peace, restoration, and equality to America. Even if that were all true, which Matthew doubted, it still didn't make the man on the same plane as the Almighty. The fact that the Yanks would even dare say so was evidence they couldn't be trusted.

The group neared the Surratt house and Matthew focused on the issue at hand. Liberator or tyrant, he was dead. And unlike Christ, he wouldn't be coming back.

Major H.W. Smith pounded heavily on the door. The curtains of the window moved, and someone called out just loudly enough for Matthew to catch the words.

"Is that you, Mr. Kirby?" The feminine voice barely penetrated the door enough for Matthew to catch it, but the woman's tone seemed to harbor no concern.

Major Smith cast a curious look at one of the detectives, who then scribbled something in a little book that matched the one Mr. Fitch carried. The major leaned toward the door. "It's not, but you are to open the door, madam."

Presently, the door opened. Mrs. Surratt stood in the entryway, her straight back and calm demeanor giving no evidence she feared the men who'd come at such an hour.

"Are you Mrs. Surratt?" Major Smith's stern voice implied he already knew the answer to his question.

"I'm the widow of John H. Surratt." Her gaze darted from the major to the men standing behind him.

"And the mother of John H. Surratt, Jr.?"

Her gaze fell on Matthew, and fire lit in her eyes. "I am." Her lip curled, but then, just as quickly as the hatred had colored her features, indifference once again settled. Her gaze slid away from Matthew and returned to the major at her door.

"I've come to arrest you and all in your house and to take you for examination to General Augur's headquarters."

With no indication of distress over Major Smith's words, Mrs. Surratt stepped back from the door and granted the party entrance. The last to enter, Matthew met her eyes as he stepped inside. She regarded him coldly, making no further effort to hide her disdain.

What did she think of him coming here in the presence of the Union Army? She thought him a traitor, most likely, and he couldn't say that she'd be wrong.

A traitor to one is but a patriot to the other. All a matter of perspective, he supposed. At the moment, however, he wished to be neither. He wanted only to see this thing finished, his brother and lady safe, and to return home. Mrs. Surratt glared at Matthew as he passed.

The men were seen to the parlor, and Mrs. Surratt, a lady identified as Surratt's daughter, and a couple of others Matthew had never seen before were rounded up to leave. Matthew watched the goings on with interest, curious at the calm the women displayed. Did they not see the peril of their condition?

After a few moments, another man entered. Matthew guessed him to be another detective. The stoic man stomped his feet and shook off his jacket before tucking his cane-reinforced top hat under his arm. His gaze landed on Matthew and he frowned. He opened his mouth to speak but a knock, followed quickly by the ring of the bell at the door, turned their attention toward the entrance. The newcomer cast one last look at Matthew and then spun and reached for the door.

From his position just inside the parlor doorway, Matthew had a good look at the caller when the door swung open. Surprise settled on them, and for a moment, no one spoke.

The man was dressed in a fine gray coat, black pantaloons, and a pair of polished boots. Upon his head the man wore a gray shirtsleeve, hanging over at one side. He'd rolled one leg of the pantaloons up over the top of his boot and slung a pickaxe across one shoulder. He looked like a man who'd tried to hurriedly construct some type of disguise and had failed quite miserably.

The odd man looked over the crowd of occupants, the smallest flash of surprise registering in his gaze. He entered, twisting the handle of his pickaxe. The strange man started toward the parlor without invitation.

"Whom do you want to see?" The detective closed the door.

"Mrs. Surratt." The man slid his gaze over Matthew and the others in the parlor and then took a seat, propping his pickaxe by his chair.

The detective followed him. "What's your business here this time of the night?"

"Work, Mr…?"

"Morgan," the detective supplied.

The man nodded. "I'm here for work. Came to dig a gutter for Mrs. Surratt." He puffed out his chest. "She sent for me."

Mr. Morgan scoffed. "In the middle of the night?"

The man looked around the room, then scratched at his curious hat. "I…was going to inquire what time she wished me to start in the morning."

Mr. Morgan's scowl deepened, a feat Matthew wouldn't have thought possible. "Do you board here, sir?"

"I have no boarding house, Mr. Morgan. I'm but a poor man." He gestured toward the axe. "I get my living with the pick."

Mr. Morgan lifted the axe, examining it closely. "How much do you make in a day?"

"Sometimes nothing at all."

Something about this entire exchange was exceedingly odd, the man's attire notwithstanding. Mr. Morgan must have displayed the same expression, because the axe man hurried on.

"But sometimes a dollar, and sometimes a dollar and a half." He smiled at Mr. Morgan confidently, as though the statement cleared him of suspicion.

"Hmm. Have you any money now?"

"Not a cent."

Mr. Morgan turned to look at Major Smith, who positioned himself by the very hearth where just days earlier O'Malley had told Matthew to end Harry. The major met Matthew's gaze as he lit a pipe. The major assessed him, and then gave a nod toward the parlor door. Matthew grunted and moved to block the exit.

Once again it seemed his stature had somehow positioned him in a precarious situation. If he'd been born a man of average height, maybe he would've been left to live a life of predictable normalcy.

The odd man noticed Matthew's movement and shifted in his seat, licking his lips.

"How long have you known Mrs. Surratt?" Mr. Morgan

asked.

"Don't, sir. Never met her."

Mr. Morgan leaned closer. "Then why would she select you?"

That gave the man pause, but only for a moment. "She knew I was working around the neighborhood and that I'm a poor man, so she sent for me." He smiled, seeming satisfied with the response.

Mr. Morgan grunted and stepped away, putting his hands behind his back. "How old are you?"

"About twenty."

"About? You don't know?"

The other man cringed as Mr. Morgan closed the gap again, leaning down close. He narrowed his eyes. "Where do you hail from?"

"Fauquier County, Virginia."

Mr. Morgan's eyes darkened. "A Southerner."

The man quickly pulled out a piece of paper from his jacket pocket and waved it at Morgan, who ignored it and instead turned on his heel to give a meaningful look to the major. The major nodded, and Morgan looked back at the squirming man in the chair.

"When did you leave there?"

"Some time ago. February, I think it was."

The same time when Matthew had been drawn into O'Malley's plot. Interesting. He'd never seen this man before, but O'Malley had often enough bragged about a far-reaching group. What part did this man play?

"I didn't want to join the army, you see," the man finally said, his voice strained. He cleared his throat. "Prefer to make my living by the axe. So I left." He wagged the paper again. "I have oath papers."

Matthew watched with more interest now. What would the traitor papers really gain a man under obvious suspicion? Mr. Morgan took the paper and scanned the contents, then passed it to Major Smith. The major read it over and then took another puff on his pipe, seeming content to let Mr. Morgan have the run of things.

"Lewis Payne, is it?" Mr. Morgan took the paper and shoved it in his jacket pocket.

"Yes, sir."

Mr. Morgan patted his pocket. "You'll have to go up to the Provost Marshal's office and explain."

Mr. Payne shifted in his seat, then he turned his gaze onto the rug and remained silent.

Before he could come up with anything else to say, Mrs. Surratt and two other women came down the stairs in a waterfall of ruffling skirts and petticoats.

Mr. Morgan gestured for Mr. Payne to rise, and Matthew stepped aside as Mr. Payne hurried out of the parlor. Morgan gestured toward Payne. "Mrs. Surratt, do you know this man and did you hire him to come dig a gutter for you?"

She looked at Payne and sniffed, then raised her right hand. "Before God, sir, I do not know this man and have never seen him before."

Payne stared at her.

So she did know him then. Why else would she display such unnecessary histrionics?

Morgan grabbed the man by the arm. "You're under arrest as a suspicious character and will have to go to Colonel Wells for further examination."

If the news distressed Mrs. Surratt in any way, she gave no indication. How had Payne been involved in the plot, and why had Mrs. Surratt denied she knew the man? For that matter, why did she pretend not to know Matthew either?

The women were ushered outside to a waiting carriage without further questioning, and after a moment they rolled away. The clack of the wheels seemed loud in the quiet street, the bell ringers having finally retired from their doleful duty and leaving the somber city to rest.

Morgan turned to the other men. "Mr. Samson, Mr. Rosch, take him." He waved a hand at Mr. Payne, and they escorted the strange man away.

"Mr. Daniels," the major barked. "Did you know that man?"

"He wasn't one of the conspirators. To my knowledge, at least."

The major stood at stiff attention. "Do you think it *possible* he was a part of this plot?"

Matthew rubbed the muscles at the back of his neck. "He seems suspicious, and his story doesn't hold up. It's possible."

The major regarded him thoughtfully then gestured toward the narrow staircase. "Show me which room belonged to O'Malley."

Matthew led the major up the stairs, and for the next two hours he aided in the search of the Surratt house, solidifying him as a turncoat.

Five

"My name is mentioned as connected with this affair.
The States is no longer a safe place for me especially as
Mother has been arrested."

John H. Surratt

Old Capitol Prison
Washington, D.C.
April 18, 1865

*A*nnabelle rose and brushed the dust off her skirts.
Kneeling to pray had only further ruined the dress,
but she couldn't bring herself to care. She'd prayed until her
knees ached, but she didn't feel any more at peace. What was a
dirty dress compared to a distressed heart?

Her cell mate paced again, wringing her hands and muttering about lost employment. The woman's constant fretting
frayed the last of Annabelle's nerves.

Annabelle opened her mouth to offer some kind of reassurance but gave up before any words could form. What difference
had any of those words made these last three days? If anything,
her attempts at consolation and friendship had only crumbled
into a smoldering pile of hatred. Alice wanted nothing at all to

do with her.

Three days. She smoothed tangled locks that she'd lost all hope of keeping in pins. Her clothes were dirty, and she desperately needed a bath. Yesterday she'd used half of her drinking water and the hem of her petticoat to wash her face and neck. Not that it had helped much. She used the lace hem of her blouse sleeve to scrub some of the grime from her teeth.

A loud clanging sound hammered on the bars from somewhere down the hall.

Oh, no. Not again.

She waited with tensed muscles, but all remained calm. Finally, she resumed her scrubbing, hoping that horrid man had grown tired of his game.

That hope shattered a moment later. "Hey! Hey, you! Do you hear me?"

Annabelle shuddered and dropped onto the floor in the far corner of the cell. She lowered her head and straightened the skirts around her feet. Perhaps no one would join him this time. Certainly after yesterday they must have grown tired of such cruel nonsense.

Alice stopped her muttering and looked down the hall. Her face crumpled into a frown, and before Annabelle could look away, the other woman's gaze locked on hers.

"You!" She sneered. "This is all *your* fault!"

No amount of logic, pleading, or attempts at polite conversation had swayed the woman's opinion yesterday, so what good would it do to try now?

Alice stepped closer and spat at Annabelle's feet. "I hope they *never* let you out. It's traitors like you that ought to be in here, not hardworking, loyal folks like me."

Annabelle squeezed her eyes shut, but this time Alice said nothing more.

"Hey! You! Rebel traitor!" The man's voice shouted again.

He wanted her to answer, but she wouldn't. It made no difference what she said. All her arguments and attempts at explanations had somehow done nothing more than stoke ire. That man thrived on instigating trouble. Well, she wouldn't be taken in this time. It was better to ignore him.

"She's too uppity to answer you, Tom. Stop all the yelling." Alice cast a hateful glance over her shoulder at Annabelle.

Annabelle pulled her knees up to her chest and wrapped her arms around them. At least the others hadn't joined in. Not yet, anyway.

"Guard! Guard!" Tom yelled again.

No one answered.

They sat in silence until the shaft of light that fell through the only window snaked its way almost to the center of the cell. Their first afternoon here, she and Alice had taken turns standing on the cot and looking out the small rectangular break in the stone wall. If they stood on their tiptoes, they could reach just high enough to get a glimpse of the yard out back.

But that was before Annabelle had made the mistake of telling anyone she was from Mississippi.

The metallic clang of the metal door at the end of the hall signaled the return of the guard, likely with their noon meal. Annabelle listened to the clinking and shuffling sounds as the guards opened the doors and pushed the metal trays inside. Finally, one of them reached Annabelle's cell.

"You have to let me out of here!" Alice wailed.

The guard pushed the metal key into the lock and wrenched

it open. "You know the answer to that, lady. No one's leaving until the murderer is caught." He thrust the tray toward her.

"I know, I know. Not that." She cast a scathing look at Annabelle. "Just move me to another cell."

The guard frowned at Annabelle's huddled form. "Why?"

Alice crossed her arms over her chest and jutted her chin. "I don't want to be stuck in here with that *Rebel* a moment longer."

The guard scowled and gave Alice an apologetic nod. "I'll see what I can do."

"Don't none of us want her in our cells either!" a man shouted from somewhere down the line.

The guard ignored him. "I'd have to put you in with two other women. Three might make it kind of tight."

Alice nodded as though Annabelle had the pox. "Better than being stuck with one of *them*."

Annabelle gulped and tried to understand the look of pure hatred tightening the features of the people in front of her.

"She was there, you know. At the theatre. I bet she laughed when the fiend shot Lincoln, too."

Heat slithered up Annabelle's neck. "I did no such thing! I tried to *help*!"

The guard grasped Alice's elbow and led her out of the cell. "I bet you did. What happened, didn't get close enough to finish him off?"

Annabelle opened her mouth, but no words could find their way past her thick tongue. The guard grunted and slammed the door.

Alice squared her shoulders, the look of relief on her face sending stabs of anguish through Annabelle's gut. The key had already ground out its screeching chorus before Annabelle found her words again. "Wait!"

The guard looked at her over his narrow shoulder, beady eyes crawling over her as though she were fetid milk left out in the sun.

"What…what…about my meal?"

The guard laughed, joined by the eerie echo of hollow chuckles down the line of cells. "Want to eat, do you? Well, maybe you should have thought of that before your kind murdered our president."

Annabelle sprang to her feet and scurried over to the door, clasping the cold bars in her trembling hands. "No! I tried to help. Tried to save him."

Alice jutted a pointy chin at Annabelle. "All those Rebels are nothing but liars and thieves."

Someone cheered and the prisoners banged on the bars. Alice made a crude face at Annabelle before the guard led her farther down the hall.

Tears slid down her cheeks.

Oh, Lord. Help me.

She stood there trembling at the cell door while calls of "Rebel harlot!" and "lying wench!" reverberated down the hall. A few other names flung at her were so foul that she finally covered her ears and dashed to the cot, flinging herself onto the stiff bed.

Alone, at least she'd no longer have to sleep on the floor. A small comfort. Finally, the other prisoners grew tired of their jeers. Annabelle's stomach rumbled, but she curled herself into a tight ball and ignored it. Maybe if she pretended they weren't out there, they'd forget about her and leave her in peace. But how long could she survive if they refused to give her any water?

A shiver ran down her spine and she dug the heels of her hands into her eyes to keep back the sobs. She wasn't sure how long she lay curled up on the cot, but it was long enough that her tears had dried on her cheeks and she'd drifted into a tense sleep.

The bars rattled.

"Miss Ross!"

The male voice chased the cobwebs from her mind and Annabelle lurched off the cot but hung back in the shadows. Three figures stood in the gloom of the hallway.

Suddenly one of them squealed and leapt forward, thrusting an arm through the bars. "Miss Belle! Oh, baby girl!"

Horrified by the sound of Peggy's voice, she rushed forward and grasped Peggy's outstretched fingers. "You shouldn't be here!"

"Neither should you," Eudora scoffed, stepping closer. Her nostrils flared and she looked up at the man standing at her side. "Mr. Crook! Is this how you've treated my granddaughter? She looks a fright!"

He gave a grunt. "I apologize. We're quite overrun, you know."

Eudora pointed a finger at the man. "You let her out this instant."

Mr. Crook hesitated, scratching at the scruff on his chin. Annabelle's heart pounded in her chest, and Peggy clutched her fingers so tightly her bones ached.

"Come now, William. We've been through this."

Bless her grandmother. If anyone could get her out of this, it would be Eudora Smith.

Mr. Crook's features tightened, and he seemed about to protest, but he finally pulled a ring of keys from his belt and slid one of them into the lock.

Relief swept over Annabelle so powerfully that her knees buckled, and she swayed.

"Hey! Who's letting out the Rebel scum?" Tom shouted.

The hall filled with the angry buzz of dozens of other prisoners as they pushed their bodies to the bars, many waving their hands out into the hallway.

Annabelle grabbed the bars to keep from crumbling.

Eudora pinned Mr. Crook with a glare that could melt iron. "Don't make me remind you of your debt, William."

Mr. Crook turned the key with a jerk and yanked the door open. Peggy rushed inside, looping her arm around Annabelle's waist and pulling her close. "Come on, now, honey. I got you."

Annabelle trembled and stepped out into the hall, not daring to look at Mr. Crook lest he change his mind. Eudora offered no comfort, but the anger in her eyes gave Annabelle courage. She straightened herself. She would not cower.

Eudora offered a slight dip of her chin by way of encouragement, then stalked toward the door. Mr. Crook made an odd noise in his throat and then stiffly followed after her. Peggy clasped Annabelle's arm.

She forced her chin high as she walked down the line of cells.

"Rebel tart!"

"Murderous traitor!"

"Filthy liar!"

Each call built onto the other until pain that burned her like the brander's iron began to stoke a flame of anger. How dare they! They knew nothing about her. They didn't know that she'd long been a Unionist at heart. But looking at the loathing in their eyes, the fury they flung from uncivilized mouths, she almost wished she hadn't.

Maybe Matthew had been right all along. He called them Blue Devils. Evil men set on nothing but coming down to the South and burning, pillaging, and stealing everything from them. All they wanted to do was destroy!

Heat burned in her stomach until it sizzled along her skin, racing like currents of lightning across a sinister sky. The *Yankees* did this. *They* were the ones that invaded her state! They were the ones who couldn't just leave the South alone. Leave them to their way of life and…and…

Her breath caught, and her vision cleared. She clutched Peggy's arm tighter, and the older woman patted her gently. "There, there. Don't you pay them no mind. They just scared, and they're taking it out on you. They know ain't none of this your fault."

Annabelle's heart swelled. The South had fought to keep Peggy a slave, and Annabelle couldn't agree with them. It'd been a long time since she'd thought about that horrible day.

Amid the shouts of hateful Yankees, Annabelle's mind traveled back to that sunny spring morning in '63. The day when the traders came.

"No! Please! Please, no!"

Lacey's howl had brought Annabelle running down the front stairs and out onto the porch. Men dragged Eli, Lacey's young son, across the yard.

Peggy grabbed Annabelle's elbow, drawing quick breaths from chasing her through the house. "Inside, Miss Belle!"

Annabelle snatched her arm away. "No. I want to know what's going on."

A pained look skittered across Peggy's face as she looked at Lacey. Two of the field foremen held the kitchen woman's arms as she thrashed between them. "Please! Please, don't take him!"

The hairs on the back of Annabelle's neck stood on end as another group of men rounded the side of the house, prodding a group of dark-skinned boys—ranging from about seven years to young men almost to a man's full height—with long metal pokers. The boys' eyes looked wide and white in their dark faces, and they kept glancing at the wagons waiting at the end of the walk.

Father came around behind them, talking to a white man in a wide-brimmed hat. The man looked like a bull. Thick, burly arms stuck out from his rolled sleeves, and a massive neck bulged from his open collar. Annabelle could only stare at him as Peggy tugged on her arm.

She shot Peggy an impatient look. "Stop it! I'll stay right here until I know what's happening."

Peggy dropped her gaze. "Yes, mistress."

Annabelle gathered her sage silk skirts and hurried down the stairs. When Father saw her, he quickly excused himself from the beefy man. "A moment, Byram."

The man gave Annabelle a look that made her feel odd.

Father grasped her arm and leaned close to her ear. "What're you doing down here, darlin'? You're supposed to be tending to your pianoforte lessons."

"What's happening, Father?" She threw a curious gaze over to Lacey, who'd ceased protesting and now stood wailing between the men who held her.

Lacey's anguished cries shook Annabelle's nerves to the point that she'd needed her fan, lest she faint of this heat and noise.

Father pointed to Lacey. "Get her out of here!"

The two foremen hooked their arms under Lacey's elbows and dragged her around the side of the house. Annabelle watched them go until they disappeared behind the rose bushes.

"I'd hoped to discuss this with you before they arrived, but they've come two days early."

"Early?"

The beefy man shouted orders to three other men, and they started loading the boys on the backs of the wagons.

Father cupped her elbow and led her back to the front porch. "Darlin', you know that we're at war and—"

Annabelle waved her hand. "Oh, yes, Father. But surely they're nearly finished with all that fighting off in Virginia."

Father's eyes softened. "I'm afraid that's not the case."

Annabelle tilted her head. "Whatever do you mean? You said the war would be over soon. You said it wouldn't possibly go on once the North saw how well the South was holding its own."

Father guided her over to the chairs on the porch and gently eased her down into one. He looked so handsome in his ivory broadcloth jacket, but she didn't like the way his frown marred the strong lines of his face. She rarely ever saw Father upset.

She glanced back over at the wagon where they had loaded the rest of the boys. "Where are they going?"

He tugged on his collar. "I'm selling them."

"To where?"

He ran his fingers through his hair, and only a few streaks of silver shimmered in their auburn waves. "I don't know, darlin'. They're going to auction."

Annabelle's brow gathered. "But what about their families?"

Father patted her hand. "Don't you worry yourself over things like that. Slaves aren't like us. They don't think of families in the same way we do."

Annabelle's frown deepened. Peggy had been her mammy since she was born. Had loved her and comforted her when she lost her mother. Peggy certainly seemed to love in just the same ways as Annabelle. Surely Father must be mistaken.

The boys sat in the wagons, hanging their heads. Lacey sure seemed upset. "Are you sure, Father?"

"Of course. You don't worry yourself. Such things aren't for a lady to fret over."

Annabelle offered the smile she knew he wanted, but she still wasn't so sure. Something seemed terribly wrong. "But *why* are you selling them? None of them have ever left before."

Father looked out to where the beefy man stood and then turned his azure eyes back on her. The worry she saw within them sent her heart fluttering. "This war's changed things. I've already lost a dozen of the field hands. They took off during the night last week to run north."

Annabelle put a hand to her throat. Peggy wouldn't leave her, would she?

"Don't worry," Father said, misreading her concern. "I have men looking for them. There's a fugitive slave law. We'll get them back."

Why would they want to run away? This was their home. Annabelle couldn't fathom wanting to run off to the hostile northern lands.

Father sighed, drawing her attention. "I thought it better I go ahead and sell off some of the younger ones. Get a good price for them while I still can. But don't you worry. There'll still be plenty here to keep things going when I'm gone."

Annabelle's heart thumped wildly. "Gone?"

"It's time I join the fight," Father said softly, his eyes begging her to understand something she could not.

Annabelle jumped to her feet. "You can't! You're supposed to stay here. The law says any man who owns more than twenty slaves doesn't have to join."

Father rose slowly and placed his hands on her shoulders. "I can't let other men fight for me, now can I? What kind of man does that make me?"

Annabelle looked down at his polished boots.

"The war is coming closer." A hint of frustration snaked through his words and settled heavy on Annabelle's ears. "I have to go and protect our home. Protect you."

Tears spilled over despite her effort to contain them. "But who will stay here with me?"

He smiled. "Sarah's father is coming. He'll take good care of everything when I'm gone, and in a few months, when I get home, everything will go back to just the way it was."

Just the way it was....

The shouts in the hall grew louder as Annabelle neared the prison door, jarring her out of her thoughts. Nothing had ever been the same after that. In some ways, she was glad. How could she have been so blind? How had she looked upon the people of Rosswood for all those years and never really seen them? She'd even been mad when they'd first run away. She shook her head. How foolish she'd been. How childish.

The main door slammed behind her, muffling the screams in the hall. Annabelle kept her eyes down as the stone floors turned to the gravel drive and finally to the welcome steps of Eudora's carriage. But it wasn't until the door latched her safely inside that she finally believed she would be free.

Rocks crunched under the wheels as the carriage rolled. When gravel turned to the steady rhythm of the cobbled streets, the air left her lungs in a rush.

"Peggy! Grandmother!"

The spell hanging over them dissipated like fog under the morning sun, and the three women fell into each other's arms on the floor of the carriage and cried the rest of the way back to the hotel.

Six

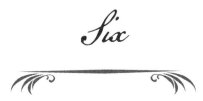

"What must be Mother's feelings at this time? Herself in prison, and unaware of my safety. How did they discover her connection with the affair? Some one must have betrayed her."

John H. Surratt

*S*houts drifted on the air like languid seagulls, floating in and out of George's consciousness like oscillating lights. He groaned and put his arms over his head, trying to get the foul things to cease pecking at his brain.

"Rebel tart!"

George shifted, removing his arm from over his head and using his fingers to massage his temples. When he'd awoken on the cold cell floor after his first night in the prison, it had been to a searing pain at the base of his skull. He'd pulled himself up onto the cot and sought the solace of sleep to leach away the ache. Somewhere in the back of his memory an army doctor warned about sleeping with head injuries, but George simply couldn't bring himself to care.

Besides, little good it would have done him. He'd tried to stay awake and had only gained the injury because of it. The

STEPHENIA H. McGEE

muffled shouts grew louder, accompanied by banging metal. George turned himself onto his back and willed his crusted eyes to open. It took several tries and a bit of scrubbing, but after a time he was rewarded with the dismal view of his prison cell.

Stone walls, stone floor, and cold bars without even the comfort of a window to let in fresh air or a bit of light. Judging by the way the gloom filtered through the shadows, George guessed it to be sometime in the day. When he'd awoken at night, the darkness had only been broken by the single lantern hanging somewhere farther down the hall, its meager light scarcely enough to be a tiny lighthouse on a sea of inky shadows.

George swung his feet over the side of the cot and sat up, waiting a moment as his vision fuzzed and then finally cleared. Two trays of food had been left by the bars. Running a dry tongue over cracked lips, George slowly gained his feet and took an unsteady step forward.

The shouts coming from somewhere on the far side of the prison had gained the attention of the others on his wing. Two men in the cell across the hall stared at him. Neither said anything. George dropped down to his knees beside the nearest tray and studied the contents. Two bits of stale bread that had been nibbled by rats and a pile of mush that even they wouldn't eat gave off a faint putrid odor that twisted his stomach. He plucked the tin cup of water off the tray and pushed the rest of it away.

The cool, stale water cut like a river through his desert throat, and he gulped it so quickly he coughed.

"See, I told you he wasn't dead."

George wiped a dirty sleeve over his mouth and darted his

52

gaze over to the two men shrouded in shadows across the hall. One of them poked a hand through the bars and wiggled his fingers at George.

"You, there. You all right?"

George stared at him for a moment before turning to search out the other tray. Perhaps it had some water as well. He crawled across the floor, feeling out with his hand until his fingers touched the smooth metal. It had slid almost to the far back corner, coming to rest next to the chamber pot. He groped for the cup and touched the rim, knocking it over with a faint clang. George yelped and scrambled to scoop it up, but the damage had already been done. He put the cup to his lips and downed the last remaining swallows, then leaned back against the wall.

"Hey, you. Over there. The fellow kneeling at the pot."

George rolled the back of his skull against the stone wall. Silence went on for so long that George thought he must have imagined someone had spoken.

"He can't even hear you, you fool. I told you. If he ain't dead, then he's some kind of dumb mute without his wits." The harsh whisper plucked at George's ears, and he narrowed his eyes to try to get a better look at the two figures across from him.

"I can hear you," George said, his thick words coming out in little more than a rasp. He cleared his throat. "I can hear you," he said again, stronger this time. His voice sounded foreign to him, the scratchy croak of an old man. "I'm not a mute." *Or a man without wits.* He hoped.

"See? I told you," the other one said. "Hey, fellow, come over here."

Deciding that speaking to someone else might keep his sanity in check, George shifted onto his knees and crawled over to the bars.

The back of his skull throbbed. He waited, but neither of them spoke again. Had he imagined their presence?

The one who'd claimed George was a witless mute spoke up. "We thought you were dead over there, seeing as how you ain't moved in two days."

"Two days?"

"Yeah," the other prisoner said. "You were standing in the middle of the cell when we were brought in."

"Kind of creepy, if you ask me."

"Sorry," George mumbled. Neither seemed to have heard him.

"Then you dropped to the floor and we thought for sure you were dead."

George was as surprised as they were that he wasn't, in fact, dead. Unless, of course, he *was* dead and this was hell. Panic swelled for a brief time before he shook his head. No. He'd put his faith in the Savior two nights after the battle of Corinth.

This might be a version of Hades, but it sat deep in Yankee territory and not somewhere below the earth. Fitting, really, if you asked George. In his experience, everything north of Virginia bore a mark of Hades. Except for that one little place in New York where an angel resided.

"I hit my head. Must have knocked me out." George gently prodded the sore place on the back of his head.

One of the men grunted. "When we woke up and saw you on the cot, we started taking bets on if you'd get up again." He nudged his companion. "You owe me your bread."

The other man waved him off. "Fine, fine."

"Why are you here?" George asked.

Both men scooted closer and pressed their faces to the bars, enough so that George could see their sparse whiskers poking through the slats. "We work at Pumphrey's Stable," the one on the left replied.

George just stared at them.

The one on the right nudged the other. "Maybe he don't know."

"Know what?" George asked.

"The president's been assassinated."

George sighed. "*That*, I do know. I was there."

"In the theatre?"

"Saw Booth jump down onto the stage and run out the back. I tried to catch him, but he took off on a horse before I could."

One of the men let out a low whistle. "That explains it. They've brought in everyone who might have anything to do with it or know anything at all. And they ain't letting anyone go until Booth is caught."

George groaned. "What if they never catch him?"

The one on the right pushed his face through the bars. "They'll get him. Every soul in the nation is looking for that Rebel scum."

"Rebel?" George snorted. "I thought he was a Yank."

Both men grew quiet. Finally, when one of them spoke, steel filled his voice that hadn't been there before. "You fight in the war?"

Something told George to be cautious in his answer, but his ability to care much about anything seemed to be malfunctioning at the moment. "I did. Mississippi infantry."

"Dirty rotten—" One of them cursed.

George just kept talking. "I fought in a dozen battles, at least, and I don't know how many skirmishes. Then I was sent to prison in Elmira for the crime of defending my home against soldiers who would as soon murder my family in their beds and burn my lands than simply leave us alone."

"You ignorant traitors and all your talk of rights."

George ignored him. "Then, after it all, after losing two of my brothers and my father in a hopeless endeavor, I betrayed all of it and signed oath papers to the North. Now, I'm a traitor to my own country." He pressed his face against the bars, baring his teeth. "And a *loyalist* to yours. One who, I might add, tried to warn you Yankees about a plot to take your precious Lincoln and who desperately tried to stop that from happening.

"Even after, when I could have simply gone home and left you fools to your folly, I stayed and came to the law, trying to do everything in my power to see that Booth was caught and brought to justice." He snarled. "Fat lot of good it did me."

The other two men stared at him for a long time until finally George sighed and dropped his head back against the wall. He closed his eyes and tried to picture Lilly's face, hoping the way her rosy lips curved would chase away the demons that threatened to claw at him.

"So what did you know then?"

"Don't talk to the *Rebel*, Sam." The other man spat out the word like rotten meat.

Sam grunted. "Rebel, Yank, does it really matter? War's over anyway. And he signed papers. Said he was loyal now."

"He was in the army that killed Jimmy!"

"Yeah," Sam said. "And we were with the army that killed his kin. Don't see how that makes much matter now, seeing as how we're all in this prison together. Union prison, I might add."

"While they search for a Reb!"

George watched them closely, as best he could in the shadows, anyway, and realized they were younger than he'd first assumed. "You said you worked in a stable? Why would that get you here?"

Somewhere down the line of cells, someone whistled a haunting tune.

The two boys stopped bickering. "When we came home, we started back to work at the stables. We'd gone out to help the cavalry, seeing as how horses are what we've known all our lives."

"And they said we were too young to fight," the other interjected.

"Yeah, like Bob said. Anyway, when Lee surrendered, they sent us home. We were working at the stables, and apparently Mr. Pumphrey had words with Booth over one of his horses. Man wanted to buy one, and Mr. Pumphrey didn't agree on the price."

George's brows knitted. "What does any of that have to do with why you two boys are locked in here?"

Sam chuckled. "Maybe they think Mr. Pumphrey is lying about when he saw Booth or something, because they kept asking us all these questions about where Mr. Pumphrey was, who he talked to, things like that. I don't think he was lying, and I sure don't think anything we had to say was worth much, but we're in here just the same."

George didn't have time to contemplate the oddity because a barrage of shouts galloped down the hall and drew their attention. George lurched to his feet, pressing the side of his face to the cold bars. The sounds came from some distant part of the prison.

"They've been doing that on and off for the last two days," Sam said.

Bob whistled. "Yeah, they must have someone pretty bad over there, way they keep carrying on about it."

A shout separated itself from the angry horde and sailed over the others. "Why is the traitor going free?"

George looked back at the two Yankee boys and from this angle could now see that there were a couple of women in the cell next to the boys, their worried eyes darting around in the gloom.

The sight of them chilled his blood. The Yanks had sunk to imprisoning women? Fire stoked in his gut as the calls around the bend brought more faces from the shadows and into his view. Most on this hall were men, but George counted at least four feminine silhouettes before he could no longer distinguish anything in the murky light.

"What's happening?" A male voice called out from a few cells down.

George clenched the bars, the bite of the cold metal stark against his sweaty palms.

"Seems like they have a Rebel woman down there no one wanted to be around," came a reply.

A bunch of grunts echoed agreement. How many on his wing had heard his conversation with the boys? Would they start jeering at him, too?

"Looks like some people came and got her out!" a voice shouted from the middle of the hall. From what George could tell, the people were relaying the information down the line.

"Maybe she was one of them! The traitors who murdered the president," another voice offered, this one probably only a cell or two removed from George.

"That was just Booth," Sam said with a snort. "Everyone knows that."

"Then why are they holding so many people?" another man bellowed. His question silenced the others.

They stood there listening for several moments as bits of the jeers and clamor reached their ears. Finally, the sounds faded and the despondent silence settled on them again.

"Whoever she was, the people on the east side sure didn't seem to like her," Bob said.

"Sure enough," Sam agreed. "Must have been pretty bad."

They're holding women.

The single thought bounded around in George's head as he stumbled back to his cot, ignoring the boys across the hall as they came up with wilder and wilder tales about who the woman was and what she might have done.

If the Yankees were holding women, then Annabelle Ross was in danger. Matthew would never forgive him if they threw Annabelle in this place. George had insisted they come to the law—insisted they not waste a moment in sharing what they knew.

When he'd found Matthew with Annabelle in his arms, he'd patted his brother on the shoulder, glad he'd finally been truthful about his feelings. Then he'd tugged on them both, bringing them into a night crackling with as much energy as any battle. He'd been the one to convince them to go to the police.

It had been the right thing to do. Hadn't it? Now, he wasn't so sure. He never dreamed he'd put the lady at risk of imprisonment. Those Blue Bellies and their blind drive toward their goal had cost this country too much already. Now the Yanks threw women in jail just because they might have information on a missing man? Barbaric!

George rubbed at his throbbing temples. If they locked her in here, Matthew would go mad. He'd never seen his brother look at another woman the way he regarded Miss Ross, and if George didn't know his brother's fierce protectiveness, then he didn't know his own name.

The two boys across from him fell silent, leaving the only noise a haunting tune one of the prisoners whistled down the line. George rolled over on his back and stared at the ceiling, praying that Annabelle and Matthew were not trapped in Hades dungeon with him.

Seven

"But the assassin—Savior—is being pursued. If he takes
the road planned out, he will certainly escape."
John H. Surratt

nnabelle walked into the National Hotel with her head
ducked, afraid that at any moment someone would
snatch her out of Eudora's grasp and haul her back to prison.
She shuddered, and Eudora pulled Annabelle tighter against her
widow's blacks. Peggy trailed along behind them, and Annabelle
could practically feel the tension rolling off her.

Eudora must have felt the same, because she bustled
through the lobby faster than Annabelle had ever seen the lady
move. It felt like they traveled miles before finally making it up
the massive main staircase, down the carpeted hall, and into
Annabelle's room. The door fell closed with a click before she
felt as though she could draw a full breath.

Everything stood exactly as she'd left it that night they had
gone to the play. Her combs were still sitting on the vanity
where Peggy had pinned her hair in the coiffure with the braids
wrapped around her head. Braids that had long since fallen and
had been worked through with trembling fingers.

Oh, her pins. What had happened to the pins? Annabelle reached up and prodded the messy bun tied at the back of her head. *Only loose women go about with their hair free*, Father had said.

Peggy grabbed Annabelle's wrists, gently tugging her hands down from her hair. "There, there, Miss Belle. Don't you be worryin'. I'll get that hair fixed up for you real nice once we get you bathed and into a clean gown."

Blood stained her white sleeve. "This one's ruined."

Eudora gave her shoulder a squeeze. "I'm so terribly sorry, dear. I got you out of there as fast as I could." Her eyes glistened.

Annabelle offered a wobbly smile. "I'm deeply thankful. I don't know how much longer I could've taken it. To think poor George endured…" Guilt flooded her heart. "Grandmother! Where are Matthew and George?"

"I wasn't able to get George free." Eudora fiddled with the black fringe on the sleeve of her dress. "There's still that matter of his oath papers, you see."

"What does that have to do with Lincoln's assassination?"

She dropped the fringe. "Apparently quite a lot. There's talk of holding him for war crimes, since he escaped prison."

"But he…he…" She stomped her foot. "Insufferable Yankees!"

Her outburst startled both of the other women, making Peggy yelp and drop the clean stockings she'd fished out of Annabelle's trunk.

"Annabelle!"

Eudora's shocked tone drew Annabelle back to her senses, and she placed a trembling hand on her heart. "Forgive me."

Curiosity flitted across Eudora's wrinkled features before

compassion settled in its place. "Let's get you cleaned up. Then we can discuss my plans to get George freed."

Annabelle allowed Eudora to slip the embroidered jacket from her shoulders. "And Matthew?"

"The Captain's currently assisting the Federal Army in apprehending Mr. Booth."

Eudora's words settled like the heat of a Mississippi July. "He's doing what?" Try as she might, she couldn't reconcile Matthew donning Yankee Blues. "Surely you must be mistaken."

"Nope," Peggy chimed in, laying a fresh cream gown and two lavender petticoats across the bed. "That's exactly what he be doin'."

Matthew with the Union Army? What on earth would have caused him to do that? "I'm afraid I don't understand."

Peggy slipped past her and cracked open the door. "I'm goin' down to the kitchen to fetch you a bucket of hot water."

"Thank you," Annabelle murmured as Peggy slipped through the door.

Annabelle stood in her chemise and pantaloons.

Eudora tsk-tsked. "It's a good thing I already sent for Lilly. Gracious, we'd never be able to make it on so few remaining clothes."

"Lilly's coming?"

"Of course, dear. Who else would bring the rest of my things?" Eudora dropped the gown with a sigh. "We can't leave. That's part of the deal I made with William. The police finally agreed to let you out of that awful prison on account of my personal relations with city officials and my husband's good reputation, but neither of us can leave the city under any circumstances unless the Washington police say so."

Annabelle wrapped her arms around herself and plopped onto her dressing chair. "So we're to stay at the hotel, George remains in prison, and Matthew is aiding the search?"

"That sums it up."

Oh, poor George. As cruel as they'd been to her, she could only imagine what they must be doing to George. She pinched the bridge of her nose. "We have to get George out of there."

"Yes, I know. But until his papers arrive from Elmira, there's little we can do."

Annabelle groaned. "I doubt that major will be in any hurry to deliver them." She remembered the way his face had reddened and the tight grip he'd had on her elbow when he'd all but tossed her out. No doubt by now he'd discovered she'd been lying about her relation to George. Her heart hammered. What if her lie had somehow caused them to deny George's allegiance papers?

Oh, Lord. Forgive me. Help me to keep my words true. And, please, don't let my foolishness bring George harm.

"Then it's a good thing I already sent Günter to collect them and bring them with him when he escorts Lilly to Washington." Eudora grinned.

"Oh, Grandmother! You're simply brilliant."

"Yes, dear. I know."

The twinkle of humor in her grandmother's eyes made Annabelle chuckle. "I'm still having a difficult time understanding how Matthew ended up with the Union Army. He's not exactly…warmhearted toward the Union."

Eudora quirked a single eyebrow in that funny way she had. "Seems to me like you might be harboring some of those same sentiments."

Heat crept up Annabelle's neck. "You wouldn't believe what they called me in there. I've never seen such looks of pure hatred."

Indignation sapped the humor from Eudora's eyes. "I heard plenty."

Annabelle rubbed the stiff muscles in her neck. "I know they're hurting, and they needed someone to blame for them being stuck in prison, but, gracious, I didn't think it would be me."

"I'm shocked they're holding so many. How many people do they really think are involved?"

O'Malley had said the group had fingers in everything. She shuddered. "I really don't know. Maybe it's the smart thing to do, to keep anyone from getting away that might be secretly aiding him. Even if they may have taken the idea too far."

"Too far, indeed." Eudora huffed.

There was a small tap at the door, and Eudora opened it for Peggy. The woman swept in with a swish of pale green silk, her freedwoman's clothes still unfamiliar.

Peggy lifted up a bucket with a smile. "Good news. Some of the girls in the kitchen's bringing up more water for a real bath."

Annabelle had to smile at Peggy's enthusiasm. The dear woman thought that all of Annabelle's problems could be solved with warm water and scented soap. Her smile faltered when she thought back to the girl she'd been before the war. So petty, so absorbed in her own comforts and whims to notice the truth of plantation life.

Things had seemed so simple then. They never discussed slavery. The servants were just always there. Tending, cleaning, and caring for things. Peggy had always loved her as any mother would, even though her father had owned Peggy like property.

The day Annabelle received word of his death, she'd officially freed Peggy. Grandfather had been furious when he'd discovered she'd signed freedom papers for the two remaining stable hands and let them go.

"You all right, child?"

Peggy's words plucked Annabelle from her contemplation and drew her back to the present. "Why did you stay?"

Peggy tilted her head. "What you talkin' about?"

"When the rest of your people ran off, or when I signed your papers. Everyone else went. You didn't. Why?"

Peggy grabbed her hands. "I weren't going to leave my girl."

She said it so firmly, with such conviction, that it brought tears to Annabelle's eyes. "Thank you."

"And look at me now." She chuckled. "In Washington City wearing all these fine silks like some kind of lady."

"Why, Peggy, you *are* a lady."

Peggy rolled her eyes and flapped the washing rag. "You hush now."

Someone knocked and soon a procession of young girls entered the room carrying buckets of steaming water. They filled a tub by the hearth.

When everyone left, Annabelle shrugged off her remaining clothing and stepped into the delicious warmth. She rested her head on the back of the tub with a contented sigh. But even as her muscles relaxed and she relished the smell of lavender soap upon her skin, her mind continually drifted toward poor George locked away and to Matthew out there somewhere looking for Booth.

Matthew swatted a mosquito and tore his focus away from the frowning Blue Belly to his left. All of the Federal soldiers watched Matthew's every move with calculating eyes, but this Yank in particular seemed ready to attack at any moment.

Their horses clomped down the road just outside of a town in Maryland by the name of Bel Alton. Someone claimed Booth went this way. They'd placed Matthew in one of the search units, the Sixteenth New York Cavalry, and sent him out of Washington.

Maybe they wanted his knowledge or just wanted to keep him close. Or maybe they intended to murder him in the woods. He eyed the man next to him again. Wouldn't put it past a Yank.

"What're you looking at, Reb?" The man lifted his hawkish nose.

One side of Matthew's mouth twisted into a sardonic grin. "Just wondering if your face always looks like that, or if you've got a bee in your britches."

The man snarled and nudged his mount closer. "Why you sniveling—"

He reached to grab Matthew's collar, but Matthew had his wrist in a firm grasp before the Yankee's fingers even brushed fabric. The fellow's eyes widened. Matthew leaned close and lowered his voice. "I don't much like the way you've been looking at me, fellow. You got something you want to say?"

"Go boil your shirt, Grayback."

Matthew hauled him closer until the man nearly came out of the saddle. Matthew's fist itched to give the Yank a taste of his frustration, but he forced his fingers to relax and shoved the fool away. He wouldn't give them the opportunity to string him up for giving a lick to this uppity, pointy-nosed dandy. "Just a lot of parlor soldiers invading good folk who only wanted to be left to their own."

The man straightened his crisp blue uniform and pointed a finger at Matthew. "Now, look here, you—"

"That's enough!"

The major's stern voice silenced the man. The Blue Belly narrowed his eyes, but Matthew only grinned, further infuriating the Yank.

"Daniels!" The red-faced major swung his horse around and pulled to a halt.

"Yes?"

"Stop aggravating my soldiers or I'll see you sent back to Washington to rot in prison."

Matthew sobered. "Understood."

The major arched his spine and nudged his horse forward. Two soldiers scrambled to get their horses out of his way. The rest of the dispatch hauled up on the reins, bringing everyone to a halt. The rocks on the road crunched underneath polished hooves as the major's roan stallion pranced forward.

The officer came to a stop about four paces away so as not to have to lift his chin to regard one lower in rank. The corner of Matthew's mouth twitched. Here sat a man accustomed to being in power.

"You will address me as Sir or Major, Private. Is that understood?"

His jaw clenched. He'd been stripped of his Captain's rank as soon as they'd forced him into blues. Matthew had earned his rank in his four years of service. How he loathed these Yanks for knocking him to the bottom of the rank structure. Underneath nearly every one of these scoundrels.

"Yes, *Major.*" Try as he might, he couldn't keep the disdain out of his tone.

To his surprise, however, the major said nothing of it. He looked at the other men in the group. "You boys leave him alone. He's signed papers."

The Blue Belly Matthew had grabbed spoke up. "But he's still a Reb!"

"Not according to the law or orders from the White House."

The words hung heavy in the air, and Matthew could feel all the Yanks' eyes on him. His skin crawled. What orders?

"No more bellyaching," the major snapped. "If you don't have something pertinent to say, then keep your blasted mouths shut!" He snatched the reins and spurred the horse back to the front of the line. The rest of them fell into step behind him, reforming their two lines.

Matthew refused to look at the man next to him. Orders had come from the White House. A bead of sweat gathered at his nape and scuttled down the back of his collar.

Orders pertaining to him. Whatever it meant, he knew one thing. It probably wasn't good.

Eight

"One thing will at once be conceded by all generous minds; no people or class of people in this country, have a better reason for lamenting the death of Abraham Lincoln, and for desiring to honor and perpetuate his memory, than have the colored people; and yet we are about the only people who have been in any case forbidden to exhibit our sorrow, or to show our respect for the deceased president publicly."

Frederick Douglass

Washington, D.C.
April 19, 1865

*A*nnabelle tugged on the skirt of the black velvet dress she'd borrowed from Eudora and hoped no one would notice that her petticoats didn't match. Her grandmother's dress was too tight, too short, and much too warm for the balmy spring day, but one did not attend a funeral in a colorful gown.

She popped open her black lace fan and tried to stir the air around her face as she and Peggy waited for Eudora. Outside the hotel carriages rolled down the street, horses clopped by, and people went about their business. Yet the somber mood of the town hung like a leaden cloud over them all, drenching them in sorrow and making even the children appear subdued.

Peggy leaned close. "Don't worry. No one's gonna notice them petticoats is dark blue."

Annabelle tore her gaze away from a family dressed in black walking down the street. "What? Oh, yes." Dressed in crinoline and two navy blue petticoats underneath the velvet gown, Annabelle already grew uncomfortable. The ruffled hem of the petticoats gave her enough length to make up for the shortened hem of the skirt, and she didn't suppose anyone would look close enough to notice the colors were off.

What did it matter if they did? She didn't care. She tightened the bow on her bonnet and gave Peggy a tired smile. "It's fine. Lucky for you, Grandmother's wardrobe fits you quite nicely."

Peggy smiled at the dyed muslin. She'd insisted on wearing the plainest of Eudora's gowns, but even then she stood out with her pearl buttons and Chantilly lace collar.

Eudora swished out of the hotel in a flurry of ebony silk and lowered her bonnet against the bright sun. She scowled as though the very notion of a chipper late spring day was the foulest of poor manners. "Come along now, girls. We don't want to be late."

Peggy's face twisted in confusion. "I ain't no girl, Mrs. Smith."

"Pish. Twenty years beneath me is as good as so." She ignored Peggy's grunt and led the way down the crowded street.

People flowed around them in a sea of inky mourning attire. When would this ever come to an end? How many years would it take for the people of this country to feel united again, to feel hopeful and joyous over anything other than the slaughter of their fellow man in battle?

Tears gathered in Annabelle's eyes, but she blinked them away. The closer they got to the White House, the more the crowd thickened. Women sniffled, men wore stoic expressions, and children stood numbly at their parents' sides. For as many people who milled about, the air remained eerily quiet. People spoke in muted whispers, apparently afraid too much noise would disturb the dead.

The three women made their way with the crowd until they reached the White House, which appeared to be so full they were beginning to turn mourners away. People gathered on the lawns to await the end of the funeral. Annabelle turned toward the shade of a large tree to shield her from the relentless sun.

"What are you doing?"

Annabelle blinked at Eudora's brisk tone. "I'm choosing us a cooler place to wait. This velvet is getting rather warm."

Eudora grabbed her arm and tugged her out of the comforting shadow. "Nonsense. We're going inside."

The Executive Mansion's white walls were covered in yards of black cloth. The balconies were draped, and every window was darkened with inky fabric. Where had they acquired so much material?

Telling her grandmother they'd only be turned away wouldn't do any good, so Annabelle allowed herself to be guided all the way to the front door.

A sour-looking Union soldier stood guard. He opened a mouth hidden in his ample beard and mustache to protest Eudora's determined gait, but she spoke before he had the opportunity.

"Eudora Smith, widow to Franklin Smith of New York."

She thrust tickets she'd plucked from her reticule at him.

The man snapped his mouth closed and gestured inside.

Suddenly there was a great *boom* and Annabelle startled, grasping at the fabric about her throat.

"Don't worry, miss," the soldier said. "It's just the minute guns from the forts giving salute."

Annabelle willed her trembling heart to slow, her nerves hanging by a fraying thread. "Oh."

The startling sound fractured the air again, disrupting the ever-present doleful toll of the church bells. Annabelle offered the man a friendly smile as she moved to step past him. It faltered when the man's cold glare landed on Peggy.

"No Negroes allowed inside."

Peggy's gaze darted between the soldier and Eudora.

"This woman is freed, soldier." Eudora waved her hand.

The man emphatically shook his head. "All Negroes remain outside."

Storm clouds gathered in Eudora's eyes, and Annabelle feared lightning would soon spark from her tongue.

"I'll wait for y'all under that shade tree."

"Now, wait just a moment—" Eudora started.

Peggy regarded her with pleading eyes. "Don't want to cause no trouble here."

Although clearly displeased, Eudora said nothing further. Annabelle gave Peggy's hand a squeeze as she hurried off the portico. She shot the soldier an annoyed look, but he was already addressing the people in line behind her.

The inside of the mansion was covered in so much heavy cloth that Annabelle could scarcely tell what the house would have looked like on any other occasion.

They passed into the darkened East Room where people filled the space. Another soldier at the door looked at Eudora's tickets and gestured to a place on the raised steps that occupied three sides around the catafalque. Whoever heard of such a thing? Tickets to a funeral?

The platform with four large posts draped in heavy black cloths held the open coffin at the center. The still form inside looked not much different from the face she'd seen lying in the bed after the assassination.

Memories of that evening raw upon her senses, she shoved them away.

Little of what Annabelle assumed to be a luxurious carpet could be seen under the black-wrapped risers surrounding the coffin. Those must have been constructed so all the invited attendees could have an adequate view of their murdered leader. She averted her eyes from his still form. Mountains of black fabric hung over the windows, gilded frames, and even the chandeliers. Her dear friend Molly had to dye old fabric to make mourning clothes for all the widows around Lorman. Seemed the North had a massive abundance of material.

The tight features of all those pressed in the room remained fixed on the grand and gloomy catafalque. In the space immediately surrounding it sat what appeared to be four clergymen, two men she did not recognize, Lincoln's two living sons, and a handful of others Annabelle guessed to be family or close friends.

Mary Lincoln was nowhere to be seen. Remembering the woman's wails from the Petersen Rooming House across from Ford's Theatre, Annabelle wondered if the First Lady's fragile state kept her away. She'd heard many rumors that Mrs. Lincoln had been volatile in her moods, though Annabelle would guess that any wife with a great love for her husband would have reacted in the same manner.

She couldn't imagine seeing Matthew shot right in front of her. That poor woman. Tears gathered in her eyes, and she didn't bother to brush them away when they fell down her cheeks.

Her gaze drifted over the dark-clad mourners to a group of brightly attired gentlemen, their foreign costumes in stark contrast to their surroundings. Like peacocks amid a flock of ravens, their bright, formal attire made Annabelle wonder at the funeral customs of other countries. People's attention swung toward the door, drawing Annabelle's gaze off the foreign dignitaries and onto the new president, who entered along with a group of men who were obviously members of his new cabinet. After the men had found their places, a pastor entered and stood at the head of the coffin and announced the commencement of the funeral rites.

"Dr. Phineas Gurley," Eudora whispered in her ear. "He conducted the funeral for Lincoln's boy Willie as well."

Poor Mrs. Lincoln. Was it any wonder the woman was more nervous than a starved cat? Not only had she endured the constant threats against her husband, but the loss of a child as well?

After a brief speech no doubt meant to comfort but laced with pain, the preacher stepped aside and another took his place, opening a book and reading with a strong voice.

"The words of our Lord Jesus, as recorded in the book of John. 'I am the resurrection and the life; he that believeth in me, though he were dead, yet shall he live, and whosoever liveth and believeth in me shall never die.'"

Annabelle breathed in the words as a manner of comfort, knowing that a man who'd so often professed his faith in God surely now lived in His presence.

The preacher listed a great number of Lincoln's virtues, but Annabelle's mind flitted to the horrors of war instead. Why would God allow it all? Did He really raise Lincoln up for a great purpose? A man who so many claimed brought the war? Annabelle crossed her arms and tried to push unanswerable questions from her mind.

"Our president's greatest virtue of all, however, was his abiding confidence in God and in the final triumph of truth and righteousness."

Righteousness? How righteous could a cause be that laid waste to the South, burning cities to the ground, ravishing women, and murdering families in their beds? The thoughts clawed at her until she shook her head violently.

Eudora's fingers dug into her arm.

Another man stepped forth and delivered a long-winded prayer in the old English of the Bible, and Annabelle soon lost his words in the churning waters of her own thoughts.

Why, Father? Why this war of pain and destruction? Both sides were wrong.

Precious daughter, I give the gift of free will.

The thought came at her from every direction, yet from no direction. Her eyes popped open. The voice hadn't come from outside of her, yet neither had it been her own.

Peace flooded over her, and tears welled anew. They flowed down her face, though this time not in sorrow, but in the joy of feeling a peaceful presence so near that the rips in her soul began to knit together. She breathed deeply, enjoying the warm feeling that cascaded through her.

A chorus of "Amen" bounded around the room. Annabelle lifted her head. Among the heavy air of the funeral, she felt a new lightness in her soul that battled against her dark thoughts.

After the conclusion, people filed out of the room. It took some time to reach the freshness of the outdoors. Below the portico, the crowd had thickened since they had been inside. Annabelle glanced up at the sun and guessed it to be around two in the afternoon. She spotted Peggy under the shade tree and joined her there.

"Are you well? You've been standing here nearly two hours."

"I'm fine. Don't be worrying on account of me."

"The procession will come down Pennsylvania Avenue and to the rotunda at the Capitol," Eudora said as she tugged the bow of her bonnet tight.

"Another service?"

"Yes, dear. From what I understand, there are to be many in the coming days. They're going to transport him by train across the country. They'll have services along the way until he's returned to Springfield."

Annabelle nodded dumbly, ashamed that she dreaded another service.

"We shall watch the procession come by, but then I'll need to retire. You two are welcome to remain."

"I've paid my respects," Annabelle said. "I'd like to return to the hotel."

"Yes, of course, dear."

After a few moments, they watched the president, hoisted

by several men, being carried out of the White House. The pallbearers joined the lines of formed ranks of Union soldiers in the street. The tired trio of women stayed until the last of the procession passed by, and then began the long trudge back to the hotel.

Nine

"The country is not what it was. This forced union is not what I have loved. I care not what becomes of me. I have no desire to outlive my country."

John Wilkes Booth

Washington, D.C.
April 24, 1865

*A*nnabelle stared at the notice posted outside the National Hotel. She'd not heard from Matthew since they'd parted ways at the police station, and this poster only deepened her concern. The longer Booth remained free, the longer Matthew would be out there.

> *War Department, Washington*
> *$100,000 Reward!*
> *The Murderer of our late beloved president, Abraham Lincoln, is still at large.*

At least the Union government spared no expense in seeing the man captured. One hundred thousand! She could only imagine. That kind of sum could restore Rosswood—could give her the chance to start over. She studied the faces of the men printed on the broadsheet. Perhaps if Matthew received something for his part.

But no. He served the Union Army now. Anything he found would belong to the government. Wind tugged at her hair, and she adjusted her bonnet. Each clop of hooves and crunch of carriage wheels drew her glance, but so far Lilly and Günter had yet to arrive. It seemed to have taken Günter longer than expected to secure George's papers, but the last telegram said that they would arrive on the train today. Annabelle insisted she be the one to greet them.

A black carriage pulled by a mismatched pair of horses rolled to a stop in front of the hotel. Annabelle took a step closer as the driver ambled down from his perch. Before he had a chance to reach the door, it swung open and Günter's large frame squeezed out.

His gaze immediately landed on Annabelle, and she offered him a bright smile. He lifted his hand in greeting and then turned to offer assistance to the lady inside. Lilly Rose emerged from the carriage and shielded her eyes from the bright sun. The driver, who had just reached the door, shot an annoyed glance at Günter as he took Lilly's arm.

Annabelle hurried forward and threw her arms around Lilly. "You've finally made it!"

Lilly stiffened, then gave a small pat on Annabelle's arm before pulling free. Despite her rigidity, Lilly's eyes filled with a mixture of surprise and amusement. "Well, now, it's nice to see you too, Miss Ross."

The driver and Günter hefted three traveling trunks and plopped them on the ground, causing a flurry of activity from the hotel boys at the door. In a matter of moments, all three were plucked from the ground and disappeared inside.

Günter fished money out of his pocket to press into the waiting hand of the driver. Without a word, the man swung back into his seat and slapped the reins across the horses' backs. Günter watched him go, then looked up at the National Hotel.

He let out a low whistle. "I never see such a hotel," he said in his thick German accent.

"Nor I," Annabelle agreed, tugging on Lilly's hand. "Come, Grandmother is eager to see you."

Lilly allowed Annabelle to pull her along, and the three soon caught up to the boys carrying the trunks on the staircase.

Lilly looked up at the massive chandeliers glittering overhead with much the same awe Annabelle had felt when she'd first arrived.

"Where is Frankie?"

Lilly's features tightened. "Anka is keeping him until I return."

Of course. Such a trip would be difficult on a little one. Still, Annabelle would have liked to have seen the little cherub.

Eudora's door stood open. One boy delivered one trunk to her room while the other two stood waiting outside Annabelle's. She fished the key from her pocket and turned it in the lock, gesturing for them to enter.

After she thanked the boys for delivering the items, they hurried off.

Günter's robust laughter drifted from Eudora's room.

The sound warmed Annabelle's heart, even if it felt out of place among the hushed mourning of the city. Lilly trailed along behind her, eyes downcast.

Inside, Eudora dug through the trunk on the floor. "Did

you get everything I asked you to bring, Lilly?" Eudora asked without looking up.

"Yes, ma'am. I made sure of it." Lilly slipped around Annabelle and leaned close to Eudora's ear.

Eudora gave a nod and closed the lid, straightening her back. "Very good." She turned to Günter. "And you have the papers?"

Günter reached into the inner pocket of his silk-lined jacket and plucked the papers free.

Odd attire for a stable man.

"This fancy coat's as slick as a new foal, Frau Smith."

"I needed a gentleman to escort Lilly Rose." Eudora made a sour face. "Not a stable hand."

Günter grunted. "But stable man is what I am, Frau."

Eudora plucked the papers from Günter's hand. She unfolded them and scanned the contents. "Good. This is exactly what we need."

"May I see them?" Annabelle asked.

She handed the papers over, and Annabelle studied the scrawled name at the bottom. George Daniels. She drew the papers to her chest. "Let's be on our way."

"Shall I wait for you here, Mrs. Smith?" Lilly asked.

Eudora paused on her march out the door. "I expected you to come with us."

Lilly's eyebrows pulled together. "Why?"

"Don't be silly, girl. Let's go."

Lilly stared at Eudora a moment, then clenched her jaw and hurried out the door. Annabelle shot Eudora a curious look, but the older woman only smiled. Shaking the oddity off, Annabelle pulled the door closed behind her.

She wished Peggy was here, but she'd asked to have the morning to herself. Annabelle had been both surprised and glad at the request, and she'd offered Peggy a smile and embrace before sending her on her way.

But now she missed the comfort of Peggy's presence.

After a short carriage ride, they arrived back at the place Annabelle had hoped never to see again. The old capitol building, which they had turned into the Old Capitol Prison, loomed in front of her as she took Günter's hand and stepped down from the carriage. Her heart pounded so rapidly Annabelle feared it would gallop right out of her. She placed trembling fingers on her throat and tried to steady her breathing.

"Are you all right, dear? You're looking rather pale." Eudora's face filled her vision, concerned eyes narrowed into slits.

"I'm…fine."

"I think not." Eudora gestured to Günter. "Günter, would you stay here with Annabelle while Lilly and I go inside?"

"Grandmother, I don't need…"

Eudora waved her hand, and Annabelle snapped her mouth closed. When Eudora Smith got that look, there was no point in arguing with her. Besides, Annabelle couldn't deny the relief she felt at not having to go inside.

Without waiting for her reply, Eudora lifted her hem and strode for the door with Lilly on her heels. Annabelle watched them go, praying that the papers would be enough.

A rat gnawed on the wooden leg of his cot. Curious, George

shifted his weight and let his head fall off the edge. The creature paused and turned a beady black eye on him, the tiny whiskers around its nose quivering. After a moment, it returned to its chewing. George shifted again, bringing his arm over the side. The rat scurried away a few steps, regarding him with that glassy eye.

George shot his hand out and the rat fled. His fingers grazed the slick end of the tail before the rodent shot out of the bars of his cell and down the hall. George sighed and fell back on the cot, wishing he could dart out of here so easily.

How many days had he been here? He didn't know. Unlike Elmira, he didn't have a place to scratch a record of his days. Nothing here but stone. Stone walls, stone floor, and a bed that might as well be stone.

Groaning, he swung his feet over the side of the cot and let his bare toes touch the floor. Cold and smooth. George trailed a toe along the cracks between the stone, wondering if he could free the dirt caught in between.

After a few moments, nothing much came free, and George gave up on the game. He rose, stretched his arms over his head, and padded to the iron bars. He glanced down the hall and suppressed a shiver. The two boys across from him had left some hours ago. He couldn't be sure if they'd been released or simply moved to another place. Any hope for human connection had left with them.

When was the last time someone had brought a tray?

A scuffling sound drew his attention. Something shifted in the shadows, and a form emerged. George tilted his head, watching as it glided down the hall. Wide at the bottom and narrow at the top, the shape resembled a bell. George tilted his head. How strange. The figure continued to glide his way. He narrowed his eyes, trying to separate the form from the gloom.

Ah. Of course. A slow smile drifted onto his lips. She was returning to him again. George had almost thought she wouldn't.

The dreams were becoming more real. Sometimes, the Yankees came to stab him in his bed. Other times, the drowning soldiers at Elmira drifted through his cell, clawing at him with their cold, shriveled fingers. But sometimes, she came.

Those were the good dreams. She'd offer him a gentle smile and her presence would fill him with a measure of hope. It'd been many nights since he'd seen her. He didn't remember falling asleep, but that meant little.

She neared the cell, escaping the shadows that threatened to swallow her. The dream angel came to a stop in front of him. So beautiful. Her ebony hair twisted away from her face, leaving only a single curl hanging down by her ear. Such a lovely curl. He reached through the bars to caress it.

She frowned and took a step back. "Mr. Daniels?"

George blinked. She'd never spoken to him before. Her voice drifted to him like a soft breeze, delicate and sweet.

The vision cocked her head and her almond-shaped eyes narrowed. "You all right?"

She seemed so real he could smell her. He drew a long breath. Yes. The scent of honeysuckle and cinnamon. His dreams had never included aromas before. He suddenly straightened. "Lilly?"

She glanced back down the hall and took a step away from him.

"No! Please!" George stuck his fingers through the bars,

desperate not to lose her. "Don't go. Don't leave me!" Fear flooded his voice, and he hated himself for letting her see him so weak. But he couldn't lose her. Not when she was so close!

Concern flittered over her smooth features. "You're scaring me."

"I...um...may I touch your hand?"

Lilly shied away. "Why?"

"I need to know."

She crossed her hands over her chest and glanced down the hall again. "Know what?"

"If you're real." The whispered words grated against his throat.

She stared at him. He feared that at any moment she'd vanish, so he stared right back, hoping to memorize every detail of her striped gown, pursed lips, and questioning eyes. Finally, she took a small step forward and lifted her hand.

George snaked his fingers through the bars. They quivered.

Lilly must have noticed, because she took another step forward and grabbed his hand. "It's all right, Mr. Daniels."

His knees buckled and he had to catch himself on the bars. She made a small sound and came up against the cell. Worry danced in her beautiful eyes, and it warmed the frozen places within him. He ran his thumb over the back of her hand. "You're really here?"

"I am." She pulled her fingers from his grasp. "Mrs. Smith will be here any moment."

She was really here. In the prison. Alarm shot through him like a cannon blast. "Tell me they haven't arrested you!"

Her nose wrinkled. "We've come to get you out."

"Out?"

"Are you sure you're all right, Mr. Daniels?" She looked at him as though he had lost all his wits.

He pulled his face away from the bars. "I...oh, forgive me, Miss Rose. I'm afraid returning to prison has done...unpleasant things to me."

The concern returned to her face, and she came close again. She reached a hand out to him.

George turned his face away. "I didn't want you to see me like this."

She dropped her hand and wrapped her arms around her tiny waist. Heavy footsteps sounded down the hall, and in a moment, Mrs. Smith appeared with the lawman George remembered meeting at a dinner prior to the assassination. How long ago had that been? Weeks? Months?

"My, but you do look a fright." Mrs. Smith clicked her tongue. "And again I find you without shoes."

George raked a hand through dirty hair that hung limp around his ears and ducked his head.

Metal scraped on metal and the door swung open. George stared at it in disbelief. A trick. The Yankees were playing a trick on him.

"Come along, Mr. Daniels," the man said, his gruff voice laced with annoyance.

George scrambled through the door and stepped into the hallway, his heart pounding. Run. He had to run.

Something touched his shoulder. Alarmed, he looked down. Lilly's fingers grazed his arm. He bent his elbow to escort her. A lady shouldn't be in this place. Behind him, the lawman mumbled something about boots and went into the cell to fetch them.

George took a step forward. No one stopped them. Faces peered at him through the bars, faces scorning him for leaving them behind again. But he couldn't feel the press of guilt now. He must protect the lady at his side. See her freed from this place.

He placed a hand over her cool fingers and gave them a pat of reassurance but didn't remove his eyes from the door at the end of the hall. To his astonishment, no one stopped him when he touched the knob or even when he pulled the door free.

Glaring sunlight washed over him, stinging his eyes with the promise of hope. Voices stirred around him, but he couldn't see. Hands gripped him, but all he could feel was the loss of the delicate one who'd been on his arm.

The hands guided him, and gentle words fell on his ears. He climbed into a carriage and settled onto a soft cushion. His heart hammered a rhythm in his chest, the rat-a-tat of the drum line signaling the battle to come. He tensed, grabbing the sides of the plush cushion underneath him as he began to sway.

"George!"

A voice broke through the sea of muffled sounds and snapped him awake. George blinked at the figure in front of him. The frayed edges of his vision began to clear. Like having his head ducked in winter water, George awoke from his stupor. "Miss Ross!"

A wide grin split her face. "Oh, thank goodness. Are you all right?"

His gaze darted around the inside of the carriage at Annabelle, Mrs. Smith, the stable hand Günter, and finally at the beautiful vision sitting at his side. He pinched the bridge of his nose. "I believe so. Forgive me."

Miss Ross leaned forward. "No forgiveness needed. I regret it took us so long to get you out."

"Indeed." Mrs. Smith watched him in that knowing way of hers. "Any longer and you might not have been the man we brought to Washington."

Heat crept up his neck, but he couldn't deny the truth of her words. "How?"

Mrs. Smith waved some papers at him. "We got these from Elmira."

George took the papers and unfolded them, the words jumping off the page.

Oath of Allegiance.

The words trembled in his fingers and he clutched them tighter to steady their shaking. "My papers were accepted."

"You're not being charged." Annabelle watched him intently.

Suddenly realization slammed into him. "Where's Matthew?"

Fear flooded Annabelle's eyes and nearly brought his pulse to a halt.

"He's gone to help the search, "Mrs. Smith interjected. "He'll return as soon as Mr. Booth is captured."

"He signed the papers, too," Annabelle said softly.

"Matthew signed oath papers?" George studied Annabelle but could find no deception in her open expression. "Why?"

The question hung in the air for a moment.

"We're not entirely sure," Annabelle said, "but it would seem that his helping in the search kept him from being held in the prison like the rest of us."

"They arrested you as well?"

Annabelle nodded, and the look of fear that flashed across her eyes stirred the fire building in his belly. "What kind of people imprison a lady? Is there no end to the Yanks' deplorable—"

Mrs. Smith cleared her throat in a most unladylike fashion, bringing George's words to a halt. "Perhaps, Mr. Daniels, you might recall that all of us present, yourself included, happen to fall beneath such a category?" She plucked an apple from her lap and held it out to him.

Lilly turned questioning eyes on him. Eyes that searched him in such a way that he somehow sensed his reply had a greater meaning than he could fathom. The ire rising within him dissipated with each blink of those silky lashes.

He took Mrs. Smith's offering and gripped the fruit tightly. "Forgive me. You're correct. We are a whole nation once again."

He was rewarded with a flash of joy in the mahogany eyes shining up at him. Something twisted in his heart, and he knew he'd do nearly anything to keep that look in her eyes.

Heaven help him. He was falling in love with a Yank.

Ten

"After being hunted like a dog through swamps, woods, and last night being chased by gunboats till I was forced to return wet, cold, and starving, with every man's hand against me, I am here in despair. And why? For doing what Brutus was honored for and what made Tell a hero. And yet I, for striking down a greater tyrant than they ever knew, am looked upon as a common cutthroat."

John Wilkes Booth

The days following the assassination
Philadelphia
April 15, 1865

*D*avid O'Malley groaned and shifted in his bed. His head felt like it'd been beaten with a hammer. He rubbed his temples, hoping the motion would ease some of the pounding. Perhaps he should dress and go downstairs to inquire if Mrs. Surratt had a tincture of opium to ease this pain.

Swinging his legs over the side of the bed, he forced his eyes to open into slits, admitting the light in a small measure. As his eyes began to adjust, the room around him became clearer— small, poorly furnished, and most certainly *not* his boarding room at Surratt's.

David lurched to his feet. Placing a hand to the throbbing in his head, he took the three strides required to reach the door and pulled on the knob.

It remained firm. His vision swam, and he stumbled backward, nearly falling before he reached the bed again. His stomach roiled, filling his mouth with acid. He swallowed down the foul liquid and crawled on top of the tangled mess of bedclothes, squeezing his eyes tight against the pain.

Some hours later, David awoke to pounding on his door. He opened his eyes. The pain pressing against his skull had lessened. He sat upright without losing vision.

The knock came again. David looked about the room for a weapon. Finding nothing, he rose and crossed to the door, but again found it locked.

"Open up," called a woman's voice from the hall.

David wrenched on the door. "It's locked."

A heavy sigh. "Then use your key."

Key? He patted his rumpled vest. "I don't have a key, as I did not acquire this room. Now let me out!"

After a moment, the lock rattled and the knob turned. David grabbed the door and yanked.

A startled yelp, and then a portly woman frowned at him from the other side of the door. "Your coin only paid for one night, mister. You're going to have to get on now." She wagged a finger in his face.

David looked past the woman and out into the hall. "Where am I?"

The woman crossed her arms over her ample bosoms. "Been sleeping off your drink at the Silver Maiden."

"What drink?"

The woman laughed, a robust sound more suited to a man than a woman. "My Joe said you'd be a bear today. Sure right enough, he was." She sobered and regarded David with a frown. "Now, I'm not one to condemn a man on taking his ale. But when he can't even remember his drink, I say it might be time he stayed away from it."

Memories came crashing down on him. The Grants. The train. Matthew Daniels. The plot.

David's jaw convulsed. Trying to remember his charm, he smoothed his features and hung his head. "Apologies, madam. I'm sure you're right. Tell me, in what town have I landed this time?"

"Philadelphia."

"I was with a companion. A giant of a man. Do you remember him?"

She bobbed netted curls. "He paid for your room."

David's grip on the door tightened. "And where is he now?"

She shrugged. "Left last night. Covered the room and breakfast for you, then took off."

David suppressed a growl that gurgled in his throat. He'd been deceived! He forced a friendly smile, but the bothersome woman still narrowed her eyes.

"You feeling well, mister?"

"Not at all. But I'll be out of your way, madam." And on to the nearest train station.

She looked relieved. "I'll be back in a bit, then, to clean your room." Without waiting for his reply, she hurried away.

David thrust his hand into his vest pocket. Cursing, he searched his trousers. *Robbed!* David whirled and slammed his fist into the wall. The traitor. The thieving, dim-witted, blasted traitor! There would be no more mercy for Matthew Daniels.

He traipsed down the stairs a few moments later to find the husky barkeep giving the plump woman a squeeze on the rear. He turned his eyes away from the crude gesture. He would have never dreamed of treating Eliza like a common tart. The barkeep must have noticed David, because the bear gave the trollop a pat and sent her away.

"Need anything, mister?"

David rubbed his forehead. "Got anything for the throbbing?"

The man chuckled. "Got some coffee. Might help."

David eased onto one of the barstools. "I didn't drink too much."

The man grunted and went around the end of the bar, disappearing to a room in the back. After a moment, he returned with a chipped cup of steaming liquid and handed it to David. "Heard many a man say the same. But you were sure enough wallpapered last night, friend. Saw you myself."

David sipped the bitter liquid, ignoring the comment. "David O'Malley."

"Joe Foster." He took a rag and wiped the polished surface of the bar.

"Tell me, Mr. Foster, what exactly did you see?"

The man flipped the rag over his shoulder. "Fellow brought you in here, all limp like, and said you'd had too much ale. Paid for a room and breakfast, which you missed, and said he had business to return to."

David's insides heated with fury. "And you believed him?"

The man paused, taken aback. "Why not?"

David slammed the mug down on the bar, sending coffee splashing out. "That man assaulted me on the train, suffocated me to unconsciousness." He patted his pockets. "And apparently stole all my money!"

Foster rubbed his thick chin. "But he paid for your room. If he'd done those things, why not just leave you on the street? Seemed like he cared."

"Guilt, I suppose, over his betrayal."

"I'm right sorry for that. It's a bad spin of things."

David snorted and picked up his mug.

The barkeep quickly soaked up the spilled liquid and then leaned on the bar. "There's a telegraph station just down the street, and a bank just past that. You can stay another night, if you need."

David thanked him. He needed a plan. What to do about the failure with the Grants? And the tyrant.

His thoughts ground to a halt. He looked up at the barkeep, who was busy polishing glassware. "Say, you haven't heard any sort of news, have you?"

The man tossed the rag over his shoulder again and stepped closer. "None yet today, but you can probably go down to the post and get the latest. Word last night was they didn't think he'd make it."

David's pulse slowed. "Who wouldn't make it?"

The man's bullish face crumpled. "Sorry, friend. Forgot you missed it. Right tragic."

David leaned closer. "Missed what?"

The big man shook his head, looking despondent. "The president. He was assassinated."

Philadelphia
April 16, 1865

Birds warbled overhead, their bright, incessant chirping in contrast with the storm clouds gathering in David's soul. Across from him, the Silver Maiden stood quiet, an almost amusing disparity to the noise that had pricked at him until the wee hours of the morning when the Yanks had finally ceased their bluster and returned to their homes. He rubbed his shoulder, the muscles tense from sleeping on the stone floor with nothing underneath him…if his fitful time on the floor could be called sleep. A few stolen winks had been all he'd managed prior to the cook kicking him out before the first light of dawn. The barkeep's pity wouldn't see him on the street in last night's rains, but it didn't result in comfort.

This morning he'd been told he wouldn't be allowed back inside without payment, nor would they allow him to claim the breakfast Daniels had supposedly paid for.

Dismissing his ire over the lack of human compassion—what else did one expect from Yanks?—he turned his attention back to the matter at hand. More news had arrived in waves yesterday, flooding the Silver Maiden and crashing upon his throbbing brain until it all became a jumbled mix of tales, rumors, and bad piano music. After hearing that the tyrant no longer besmirched this world and had moved on to his punishment in the next life, David had returned to the pub. The patrons who'd gathered there railed about murder, called for retribution, and lamented in their ale until he longed to see them silenced.

The scent of bread wafted across the road and tickled his nose. David grunted and turned his attention back to the newssheet he'd plucked when the newsboy wasn't looking. He trailed his fingers along the pages. "That cut-rate actor!"

His outburst sent a pigeon squawking and fluttering away in an explosion of feathers. David clamped his mouth shut, but no one seemed to take notice of him, save the riffraff. A few urchins slinked around in the shadows, probing at him with caustic, yet impotent, glances. They would be of no concern, and the few people who were about this early in the morning were more interested in their work than in the rumpled fellow sitting on the bench. They likely thought him a drunkard who'd stumbled out of the pub.

His eyes darted back to the broadsheet, still stunned that Booth had actually prevailed. He'd shot the tyrant right in the middle of Ford's! What a scene it must have been. David inhaled with exuberance over the knowledge that the reign of the tyrant had come to a blessed end, and then he exhaled with a surge of frustration. He'd been played for the fool.

He could see it so clearly now. Booth had sent David on a frivolous errand to keep him from achieving his goal! While he chased the Grants, Booth plotted and absconded with the glory of felling the true prize for himself! David had been robbed of the glorious justice that had been his to serve, the grand dessert on the buffet that fate had spread before him.

Booth had taken it all! In cahoots with Daniels, no doubt. How had he not *known* that someone else might turn his dog against him? What had Booth offered Daniels?

David scanned the reports again. No mention of Daniels in the papers. What had Booth given him to make him betray O'Malley, and how had the man avoided suspicion? Daniels had been putty in his hands, doing everything David had commanded. He grunted and flicked his hair out of his eyes. That lout wasn't bright enough to have come up with such duplicity on his own—it had to have been Booth's doing. The cur.

David narrowed his gaze at the paper once again, forcing his eyes to focus on the news it contained. Booth had gotten away. That could not be considered news at all. Of course he had escaped. They'd planned out the routes to get them back into Confederate territory.

In fact, it had been David's maps that had aided the escape. David had shown that traitor the new paths through Maryland and across to Virginia. The paper crumbled in David's fist. He had no doubt that even now Booth followed David's course, further adding insult to his treachery.

Soon, if not already, Booth would be crossing the river into Virginia, where the South would welcome him with a hero's celebration. A celebration that should have been David's!

Well, not if he had anything to say about it. Take his glory, disappear using his map? There Booth had made his fatal error—an error that would cost him dearly.

Potomac River
Maryland
April 21, 1865

David scanned the muddy banks again, but still no sign of Booth. Grinding his teeth in frustration, he tried not to contemplate the possibility that Booth had not followed his maps after all. The very notion was absurd, of course. Besides, he'd been following the route for days now and had twice seen swarms of mounted Yankees crawling over the land like ants. No doubt they were scurrying around on Booth's trail.

Unfortunately, it had been necessary to swipe a lady's valise in order to get the funds he needed. He'd slipped away unnoticed and, as he'd hoped, found a small purse with Union bills and, better still, a pouch of gold coins buried beneath bits of lace and taffeta. Thanking fate for shining on him once more, he'd pocketed the money and left the lady's belongings for her to recover.

According to the paper tucked under David's arm, Booth remained at large. He swatted away a mosquito and opened the page again. One hundred thousand for his capture. The temptation swirled in him. Two options, but which to take? See Booth dead, or turn him in and use the money to start a new life?

The sun cast rays of violet and crimson across the glittering waters of the river as the day settled into evening. A new life was impossible. Nothing mattered now anyway. The South had laid herself down at the feet of the North, and his Cause had died with the army's cowardice. He had no home to return to, no family to try to wash away the stains of war. His only consolation in this horrid affair was that at least the tyrant laid cold and dead while the imbeciles flocked around his coffin.

David sat among the reeds and propped himself against a tree, watching a Union gunboat make another pass. He had no way of knowing if Booth had already crossed or, like David, simply waited for the Yanks to give up on this area and move to another. He plucked a blade of grass and twisted it between his fingers, watching the green stain his fingertips in the same way that war had stained his soul.

"Forgive me, Liza. I've failed you again."

Why wait here for Booth? He remained undecided. To

capture the man and see him humiliated had its merits, as would watching the expression on his face as David gunned him down. His chest tightened. Did he really want to do that? Murder a fellow Southerner in cold blood?

He stole your glory. It belonged to you.

The thought pounded in his head, almost audible. David pulled his pistol and waved it at the deepening shadows. Crickets began their symphony, undeterred by David's pounding heart.

"Who's there?"

No answer came other than the croak of frogs. David sank to the ground. Just his own thoughts. He chuckled. Thoughts so real they seemed to come from someplace other than his own head. Something in the back of his mind warned he struggled with his grip on sanity, but he pushed the feeling away.

He dropped his head back against the tree and let the inner voice work through his tangled emotions.

The tyrant had to be punished. Such a shame, though, that the glory was stolen.

Anger began as a slow simmer in David's gut. He plucked a stone from the ground and tossed it in the river. It hit with a *plop* and then sank to the murky bottom.

Very little light remained, and this was nothing more than a fool's errand. He no longer cared if Booth crossed, drowned, or was captured. If he didn't stop this obsession, he would become nothing more than a blithering idiot in an asylum. Liza wouldn't have wanted that. He straightened his coat and turned to leave the water's edge.

But then, truth be told, he did care. Booth deserved to pay for his betrayal. Just as Lincoln deserved to pay for Liza's death.

Off to his left, three shadows emerged, scurrying like mice along the water's edge. Two of them pushed a small boat into the edge of the river, then assisted the third. David narrowed his eyes, focusing on the man hobbling on a crutch. One man got into the boat, and the other helped the cripple.

The fire inside intensified, swallowing him up and melting every thought but one—he'd found his quarry.

Eleven

"I hoped for no gain. I knew no private wrong. I struck
for my country and that alone. A country that groaned
beneath this tyranny, and prayed for this end, and yet
now behold the cold hands they extend to me."
John Wilkes Booth

Bowling Green, Virginia
April 24, 1865

*M*atthew raked a hand through his hair, loosening it from
the leather tie at the nape of his neck and letting it fall
free. He would need to cut it before his wedding. He'd not given
much thought to having his hair in a fashionable style, but if he
could, he'd like to surprise Annabelle by having their image
captured on that joyous day. His cousin Charles had done it for
his Lydia, and Matthew wanted to give Annabelle the same
treasure.

Matthew rolled his shoulders to loosen the tension. How
long until they could be wed? Hopefully, before summer came
in force, he and Annabelle would be sipping lemonade at
Rosswood as husband and wife. The thought stirred his blood,
and he ached for this quest to be over.

They had been running around for days, and it seemed to Matthew that the fool would never be caught. Likely, too many Southerners would hold Booth in secret, and he would dive ever deeper into the South. How long would the Union chase him? To the gulf coast, no doubt. Even if it took months, the Yanks would have their revenge.

Matthew stretched his shoulders and adjusted himself in the saddle. No one seemed to worry about him much anymore, and for the most part the Blues simply ignored him. No one even glanced back at him to see if he still followed. Part of him wondered how far he would get if he turned the horse around and galloped away. He grunted. Not far enough. Besides, that would only put the people he loved in further danger.

The detachment of Yanks in front of him looked every bit as tired as Matthew felt. They'd traipsed through the woods looking for Booth until they'd decided he no longer hid anywhere in the area, only to find they'd missed him, and the murderer had likely already crossed into Virginia. Matthew scooped up the loose strands of his hair and retied the bit of leather to keep the wind from sending locks into his eyes.

His thoughts returned to Annabelle, as they most often did. Worry churned in his gut each time he pictured her waiting in a cold prison cell for him to find the assassin and see her freed. Each day, each hour the man ran free, the more Matthew hated him.

He slipped a flask from the inside of his coat and turned it to his lips. The hot liquid slid down his throat and pooled in his belly. Three more sips, and his frayed nerves began to calm. Four years of war without taking a swig, and this mess had sent him reaching for the flask.

He pushed the hardened wooden stopper back into the flask and tucked it inside his coat. He only needed a little. The ale the Yanks gulped every night hadn't been enough to soothe, and he'd needed the whiskey to make it through the long days with them.

And the nights. The nightmares were the worst of it. Boys too young to be in uniform melted beside him, their faces contorted in pain and fear. Boys he could not save. Other nights it was the prison. Watching the walking bones of Elmira usually sent him into a fever, and he woke in a cold sweat.

He plucked the flask out again. One more sip wouldn't hurt. The prison dreams were the worst. Last night he'd not only seen George's shivering bones along the river at Elmira, but in the midst of it all stood Annabelle, her dress in rags and her pleading voice calling for him to save her.

A shiver snaked down his spine as one sip turned to a gulp. The liquor's fire would numb him. He tucked the flask away and pulled up on the reins, noticing the others had come to a stop.

"Where are we?"

A Yankee about twenty years his senior twisted in the saddle. "Star Hotel. Got a tip a man here knows where Booth is."

"Let's hope that's true, so we can see the fiend captured and this thing finished."

The Yank appeared pleased with the cold steel in Matthew's voice. "Indeed."

They dismounted, tied the horses, and in a few moments filled the small lobby of the hotel with a wave of blue wool. Matthew plucked at his collar, the fire in his gut and the warm spring weather making him wish he could shed the coat and toss it in the street.

"We're looking for a man by the name of Jett," Lieutenant Baker called out.

Matthew looked over the heads of the soldiers and to the main receiving desk for the hotel, where a wide-eyed proprietor gestured upstairs. Nodding, Baker scanned the soldiers.

"Doherty, Conger...and Daniels, come with me."

Ignoring the looks he received from the soldiers he passed, Matthew wound his way through them, followed the lieutenant up the stairs, and waited in the hall as the officer pounded on the door. After a few moments, it swung open, and a dark-haired man stared out at them.

The fellow, apparently Mr. Jett, appeared to have been roused from his bed, though the day was more than half spent. He stroked a narrow chin, his smooth face delicate. He reminded Matthew of a man meant for books rather than war.

"Yes?" Jett asked, his gaze skittering over their company.

"Where are the two men who came with you across the river?" Conger demanded, not wasting a moment on introductions or pleasantries.

The man's dark eyes rounded, and he took a small step away from the door. Baker turned and motioned to Matthew. Knowing his role, Matthew straightened his spine—taking advantage of his height and bearing—and took a commanding step forward.

Jett gulped. "I know who you want, and I can tell you where they can be found."

Baker nodded. "Tell us, and you won't be held for treason."

Jett glanced at Matthew once more, and then his shoulders drooped. "I was on my way to Caroline County, Virginia, in company with Lieutenant Ruggles and a young man named

Bainbridge."

Conger, the detective, held up his hand. "Union or Confederate?"

"I was formerly a member of the Ninth Virginia Cavalry."

Confederate.

Conger grunted. "Go on."

"At Port Conway, on the Rappahannock, I saw a wagon down on the wharf—at the ferry—on the Monday a week after the assassination of President Lincoln." He tugged on the collar of his shirt, releasing the first button. "A young man got out of it, came toward us, and asked us what command we belonged to. We were all dressed in Confederate uniforms. Lieutenant Ruggles said that we belonged to Mosby's command. The young man then asked where we were going, and I replied that it was a secret."

Baker frowned. "Why?"

Jett shrugged. "After that, we went back on the wharf, and a man with crutches got out of the wagon. We asked him what command he belonged to, and he replied, 'To A. P. Hill's corps.' The young man then said that their name was Boyd, and that his brother there was wounded at Petersburg, and he asked if we would take him out of the lines."

Baker and Conger exchanged a glance.

"We didn't tell him where we were going," Jett said again, noticing the exchange.

The lieutenant declined to reply and the muscles in Jett's jaw tightened. He cleared his throat. "Then he asked us to go and take a drink with him, but we declined. We went up to the house and sat down, conversing among ourselves. We'd only sat a few moments, however, when the man called Boyd came and asked me to speak with him privately."

"And did you?" Baker inquired.

"I went down with him to the wharf, and he said, 'I suppose you're raising a command to go south?' and added that he would like to go along with us. At length, I said, 'I cannot go with any men I don't know anything about.' Then he seemed agitated. He said, 'We are the assassinators of the president!'"

Baker's features tightened, and he leaned closer to the wide-eyed Confederate. "And what then?"

"I was so confounded that I didn't reply. Not that I remember." Baker narrowed his eyes, and Jett hurriedly continued, "Lieutenant Ruggles was very near, and I called to him."

"I thought you stated he was up at a house," Conger interjected.

"He was watering his horse," Jett replied, his brown eyes landing on each of them before returning to Baker. "I called to him, and he came, and Boyd said again that they were the assassins. Then the young man said that the other was Booth, and he was Harold, but that they wanted to pass under the name of Boyd."

"And you believed this to be true?" Conger asked.

Jett nodded. "He didn't seem very self-possessed, and his voice trembled, but he clearly pointed at the other man and said, 'Yonder is J. Wilkes Booth, the man who killed Lincoln.'"

Matthew shifted in his stance, eager to be on with the hunt, lest the man continue to slip past them. Baker, however, remained calm and gestured for Jett to continue his tale.

"They went across the river with us, and then we went on up to the road to Port Royal and on to a Mr. Garrett's. That's where we left them."

"So you aided them?" Baker boomed.

Jett shifted his stance. "I'll go there with you. Show you where they are."

Conger scowled. "You have a horse?"

"Yes, sir."

"Get it, and be ready to go." He turned to leave and then paused. "You say they're on the road to Port Royal?"

"Yes, sir, about three miles this side of it."

Matthew groaned. They had just come that way and had missed him. Likely, he'd be gone before they could double back.

"We've just come from there," Conger said, voicing Matthew's thoughts.

Jett appeared embarrassed and scratched his head. "I thought you came up from Richmond. If you came that way, then you went past them. I cannot tell you whether they are there now or not."

Conger grabbed Jett by the shoulder and the man winced. "It makes little difference. You'll take us back, and we'll see."

Jett closed the door while they waited outside for him to dress, and then they returned to the rest of the men waiting below. All eyes followed Jett, and in a few minutes, the man had his horse saddled and rode beside Matthew.

Matthew regarded the man openly, but he wouldn't meet his gaze. "I was in the Mississippi," Matthew finally said.

Jett turned his narrowed brown eyes on Matthew's uniform. "Yet you wear blues?"

"I must see this fiend captured, or else they won't release my… *intended*." The word felt good on his tongue and brought soothing warmth to his insides not brought on by the drink. He counted the days until he could make such a claim in truth.

Confusion marred Jett's features.

"They're holding people," Matthew explained. "More than a hundred, if I were to guess, until Booth is caught. Anyone who might be connected with him."

"And your lady? Is she involved?"

Memories of everything they'd endured crashed on him like a foaming wave, but he shook his head. "She and my brother were simply at the theatre that night," he said, too low for the Yanks riding in front of him to hear.

Jett pursed his lips. "Our country is lost. I see no option other than to attempt to live under the rule of this one. Do what we must."

Matthew tilted the kepi on his head and cast a long glance at Jett. "So you know why I wear blue."

"I hope for your lady's sake, then, he's still where we left him."

Matthew's shoulders tightened and he curled his fingers into his palms, hoping that at long last they'd come to the end of the chase and he could return to collect those he loved.

Twelve

"For my country I have given up all that makes life sweet and holy, brought misery on my family, and am sure there is no pardon for me in heaven since man condemns me so."
John Wilkes Booth

National Hotel
Washington, D.C.
April 25, 1865

*G*eorge laid aside the razor and assessed his reflection in the mirror. Tired, amber eyes stared back at him, taunting him with flecks of desperation he couldn't hide. Nor ignore. What would he do now? They had strict orders not to leave the city.

He ran a comb through his damp hair. A few limp strands of straw-colored locks flopped back down across his forehead. He needed some oil to keep them back, but what did it matter? Still lanky from his stint in Elmira, he'd not had adequate time to regain his health before being thrown in prison once again. Now he looked like a walking scarecrow. Last night's hearty meal and Mrs. Smith's never-ending thrust of foodstuffs in his direction today had eased the pains in his stomach but had not yet put meat on his bones.

Thank God for Mrs. Smith sending the stable hand to fetch his loyalty papers. He'd feared his sanity may have very well been lost if he'd stayed at the Old Capitol much longer. Hour by hour he could feel his mind slipping away, eroding under a volley of memories he couldn't shake. He strode to the bed and dropped to his knees.

Lord, I need someone. I know Your love is complete for me, but, please, Father. I need someone to share my life with, to be there to hold and love. Someone to temper these pains.

Immediately Lilly's sweet face filled his vision. Her eyes held equal amounts of spark and kindness, and he desperately wanted her to be his anchor. But he'd vowed that he would take all decisions to the Father first. He couldn't stand to make a wrong decision that might thrust him into further heartache. He forced her vision aside.

Lord, you know what that lady does to my heart. She calls to me in a way no other ever has. But I will not move unless you say it's right.

George sat quietly, letting his heart praise his maker for His goodness. Then gently, like an unmoored ship drifting on the current, Lilly's face returned to him again, along with a warm feeling of peace that drifted over him.

Feeling he knew his answer, George spent a few more moments giving praise to the Father for answering his plea. Finally, he rose and pulled on a clean coat, his heart lurching inside him.

Now, to make God's will known to the lady.

Lilly Rose shook out another of Mrs. Smith's gowns and spread it across the bed. All these wrinkles! Mercy, she'd have a time getting them out.

"Smooth your brow, Lilly, or you'll find yourself with permanent furrows." Mrs. Smith didn't even look up from the paper across her lap.

How had she known? She swung her gaze to her employer's granddaughter, a young woman whose mixture of sweetness and spunk Lilly admired. The lady's sparking blue eyes met her gaze.

Miss Ross scrunched her pert little nose. "At least I'm not the only one scolded about wrinkles."

Lilly couldn't help but smile, or like the woman. Perhaps they could even be friends. Lilly pushed the thought away. There she went forgetting her station again. It became harder and harder to remember she was nothing more than a poor working-class woman, though, when she swished around in silk gowns.

"Yes'um," she mumbled in mock petulance.

"Yes *ma'am*," Mrs. Smith corrected, waving her dainty hand.

Miss Ross giggled, and Lilly joined her. Then, remembering herself, she sobered and plucked another black gown out of the trunk. Why Mrs. Smith owned so many when she seldom left her home still baffled her.

"We're going shopping today," Mrs. Smith announced. She folded the paper and smacked it against the table as though daring anyone to argue.

Surprisingly, Miss Ross did just that. "You can't be serious. We've enough gowns already."

Mrs. Smith rose from her seat and looked through all that Lilly had brought. "I'm tired of sitting in this room. Besides, you'll need just the right dress for the trial. Modest, certainly, and delicate. Something that shows your innocence and sincerity."

Miss Ross puckered her lips. "But my words will show my honesty and sincerity, Grandmother, not a gown."

Lilly cocked her head. "What trial?"

"Why, the trial they will hold for the assassins, of course," Mrs. Smith answered.

She dropped her gaze to the patterned carpet underfoot, still not used to the finery she always found herself in, even after nearly three years. Some mornings, she still awoke before dawn to head to her work in the factory. She rubbed her fingers as though they still ached from the stitching she'd done from before the day began until after the sun had bedded at night.

Suddenly, one of her hands disappeared inside a creamy white one. Lilly startled. Odd, how a wealthy white lady had such rough hands. These were not the hands of the delicate dolls that never lifted a finger. They felt like the fingers of one accustomed to hard work. Lilly looked up into kind eyes that reminded her of a smooth lake.

"I wondered the same." Miss Ross gave her hand a squeeze and then released it. "How do you know they'll hold a trial, Grandmother?"

The older woman scoffed. "It seems rather obvious, I would think. It's just a matter of how many of Booth's plotters they'll sit beside him."

Miss Ross's face paled to a milky white. "Oh, dear."

"Don't worry, child." Mrs. Smith patted her granddaughter's arm. "I'm sure your Mr. Daniels won't be among them. His work in the search is evidence enough."

Miss Ross offered a weak smile, though Lilly could tell the lady only did so to appease her elder. The poor woman feared for her man. Lilly pressed her hands against her stomach, remembering the infant she'd carried inside as the thoughts of her late husband surfaced. She needed to get home to her sweet boy.

She dropped her hand and addressed her employer. "When will I be returnin' home, Mrs. Smith?"

"Whenever you're ready, I suppose."

Relieved, Lilly smiled. "Thank you, ma'am. I'd like to go today."

"Hum? Oh, no, it'll have to be in the morning, at the earliest. We're shopping today, remember?"

Lilly let out a long breath, swinging her gaze to Miss Ross, who returned her look with matching annoyance and resignation. There'd be no sense in arguing.

A knock sounded, and Lilly hurried across the room. She found the elder Mr. Daniels on the other side of the door. As soon as his gaze landed on hers, his eyes lit up, turning them from a warm honey to a bright amber. A smile played on his mouth, sending a swarm of butterflies dancing in her stomach.

Remembering the strange way he'd looked at her in the prison, those fetching eyes so full of adoration, she dropped her gaze. Mercy, what was wrong with her? This here was a plantation man. The worst kind! So why, then, did his smile melt her and his touch make her legs as wiggly as blackberry jelly?

She turned away from him before he could see anything he shouldn't in her eyes. "Mista Daniels is here to see y'all."

Surprise tumbled through her. She'd suppressed that talk for years, carefully molding her speech the way Mrs. Smith had directed. Why did it bubble from her lips now?

Mr. Daniels cleared his throat. "Actually…I've come to speak to you, Miss Rose, if you'll allow it."

Her eyes darted back up to his. Yes, like warm honey with flecks of gold. His intense gaze studied her as if searching for something. She blinked. "Me? What for?"

"Go on, dear. The lobby is a perfectly acceptable place for entertaining the gentleman."

How could she imply such an improper thing right in front of the man? Heat crawled up her neck, but Mrs. Smith only flicked a knowing smirk at the man standing behind her.

Drawing her lips into a disapproving line, Lilly focused on Mr. Daniels, schooling her features into the sophisticated look she'd worked to perfection. "What, exactly, do you wish to see me about, sir?"

The confounding man dropped his gaze to the floor, shifting his stance like a nervous suitor. Panic seized her gut, while at the same time her traitorous heart gave a mighty leap. What foolishness!

"I'd hoped we could discuss it downstairs. First, however, I'll need to have a word with Mrs. Smith."

Lilly's heart pounded so fiercely she feared everyone could hear it. Numbly, she gestured for him to step inside. Before she could think to do anything else, Miss Ross grabbed her arm and swept her into the hallway, pulling the door closed behind them.

Miss Ross clapped her hands, and the unexpected sound made Lilly jump.

"I knew there was something in his eyes when he looked your way." Miss Ross laughed. "I just knew it."

The woman had lost all her senses.

Miss Ross paced the small space between the doors lining the hall. "I thought perhaps the look was because he remembered his own wife and child, but now I see I was mistaken."

Lilly opened her mouth to speak, but it felt like someone had stuffed it with cotton. She swallowed and tried again. "What in tarnation are you talkin' about?"

Miss Ross cocked her head, her face palling. "Oh, I didn't think! I shouldn't have told you, as it wasn't my place to do so." She pinched a pink lip between her teeth. "Please don't let on that I told you, but George lost his wife in childbirth before the war."

Sympathy washed over Lilly. She couldn't imagine the pain of losing both her marriage partner and her child. True, her affections for Bernardo had never been immense, but she'd still been drowned in sorrow with the loss of her husband. And at least she had little Frankie to remember his smile by. Poor Mr. Daniels had lost everything. "I won't say anything, Miss."

"Please, do call me Annabelle."

A rustle of fabric made both women turn before Lilly could reply. Peggy bounded down the hall with the energy of a much younger woman. "There you is, Miss Belle. The carriage is waitin'."

Annabelle lifted her thin brows. "What carriage?"

"The one your grandma told me to fetch for shopping."

Annabelle sighed and glanced at Lilly. Then she brightened. "Tell him to come back in about an hour. We'll be a bit delayed."

"Is everythin' all right?"

Mr. Daniels stepped out of the room, looking brighter than Lilly had seen him since they'd left the prison.

He offered her his arm. "Shall we go to the lobby, Miss Rose?"

Lilly's gaze slid over the two women in front of her. Peggy wore a mask of confusion that burst into a look of surprise, and Annabelle gazed at her with a gentle satisfaction. Her blue eyes left Lilly's face and landed on Mr. Daniels, and Lilly's heart jerked.

Mercy, hadn't this man courted Annabelle in New York? What must she think about him offering his arm to a mulatto? But instead of the piercing anger she expected, there seemed to be a look of understanding pass between them, and Annabelle's pink lips turned up.

Everyone looked at Lilly, and she pressed a hand to her heart, hoping to calm it. Her gaze darted to Mr. Daniels, who still stood with his arm extended to her. Despite her better judgment, Lilly tucked her fingers into the crook of his arm and allowed herself to be led away.

A thrill ran through him at having such a rare beauty on his arm. Her golden, sun-kissed skin and dark hair were exotic.

Lord, Your match for me certainly comes with a fetching face!

He nearly chuckled but caught himself before he had to explain his mirth to the lady. She already must think him mad, and the hesitation in her step proved that he'd need to proceed with caution. He did not mind taking his time, though. God had already shown him his anchor, and he would not ruin anything by being impatient.

They descended the staircase and found a settee, two chairs, and a small table just off from the receiving desk. George chose this location in part because no one else currently occupied the space, and partly because he assumed the proximity to the main desk might ease the lady's nerves.

He'd chosen wisely. Lilly's shoulders relaxed a bit as she took a seat in one of the single chairs and arranged her skirts. The shimmering blue fabric with bits of lace reminded him of what it had been like courting fine ladies when he was a youth. Now, at twenty-eight, he had almost forgotten what the flutter of excitement had been like.

He cleared his throat. "Um, Miss Rose..." he began as he sat on the end of the settee closest to her.

She tilted her head, drawing his gaze to the curve of her smooth jaw and the lines of her neck. "Why do you keep calling me that?"

His gaze snapped back to her chestnut eyes. "Isn't that your family name?"

"No. I don't have one."

"You don't have a family name?"

She shook her head, and a stray lock dropped from her modest bun. His fingers itched to reach out and test its softness, so he clenched his hand into a fist instead.

She looked sorrowful, and George could not bear to pry. She'd tell him in time. He offered an encouraging smile—one she'd see if she ever turned those beautiful, almond-shaped eyes back up to him.

"Everyone just calls me Lilly."

A tingle slid through him at the implied familiarity of using given names. What had overcome him? Never had a young woman affected him this way. He ran his tongue over his dry lips. But he wouldn't use the familiarity, not until she understood he spoke her given name with intimacy and not because he saw her as merely a working-class woman.

Still, the idea tempted. "You could call me George."

"Oh, no, sir. I can't do that."

Disappointment scurried over him like a scalded rat. "Why not?"

"It ain't proper." Her eyes widened and she put her fingers to her lips as though she'd said something wrong. *Curious.* Tamping down his discouragement, George folded his hands in his lap. "Miss Rose, I've spoken to Mrs. Smith, as I didn't know who else might speak for you."

Her eyes flashed. "What do you mean, speak for me? I speak for myself."

This wasn't going well. He pulled in a long breath to steady his nerves. He must remember that Lilly wouldn't be accustomed to the ways of the elite. No matter. He'd help her become a proper lady for Westerly.

She stared at him with narrowed eyes, and he realized he took too long answering. "Forgive me. However, that's why we're here." At her confused look, he continued. "So that I might speak to you as well."

Her features softened.

"I'd like to ask if you'd accept my suit." His heart thudded like a thoroughbred, and he found himself holding his breath.

He stared into her eyes, trying to judge her reaction. What he saw there made his pulse quicken further. Hope, excitement—and dare he believe it—attraction darted across those warm depths before she lowered her lids, splaying dark lashes across her smooth skin.

Anticipation swirled within him as he waited. Finally, she turned her eyes upon him again, but the determined glint he found there shot holes in all his hopes.

"I can't do that. I'm sorry."

"Why?" Hating himself for playing the begging fool, George nonetheless had to know the answer.

"You really don't know, do you?" The disappointment in her tone sent shards through him. Uncertainty crinkled the corners of her eyes, then resignation turned golden chestnut to a dull brown. "You're a plantation owner, sir. One who had, or has, slaves. I could never hold affections for such a man."

Without waiting for his reply, she jumped to her feet and dashed away, leaving George with a devastating feeling that threatened to reduce all his hopes to ash.

Thirteen

"God try and forgive me and bless my mother. I do not repent the blow I struck. I may before God but not to man. Tonight I try to escape the bloodhounds once more. Who can read his fate? God's will be done."

John Wilkes Booth

April 26, 1865
1:00 a.m.

*M*atthew's nerves felt nearly as taut as his muscles. He itched to pull the flask from his jacket, equally loathing himself for becoming dependent on it and at the same time desperately wanting its numbing comfort.

He'd quit once this mess came to an end.

The horse pranced underneath the saddle that Matthew tried again to tighten. The animal likely sensed Matthew's own distress. He forced his shoulders to lower, released the girth, and paused to stroke the animal's thick neck. The mare had shed her winter coat, and the slick white hair underneath felt good under his fingers. He gave her a good scratch along the mane, and after a moment, she relaxed and turned her head into his fingers. Matthew gave her a good pat, then returned to saddling. He couldn't blame her for detesting being saddled again so soon, but they had little time to waste on sleep. Better to try to catch Booth when he'd least expect it.

The mare stood for Matthew this time, and he pulled the girth tight and cinched it. He swung up into the saddle and waited for the rest of the men. Tension seethed in the air around them, reminding Matthew of the energy before a battle. He scanned the faces of the group. Had he ever fired on any of these men? Shot down those in their ranks?

Matthew scrubbed a hand over his face. How he longed to see Annabelle. Pull her close against him and breathe in her sweet smell of lavender and femininity. Too soon he had gained and lost her.

Would these fools hurry up? They were wasting time! If Booth escaped this time—

No. They would find him. Had to. He couldn't stand it much longer knowing the two people he loved wallowed in filth and unjust containment.

"Looks like your head's about to start smoking, fellow." A boy who looked barely old enough to be called a man regarded Matthew thoughtfully.

He narrowed his gaze and gave the boy a look that had made more impressive men cower.

The young soldier merely sucked at his teeth. "Anxious to see the murderer brought in, are you?" Matthew opened his mouth to reply, but the auburn-haired young man kept talking. "Yes, sir, I sure am, too." He eased his horse closer and into the circle of lamplight provided by the post above them.

The two animals touched muzzles, giving one another a good sniff. Matthew's horse bobbed her head.

"You think he'll still be there?" the boy asked.

Matthew's muscles bunched again. "He'd better be."

The boy gave Matthew a look of approval. "You're right patriotic for a Reb."

Matthew planned to snarl, but the look of innocent sincerity on the boy's face melted his ire into a chuckle. "Boy, that fool's caused nothing but trouble for all of us. Don't do much for rebuilding relations between the states, that's for certain."

"You're right about that, mister. Sure enough."

The call came for them to move out, and instead of taking his customary place at the back of the pack, Matthew allowed his horse to fall in stride with the boy's, and they settled into the middle of the procession.

Last night they'd received word that more men had joined the search, and hounds were scouring the countryside.

The fresh scent of Virginia air drifted over them, reminding him of the peaceful evenings at Westerly he'd taken for granted. Bullfrogs croaked as they passed, annoyed by the clip-clop of hooves at such a witching hour. Up ahead, Matthew could just see the tops of a cluster of buildings in the moonlight, and he hoped they belonged to the farm they sought.

The man they'd brought along, Jett, waved his hand at Detective Conger. "We're close. Let's stop here and look around."

Conger narrowed his eyes. "Lieutenant Baker! Come with us."

The officer scowled, as though resentful of being under the orders of a policeman outside their military structure, but begrudgingly obliged. Did the man plot to separate the leaders from the group and snare them in a trap?

A buzz of energy thrummed through the group of men as

the two rode off together, leaving the cavalry to stew in anticipation as they shifted on their mounts in the wash of silvery moonlight. Matthew brushed away a bead of sweat that threatened to drop into his eye.

After what felt like an hour, but surely was only a few minutes, the men returned, and Conger seemed agitated. "We may have found him. Spread out and surround the farm. Take any man who tries to run."

The men spurred their horses into action, and like a coming storm of wrath they galloped toward the Garrett farm. Reaching the outskirts, they dismounted, tied the horses, and fanned out.

Gravel crunched beneath Matthew's boots as he stepped through a small gate and came upon a clearing with a modest house, a large barn, and a few other outbuildings. The hairs on the back of his neck rose. Crickets increased their song as though warning away any who sought shelter here. Remembering O'Malley and the barn he'd instructed Matthew to wait within, Matthew turned in that direction. If the pattern held true, the men would have given the owners a signal and then remained in the barn.

Conger glanced in Matthew's direction, the light of the full moon making his stern features clear. Matthew gave him a knowing look and gestured toward the barn. Conger motioned for Lieutenant Baker to go to the door of the house, and then nodded for Matthew to take a position near the barn. He kept an eye on the house as well, just to be certain. He couldn't allow the miscreant to get away again.

Lieutenant Baker pounded on the door, and after a moment an older fellow appeared, his gray hair disheveled and his hastily thrown-on robe evidence he'd been roused from his bed.

"Are you Garrett?"

The man's Adam's apple dropped at the lieutenant's booming voice, then he gave a small nod.

Conger strode up to the house, though he didn't mount the porch steps. "Where are the two men who stopped here at your house?"

Garrett shifted his weight and glanced off to the side. "They're gone."

"Gone where?"

Garrett tugged at his collar. "Gone to the woods."

Conger, growing increasingly more agitated, pointed a finger at Garrett. "Well, sir, *whereabouts* in the woods?"

Garrett's eyes widened and his nervous gaze darted around the stony faces of the men gathered in his yard. Then he threw up his hands. "They came here without my consent. I swear it! I had nothing to do with those fellows. I did not want them to stay! I—"

"I don't want any long stories!" Conger held up his hand. "I just want to know where these men have gone."

Matthew glanced back toward the barn, his suspicions growing.

"I tell you, I…I didn't want them here." The old man stumbled over his words, his voice becoming a higher pitch and more garbled with each plea of innocence.

Conger shouted to the men behind him. "Bring a lariat rope. I'll put that man up to the top of one of those locust trees."

The man stopped his babbling and stared at Conger with wide eyes. Matthew had no doubt he'd do it. Leave it to the Blue Devils to string up an elderly man.

A lanky young man suddenly darted out of the house, and

STEPHENIA H. McGEE

the lieutenant and several others of the cavalry drew pistols.

"Please, don't hurt the old man!" He lifted his palms. "He's scared. I'll tell you where the men are."

The Yanks lowered their weapons but didn't put them away. Matthew, not having been given a weapon, simply watched the young man.

His gaze darted to the barn, confirming Matthew's suspicions. "They're in the barn."

Matthew turned on his heel and strode for the structure as the rest of the Blue Bellies scurried into position. He took a place near the door. The old barn had weathered until the planks no longer touched, leaving cracks in between wide enough for any mouse.

A shadow too large to be a rodent scurried across one of the cracks. Matthew narrowed his eyes and took a step closer, but hurried footsteps behind him made his head swivel to the rear.

Another young man, similar in form and appearance to the one who'd told them to look in the barn, scuttled around a large oak.

Conger pointed at the newcomer. "You! Go in there and take the arms from those men."

The boy shook his head, eyes wild with fear. "Oh, no, sir. I don't want to go in there."

Baker stepped past Matthew and clamped a hand on the boy's shoulder. "They know you. You can go in." Without waiting for the Garrett boy's reply, Baker raised his voice and shouted at the barn. "We're going to send in this man, whose premises you're on, to get your arms. You must come out and give yourselves up!"

The boy gulped and nodded, then slowly marched to the

126

door. He slipped inside. Conger waved his hand, and the cavalry men all came in closer, tightening their noose on the barn.

After a moment or two, the boy scurried back outside. "The man cursed me and said I betrayed him. He threatened to shoot me!"

Conger, looking none too convinced, widened his stance. "How do you know he was going to shoot you?"

The boy threw up his hands. "He reached down to the hay behind him to get his revolver, so I came back out!"

Clenching his jaw, Conger nodded to Lieutenant Baker.

"Come out here and deliver yourselves up!" Baker shouted. "If you don't, in five minutes we'll set this barn ablaze."

Matthew withheld a humorless laugh. The Yankee solution for everything. Burn it to the ground.

A voice rang out from inside, thick with desperation yet still laced with arrogance. Matthew recognized the slick tongue of John Booth instantly. "Who are you and what do you want?"

Baker's eyes blazed. "We want *you*. Give up your arms and come out."

There was only a slight hesitation. "Let us have a little time to consider it."

Matthew snorted. More like time to figure out a way either to escape or bring down as many of their numbers as he could.

Baker, however, foolishly agreed. "Very well. Five minutes."

They stood there in silence, all eyes fixated on the barn for the slightest sign that the man would make a move, but all remained quiet. Frogs and crickets sang, their lives unaffected. Some of the fellows poked the toes of their knee-high boots into the moist earth. Others fingered their weapons, itching to release pistols and swords from their confines.

Finally, after nearly a quarter hour of the men heaping further tension on top of their already fraying nerves, Booth called out again, "Who are you, and what do you want?"

Conger growled and pointed a finger at Baker. "Don't tell him who we are. If he thinks we're Rebels…" His gaze crawled across Matthew. "Or thinks we're his friends, we'll take advantage of it."

Matthew glared at him, not bothering to hide his disgust. He wanted the man brought out as much as any of the rest of them, but the Yanks' unfathomable lack of honor soured his gut.

Conger hurried to add, "We won't lie, but we needn't answer any questions." He turned his back to Matthew, but Matthew could still hear the man's words. "We simply insist on his coming out, if he will."

"Don't make any difference who we are," Baker shouted back at the barn. "We know who *you* are, and we want to take you prisoner."

Conger groaned, and Baker cast him a curious glance.

"This *is* a hard case." The voice drifted from the barn, just as smooth and utterly convinced of his own merit as the fervent voice Matthew remembered from that day they'd tried to overrun Lincoln's carriage. "Maybe I am to be taken by my friends?" Booth asked.

Conger and Baker exchanged a look, and Matthew wondered if Booth had heard their earlier exchange.

After a moment, Booth shouted, "Captain!" A tingle ran down Matthew's spine. "I know you to be a brave man, and I know you're honorable."

Conger and Baker both stared at Matthew. Booth had recognized him. Did he think Matthew had come here under disguise to help him?

"I'm a cripple. I have but one leg. If you'll withdraw your men one hundred yards from the door, I'll come out and fight you."

Matthew opened his mouth, but Conger silenced him with a glare. Lieutenant Baker lurched forward before either of them had a chance to respond to the foolish notion. "We didn't come here to fight you! We have simply come to make you our prisoner."

A frustrated reply shot from between the wooden slats. "If you'll take your men fifty yards from the door, I'll come out and fight you. Give me a chance for my life!"

Conger snarled. "We will not withdraw, nor fight. Come out and surrender and be done with it!"

The theatrical voice rang out over them. "Well, my brave boys, prepare a stretcher for me!"

Conger's forehead furrowed and he stomped away from the barn to motion for the young Garrett boy. "Gather up some brush and pile it around the barn. Pine boughs, if you've got them."

The boy hurried away, the terror in his expression sending a wave of pity through Matthew's gut. After the boy placed limbs nearly all the way around the structure, he came running back up to Conger, a few paces off to Matthew's left.

"That man inside says that if I put any more brush in there, he'll put a ball through me."

The tight lines around Conger's mouth softened. "Very well. You need not go there again."

Conger motioned to Baker, and the two men stood hunched low together, their conversation too hushed to reach Matthew's ears.

"There's a man in here who wants to come out!" Booth called.

Looking satisfied with himself, though Matthew couldn't fathom why, Baker's lips curled into a slow grin. "Let him throw his arms out and come outside."

Voices bounced around in the barn, as a discussion passed between at least two men inside.

"You coward!" Booth suddenly shouted. "Will you leave me now? Go, go!"

There came a fervent reply, though Matthew couldn't make it out. He took another step closer to the barn, and Conger pinned him with a glare. He halted.

After a few more moments, a face pressed to the door. "Let me out!"

Baker strode forward, pausing only a pace or two away. Matthew, along with most of the other men, drew closer to the barn.

"Hand over your arms," Baker said.

A shaved chin, followed by worried eyes topped with a mop of dark hair, appeared through the crack of the door. "I have none."

Baker shook his head. "You carried a carbine, and you must hand it out."

Booth's voice snaked around the man at the door. "The arms are mine."

Baker fingered the pistol at his side. "This man carried a carbine, and he must hand it out."

Sounding perturbed, Booth retorted, "Upon the word and honor of a gentleman, he has no arms! The arms are mine, and

I've got them."

Honor of gentlemen? Who stood here but a misguided assassin, a score of government-sanctioned murderers, and a failed deserter who'd somehow managed to be part of the deadly scheme? The irony made Matthew shake his head. There were no gentlemen here.

He grew tired of this game. If not for strict orders to remain firmly under their command or risk losing his deal to see Annabelle and George freed, Matthew would march right in there and haul Booth out himself.

Conger, apparently sharing Matthew's thoughts, clamped a hand on Baker's elbow. "Never mind the arms," he said in a harsh whisper that still carried to Matthew's itching ears, "If we can get one of the men out, then let's do it."

The man inside thrust both hands through the door and revealed his palms. Baker lurched from Conger's side and clamped the man's wrists in an iron grasp. He tugged the man from the barn and sent him stumbling toward the rear, where the soldiers waited with eager hands to subdue him.

Conger, seeming to have lost all patience with the situation, strode to the edge of the barn and picked up a bit of straw, twisting it in his fingers. Before anyone could think to say otherwise, he lit the tube of straw on fire and thrust it through the barn and onto a stack of hay.

It caught rapidly, filling the barn with thick smoke. Visions of the fiery blasts of cannons assaulted Matthew. He pushed the heels of his hands into his temples.

Not now. Focus!

He tried to push aside the memories of fire streaking across the land and balls of iron ripping men only an arm's length away from him to shreds. But the vision only grew, becoming nearly real.

Please! Help me!

The vision of mangled bodies around him began to fade, and the screaming Yankees settled into the confused expressions of the men he'd spent the past days among. Matthew swallowed hard, the acrid taste of smoke burning through his nostrils and down his throat.

Conger pressed his face against a crack in the barn, his hand resting against the wooden slats. Matthew focused on him and not on the glowing fires of Hades within. After a few moments, Conger jerked away and turned toward the door. He flung it wide.

Inside, Booth stood defiant of the defeat surrounding him.

Conger scrambled around the side of the barn, though whether to stop Baker or Booth, Matthew couldn't be sure.

Boom!

The crack of the pistol turned Matthew's veins to ice. Then Booth fell to the ground.

"I have too great a soul to die like a criminal. Oh, may
He, may He spare me that, and let me die bravely."
John Wilkes Booth

*H*e shot himself!" Conger shouted above the pulsing
blood in Matthew's ears.

Baker shook his head. "No, he didn't."

The faces around Matthew swirled into a mixture of confusion, anger, and worry. Then, as though thinking as one, they
moved forward in a scramble of shuffling boots and muttered
curses. Matthew used his frame to nudge past those who'd
beaten him to the door, ignoring their sneers.

"Whereabouts is he shot?" Conger asked, putting his fingers
on Booth's dusty lapel. "In the head or the neck?" He reached
under him and raised him up, exposing the right side of Booth's
neck. Blood seeped through his fingers and on to the ground.

Conger looked at Baker again and gave a somber nod. "Yes,
sir. He shot himself."

Baker shook his head emphatically. "I tell you, he did not!"

Matthew, apparently the only one concerned with the glowing dragon breathing behind them, cleared his throat. "Perhaps

he should be moved away from the flames?"

Shock registered on the men's faces, and Baker scrambled to his feet.

"Let's get him out of here. This place will soon all be burning," Conger said as if the thing had been his own idea.

The two men grabbed Booth, one under his arms and the other at the limp man's feet, and struggled to lift him. With a grunt, Matthew stepped into the barn and slid one arm underneath Booth's shoulder and the other under his thighs and hefted him up, leaving the two stunned men to scramble after him. They hurried out of the blazing heat. Matthew lowered Booth to the grass near a locust tree.

Once Matthew sat Booth on the ground, Conger returned to the barn, calling for men to help him stifle the flames. But the way the thing heaved and spit sparks, that barn was well beyond saving. The Garrett men gathered to stare at their ruined building, glazed eyes dancing with the reflected flames.

Matthew stared down at Booth and frowned. Had he imagined it? No. He leaned closer. Faint breath lifted the man's chest and lowered it, the rhythm of life still struggling against the coming end. Booth's lips moved.

Conger appeared over them. "Bring some water!"

Booth's mouth moved again, though his eyes remained closed. Matthew leaned close, trying to catch the words. Someone appeared with a damp rag, and they wiped it over Booth's face. His eyes flew wide, staring out at something beyond their realm of vision. Then a flicker of recognition lit their dark depths, and Booth stared at Matthew.

"Tell Mother...I die for my country."

"What did he say?" Conger huffed, leaning in.

Matthew gave the dying man a somber nod. "He says to tell his mother he dies for his country."

"Get him up from there." Conger spat and turned toward the house as Matthew hefted Booth into his arms once again. He couldn't imagine the pain the man must be in, but still Booth only mumbled garbled words about giving all for his country and bringing an end to the tyranny.

While the Garrett men continued to keep watch on the burning barn, Matthew carried Booth to the porch of the house and laid him down.

Booth's eyes cleared. "Water!"

A soldier, whose name Matthew could not recall, ladled water to Booth's lips from a pail near the door. Booth took a small sip, then turned tortured eyes on Matthew once more. "Turn me over to my face," he said, his voice little more than a whisper.

Conger heard him anyway. "You cannot lie on your face."

Booth shifted uncomfortably, the pain certainly becoming more than he could bear. "Come, hold your hand to my throat."

Matthew moved to oblige him, but Conger pushed his hand aside and placed his own fingers over the wound and pressed. Booth struggled to cough up the blood that surely trickled down his throat.

"Open your mouth," Conger commanded. Booth parted his lips and Conger narrowed his eyes. "There's no blood in your throat."

Booth turned his head away and pierced Matthew with pleading eyes. "Kill me."

Matthew shook his head, and again Booth repeated the plea to which Matthew simply could not comply. Booth's eyes rolled back in his head and then fluttered closed.

Conger slipped his fingers into Booth's pockets, then wrapped up what little he found in a cloth.

Booth gave another gasp, his body struggling for life, then fell still. Conger stared at him a moment, then descended the steps and called out orders detaining their prisoner, a man called Herold.

Conger threw a glance over his shoulder at Matthew. "Wait an hour and see if Booth is dead. If he seems to recover, send over to Belle Plain for a surgeon from one of the gun ships."

"Why not send for him now?"

Conger glanced between Matthew and the dying man, and then seeming to find a little humanity in his heart, gave a nod. Matthew waited by Booth's side, but the man didn't stir again, and when the doctor finally arrived, he was already dead.

About a quarter hour later, Lieutenant Baker gathered the cavalry men near the house.

"Who shot him?" Conger bellowed.

The men were quiet for a moment, and then a sergeant, Corbett, if Matthew remembered correctly, stepped forward. "I did, sir."

"For what reason?"

The man, seeming entirely unconcerned, shrugged. "He was taking aim with the carbine."

The muscles in Conger's jaw twitched. "At you?"

"I can't say. At something, certainly."

"And so you shot him?"

"It was time. I shot him through a large crack in the barn. I could see him through there and knew that he meant to kill one of us. I did what I had to do."

The sun spread sleepy light over the exhausted men, dappling their clothing as they stood there silently, none seeming overly concerned about the murder of a man who'd surrendered. Matthew looked down at Booth's still form.

What morbid poetry that this man would also receive a bullet that tore flesh from the back of his skull. Then, just as Booth's own victim had, Booth had lain struggling for a time, only to succumb to his wound at the dawning of a new day.

Sighing, Matthew turned his eyes to the trees beyond the barn, where the gentle morning dawned with a promise of a new beginning. Booth had been caught, and the Yankees had disposed of him, bringing a quick end with no need for a mock trial. Perhaps now this thing would be over.

Movement in the trees caught Matthew's attention. He focused on the woods, narrowing his eyes. There, hiding in the shadows, stood a familiar form. Matthew's chest tightened.

O'Malley smiled at him.

You could shoot him from here.

The inner voice slithered around in David's head, and his fingers reached for the pistol he'd stolen. It would be an easy shot. A bit far, perhaps, but nothing for an excellent marksman. He lifted the weapon and steadied it.

The big man's eyes swung in David's direction. Surprise flitted across his wide face. Yes, of course he would be surprised. He'd left David for dead! Then the giant's surprise melted, replaced by concern. David smiled. Concern? Perhaps remorse for leaving him?

His concern is only that you will gain your revenge. He wants you to fail.

David shook his head to dislodge the voice, but it wouldn't be silenced.

His hand trembled. Liza wouldn't have wanted this. He pressed his hand to his temple and stumbled back into the foliage behind him. He fell to his knees, the conflicting voices in his head pecking away at his sanity.

Fifteen

"Safe again on British soil, and under the protection of a
neutral power. It will give them some trouble to find
me, and still more to take me."

John H. Surratt

Washington, D.C.
April 29, 1865

"*Y*our brother and your lady friend aren't here, sir."

Panic surged in Matthew's gut. "Your people said
that if I signed your papers and helped with the pursuit, then
they'd be freed." He stepped closer to the officer, his hands
clenched tightly at his sides. "Where are they?"

The deep growl of Matthew's voice made the other man
step back. He tugged on his lapels. "They've already been
released."

Tension slid off Matthew's shoulders in a mighty wave.
"Released?"

The man scooted around him and plucked some papers
from a nearby table. "Says here that the lady was placed under
the care of a Mrs. Smith, provided she didn't leave Washington."

Thank heavens. "And my brother?"

"Released as well, on account of his loyalty papers and the word of Mr. Crook."

Matthew tugged on his collar. Crook, Mrs. Smith's friend. It would seem the woman's efforts had sufficed in getting them both out without Matthew's aid. Disgust rolled through him. They'd tricked him into signing that blasted paper. Had made it seem the only way!

Matthew's fingers inched toward the flask in his pocket, but there would be time for that later. He gave the officer a nod and turned to head out the door.

"Wait! You haven't been cleared to leave."

Matthew clamped his jaw. If this scrawny man thought he could detain him—

"Ah! Mr. Daniels, there you are!"

The voice of Mr. Fitch, the detective he'd first struck the deal with, made Matthew turn. "What's the meaning of this, Fitch? I did what we agreed upon, and your man says my brother and Miss Ross have been released. Our deal is done."

Fitch fingered his mustache. "Well, not quite." Matthew narrowed his eyes and the man lifted a hand. "I want to ask you to testify at the trial. Miss Ross and your brother as well."

Something the man had said earlier about the law not allowing accused to be witnesses surfaced. "So none of us will be charged?"

"No. We've chosen the eight who'll stand trial. The others are either dismissed or will be called as witnesses."

Matthew crossed his arms. "What if we don't wish to stay in Washington for a lengthy trial? Can't we simply pen our account and be on our way?"

The corner of Mr. Fitch's mouth twitched. "Witnesses need to be examined and cross-examined."

"Mr. Fitch, Miss Ross has been as helpful to the Union as you could ask anyone to be. I must get her home."

Mr. Fitch sniffed and brushed at his coat. "A couple of more weeks surely cannot make a difference."

Matthew rubbed his chin. "Perhaps you're right. She's probably lost it all anyway, spending so much time trying to help."

"Lost what?"

Matthew searched the man's face for mockery, indifference, or an indication that he sought information to use against them. Yet only genuine curiosity and perhaps even a speck of concern lingered in the lawman's brown eyes.

"Miss Ross came North in search of either finding her uncle, if he still lived, or her Union family to help her hold on to her land after her father died. Instead, she became tangled in this and has likely lost her home by now." He glared at the lawman. "But no different from most other families in the South, I suppose."

Mr. Fitch's mustache twitched. "Perhaps the government might be willing to aid you, Mr. Daniels."

Matthew's forehead creased. "How?"

"You three have demonstrated your loyalty. Perhaps, as Unionists, there could be certain…accommodations made that wouldn't otherwise be granted to Southerners."

Matthew shifted his stance. "What kind of accommodations?"

Mr. Fitch smiled. "Let's get this trial over with, shall we? Then we'll see what can be done."

Annabelle studied Peggy's reflection in the oval mirror as Peggy pinned her hair. Peggy looked tired. This journey had been difficult on her.

"There now." Peggy patted her shoulder and turned away.

"Peggy?"

She paused. "Yes, Miss Belle?"

Tears threatened, and Annabelle had to steady herself prior to speaking. "I wanted to thank you. For always being here for me, putting up with my foolish decisions, and making sure I'm cared for."

Peggy smiled. "And thank you for giving me my freedom and standin' up for me when folks treat me bad." Her eyes sparkled with mischief. "And for making sure I didn't die on the back of no horse."

Annabelle laughed and rose to sweep Peggy into an embrace. A knock came at the door, drawing them apart.

"Probably your grandma, wantin' us to go shopping again," Peggy said, rolling her eyes.

Annabelle sighed. "Let's hope not. I have enough clothing for the next year."

"Ain't that the truth." Peggy hurried to the door and pulled it open. She took a sharp breath, her hand flying to her throat.

Annabelle's eyes darted past Peggy, traveled to a stiff blue jacket, up to a strong jaw peppered in stubble, and finally to the dancing eyes that had filled her dreams. She let out a yelp and ran to him, barely giving Peggy enough time to jump out of the way before she launched herself into Matthew's arms.

He chuckled and wrapped his arms around her waist. "And here I thought you might not have missed me."

She pressed her ear against his chest, listening to the rapid beat of his heart. She shifted in his arms so that she could see his face. "Come now, who says I missed you?"

Amusement danced in his eyes before he lowered his head and planted a quick kiss on her forehead. "My, Miss Ross, if this is how you react to a man you didn't miss, I'll have to stay away longer next time so I can see what happens if you *do* miss me."

Annabelle swatted his chest playfully. "You wouldn't!"

Peggy cleared her throat. "I'm right glad you's back, Captain, but this here still ain't proper."

Matthew gave her a sour look.

Peggy shrugged. "Course, if you had given your intentions and were courtin' proper like…"

Matthew grinned again. "Then what, Peggy? Would I get to do this?"

He dipped Annabelle back and pressed his mouth to hers. Warmth surged from her lips all the way to her toes. She didn't get a chance to return the kiss, though, before Matthew righted her and left her breathless.

She expected a sharp retort out of Peggy, but instead only saw a twinkle in her eyes as she shook her head.

"No, suh," Peggy said, exaggerating her Southern drawl. "That there is only fittin' for folks that's gonna wed."

Mischief played in Matthew's eyes and he took Annabelle's hand. "Well, then, I suppose it's a good thing I've already spoken to Annabelle's grandmother."

Her heart tripped over itself. "My grandmother?"

Matthew ran a thumb over her jaw. "Since she's your closest

family, I thought that would suffice…?"

The lump that gathered in her throat kept Annabelle from doing anything more than nodding.

Matthew threw up his hand. "I wanted to do this with something big and romantic…." He fished something out of his pocket. "But I simply cannot wait any longer!"

Matthew dropped to one knee and Peggy gasped.

Annabelle's heart felt as though it would burst from her chest. Excitement welled up within her and then fell down her cheeks as two tears of joy. She sniffled. Oh, heavens! She was ruining the moment with her blubbering.

But Matthew didn't seem to notice. The adoration shining in his eyes made her long to stare into their depths forever.

"Annabelle Ross…" Matthew's voice hitched. So uncharacteristic for the mighty warrior she'd come to love.

"Yes?" she answered, the breathy word lingering between them for a heartbeat.

"Would you do me the great honor of becoming my wife?"

She bounced on her toes, a thrill running through her veins. "Yes! Oh, a hundred times yes!"

He slipped cold metal onto her finger, and she looked down at a bright sapphire, flanked on each side by two diamonds. Her breath caught. "Where…?"

"Like I said, I spoke to your grandmother." Matthew caressed her hand. "She insisted you have this. It was your mother's. We saw no reason not to go ahead and give it to you now, as a marker of our betrothal."

She cupped Matthew's chin and ran her thumb across his cheek. "Thank you."

He jumped to his feet and swept her into his arms. Annabelle gazed into his eyes and saw love swimming in them. She tried to push all her feelings for him through her gaze as well, hoping he would see the devotion that swelled in her heart.

Peggy cleared her throat again. "Captain—"

"But Peggy," Matthew interrupted, "Surely this can't be improper." His eyes never left Annabelle's.

"Well…" Peggy huffed. "All right. But only for a moment. I'll be right outside that door, you hear? And you got two minutes. Nothin' more."

Matthew grinned, and his lips fell on Annabelle's before Peggy even made it out the door.

This beautiful, strong, feisty woman would soon be his wife! Matthew's fingers trailed up her back, and he felt her shiver in his arms. He pulled her closer, gently exploring the lips that would be his to kiss for a lifetime.

A soft sigh escaped her mouth, and she tangled her fingers in his hair, pulling it free from its tie. Matthew's body responded, and with a groan, he gently eased her away. "We should stop."

Annabelle bit her bottom lip, still pink from his passionate kiss. After a moment, she gave a reluctant nod.

He rubbed a piece of her golden hair between his fingers. Soon he'd get to free these tresses from their pious prison and let the curls tumble down her back. "I'd marry you tomorrow, if you'd let me."

A smile bloomed on her pink lips, but she shook her head.

"Much as I'm eager to be your wife, I'd like to be married at Rosswood." She dropped her gaze. "It's the closest I can get to my parents being there."

Matthew wanted to tell her that her parents' memory would be present no matter where they wed, but he knew it was important to her. He could wait. He placed his fingers under her chin and tilted her face up to him.

Peggy knocked on the door. "All right, now, that's enough. Open up."

Matthew smirked and gave Annabelle one last gentle kiss before he opened the door. "Ah, Peggy. Right on time."

She assessed him with narrowed eyes a moment before her gaze darted around him to Annabelle. Peggy put her hands on her hips. "How we ever gonna travel now? I won't get the first bit of sleep having to watch you two."

A fetching pink tinge bloomed on Annabelle's cheeks.

"Now, Peggy," Matthew said with a mock indignation. "I'll be the most proper of gentlemen. You have my word."

Peggy studied him a moment. "Well, all right then."

Annabelle squeezed Matthew's hand. "Now that you are back, can we go home?"

Matthew hesitated, not wanting to break the joy of the moment. "I'm afraid not, my love."

"But…why not?" The disappointment in her eyes stabbed him.

"They want us to testify at the trial."

"We already told them everything!" Annabelle groaned. "Will those Yankees never let us have our own lives?"

He'd never heard her speak with such venom. He tilted his head in a silent question.

She ran her palms along her skirt. "You don't know how these...*Northerners* treated me in prison."

His fisted clenched. If anyone had hurt her, he'd—

Annoyance sparked in her eyes, turning sunny skies to storm clouds. "How could they blame me like that? Just because I come from Mississippi means this whole war is *my* fault? That Lincoln's *death* is my fault?" Her voice rose with each word.

Matthew placed a hand on her shoulder, forcing himself to remain calm. His temper would do her no good. "Don't listen to them, my love. Soon we will be able to go back to Rosswood and be gone from this terrible place."

Annabelle drew her lip through her teeth. "If we can regain it."

Matthew's grip tightened. "We will. I promise."

Annabelle wanted to ask how he could possibly promise such a thing, but the sincerity in his eyes stayed her tongue. She knew this man well enough to know that once he set his mind to something, it would take an act of God to move his course.

Perhaps she should have been praying about this. Asking God's direction. Oh, heavens. Why did she always think of that so late?

I'm sorry, Father. Please, direct us.

"Besides," Matthew said, releasing her shoulders. "There's hope that we'll have aid once we return south after this trial is done. Or, at least, after our part in the trial is complete."

Her interest piqued. "What do you mean?"

"That lawman, Mr. Fitch, implied that as loyal Unionists, there would be certain allowances granted to us. Hopefully, that will mean not only will you keep your lands from being stripped from you by the North, but that we will also receive some help in prying them from your grandfather's clutches."

Annabelle tugged on one of her curls, slipping it from a pin. "That's something, I suppose. At least our being tangled in this web might not be all horrible after all."

Matthew graced her with an approving smile, and her heart jumped. "There's my girl. All we have to do is give our account before the military court, and then…" He swept her into his arms again, "It's off to Rosswood to make you my wife!"

Sixteen

"Booth must have had some good reason for changing his plan, or he never would have done so. We had agreed on so good a scheme, that to change it seemed like tempting destiny."
John H. Surratt

Smith House
New York
May 3, 1865

*L*illy's hands shook as she stared at the letter. It had arrived two days ago, but still she couldn't open it for fear of what it contained.

"Mama." Frankie tugged at her skirt, his sweet voice smoothing her worry lines like a hot iron to a rumpled cloth.

"What's the matter, baby?" Lilly scooped him up and nuzzled her nose into his chubby neck, his scent of powder and baby soothing to her nerves.

Frankie rubbed her ear in the same habit he had of rubbing his own. He smiled at her, the little row of pearly teeth reminding her he wouldn't be a baby much longer. "Eat, mama?"

Lilly chuckled. "You must be growin' mighty fast, baby. You always want to eat." She tucked the letter in her dress pocket and took Frankie into the kitchen where Sue would be preparing lunch.

Instead of finding Sue bustling around in the kitchen as she usually did, Lilly found her staring at a shelf with her hands on her hips. Lilly sat Frankie down, and he toddled over to the quilt they kept spread out on the floor for him and picked up a carved horse.

"What's wrong, Sue?"

The other woman huffed, her shoulders lifting with an exaggerated sigh. "I'm tryin' to see if there's anything I can send to Washington City that'll keep."

"What're you talking about?"

Sue huffed. "To send to the missus, of course." She regarded Lilly as though she'd let go of her sense.

Lilly chuckled. "Have you ever been down to Washington?"

"No. What's that matter?"

Lilly stepped over to a basket by the stove and lifted the cloth draped over it. "They have restaurants, and even the hotels serve fancy food. I promise you, Mrs. Smith is doing just fine." She plucked a plump roll from the stack and replaced the cloth.

"Them places don't know about Mrs. Smith's," she lowered her voice, "delicate stomach." She glanced around as though someone might overhear.

Lilly squatted and offered the roll to Frankie. He dropped the horse and reached for the bread. Lilly pulled it back. "We say thank you, baby, when someone gives us something."

Frankie reached again. Lilly smiled and slowly pronounced, "Thank you."

"That baby too little for such stuff," Sue mumbled behind her.

Lilly held out the roll and offered Frankie a warm smile. His brown eyes looked at her, then at the roll. "Tank you, mama."

Lilly beamed. "Very good, Frankie!" She handed him the roll and sat back, satisfied. Lilly turned back to Sue with a grin. "Never too soon for him to start learning to be a gentleman."

Compassion swam in Sue's eyes, and Lilly's smile faded. She turned away. How could she teach Frankie all he would need to know about being a man?

As though reading her thoughts, Sue put a hand on her arm. "You read that letter yet?"

"No."

"Why not?"

Lilly watched Frankie finish his roll and grab up a carved wooden frog, making bubbling sounds with his mouth. "What good would it do?"

"You know Mrs. Smith been trying to find a respectable gentleman who'd make a good papa for this baby. I seen the way that fellow looked at you when he was here. Maybe that letter is asking for courtin'."

Lilly stood and folded her arms. "It's not."

Sue scoffed. "How you know if you won't open it?"

"Because he already asked to court, and I told him no."

Sue's mouth fell open. "You did what?"

Lilly pulled the letter out of her apron pocket and looked at the neatly printed letters. He'd assumed she could read. She could, but only after Mrs. Smith taught her, and she still was a bit slow. If he knew the truth about her, he wouldn't be doing these things.

"That there's a fine gentleman, and one right handsome as white folks go," Sue said with a smirk. "Even though he do need some good cookin' to fatten him up." Lilly gave her a flat stare and Sue grew serious. "He a fine gentleman, Lilly. One that could be a good papa to Frankie. You told me yourself how he played with the boy, and how Frankie took right to him."

Lilly's eyes darted to Frankie. His olive skin, so much like his father's, would never really be accepted. She shook her head. "It's not possible."

"Why?" Sue prodded.

"Why...why, because he's a *plantation* owner!"

Sue wiped her hands on her stained apron. "War's over now. Plantations ain't going to be what they were before. And you ain't never been no slave."

Lilly sank into a chair and drew a deep breath of the pleasant scents that always filled the kitchen—spices, flour, and the lingering sweetness from this morning's oatmeal. Her mind drifted back to the days in the orphanage. From what the nuns had told her, she'd been brought in because she was far too white. They said her parentage was too easy to tell. She looked up at Sue. "Do I look white to you?"

Sue placed her hands on her thick hips. "Now, what kind of question is that?"

"One I'd like you to answer."

Sue put a hand under Lilly's chin and turned her face to look at it as though she'd not spent the last nearly three years with Lilly. "You sure ain't pale as cotton, like so many of them is."

The corners of Lilly's mouth turned up. "Besides that."

Sue dropped her hand. "Yeah, I'd say so. You look 'bout

like them poor white women, the ones who go out in the sun and actually do some work." She shrugged. "Why? You wantin' to look like them rich ladies?"

"Of course not." Lilly didn't want to be anything like the women who must have insisted she be sent to the orphanage, lest anyone know their precious men found comfort in the warm arms of colored women instead of sharing their beds with frozen flowers.

"You know they ain't all bad. Look at Mrs. Smith. She got plenty of money, and she use a good bit of it to help our people."

Lilly looked at the floor. "I don't have a people."

Sue placed a hand on her shoulder. "You got people. You might even have more people than most, seein' as you got blood from both white and colored."

Lilly barked a bitter laugh. "Blood from two peoples and wanted by neither."

"Now, that ain't so. There's a fine white gentleman that's interested in you. I say you don't let that go to waste."

Lilly tucked a stray hair back into her bun. She remembered the way her heart galloped and the way Mr. Daniels had made her hands tremble. Things her sweet Bernardo had never made her do. He'd promised that the two of them working together would give them a better life. He'd been right, and they had been able to rent themselves a small room in a safer section of New Orleans. He'd been the only man who ever seemed to care about her. Sure, there'd been the salacious looks from some men, but never the looks of ardor that Bernardo had given her.

Bernardo had such dreams. His family had come through the port, looking for a new life. The hard conditions, the endless hours spent toiling to learn a smith trade, never dampened his spirits. He'd said he would make a good life for them.

Lilly sighed. "I wonder what would have happened if he hadn't died."

"Your husband?"

An unexpected tear slid down Lilly's cheek, and she swiped it away.

Sue grabbed another chair and swung it around in front of Lilly, then settled her bulk into it. "I'm so sorry. I shouldn't have been pushin' for you to see another man when you is still in love with the one you lost."

Lilly should nod and leave it there. That would be for the best, right? Instead the truth sprang from her mouth. "I never really loved him. He was a good man, and kind. And I was very fond of him. But…it was more a deep friendship than love. I still miss him, though."

Frankie spotted his mother sitting still and got up from his blanket, hurrying over to her side. He lifted his arms, and she scooped him up and placed him in her lap. Sue watched them quietly, allowing Lilly to sort through her thoughts.

"If he was still alive, maybe we would've gotten a house by now. And Frankie would have his father. A father who had the same tone of skin and would never look down on him for its darkness."

Sue tilted her head. "Mr. Daniels didn't seem to mind one bit about this baby's coloring. He got eyes, Lilly. He can see the boy got something other than white in him. And still he plays with the baby and looks at you like you be the queen of England."

Lilly laughed. "What would you know of the queen?"

Sue shrugged. "Nothing. Don't mean I can't see when a man looks at a woman like she's royalty. I know, because my Henry used to look at me that way, even though I was nothing more than a hefty slave sweatin' by the cooking fires. Didn't mean nothing to him. He looked at me like I was the finest lady in all the world."

Lilly offered a sad smile. "That sounds beautiful. I'm so sorry you lost him."

Sue wouldn't be turned from their conversation. "Now, Mr. Daniels, he look at you like that. Maybe you see mixed blood like I saw being sweaty and covered in cooking grease, but just like my Henry, that Daniels man don't see those things. He look at you different."

Frankie gently rubbed on Lilly's ear again and her heart ached. "He wouldn't, though, if he knew what I am. A mulatto who grew up in an orphanage. I'm not some white lady meant for a plantation. I can't live somewhere like where Momma came from." She shook her head. "I just can't."

It had taken her years, but after the North passed their proclamation and Southern slaves started making their runs, she'd finally found someone willing to get Momma out. The stories she'd told Lilly on the long journey to New York were horrible.

"I wonder what'd happen if a woman who knows what life be like for colored folks were to take the place of a plantation lady…" Sue left her words dangling in the air between them.

"She could make things better for the people there," Lilly finished. Could she do it? Pretend her past didn't matter and let her heart explore these strange new feelings for this man? And if she were to marry him, could she make a difference? In some small way make up for failing her mother?

"Maybe it be best if you start with openin' that letter," Sue said, gesturing to the envelope Lilly had laid on the table.

The woman made a fair point. She broke the seal before she could convince herself otherwise and unfolded the single sheet. "Miss Rose..." she began.

"Why does he call you that?" Sue interrupted.

Lilly looked at her from over top of the paper. "Because he can't fathom why I don't have a family name, so he insists on using that by way of a proper title."

Sue just stared at her. Lilly dropped her gaze back to the paper, but Frankie squirmed and lifted his head from her chest where he'd been resting it. "Mama."

"Hold on, baby." She tried to look around his head.

"Mama. Eat," Frankie insisted, putting his fingers on her face.

Lilly lowered the letter. "You just had a roll, baby. No more."

"Pish! Let that little one eat. We got plenty. No reason for making him go without." Sue got up from her chair and fished another roll from the basket and handed it to the boy. "You keep on reading."

Frankie took the roll. "Tank you!"

A smile played on Sue's mouth as she sat back down. "Yes, sir. Your momma's right, little fellow. You gonna make a right polite gentleman."

Frankie settled back against Lilly's chest and gnawed on the roll. Lilly lifted the paper again and read aloud. "Miss Rose, I am ever so deeply sorry for being so forward. I fear that my time in prison has made me appreciate life in such a way that I seek to take advantage of each breath of freedom. However, I realize that I moved things much too quickly and I have frightened you away. I know that you are of the Union, and your aversion to a man from the South is understandable."

Lilly lowered the paper. Is that what he thought?

"What did you tell him?" Sue asked, her face befuddled.

"I said I couldn't be courted by a plantation owner."

"Hmmm."

Lilly cleared the lump that formed in her throat and continued. "But since this war has come to an end, and we are once again of one nation, I ask that you try to look beyond the wounds of war. I have signed loyalty papers, and as far as the government is concerned, I am as much a…" She paused and squinted at the word. It seemed he had started a Y then an A, but he had drawn through them. Paper being as rare as it was, he'd not gotten a new sheet.

"As much as what?" Sue prompted.

"As much of a Unionist as anyone else," Lilly continued. "My plantation will be run under Union stipulations. I hope this eases your mind, Miss Rose, and that you might reconsider me?"

She looked up at Sue, who offered an encouraging smile. "What am I to do? A plantation owner and a mulatto? It isn't possible."

Sue shrugged. "Looks possible to me. 'Sides, if he can't see you's mixed, why bother telling him?"

Lilly dropped her gaze back to the page. "We must stay on in Washington for a time, since our testimony will help with finding justice for the murder of the president. I would ask that you and Frankie come back to Washington and stay while we are at trial. Mrs. Smith has given me permission to make this request and adds her wishes to my own."

Sue clapped her hands together smartly, but Lilly ignored her as she turned the page over. "She says that she would greatly appreciate you coming to help her with lady matters." Lilly laughed. "I wondered how she's managed without me doing her hair."

"Now, see there. Mrs. Smith needs you. You should go." Sue bobbed her head as though that settled the matter. But since Mrs. Smith was her employer, not to mention a dear and trusted friend, Lilly supposed Sue was right.

Lilly looked back at the page. "Miss Ross's maid has stated she would help with caring for Frankie as much as you need it." *Ah, sweet Peggy. She did take a liking to Frankie.* "And, if it is not too forward of me to say so, I would like your permission to get to know you better. I remain hopefully yours, George C. Daniels."

Sue stared at her earnestly. "What you think?"

Lilly pressed her fingers to her lips for a moment before answering. "Well, if Mrs. Smith needs me, and I can keep Frankie with me..."

Sue nodded, encouraging her to continue.

"Then I suppose I should go to Washington to help her, if she wishes it."

"And...?" Sue prompted.

"And, well, anything else will have to be determined later."

Sue rose from her seat and scooped Frankie out of his mother's lap. "All right then, you go pack. Frankie and me is going to go tell Günter to get ready to take you to the train station."

Sue hustled out of the kitchen door as though she feared

Lilly would change her mind. She should. She should write to Mrs. Smith and beg off going to Washington. But instead, her heart filled with anticipation, and for some reason, her feet bounded toward the main house with joyful steps at the very thought of seeing a man she would be better off forgetting.

Seventeen

"He has indeed gained an immortality of fame."
John H. Surratt

Washington, D.C.
May 5, 1865

G eorge ran a hand through his hair, feeling much too nervous to wipe the smirk off Matthew's face.

"My brother courting a woman. One that, I must say, is quite unexpected," Matthew said, continuing to goad George.

George tied his cravat for the third time. "I don't care she's from the working class. It's a good thing, really. Then she won't expect life at Westerly to be what it was before the war."

Matthew handed George a pair of cufflinks. "That's true. But even the ladies of means have changed, George. Look at Annabelle."

George nodded his agreement. The woman certainly didn't seem the spoiled, delicate flower that Southern women were expected to be. He slipped the links on and tugged his sleeve. "Yes, and aren't you glad you didn't keep insisting that *I* be the one to wed her?"

"Quite."

"How do I look?" He'd had a haircut and shave, and in this gray suit with black velvet trim on the lapels, he even looked like a gentleman again.

Matthew winked. "Like a woman fussing over whether every hair is in place." George swatted at him, and Matthew ducked. "You're turning into a dandy."

George paused and then when Matthew relaxed, he landed a playful punch on his beefy shoulder.

Matthew chortled and stepped away. "Geez, roused the bull, did I?" He sobered. "In truth, brother, I'm quite pleased to see you this way. You've never seemed so enamored with a female."

He stuck his foot into a boot and tugged it on. "I believe she's the one God means for me."

Matthew's expression clouded and he turned away. "I'm glad."

Too much in a hurry lest he be late, George nudged his concern over his brother's odd behavior away. He straightened his trousers and then slapped Matthew on the shoulder. "Wish me well."

Matthew's eyes danced, their old humor returning a bit more each day. George supposed he had Miss Ross to thank for that.

"Perhaps I should instead remind you to keep your wits about you," Matthew said. "Going out without a chaperone and all. My offer still stands to join you."

George rolled his eyes. "We're both widowed. Besides I'm a gentleman and she a proper lady, despite her class." George plucked his silk hat off the bureau. "Now, my lady awaits."

He left Matthew chuckling as he closed the door to their room behind him and then sauntered down the hall, feeling lighter than he had in years.

Annabelle watched Peggy pin Lilly's ebony locks in a complicated style. Lilly shifted again, her plum-colored dinner gown rustling around her fluttering feet.

"Now, see here, Miss Lilly, you're going to have to be still."

Lilly froze, her eyes darting first to Annabelle and then to Peggy. "You don't need to call me that. I'm not a lady."

Peggy shrugged and placed another pin. "Don't matter if you is or you ain't. You have to be still or this hair's goin' to be a mess."

Annabelle withheld a laugh as Lilly chewed on her fingernail, clearly nervous.

"Are you certain it's all right for Frankie to stay here with you? Because I can stay."

The baby played contently on the floor with the little silver horse Matthew had given her. She offered Lilly a reassuring smile. "Nonsense. He's just fine here with us."

"You don't got to stay here with me, Miss Belle," Peggy said. "You can go down to the lobby with the Captain. There's plenty folks down there, so you don't much need a chaperone."

Though she would enjoy Matthew's company, she had other plans for tonight. "No, I'd like to stay here. I thought maybe it might be good for me to spend some time with children. I know so little about them."

Peggy's nimble fingers paused, and sudden terror swept over her face. "You're gonna be married soon."

The disbelief in Peggy's voice had Annabelle confused. "You've known that for some time. Heavens, you were there when he asked!"

Peggy and Lilly exchanged a knowing look.

"What?"

Peggy's fingers started working again, though they seemed to be moving much too fast. What had Peggy in such a dither? "Um, Miss Belle, you need to go to your grandma and have a talk with her about the ways of being married."

"Why?"

Lilly played with the lace collar of her gown. "Since your own mother isn't here to talk to you about such things, Mrs. Smith gonna be the one to tell you what you need to know."

"But…" She looked at Peggy. "Peggy has been a mother to me since Momma died. Surely she would be best."

Lilly's eyes widened with an expression Annabelle didn't quite understand. Surely Lilly didn't look down on her relationship with Peggy. She'd helped slaves to freedom. "Is there something wrong with that?"

"Ain't proper," Peggy supplied.

Lilly's features returned to smooth glass and she nodded. "That's right. Mrs. Smith would be better."

How could she make them understand? "I care for Grandmother, but I don't know her well. And I am given to understand that what goes on between husband and wife is a…" Heat rose up her neck. "A delicate matter?"

Lilly's cheeks colored, and she looked away.

"Peggy, I know you didn't marry, but…" What else could she say?

Sorrow washed over Peggy's eyes as she placed a pearl pin

in Lilly's hair and stepped back. "Not by white law."

The ground seemed to shift beneath her and Annabelle's stomach clenched. "What are you talking about?"

Peggy studied her a moment, then seemed to come to a decision. "I had a man. He worked for your daddy down at the Natchez house. Didn't get to see him much, but we jumped the broom." A sad smile played about her lips. "He was the only one that made my heart ever flutter."

"You never told me that!"

The pain in her eyes twisted Annabelle's heart. "He was sold when you were just a little girl. Didn't ever see no reason to bring it up."

Having her husband stolen from her was a grave injustice. "Oh, Peggy. I'm so sorry."

"Don't be, baby girl. Had nothing to do with you." Peggy reached out and took Annabelle's hand, giving it a squeeze.

"What happened to him?"

"Don't know, child. He was sent to auction. I never saw him again."

Annabelle swallowed a lump in her throat. "You should have said! Maybe we can find him."

Lilly made a funny sound, and they turned to look at her. Embarrassed, the lady dropped her eyes.

"What's wrong?"

Lilly shook her head, the thin curls at the nape of her neck swaying. "It's just that, well, not many Southern white ladies are like you, you know that?"

"That they ain't," Peggy said, pride evident in her tone. "My girl is special."

Something about the way Lilly said it seemed odd, but Annabelle had other things to consider at the moment. Like avoiding embarrassing conversations with her stiff grandmother. "Since you *were* married, Peggy, that's all the more reason you should be the one to tell me what I need to know." Her gaze drifted over to Frankie, so sweet with his chubby hands and angel's face.

"Oh, Lawd. I'm telling you, that there ain't proper."

Lilly swept up from her chair. "Why not? According to the law, you're a freewoman. And if you two have this kind of relationship, why should something so silly as skin tone matter?" Lilly's tone seemed almost desperate.

At least someone agreed with her. "Yes, exactly."

Peggy groaned. "Guess you do need to know."

Annabelle laughed, her victory secured. Besides, how bad could this conversation really be?

A knock pounded on the door. "Ah!" She scooted around Peggy to grab the door. "The gentleman has arrived."

Did she imagine it or had Lilly grown pale?

She swung open the door, and her breath caught in her throat. Not George at all, but a face from her past. One that had her daddy's eyes. Her hand flew to her throat. "Uncle Michael! Is it really you?"

His hazel gaze ran over her. "Why, little Anna, you're all grown up!"

Annabelle squealed and launched into her uncle's arms. He chuckled and patted her back, then eased out of her grasp.

"We feared you were dead! Didn't you get my letters?"

His face scrunched. "No, but then I did move around a good bit there at the end, and I spent a lot of time in a hospital with a nasty head wound. Was returning to my men when Lee up and surrendered."

George appeared over Michael's shoulder, a good hand's width taller than her kin.

"Mr. Daniels, meet my Uncle Michael."

George thrust out a hand. "A pleasure, indeed! We're glad you've finally been found, sir. Your niece has been quite worried."

The men exchanged pleasantries and words of war until George's gaze found Lilly standing behind Annabelle. "Excuse me, sir. I do believe I've kept the lady waiting." He offered his arm, which Lilly accepted, and the two of them drifted down the hall.

Annabelle smiled as they disappeared down the main stair and then gestured for her uncle to enter.

He brushed a hand over his short sandy hair and proceeded no farther than one stride inside. "It's been quite an effort to find you, Anna. Imagine my surprise upon coming to Washington and seeing my niece's name listed with the witnesses for the coming trial!"

She could only imagine.

"It took a bit of asking around to find you were at this hotel."

Annabelle pressed her hands together. "It has been quite an eventful few months, Uncle."

"I should say so. Do you know what's going on at Rosswood?"

Fear squeezed thick fingers around her stomach until she thought she might lose its contents. She shook her head, unable to get any words to escape her tight throat.

"Andrew's laid claim and nearly shot me when I arrived.

Not even so much as a proper greeting! Then all that rambling on about wedding you as soon as you return."

The cad! The—Annabelle swayed.

"Come, Miss Belle." Peggy wrapped an arm around her waist. "You better sit down."

She allowed Peggy to guide her to the dressing chair. "I have no intentions of ever wedding that foul man. Grandfather secured the arrangement without my permission."

Michael growled. "I'm aware. Why didn't you contact me?"

"I did! I sent you two letters, but I don't think he allowed them to ever reach the post. I tried a telegram, and then I got desperate and attempted to get a message to an army dispatch. That…didn't work out so well."

He stroked his beard. "Hmm. After hearing his claims, I came to Washington to speak to my solicitor, who apparently has been in the city on business for some time." His nostrils flared. "Cowardly man probably stayed up here to avoid the fighting down south."

"Is there anything he can do?"

He offered her a placating smile, as though she was still the child he remembered. "Of course, my dear. Forgive me for my outburst. I have legal paperwork giving me command of all my brother's properties. Don't worry. I'll take care of you."

Unease slithered through her veins. "My father's will states that Rosswood should go to me."

Michael hesitated. "And so it shall. Once I find a suitable husband for you, of course."

Of course! How had she forgotten? "I'm already betrothed."

His face clouded. "With whose permission?"

Why would he seem displeased? "Grandmother consented."

"Grand…you mean the Yankee shrew?"

Annabelle startled, surprised by the loathing in his voice. "She's been most kind to me, and if not for her, I'd have been in quite a mess. She helped us all. Why, she even took us in after we got George out of prison and we had nowhere else to go."

Michael studied her, his hazel eyes a tempest of emotions. Annabelle glanced at Peggy, but she'd pushed herself up against the wall with her eyes lowered. Hadn't Peggy grown past such behaviors?

"I'll have to meet this gentleman. There are far too many men out there who would take advantage of a woman who can offer them something. With this war, not many plantations still stand."

Annabelle relaxed. He only sought to protect her. "Oh, not to worry. Father himself already approved him." When confusion lined Uncle's features, she added, "Mr. Matthew Daniels. The youngest of the Daniels brothers."

Recognition did not lighten his features. "We shall see." Then, as though the matter was settled, he smiled at her again. "Come along, my dear. I want to take you out for supper."

Casting one longing glance at Peggy and the baby, but knowing she could not refuse him, Annabelle rose. "Thank you. I shall be pleased to have your company."

Satisfied with her response, he offered his arm. As he led her out into the hall, Annabelle prayed that all would be made right. An idea struck her. "Mr. Daniels is staying here as well. Perhaps we should fetch him so that the two of you might become acquainted?"

Michael took so long in answering that Annabelle thought he hadn't heard her. Finally, he patted her hand. "Of course, my dear. The sooner I see what this man is about, the better."

Annabelle led Uncle to Matthew's room and tapped on the door, but no one answered. She lifted her shoulders. "I suppose he's gone out."

"Then we shall go on without him," Uncle Michel announced, sounding oddly pleased.

Matthew rubbed the glass between his hands, the damp condensation blending with his clammy palms. The visions were getting worse. No sooner had George stepped out than a shadow had darted just outside his vision. He'd spun around, but no one had been in the room. He knew, because he had nearly torn it to shreds with his searching. His hands had started trembling, so he'd come downstairs for something to ease his nerves.

One glass had done nothing more than warm his belly. Glass two, and he still saw shadows slinking just outside of his vision, disappearing every time he turned to look. This third glass, sparkling with amber liquid, had to be his ticket to relief. Throwing it back, he downed the entire thing in one gulp. The whiskey burned its way down his throat and seared into his belly.

There. Now he could return to his room and get some rest. He rose from his seat and swayed. Surprised, he gripped the back of the chair. Before the war, a few glasses wouldn't have affected him so.

Straightening himself, he carefully strode toward the hotel

lobby, and then he froze when he saw Annabelle. *His* beautiful Annabelle—on the arm of another man! She laughed, placing her hand on the stranger's arm and looking up at him with sparkling eyes. Fury swirled in Matthew's veins and he pushed forward like a lion that had spotted a rival entering his pride.

A chair fell over as he shoved past it and toppled to the ground with a thud that drew the attention of the restaurant's patrons. Annabelle's eyes turned to him, surprise blooming on her face.

How could she betray him? Was *this* the reason she'd begged off his company tonight? So that she might entertain another man? The scoundrel looked down at Annabelle with confusion, then narrowed his eyes at Matthew. Blood pounded in Matthew's ears, drowning out the other sounds around him.

He reached the man, who audaciously still clutched Annabelle's arm, and grabbed his black cravat. The man's eyes widened, and then his gaze darted to Annabelle. So, not only a lecherous fool after another's intended, but a coward who looked to a woman to save him as well. "What do you think you're doing?"

"Matthew!" Annabelle shrieked, clawing at his arm. "Unhand him!"

Her defense of the rogue seared him with equal parts pain and fury. The muscles in his jaw tightened and he squeezed the man's neck tighter. "Are you aware, *sir*, that this lady is already spoken for?"

Understanding dawned in the man's eyes, followed by disgust. "Unhand me, you drunk fool."

Matthew's fist clenched at his side, prepared to knock the smug look off this charmer's face. Annabelle desperately clawed at his arm, her words finally breaking through the pounding in his skull and exploding in his brain.

"Stop! This is my Uncle Michael!"

Matthew dropped his fist but still held tight to the man as he stared at Annabelle, her words slowly taking hold.

Her feathery lashes batted like a butterfly in a windstorm. "What's the matter with you, Matthew?"

The man, her uncle, shoved away from Matthew's grasp. "He's drunk, that's what. You can smell it from here." He tugged on his jacket, looking at Matthew with a haughty smirk. "I guess now we know where he ran off to."

Annabelle's delicate brows dropped, pulling his heart down with them. Fool! How could he have so quickly assumed her a scandalous woman? He reached for her, but she stepped back out of his grasp. Pain swirled in her icy eyes, but she castigated him with pithy words, nonetheless. "Perhaps you should return to your room."

Shame washed over him in a fiery wave. Swallowing his pride, he stuck out a hand to her uncle. "My deepest apologies, Mr. Ross."

The man eyed his hand and sniffed, looking away. Matthew clenched his jaw, his clipped words having to fight their way through his teeth. "Good evening, then."

He glanced at Annabelle again, but she only shook her head, ashamed of him. Feeling the stares of everyone he'd startled from their meals, Matthew stalked out of the room and back to the private prison of the shadows that haunted him.

Eighteen

> "...to prevent accidental discovery I will disguise myself
> by dying my hair and staining my skin. I must remain
> here for a time, and when opportunity offers sail
> for Europe."
>
> John H. Surratt

Conspirators' trial
Washington, D.C.
May 12, 1865

*A*nnabelle watched Matthew from the corner of her eye. He appeared no more uneasy than all of the other people crammed into the room. The moderate temperature did little for the nervous energy of those brought before the Military Commission. Several ladies fanned themselves while men tugged on collars and cravats.

Matthew's gaze swung across the room and landed on Annabelle. Her heart constricted.

Whatever tomorrow brings.

His words echoed in her head yet again, pounding in rhythm with her aching heart. Had he truly meant them? She twirled the ring on her finger and pushed the thought aside. Matthew's eyes swam with remorse and shame, just as they had every day for the past week.

She offered him a gentle smile, but he only hunched his broad shoulders and averted his gaze. He'd left a scrawled note under her door the morning after the incident with her uncle that begged her forgiveness, but she'd not had a chance to discuss it with him. Since then, he'd been busy with the trial and with the Union company he'd been assisting. Or maybe he simply wanted to avoid her. The thought made her stomach churn.

She snapped open her lace fan and stirred a breeze around her face, but it did little to cool the heat radiating up her neck and into her cheeks. She wished Peggy was here. Or Eudora, at least. The strict rules of the court didn't allow anyone not directly involved in the case against the accused inside.

Mumbling drew her attention from Matthew's profile and to the door, where two guards ushered in Mrs. Surratt, David Herold, George Atzerodt, Lewis Payne, Michael O'Laughlen, Edward Spangler, Samuel Arnold, and Samuel Mudd. Suspiciously absent was David O'Malley, whom Annabelle couldn't believe hadn't been captured. Booth himself...well, Annabelle couldn't be sure the man hadn't been murdered. Rumors swirled regarding what had happened that day, but she'd gleaned little. Yet knowing how fervently the Unionists wanted revenge...

She turned the thought aside. She'd not make judgments without facts.

The Union officers serving on the Military Commission entered after the accused and took their places at the head of the room. Each man wore a decorated uniform that designated him as an officer of significant rank. Annabelle closed her fan and placed it in her lap, the somber atmosphere making her fear too much movement might cause any one of those officers' stony eyes to land on her.

A tall man with a groomed beard stepped forward. "By order of the President of the United States, we hereby convene on the day of our Lord May 12, 1865, to continue in the presentation of testimony of the accused implicated in the murder of the late President Abraham Lincoln, and the attempted assassination of the Honorable William H. Seward, Secretary of State, and in an alleged conspiracy to assassinate other officers of the federal government at Washington City, and their aiders and abettors."

Annabelle swallowed the lump gathering in her throat. Her eyes sought out the detective, Mr. Fitch, but couldn't find him in the crowd. The officer had assured her this morning that she would not be charged. She must only relate information to the Military Commission and then she'd be free to go. Still, her heart fluttered like a sparrow in a windstorm.

"Brigadier General Joseph Holt, Judge Advocate General of the United States Army, is appointed the Judge Advocate and Recorder of the Commission, by order of the President."

With that announcement, the men all took their seats, and the prisoners settled on stiff chairs in front of the assembly. Mary Surratt's calm demeanor stood in stark contrast to the oppressive tension draping the countenance of the others. Did she perhaps believe she wouldn't be found guilty?

The solicitors from two opposing sides rose and began a series of proceedings that followed a strict code of operation. Men and women were called to bear witness to all manner of questioning, and Annabelle thought some of those questions seemed to have little to do with the assassination.

One witness was interrogated extensively about stealing a false mustache, presumed to be Booth's, with such intensity that Annabelle might have found the absurdity of such a thing quite humorous under different circumstances. As it was, the probing questions only added to her unease.

Annabelle glanced at Matthew again, but his eyes remained forward. She bit back her welling frustration and fingered the ring on her hand. How could she marry a man who refused to face their problems? She clenched her jaw. After his display at the hotel, Michael would never approve the match.

"Ross? Is Miss Ross not present?"

The voice pierced her thoughts and Annabelle jumped. "Oh!" She rose and brushed at her skirt, heat rising in her face. "I'm here."

The solicitor at the front narrowed his eyes as she made her way forward. *Oh, gracious!* They'd think her a dolt. She smiled sweetly at him, but the solicitor didn't return the gesture. Instead, he motioned for her to take a seat at the head of the room. Annabelle eased onto the chair, her eyes skittering over the prisoners and landing on Matthew. The concern brimming in his stormy eyes did little to drown the unease churning in her stomach.

The solicitor tugged on the lapel of his gray broadcloth jacket with black velvet trim. She shifted in her seat under his scrutiny. She dared a glance at the presiding Union officers, but finding their harsh gazes unnerving, looked down at her trembling hands instead.

"Please state your name, miss," the solicitor, Mr. Stone, said. He nodded toward the military commissioners.

She swallowed. "Miss Annabelle Ross."

"Miss Ross, can you please inform the commission of your whereabouts on the night of the assassination?"

So, they wouldn't ask about her involvement in the attempted abduction? She almost let out a sigh of relief. She straightened her posture. "I was present in Ford's Theatre on the night of the assassination. I was sitting in the lower floor and saw when the man leapt to the stage."

"And why, exactly, were you there, Miss Ross? It wasn't simply to enjoy the acting, was it?"

Annabelle clamped her hands. "No, sir. We were there because we feared there would be another attempt to abduct Mr. Lincoln."

The man raised his eyebrows, though Annabelle knew the information hadn't come as a surprise. "Another? What do you mean?"

"I became aware of an attempt to abduct the president and take him to Richmond earlier in the year. The man who planned the first attempt was seen with Mr. Booth, and we thought perhaps they would seek to try to abduct Mr. Lincoln at the theatre."

"I see. And you thought your presence would stop such an attempt?"

Annabelle ignored the sarcasm in his tone. "No, sir. But we had given Mr. O'Malley's description to the lawmen, who were to be on the lookout for the man. My grandmother, Mr. Daniels, and I went to the theatre in order to help look for him."

The man stroked his mustache and paced in front of her. She spared a glance at Matthew, who offered a small nod of encouragement.

"And was this man, O'Malley, at the theatre that eve?" Mr. Stone asked, turning back to face her.

"No, sir. Mr. Matthew Daniels detained him in Philadelphia. Though we didn't know that at the time. When I saw the assassin leap onto the railing of the president's box, I first thought him to be Mr. O'Malley."

"Though clearly he was not. What happened after you saw *Mr. Booth* jump onto the stage?"

"My grandmother and I went to the president's box."

The man nodded as though he already knew her answer. "What for?"

She twisted her hands. "We feared for him and wanted to see if we could be of any help."

"And what help could a lady provide?"

Annabelle sought to keep the annoyance from her tone and lifted her chin a fraction. "I spent two years tending wounded soldiers, sir. I'm not without skill."

The solicitor seemed mollified and placed his hands behind his back. "I see. Was there not a doctor around?"

"There was. He ran up after us and went straight to the box, though the door was locked. It took some time before Mr. Rathbone opened it."

The solicitor looked to the presiding officers. "Let the records show that the surgeon, Charles Leale, has confirmed this report." Mr. Stone turned back to Annabelle. "Once the door opened, what did you do?"

"I offered to help Mr. Rathbone, who had a long gash that ran the length of his arm, but he and the doctor sent me out, so I remained in the hallway."

The man questioned her about nearly every minute thereafter, including when she went to the police to give her account. Then, as she had feared, his questions circled back to the abduction plot and her involvement. Annabelle chose her words carefully, fearing the man might be slowly wrapping her in the silky threads of confusing questions like a spider preparing its kill.

"So, Miss Ross," Mr. Stone said, pinning her under his gaze. "You were present for the attempted abduction of the late president on the seventh of March *and* present for the assassination, including following the president over to the boarding house where he later died?"

She forced herself to hold his gaze. "Yes, sir."

He narrowed his eyes. "Yet you say you were not involved in the conspiracy?"

The spider pulled his threads close, choking Annabelle's thoughts. She drew a long breath. "No, sir."

Suspicion flared on the solicitor's face. She straightened her shoulders. "Not directly. Once I became aware of these men's intentions, I did everything in my power to stop them."

The solicitor paced, each thud of his shoes heavy in the quiet room. Then, with what seemed an air of finality, he came to a halt in front of her. "Where did you first hear of these plots?"

Her gaze darted over to Mrs. Surratt, who stared at Annabelle with open accusation. Did the commission notice as well? Annabelle swallowed. "At the Surratt Boarding House, sir. I overheard the men discussing their abduction plan in the parlor there."

Mr. Stone gestured to the widow. "And is this the woman

who owns that boarding house?"

"Yes, sir."

He nodded his satisfaction. "Miss Ross, is it your opinion that Mrs. Surratt was aware of these plots and perhaps even aided in them?"

Mary Surratt glared at her.

"Miss Ross?"

She snapped her gaze back to the solicitor. "I...well, she was often present with the men when they spoke in private. As to the nature of those conversations, however, I'm afraid I cannot comment since I wasn't among them."

She looked at Mrs. Surratt again, who regarded her evenly.

Mr. Stone glanced between the two women. "But if you were to guess, would you say that you ever felt that Mrs. Surratt played a part in these events or was at least aware of them?"

Annabelle looked into his serious eyes, seeing his suspicion of her rise. She must tell the truth. "Yes, sir, I must say that I did have that feeling. I also know that Mr. O'Malley boarded with her, and that Mr. Booth visited her on a few occasions. I believe it's quite possible, though not definitive, that she at least knew of their intentions."

The man seemed satisfied once again. She hadn't been the first to offer up Mrs. Surratt's connections, but it seemed her testimony only added to the mounting accusations.

After questioning Annabelle about her acquaintance with Booth—when she saw him at the National Hotel, and if she was certain he was present on the day of the attempted abduction—the solicitor finally turned her over to another solicitor, a Mr. Ewing.

Annabelle shot a glance at Matthew again, and this time he

rewarded her with a smile that made her chest constrict. How she loved that man. Why must he be so difficult?

"Miss Ross," Mr. Ewing said, standing in front of her and blocking her view of the man who'd stolen her heart. "Can you please tell me about your time spent in the Surratt house, and any persons whom you saw there?"

Had she not just been through this with the other? She glanced at the Union officers, and one of them, a man with stern features but kind eyes, gave her a nod.

"I resided at the house of Mrs. Surratt last March," Annabelle said. "My betrothed and I were on our way to my family's home in New York. During that time, I saw John Booth and the matron's son, John Surratt, along with Mr. O'Malley and his companion, Mr. Harry Thompson." She gestured to the other prisoners. "I didn't see any of these other men there."

The man nodded and then, without further questioning, allowed her to step down. She kept her eyes on the floor until she made it back to her seat, avoiding the gaze of two men she had to squeeze past.

The man who'd first given the introductions at the beginning of the day positioned himself at the front of the room. "The commission will now take a one-hour respite. Morning witnesses are free to go."

Annabelle's breath left with a rush. Free to go!

Oh, thank you, Lord.

She rose and turned to find Matthew, who thankfully headed in her direction. He stepped through the people hurrying to find their luncheon and offered her his arm. She slipped her fingers across the coarse material of his Union jacket and settled her hand into the crook of his arm, clinging to him as though he might slip away at any moment.

He led her through the crowd and out to the warmth of the day, where the clear spring air offered a welcome breath of freshness. "Wait here," Matthew said, slipping from her grasp, "I'll find you something to eat."

Annabelle dug her fingers into his arm. "Matthew!"

He turned back to her, pain jarring in his eyes.

"You've been avoiding me." His Adam's apple bobbed, but he didn't speak. "We need to talk about what happened."

Matthew shoved his hands in his pockets and cleared his throat, looking everywhere but directly at her. "I've been busy with the detectives."

Annabelle gave him a dubious look.

"You're right. My shame sent me slinking away like a scalded dog and has only caused further dishonor." He lowered his gaze. "Another failure I must ask undeserved forgiveness for."

She caressed the slight stubble peppering his jaw, unconcerned that they stood in public. "Matthew, look at me."

He grasped her hand, gently lowering it to her side, then released it. Fear galloped through her. His conflicted gaze roamed her face as though he sought something there that he desperately needed. "I must...sort through some things, Annabelle." His jaw clenched. "I think it would be best if you return with your uncle to Rosswood."

Her heart plummeted. "What..." She blinked back burning tears. "What are you saying?"

"Mr. Fitch promised me that George won't need to testify. Now that you've given your account, there's no reason for you to stay. Not when we need to be certain Rosswood is safe."

"But...what about you?"

He shifted his stance. "I must remain."

"For how long?"

He reached up as though to trap a stray lock of her hair that danced across her cheek but then lowered his hand and glanced away. "I don't know."

"Matthew, I—" Her voice hitched.

He grasped her hands, his eyes boring into hers. "I love you. But I must think through some things."

She stared at him, unable to force any words past the constriction in her throat.

He dropped her hands and rubbed his knuckles over her cheek. "Will you wait for me?"

She tried to hide the fear from her features and forced a smile. "Of course. But you *must* speak to my uncle. He's currently opposed to our betrothal."

The muscles in Matthew's jaw tightened. "He cannot be blamed. I acted a fool."

"Why did you?" she asked softly. She hadn't wanted to ask but needed to know.

"I misjudged the amount of drink I could handle."

Confusion puckered her brow. She'd spent months with this man and had never known him to take strong drink. "If I'm to be your wife, you must be able to tell me things."

"I needed something to numb the dreams." He tugged on his collar. "Just until they go away again."

The pleading in his tone pricked her. "What dreams?"

He lifted his chin and stared at something over her head. "I see things again in my dreams that seeing once was more than enough to endure. Now those mangled forms with their anguished screams haunt my resting hours and torture me with my failures. Twisted, bloody faces, lost limbs and the roar of the cannons—" He shook himself.

Annabelle placed her hand to her heart, but Matthew seemed to mistake her concern for contempt.

Resignation flashed in his eyes. "You deserve a man who isn't broken."

"It's not your fault." She stepped closer to him, breathing in the scent of earth and cedar and uniquely *him*. "I've learned that to find peace, we must give our worries to God. Let him heal us."

Matthew snorted. "I can assure you, the Almighty doesn't wish to concern Himself with a man whose only prayers were for the enemy to fall at his feet."

The bitterness in his words clawed at her heart. "You must turn to Him for peace or you'll never find it."

He took a step back. "I'll come to Rosswood as soon as this is finished. Don't dally and risk them bringing you back. I don't trust these Yanks to keep their word."

Regret flickered on his face. Annabelle opened her mouth to refute him, but before she had the chance he turned and walked away.

Nineteen

"The Yankees are going to mock justice by pretending
to try those whom they have captured. They cannot
revenge themselves on Booth—he is out of
their power."
John H. Surratt

G eorge studied his reflection in the mirror, finally starting to
see the man he remembered. His face had filled out, and
light once again sparked in his eyes. He'd taken Lilly to dinner
each day since she'd returned to Washington, and things had
been going quite well. He'd enjoyed spending time with her and
little Frankie. In their company he could nearly forget the
bloody war and the stench of prison. Where once he feared he
might be slipping into madness, hope now swelled like a rising
tide.

Gone were the days of gloomy tents and restless soldiers.
He could put it all behind him and focus on rebuilding his life at
the plantation. Once matters were settled here, they'd take long
rides over the lands of Westerly. In the evenings, they'd take
their leisure by the hearth in the study while the boy played on
the rugs. And then, after the wedding, he'd be blessed to spend

each night in Lilly's arms.

The thought aroused desires he had to fight to dampen. He'd been years without the affections of a woman, and the thought of rediscovering those passions with Lilly made his blood heat. He combed back his freshly cut locks and looked at the gentleman he'd known before the war staring back at him from the looking glass. His eyes brimmed with hope.

He reached into his pocket and pulled out a slim gold band, hoping the ring would fit her delicate finger. He'd wanted to give her one with an emerald or diamond, but the Confederate notes he had were worthless, and he'd need the remaining silver to get the lands of Westerly working again.

She'd understand. George smiled. A working-class woman wouldn't turn up her nose at simplicity. She'd make a perfect lady for Westerly. Mother would be so thrilled to have both her sons wed that she wouldn't begrudge him marrying below their station.

He tucked the ring back into his pocket and straightened his cravat.

Would Lilly accept him? He clenched his teeth and tried to brush the thought aside. Though she'd seemed hesitant at first, the lady had begun to soften toward him these past few days and her demure glances had given him hope.

Besides, doubt was foolish. Had he not heard a word from the Almighty? Their engagement could last as long as she needed it to, but he couldn't leave for Rosswood with Annabelle and Mr. Ross without the security of knowing he wouldn't lose her to another suitor. Though she knew his intentions, the ring would seal their relationship.

Feeling more confident in his decision, George checked the

clock on the mantel. With Annabelle's required testimony completed, they'd depart in the morning. Though George assumed Mr. Ross capable of handling their family concerns over the land, Matthew had been quite insistent that George go south with them. The concern in his brother's voice had been clear, and George couldn't deny him. Besides, he owed Annabelle a debt and would provide her with any assistance he could.

He closed the door to his and Matthew's hotel room and strode down the plush carpet of the hall, excitement growing. He came to the door of the room Mrs. Smith and Lilly shared and knocked.

Mrs. Smith smiled up at him. "Good evening, Mr. Daniels."

George bent slightly at the waist. "Good evening, ma'am."

The widow stepped out of the door with a rustle of black silk, pulling it closed behind her. "She'll be ready in a few moments." A mischievous glint entered her eyes. "I'd like to speak with you about your intentions."

She already knew his interest in Lilly. "My intentions haven't changed since you gave me permission to ask Miss Rose to return to Washington."

The woman watched him with interest, and her next words came out carefully. "You keep calling her that. You know she has no family name. She is not a lady of means."

"Yes, I know. But I don't know what else to call her."

Mrs. Smith fingered the brooch at the base of her throat. "It is a lovely name, don't you think? As fresh as flowers…for a new beginning."

George nodded absentmindedly, but then something in her tone gave him pause. A memory tugged at the back of his mind but wouldn't take root.

He opened his mouth to reply, but she held up a hand. "I'll let you discuss these things with her. All I can say is that I pray you're the gentleman I hope you are and won't be blinded like the rest of your kind."

His kind? What in heaven's name did she mean by that?

He didn't get a chance to ask. The door swung open and Lilly appeared, a vision in emerald silk and delicate bits of lace. He felt like an anxious youth courting again—a lovesick fool who still possessed a head full of plans and a heart full of wild dreams.

Lilly lowered her eyes, letting fringes of dark lashes feather over her smooth complexion. She never played the coquette, but when she looked up at him from under those lashes, his pulse quickened.

Mrs. Smith mumbled something and patted Lilly's arm before slipping back into the hotel room and closing the door.

"How's Frankie after our ride this morning?"

The smile he'd hoped for curved her pillow lips. He offered his arm, and she placed her small hand on his forearm. "He was so worn out from all the excitement I didn't have to rock him half a minute before he was fast asleep!"

The laughter in her voice warmed George, and he returned her smile. "Thank you for trusting me with him."

Her hand tightened on his arm. "Frankie is quite taken with you." She laughed again. "What was I to do?"

"I'm taken with him as well." He patted her fingers. "I truly enjoy his company."

Lilly grew thoughtful as they made their way down the stairs. They crossed through the hotel lobby and into the dining room on the main floor. Trusting him with her son and the fact that the boy grew fond of him meant a great deal for the development of their relationship.

After he had pulled out her chair and sat in his own, George offered her a contented smile and continued the conversation. "I hope someday I can teach Frankie how to ride on his own."

A flicker of worry passed over Lilly's features. Had he said something wrong?

Lilly opened her mouth, but then closed it.

"What's wrong, Miss Rose?"

She sighed. "I keep telling you not to call me that."

"Then may I call you Lilly?"

"We've had this same talk before. Don't you remember?" She shook her head, clearly finding him daft. "I already told you that *everyone* calls me just plain Lilly." She cocked her head. "Or sometimes Lilly Rose. But Rose ain't my family name. Just part of my first, and only, name."

George chuckled. "I remember. However, I was taught to call a lady by her surname until she granted the use of her given name. I want to court you properly, you see. Therefore, when I call you by your given name, I want it to be because you've given me permission to speak your name with a more intimate familiarity."

Realization sprang up in her eyes, and her mouth made a fetching little O shape. He smothered his amusement, lest she think he made light of her. "I hope you understand that I have affections for you and that my intentions toward you are directed at a permanent relationship."

Her eyes widened farther at his blunt admission. Surprise melted into a flicker of delight, and his heart warmed. But then the flicker suddenly died, replaced with a smooth formality that chilled him.

Lilly lifted her chin, resignation tightening the lines of her mouth. "I've thought long and hard about ignoring your misconceptions and simply letting myself enjoy what you're offering."

What was she talking about?

The serving man appeared, keeping George from asking her what she meant. The server told them about the evening's selection of meats and other various dishes. The words fell like muted rain on George's ears. He tugged on his collar and then ordered them the chicken, knowing Lilly preferred foul to beef, and sent the man scurrying away with an impatient look.

As soon as the man retreated, the lady leaned over the table, allowing the candlelight to dance across her bare shoulders. The dip in the neckline of her bodice exposed the hollow of her throat. George had to pull his gaze back up to the deep brown eyes that studied him.

"I cannot figure you out, Mr. Daniels. I don't know if you understand the truth of the situation and choose to pretend it doesn't exist, or if you're oblivious to something that you should be able to see without me having to say it."

George sat back in his chair, perplexed. "I'm well aware you're a woman of working stature while I'm a man of family means. However, you seem far more interested in the divide than I am. The war has a way of bringing poverty to us all." She simply stared at him, so George forged on. "To be rather blunt, I'm pleased you're a woman I feel I can rely on to help me bring my plantation back to what it once was."

She stiffened and leaned away from the table. What had he

done to upset her this time? Women were such fickle creatures. How could a man understand their moods, when their emotions so often flitted from one thing to another?

Neither of them spoke to the server when he placed their plates in front of them. When the man stepped away Lilly said, "You're a kind man, Mr. Daniels, and I must admit that if I permitted myself the fantasy, I'd be drawn to you. But I cannot allow this to continue."

Worry snaked through him, choking out the tender hope.

Lilly looked at him with tired eyes, and he sensed her deep regret. He reached across the table to take her hand, but she pulled it back. "If Frankie gets too attached to you, it'll only make things harder on him."

"Make what harder? I'm not going to come into his life and then disappear. Don't let the loyalties of a finished war make your decision." He reached into his pocket and plucked out the little ring, laying it on the table between them. "I hope to marry you, Lilly." Her name slid off his tongue like silk, and he didn't miss the little shiver that passed over her.

Before she could conjure a protest, George hurried on. "I hope to be a father to Frankie and a loving husband to you. I want to provide for you, care for you, and someday I hope that you will come to find affection for me as well."

Lilly stared at the ring on the table, and tears gathered in her eyes. "Oh, George."

The longing in her tone and the use of his name on her velvety lips sent a jolt through him.

"I'm part Negro."

The words hung on the air. He was too stunned to speak. She kept her eyes on her untouched food, her soft words pounding a stake into his heart. "Frankie's father was an immigrant from Spain, so his blood is even more mixed than my own. My father was a white man, a plantation man. My mother was a slave, also born of mixed blood." Her chest rose and fell.

How could this be? She was supposed to be the one God sent for him! How could he have been so mistaken? A mulatto? His family would disown him. He could never—

Two tears slid down her perfect cheeks, and she stood, leaving her napkin on the table. Her sweet voice clawed him to shreds. "I didn't want to tell you, because I knew how badly it would hurt to see the way you just looked at me." Her voice hitched. "Farewell, Mr. Daniels."

George stared at the ring on the table as she stepped away. He didn't turn, and he didn't call after her. The words his heart wanted to shout died on his lips. He reached out and took the ring in his hand, feeling the small, cold metal.

He slipped the ring in his pocket and turned to leave the forgotten meal. Regret, fear, and a host of other emotions he couldn't even name churned within him, making him feel like a lone soldier caught between the lines. Doubt peppered him like Minié balls, and he clutched at his chest. Hot. The room was much too hot. His ears rang, hearing the ghostly whine of bullets. He couldn't stay here. George stumbled through the dining room like a drunkard. Then he righted himself, straightened his cravat, and stalked out the front door of the hotel and into the lonely night.

Twenty

"Montreal not safe; left it, therefore, last evening.
Detectives about everywhere. I shall not be looked for
in this retired place."
John H. Surratt

*W*hat would she find upon finally returning home? It had been two months since she'd left Rosswood. Uncle Michael didn't know if Grandfather still lived or not, seeing as how Andrew had been too hostile to let Michael inside. Her heart brimmed with both anticipation and trepidation.

A warm breeze ruffled the fringes on her gown, the long northern winter finally having been vanquished by the fortitude of spring. Movement drew her eyes away from Michael's agitated instructions to the coachman loading their baggage and to Eudora.

How she'd love to have the formidable lady at her side when she returned home. "Are you certain you cannot come with me?"

"I'm afraid not dear." She regarded Michael with a down-turn of her lips.

The two were not fond of one another. Annabelle wondered

about the history between the two sides of her family, which she sensed had more animosity than could be attributed to the war.

Annabelle slipped her arm into Eudora's. "I know you've been away from home for weeks, but I shall greatly miss your company."

Concern flittered across Eudora's features. "I'll be along as soon as I can."

Annabelle wanted to argue that it was more sensible to simply to come along now, but then Lilly appeared on the outer walk and Eudora pulled away. She took Lilly's arm, guiding her away from the others as they spoke in low tones.

Someone clasped her elbow. Startled, she found George staring down at her. "Come, Miss Ross. We mustn't be late for the train."

"Well, yes, but I haven't finished my goodbyes." She shielded her eyes from the sun's glare. "And where is Peggy? We can't leave without her."

George's face tightened, and he dropped her elbow. "I'll find her."

What had gotten him all flustered? Dismissing his mood, Annabelle hurried over to Eudora and Lilly. Seeing her approach, the two women stopped their conversation and Lilly stepped forward, extending her hand to Annabelle. Annabelle grasped it and gave the other woman's fingers a squeeze.

"Please come and visit me sometime."

A sad smile tugged on Lilly's lips. "That would be nice, Miss Ross. I'm sure we will see one another again when you come to call on Mrs. Smith."

Lilly's eyes were red around the edges, and dark smudges marred the skin underneath. Annabelle glanced at Eudora, but the other woman gave a small shake of her head. Feeling compassion for her friend, Annabelle pulled Lilly into an embrace, hoping the gesture would give a small measure of comfort to whatever saddened her.

Lilly returned Annabelle's squeeze and then stepped away, dropping her gaze. Sensing Lilly's discomfort at something behind her, Annabelle turned to see George standing stiffly with Peggy at his side.

"Where have you been?"

Peggy crossed her arms, in a snit about something, and answered only with a grunt. Annabelle tilted her head. What was she missing?

"We must get going," Michael said. He snapped his pocket watch closed and stuffed it back into his jacket. His eyes held impatience, as though he couldn't fathom why everyone didn't jump at his command.

George ducked into the carriage without another word. Annabelle looked back at Lilly, understanding dawning. The two of them must have had some kind of quarrel. Poor Lilly. Anyone could see she was taken with George. What had happened to cause such a rift between them?

She'd speak to George. They'd work it out. And if things went well, then perhaps Lilly would join the family in marriage. A sister.

Lilly ducked her head and scurried back inside the hotel, leaving Eudora alone with Annabelle on the walkway.

"A quarrel with Mr. Daniels, I presume?"

Eudora pulled Annabelle close and patted her back. "If only it were so simple," she mumbled.

Annabelle made a move to pull away to question Eudora's

meaning, but the woman held firm, continuing to speak in Annabelle's ear. "Right now you need to worry about your lands. I'll be along in a few weeks, once I get Lilly and Frankie settled back at home."

Without waiting for Annabelle's reply, Eudora pulled away and strode back into the hotel. Michael held the carriage door while Peggy darted her gaze around the streets of Washington as though some foul creature might pounce at any moment.

Annabelle took Peggy's elbow and guided her closer to the carriage.

"What are you doing, Anna?" Michael's tone held bewilderment. "That slave cannot ride in the carriage."

Annabelle tightened her grip on Peggy's arm. "Peggy is a freedwoman."

His brows knit. "On whose authority?"

"On mine, foremost. I set her free as soon as I learned of my father's passing. Secondly, in case you've forgotten, the Union government abolished slavery."

Uncle grunted. "They'll not take what's ours, neither by their army nor their politics."

Annabelle bit back her retort at the preposterous statement.

The lines on his face deepened. "To say so would be to say that all we suffered was for nothing."

Compassion tugged at her. What had her uncle endured? She knew how the war had weighed on the Daniels brothers. Men were so stoic and adept at burying emotions. There would be no judging just how many wounds would linger long after the flesh had healed.

Annabelle offered Uncle a gentle smile and guided Peggy to the carriage. "What matters now is rebuilding peace and a new future in this changed land. We must all learn to move with this current, lest it overtake us."

Michael's features softened slightly, but his posture remained stiff.

"And so she'll ride with me."

Uncle said nothing further as the women settled on their side of the carriage, nor anything when Annabelle took Peggy onto their traveling car on the train. The four took their seats and the steam engine gave off its shrill whistle. Annabelle stared out the window and watched Washington pass by, her heart aching as she left Matthew behind.

George swallowed bile that rose in his throat. His stomach remained in constant turmoil, as though it thought to mimic the unrest in his heart. He'd lain awake all night, picturing Lilly's face. He felt ripped in two different directions. He still saw her as his light, and the joy at the thought of their life together waged a bloody war with all he'd ever known. No respectable Southern gentleman could marry a woman of color! He nearly groaned, shifting in his seat and looking at Michael Ross from the corner of his eye.

What did the man think of his niece's predicament? Matthew hadn't been in their room when George finally returned last night, nor had he been here this morning to bid his betrothed goodbye. Had it not been for his brother's scrawled note thanking George for accompanying Annabelle while Matthew stayed for the trial, George would've thought him missing.

He'd not known Matthew to stay out all night since before the war, and the idea troubled him. Something seemed amiss.

A pang of guilt nipped at him. He'd noticed something out of place with Matthew, but he'd been too preoccupied with his doomed courtship to pay him much mind. Now he feared that something pushed his brother toward a precipice.

The train chugged farther south, back toward homelands that would never again be the same. George's thoughts shifted to Westerly. He'd sent Mother a long letter, letting her know all that had transpired and telling her that he'd be returning soon. He prayed all would be well when he finally made it back home.

Home to run Westerly alone, with no gentle anchor at his side to keep him steady.

Soon the rhythmic cadence of the train lulled him into an overdue sleep. As though outside of himself, George watched the train fade away. A blink, and then he found himself standing in his personal bedchamber at Westerly, surrounded by things he hadn't seen since his last furlough three years ago.

Curiously aware that he *must* be asleep, yet feeling as awake and alert as ever, George walked around the room. He fingered the blue quilt his mother had made by her own hand and then stepped over to the window to look at the grounds below.

The yard sprouted with an abundance of budding flora, and out on the hill a mare with a new colt at her side bent to graze on tender grass sprouts. George turned from the window, meaning to go out of the room and seek out his mother. He passed by his bureau and his eyes caught on the mirror. What he saw there sent him stumbling to a halt.

What in heaven's name...?

The face before him stared back with wide eyes. He touched his open jaw. The reflection did the same, the stranger there imitating his every move.

George stared at the looking glass in disbelief. It must be some trick of the mind! He stepped closer, and the figure in the mirror did the same. He forced a nervous chuckle. Whoever stood trapped beyond the glass wasn't him. The other simply copied George's movements.

Just a dream.

The thought did little to reduce his pounding heartbeat.

Slowly, George turned his gaze from the startled face in the mirror and to his hands. Panic surged anew.

These were not his hands!

Where he'd thought to regain reality, here was only further evidence of what his reflection foretold. He studied the hands before him…hands the warm color of mahogany.

His eyes darted back to his reflection. His face, yet not his own. His nose was a bit wider, his eyes a deep, rich brown. George stumbled away from the looking glass, slick sweat making his skin shine. He dropped to his knees and put his hands against the sides of his head.

"Lord! What's happened to me?"

I Am here, my son.

The voice flowed over him, caressing the worry away and settling on his spirit. "I'm still me, Lord, yet not."

He could feel a sense of amusement fill the room.

The same, yet not the same. Why is that?

"You can see me, Lord. You know."

Indeed I do. Do you?

"My skin, Lord. It's not me."

Is it not? the Voice said from somewhere deep inside. *Look again.*

George lurched to his feet and hurried to the mirror. The dark tones of his face faded right before him, past his usual coloring and not stopping until his skin was as pale as milk. The dark, coarse hair on his head faded and lengthened. For a moment, his natural locks appeared and then transformed into a bright fiery red. Stunned, George could only stare as his eyes turned from deep chestnut to stark emerald, staring back at him from a face that once again was somehow his own, yet completely strange.

George cried out, leaping away from the mirror. "This is not me, either, Father! Have you forgotten me?"

Peace swirled around him. *Be calm, my child. I know every hair on your head.*

How could the Lord know every hair on his head, when this was clearly not the same features? Though he dared not voice the doubt, an answer came anyway.

I know every detail of the ones I create. I make all people in the way I want them. Who are you to say which form I give you is best?

George shrank from the voice, strong and corrective, yet at the same time loving and kind. Still, he could not pull his eyes away from the reflection as his features shifted again and returned to the familiar ones he'd always known. George looked down at his hands, relieved to see them the proper color, and then felt a sudden wash of shame.

"I was still me on the inside, wasn't I?"

It is beyond what you can understand, but know that you are more than just the body I form in the secret places.

George's image faded from the mirror, replaced by the

pained eyes and sorrowful features of Lilly Rose. George turned to look over his shoulder, but she didn't stand in the room with him. The mirror showed only her portrait, as though she were frozen on the other side.

George hung his head.

My daughter, the voice said, so filled with love that George's heart constricted. *So precious to Me.*

That voice, laced with disappointment, dug deep into George. All the arguments he wanted to claim…the ways of society, the hardships they would endure…all died before they could form. Who was he to say any of those things to the Almighty?

"I'm sorry." What else could he say? The woman in front of him was so beautiful with those eyes that spoke of a depth of soul he longed to explore. He'd always found her golden tones so appealing. Why would knowing her mixed parentage change that now? He reached out and touched the mirror. Her image disappeared, leaving him looking only at his own haunted eyes.

George dropped to his knees, feeling the loss of her so heavily that he ached. "What do I do?"

No voice answered him. Desperately, George looked around, but the room no longer felt like home. Though in all appearances the same, it seemed nothing but cold and empty. Lonely.

"Help me." His head swam, and he squeezed his eyes against the wave of anguish that washed over him, drowning in him self-made sorrow and—

George jerked awake, bolting up in his seat.

"Mr. Daniels!" Mr. Ross eyed George sternly. "Gather yourself, man!"

"Are you well?" Annabelle asked. When he didn't answer, she leaned nearer, lowering her voice. "Do you have the same dreams of war that plague Matthew?"

He nodded, thinking the lie easier than the truth.

She offered him an encouraging smile. "I'll pray these dreams leave you be, as I'm praying they leave Matthew."

"I...thank you."

As though her prayers settled the matter, she smiled and looked back out the window. Mr. Ross had returned to his paper, ignoring the others in his company. Peggy stared at him. He shifted uncomfortably. How much did she know? From the look of regret on her face, he guessed a good deal more than Annabelle.

George suddenly wished he could jump from the train. "My apologies. It seems I must guard against sleeping in public."

Despite his effort to make light of the situation, Mr. Ross offered nothing more than a cursory grunt and the women, placating smiles.

Images from his dream peppered him like lead, and no matter how hard he tried to dislodge them, they buried deep into his heart causing a flow of emotion he could not staunch.

Twenty-One

"I wonder what is intended to be done with mother.
Surely they will not hang a woman! Should they do so, I
will live only to bide my time."
John H. Surratt

*M*ichael snapped his pocket watch closed and leaned closer to George to look out the window. Annabelle's gaze drifted from Uncle's tight features to George's blank stare. She forced levity into her voice. "I'm sure it won't be much longer, Uncle. See how close the trees are here?"

He mumbled something under his breath and didn't look at her. What were they to do but wait? The train couldn't go without the wood, and it took time for the locomotive crews to chop and load the fuel into the supply car.

Ever since they'd crossed into the southern parts of Virginia, train travel had become burdensome. The Confederate lines had been destroyed in several places, making their progress slow and cumbersome. She'd heard some of the other passengers say that Sherman had even diverted tracks into the trees in order to destroy the engines as they chugged unwittingly down the tracks.

Fuel stores and depots had been destroyed and train crews were severely understaffed. The remaining engineers often had to stop along the route to chop wood to burn in order to keep the train moving.

"We'll be in Mississippi again soon," Annabelle said.

Michael smoothed his furrowed brow. "Yes, but we'll have to stop north of Holly Springs and disembark. Coaches for hire have been gathering at the end of the tracks to take passengers on into town."

A grim expression tightened the lines around George's mouth. "Van Dorn destroyed the tracks when they forced Grant back to Tennessee."

Annabelle shook her head, not bothering to ask the details. They'd been on trains for much longer than she liked, and the prospect of switching to a coach to take them the rest of the way home sounded quite appealing.

Another hour or more passed before the whistle blew and they started south again. Four hours later, the passing scenery of burned fields, half-standing homes, and towns left to ruins finally slowed to a stop. Annabelle stood and raised her arms over her head, trying to get some of the stiffness to ease from her shoulders.

Michael and George gathered the bags, and they all descended the steps out onto an open patch of ground. Annabelle knotted the ties on her bonnet, though only a whisper of a breeze stirred the seeded tops of the grass underfoot. Despite what Uncle had said, Annabelle didn't see any coaches waiting for them. Knowing better than to raise his ire by saying so, she waited on the grass with about ten other passengers as the engine crew began preparations for returning north.

Peggy leaned close and whispered in Annabelle's ear. "They ain't just gonna leave us out here in the middle of this field, are they?"

"Surely not." The other passengers appeared uncomfortable as well. "Why, I imagine a coach or two has already seen the engine smoke and is on the way now."

Peggy grunted. The sun bore down on them, causing sweat to dampen Annabelle's face and slide down underneath her bodice into places it had no business going. They must have missed the brief Mississippi spring and plunged right into the boiling summer.

"Where'd we put that parasol? You gonna be blistered out in this here sun." Peggy plucked the fan from Annabelle's fingers and waved it fervently in Annabelle's face as though she could shoo away the sun.

"Peggy! Stop that."

"I'm going to walk to town to see what I can find," George said, removing his hat to wipe his brow. "Your maid is correct, Miss Ross. A lady shouldn't be subject to the afternoon's sun."

Michael twirled his pocket watch. "It's not your responsibility to look after my niece."

They all turned to stare at him. Why would Uncle say something so rude?

"As I know you're aware, my brother asked me to look after his intended until he's able to do so himself. So, yes, it is in fact my responsibility." Uncle's face reddened, but George simply pulled his shoulders back and continued. "I say we need to stop standing around like a bunch of dolts and make our way to town."

Michael puffed his chest and stepped closer to George,

lowering his voice. Annabelle heard him anyway. "I haven't approved of your brother's suit, let alone consented my niece's hand. Therefore, you have no reason to be here and are welcome to return to your own lands. Surely they require your attention."

George's hands clasped into fists and Annabelle hurried over to the two men, fluttering her fan. "Oh, dear, but I do believe I'm growing weary in this heat." Both men turned to regard her, the two of them the very image of competing stags prepared to clash. She batted her lashes and put a hand to her throat, pretending to sway. "Perhaps we all might walk together to meet the coaches?"

The tactic seemed to suffice because they both leapt forward to take her elbows.

Michael patted her arm. "There, now, Anna. Don't fret. Why don't you and the maid stay here, and we'll find you a bit of shade? Then I'll hoof it to Holly Springs and bring you back a fine coach."

Annabelle smiled, feeling the two men glaring at one another above her head as they turned her toward a cluster of trees that a few of the other displaced passengers already walked toward. "Thank you, dear Uncle."

"Quite generous of you," George quipped. "Of course, the women will need protection out here in the wilds, so I'll stay with them until you return."

Annabelle pressed her lips together to contain the chuckle she knew would annoy her uncle and focused on the grass slipping underneath her green skirts as they walked. She couldn't help but cheer George's victory, if only because she'd been wanting a few moments alone with him. She wanted to discuss the strange parting he'd had with Lilly.

They reached the small stand of trees, a lone oasis in an otherwise abandoned tobacco field. An elderly couple, a family with four youthful daughters, and two men who appeared to be members of the clergy joined them under the shade.

Uncle cleared his throat and spoke as one accustomed to authority. "I'm going to locate a coach for myself and my company. Would any of you men care to join me in securing additional coaches of your own?"

The people exchanged glances, and the man with the four daughters stepped forward. "Don't want to leave my wife and girls out here alone. No tellin' what Yankee raiding parties might be about."

The others nodded in consent. The man's wife reached for the youngest of their girls, a dark-haired darling of about ten, and drew her close.

George stepped forward. "I'll remain behind to provide protection. You have my word as a Confederate officer that no harm shall befall any here."

Uncle shot George a disgusted look, though Annabelle couldn't fathom why. "Very well," Uncle said. "Shall we go then?"

The two men who looked like either clergy or clerks by way of their spindly frames and bespectacled faces opted to join Michael and the girls' father, leaving the elderly man and George to watch over the women and girls. Leading them like he was the head of a military scouting unit, Michael marched off in quick fashion, leaving the others to hurry along behind him.

"What's got that man all up in a bind?" Peggy asked.

Annabelle tugged the bonnet off her head. "I don't know.

Perhaps he's just worried about what will become of Rosswood."

Goodness, but it was hot out here. She tugged out two of her hairpins.

"Miss Belle! What you doin'?" Peggy snatched the bonnet from Annabelle's hand and moved to place it back on her head.

Annabelle ducked out of her reach. "I have sweat sliding through my hair. These pins are slipping and pulling and, oh, they simply must be redone."

Peggy clicked her tongue. "No, ma'am. We ain't lettin' your hair free out here."

"Why not?"

"Too many folks around."

Annabelle regarded the somber people trying to cool themselves in the sweltering heat. "I'm sure these women won't mind if I take my hair down a moment and then replace my pins."

Peggy's eyes widened as Annabelle shook out her long locks, relishing the feel of freedom. "There's men here, too, child," Peggy protested, trying to place herself between Annabelle and the others.

"A grandfatherly gentleman and a man who'll soon be my brother are of little concern. Besides, it's already loose. Stop grumbling and help me get it pinned back up."

Peggy wasted no time getting Annabelle's hair properly stuffed back underneath a straw bonnet, mumbling under her breath the entire time about stubbornness and Annabelle's lacking sense of propriety.

When Peggy deemed her presentable again, Annabelle straightened. "Now, if you'll excuse me a moment, I need to speak with George."

Peggy clutched her arm, shaking her head like a bee had gotten underneath her headscarf. "No, you don't, either. You let that alone."

Annabelle stopped. "Leave what alone?"

Peggy steered her away from George and to an oak at the edge of the cluster, farther away from the others. George stood with his back to them, staring out at the open field with his hand on a pistol she hadn't noticed before.

"You was gonna ask him 'bout Lilly."

"Well, yes." Annabelle smiled. "Surely whatever they quarreled about can be overcome."

Peggy pursed her lips in that way she did when she wanted to say something but thought it better if she didn't.

"What do you know that I don't?"

"Ain't none of our business, that's what."

Annabelle just stared at Peggy until the other woman grew uncomfortable. Finally, she relented, leaning close to Annabelle with a conspirator's whisper. "What I'm goin' to tell you ain't for other ears. Don't you go runnin' to that man telling him you know, you hear?"

Curious, Annabelle leaned closer. "Peggy," she whispered, "you're being outright mysterious. What's going on?"

"Lilly ain't all white," Peggy said softly, a heavy sadness threading her voice.

Annabelle tilted her head. "She's got a darker complexion than I do, but that doesn't mean she's not a white lady."

"Miss Belle, there's a lot of areas of life where you's still innocent." Peggy offered her a gentle smile. "But I'm afraid you're gonna need to understand the ways of this world."

Flustered, Annabelle threw up her hands. "You're not making a lick of sense."

"Lilly Rose ain't her real name, you know that?"

"What…?" Annabelle sighed. This conversation started one thread only to pick up another. "How do you know that?"

Instead of answering right away, Peggy plucked a ripe seed head from a nearby grass stalk and fiddled with it. "You remember when we was traveling back to Washington City with your grandma, and we stopped at that funny little white lady's house?"

"Miss Wesson." Annabelle smiled. "The lady with the flowers."

"Uh-huh. And you remember what that woman said 'bout the slaves that came to her and how she helped them…" Peggy let the words trail off, leaving Annabelle to piece together something on her own.

She tried to remember conversations she hadn't been paying much attention to, sick with worry over Matthew as she'd been. The thought of him sent a stab of pain through her heart but she smothered it and tried to focus on Miss Wesson. She tapped her chin. "She said something about giving them new beginnings. But what does any of that have to do with George and Lilly?"

Peggy regarded her evenly. "Lilly Rose."

Annabelle huffed, exasperated. "What does Miss Wesson have to do with Lilly *Rose*—" Realization hit. She glanced at George's stiff shoulders. "Lilly Rose. Like the flowers. A name given to her by Miss Wesson when she arrived with slaves. Like Miss Wesson gives to all the new flowers."

Peggy nodded, her mouth a tight line.

Annabelle fanned herself. "It can't be! Lilly isn't a colored woman, Peggy."

"Not all, child, but enough. Your grandma told me Lilly was sent to the orphanage when one of the master's slaves birthed a child far too white."

Annabelle placed a hand to her heart. "But that would mean…" she shook her head, dislodging the thought.

Peggy grabbed her hand. "It means that the master had mulatto slaves, and when he fathered a child with one of them, the baby came out showing his sins."

Annabelle turned her face away. "How terrible for Lilly."

"Now it ain't my place to say, but before you go waggin' your tongue to Mr. Daniels, it's best you know that Lilly's momma was a slave and Lilly came up with her from Louisiana."

"So Lilly told him the truth?"

Sadness filled Peggy's eyes. It was all the answer Annabelle needed. "But, Peggy, you saw the way he looked at Lilly. My gracious, anyone could see he was smitten with her. Why should her parentage make any difference to him now?"

"I wish all white folks thought like you do." Peggy squeezed Annabelle's hand, her voice sad. "But truth of it is, when he found out she has Negro blood, that man left all his intentions behind."

Anguish had practically poured off of George these past days. Had he wanted to go after Lilly, but been obligated to stay with Annabelle instead? "What if he wanted to go to her, but Matthew insisted he come with me? I have to tell him that he doesn't need to go with me."

Peggy grabbed her arm. "No, ma'am. You ain't doin' that."

Annabelle shrugged her off. "Why not? I won't say anything

about what you told me."

"That man's got a lot of thinking to do. And if he change his mind—" Peggy shook her head as though that were as likely as one of her fried chickens sprouting feathers again and flying out of the pan. "Well, then he knows where to find her. Ain't for you to go sticking your nose in."

Twenty-Two

"Hush'd be the camps to-day, / And soldiers let us drape our war-worn weapons, / And each with musing soul retire to celebrate, / Our dear commander's death. As they invault the coffin there, / Sing—as they close the doors of earth upon him—one verse, / For the heavy hearts of soldiers."
Walt Whitman, "Hush'd be the Camps To-day" (first and last stanzas)

Washington, D.C.
May 16, 1865

*M*atthew watched the boys in blue as they downed cup after cup of ale. He tried to ignore the need in his gut.

Just a little to numb the pain. Just a little to make sure I get a full night's sleep.

The din of the tavern filled with laughter that danced on smoke tendrils and slithered across Matthew's ears. Another day of military trials, another stiff day of endless questioning as the solicitors fluffed and postured themselves against one another.

From his spot here in the far corner, he could see many of them, the folks whose lives had been upended by the simple fact that they'd been near when the assassination happened. How many had he watched give their tales?

Yes, sir, I was standing in the street that night….

No, sir, I didn't see anything….

I was in the theatre. I saw him jump onto the stage….

I met John Booth once, about five years ago….

Around and around they went until Matthew wanted to strip the hair from his scalp. His fingers slipped into his coat and caressed the smooth metal flask.

No. He mustn't. Not after the last time.

Shame rolled through him again at the thought. Curse this weakness! Before the war he'd enjoyed the drink, though never to overindulgence. Then during the war he'd not touched a drop, even when others had relished the few times they were allowed a ration or two of whiskey. Why did he need it now? Why had his head filled with so many horrid visions that he feared he'd slip into madness?

He closed his eyes and Annabelle's face returned. She looked at him with questioning eyes, their blue depths flashing from uncertainty to disgust. He groaned and hung his head. Not only had he become a man tethered to the drink, he'd become a traitor, a coward, and a scoundrel—a scoundrel who ruined his first meeting with Annabelle's kin and had since gone back on his word to her.

Whatever tomorrow brings.

He'd meant it. He had. Why, then, had he disappointed her yet again? Why had he distanced himself? The answer prodded him like a hot iron. Because he'd failed. Again.

The raucous laughter swelled as a serving girl in a dress cut far too low giggled and plopped down onto the lap of one of the Union officers. The man whispered something in her ear, and she gestured toward the staircase just off to Matthew's right.

His stomach churned. He shouldn't be here. What would Annabelle think? He'd come at the insistence of the other men in his detail, fellows who curiously had begun to act more friendly toward him as the trial dragged on. He'd obliged because he'd wanted to find something to relax him at the end of another tedious day and his lonely room at the hotel held no appeal.

He slipped the flask free and tipped it to his lips as the couple slipped up the stairs, the woman's bodice dipping low enough that he could see curves he shouldn't look upon. Matthew averted his gaze and stared at the scarred table.

Lord, help me.

He rose and nodded to some of the men, two of whom lifted foaming mugs toward him, and then weaved through swaying patrons and smiling women.

Outside, he drew a deep breath of the night air, wondering how long he'd been inside. No matter. Enough of the night was gone that he could make it until morning. He turned toward the hotel, the quiet streets in opposition to the noisy building he left behind.

Matthew trudged down the street, his self-deprecating thoughts nagging at him. He turned a corner and the hairs on the back of his neck rose. He glanced over his shoulder but didn't see anything. Still, he felt watched. Matthew quickened his pace, increasing his stride until his legs stretched to their full length with every passing step.

"Hello, my friend."

Matthew jerked to a halt. He stared at the empty street behind him. Impossible. He was hearing things now! He took another step forward.

"I see you were nothing but a rat jumping a sinking ship. Ah, well, it's to be expected."

Matthew turned toward a shadowed alleyway. "O'Malley?"

Something moved, and the shadows parted. A figure stepped forward, a hat pulled low on his head. "Hello, Daniels."

Senses on edge, he squared his shoulders and planted his feet. "Come out of those shadows."

O'Malley chuckled and stepped forward into the wan light of a half-moon. His grin made Matthew's throat turn dry. Despite himself, he took a step back.

"No greeting for your brother in gray?" He clicked his tongue.

"I thought you were on the run. If they catch you in Washington, they'll put you on trial with the others."

"Daniels, you always were a slow one." O'Malley laughed like a madman. "Do you truly think I'd be here if I feared for my skin?"

Matthew took another step back. If O'Malley had a gun, could he get away before the man shot him?

"You see, they can't do anything to me. My purpose is of a different nature."

Suddenly O'Malley grasped the sleeve of Matthew's coat. "Come, my friend. I've got something to show you."

Sweat sprang onto his brow. Matthew spun and sprinted down the street. O'Malley spewed a string of curses that any sailor would deem foul, his voice following Matthew around the corner and onto the next street.

He dared a look over his shoulder, but no one followed. Matthew lowered his head and ran harder anyway, darting down the streets in a nonsensical pattern.

Sides heaving, he didn't slow until the cold metal of the

hotel doorknob filled his clammy palm. Ignoring the startled clerk and the comments of gentlemen enjoying their brandy in the lobby, Matthew took the main staircase two steps at a time.

Inside his room Matthew stumbled over to the chair by the cold hearth and nearly fell into it. He couldn't take it. The ache, the fear, the shame. Too many emotions hung on him like boulders about his neck, and there was nothing he could do to escape them. The whiskey had promised relief but had only brought him further grief. He clutched his chest.

Would he ever find peace? Or would one war or another continue to shred his soul?

"I need You..." Matthew whispered, dropping down to his knees. How had he been so blind? His near misses at death, the miracle that saved George—all along the Creator had shown His presence, yet Matthew had ignored Him.

Matthew leaned forward and dropped his head to the floor, a gush of anguish exploding from within him. Memories of the men he'd killed in battle, the compromises he'd made, the false truths, and a myriad of other failures flooded him until he thought he would crumble beneath the weight of them all.

"Please, forgive me," Matthew whispered, his voice raw with the emotions he could no longer suppress. "Make me a better man. One who follows You. One worthy of leading an honorable life."

Matthew shuttered as peace began as a kernel, then sprouted in his soul and filled every dark corner he'd tried to conceal. He felt completely known, but no longer ashamed.

"Thank you."

Matthew remained on his knees, and for the remainder of the night, poured out his heart to the One who'd created him.

Twenty-Three

"I find the Yankees are commencing what they call the trial with closed doors. Secret plotting to take the life of a few poor victims, and one a woman. The people and the press will cry such a thing down, or I am much mistaken."

John H. Surratt

Lilly Rose toyed with the lace on her fan and wondered again just how she'd ended up here. Not here at Miss Wesson's, as ending up at the lady's home resulted from a train ride and an unwavering insistence from her employer. No, what baffled her was this fan. The fan, the dress, and, yes…the woman in it. How had she gone from a dirty orphan struggling with her peers over too little food to this lady dressed in silks leisurely passing away the late afternoon hours?

Frankie plucked another bloom from Miss Wesson's azalea and scurried over to her. He'd gotten fast! No longer did he wobble with teetering steps but ran with a solid gait that showed how quickly time passed.

"Mama! Pretty!" He thrust the snatched flower toward her face, and she smiled.

"Thank you, baby." She added it to the pile in her lap. "But let's not pick more. We don't want the bush to be bare, now, do we?"

His little forehead crinkled and he looked back at the enormous bush covered in bright pink flowers. Then he grinned again and hurried over to another, grabbing a fistful of white petals from a blossom and yanking them from the stem.

The door opened and Miss Wesson bustled out, a tray of glasses with lemonade in her hands. Behind her, a young girl of about fourteen years hurried out sputtering about how the lady shouldn't be toting the tray.

Miss Wesson giggled in that childlike way she had. "Hush, Violet, and close the door. We don't want any bees in the house, do we?"

The girl's eyes widened, and she leapt to pull the door closed. "I's sorry, Mistress!"

"Oh, fiddle. No harm done, darling." She swung around. "And I've already told you, I'm not your mistress."

The girl watched as Miss Wesson hummed to herself and placed the tray on a low table by the circle of chairs in the garden. The bits of chipped ice floated in the sunny liquid and Lilly relished the idea of a cold drink.

Frankie spotted Miss Wesson and dropped the cluster of leaves in his hand. He ran toward her with outstretched arms. "Missy! Cookie!"

Lilly made a move to reach for him, but he dodged out of her grasp. "Frankie! That's impolite."

Miss Wesson giggled and waved away Lilly's concern. "Nonsense!"

Frankie tugged on her patterned skirt. "Cookie!"

"Now, where did I put that…?" Miss Wesson made a show of thinking, patting her skirts.

Frankie grinned and pointed to her pocket. "Cookie!"

"What? You think I have a cookie in my pocket? Why, what would a sweet be doing there?"

The joy on their faces kept Lilly from saying anything as they finished the game they'd already performed three times today. She produced the cookie and held it out to him.

He grinned. "Tank you!"

Miss Wesson beamed. "You're quite welcome, young sir."

Frankie plopped onto the grass at their hostess's feet to enjoy his treat.

The older lady watched him with a hint of sadness in her eyes, and Lilly wondered if the lady regretted never having little ones. As though feeling Lilly's eyes on her, she glanced up and the sadness was gone, replaced by the joy Lilly so loved about her.

"Now, then, let's see…oh, yes. Refreshment!" Miss Wesson gestured toward the glasses and then retrieved one for herself.

Lilly grabbed one of the remaining three glasses. "Thank you, Miss Wesson."

"Uh-huh. Of course, dear."

Lilly tipped her glass and relished the feel of the cold liquid sliding down her throat. Such luxuries!

Miss Wesson glanced around, twisting in her chair until her eyes landed on the shy mouse standing behind her with downcast eyes. "Violet! There you are. What are you doing back there?"

The girl lifted her chin, her curious gaze darting over Lilly for an instant before her light-brown eyes hid beneath thick lashes once more. She stepped around to the side of Miss Wesson's chair with a rustle of fabric. "Yes, mistress…I mean, ma'am…I mean…"

Lilly's heart lurched. Poor girl. Lilly had been in the same state of confusion when she'd first arrived here. And she'd been grown. This poor child seemed about to faint.

Miss Wesson smiled gently and reached out to take the girl's soft brown hand into her own pale one. Violet's eyes flew wide, fear streaking across her face.

"Easy, sweet one," Miss Wesson soothed. "No one's going to hurt you here."

The girl flicked her eyes to Lilly again, and Lilly offered an encouraging smile. Violet's shoulders relaxed but she remained as still as a pine on a windless day.

Miss Wesson clicked her tongue. "Sit over here by Lilly Rose, dear, while we wait on old Eudora to join us."

Violet hesitated a moment and then dropped to the very edge of the chair, looking as though she might take flight any second.

Filled with empathy, Lilly reached across and patted the girl's hand. "It's nice here, Violet. You'll see. You get a new life when you come to the flower house. Just as I did."

Violet turned bright eyes on her. "*You* came through here, like me?"

"I did."

Violet's jaw unhinged for a moment before she found words. "But…but, you's a lady."

A sadness welled in Lilly's chest, nearly causing tears to spring into her eyes, but she managed to shoo them away. "Oh, no. My momma was a slave. I was brought up in an orphanage, until Momma and I made it to Maryland and then on to New York, where Mrs. Smith gave me a way to make my own pay."

Violet glanced back to Miss Wesson. "That so?"

"Yes, dear." Miss Wesson snapped open a feathered fan and waved it around her face. "Lilly Rose is one of my many precious flowers."

Violet looked back at Lilly. "But…you's…" She clamped her mouth shut.

"I'm what?"

"You's a white lady."

Lilly fought down emotions that struggled for freedom. "Partly, yes."

Violet seemed to consider this but said nothing more. A moment later Mrs. Smith flung open the door and waltzed outside in her self-assured way. Without awaiting invitation, she scooped up a glass of lemonade and settled in the chair next to Miss Wesson.

"My goodness. This heat!" Mrs. Smith said, fluttering her hand in front of her face. Her gaze darted to Violet. "Why are you sitting there like a starched twig, girl? Get your glass and drink before all that good ice goes to waste."

Violet jumped, but then the gentle smile on Mrs. Smith's face drained the tension from her. She tentatively reached out and plucked the last glass from the tray. Lilly couldn't help but smile when the girl placed the glass to her lips and surprise lit her willowy features. She'd probably never had a chilled drink before.

Thrilled, the girl settled back into her chair with her prize and savored each sip. Lilly took another sip of her own, again marveling at how she'd become accustomed to such things. Fine silks, dainty fans, and an afternoon of leisurely company with cool refreshment had become nearly normal to her. What would the young girl she'd been think of the woman she'd become?

Probably more than George thought of her. She straightened herself. He'd cast her aside but she wouldn't let him steal her happiness. She had been happy before he'd shown up at their door and rattled her finely crafted life. She would be so again. Someday.

The mention of her name brought her attention back to the two ladies across from her. "Isn't that right, Lilly?"

Embarrassed, she snapped open her fan to hide the heat in her cheeks. "Oh, I'm sorry. What did you say?"

Mrs. Smith and Miss Wesson exchanged a glance. "She's still lost in thought over that gentleman, isn't she, Eudora?" Miss Wesson asked, though her gaze didn't leave Lilly.

Glad for the fan to hide behind, Lilly pressed her lips together to keep herself from spouting unkind words about minding one's own business. That simply wouldn't do. She owed both of these women too much to sting them with cross words. Unable to deny Miss Wesson's claim without lying, Lilly chose to say nothing.

Mrs. Smith's eyes swam with compassion. "That fool will come around, you'll see."

Lilly shook her head. "No, ma'am, I already done told you—"

"It's *I already said*, dear. Not 'done told.'"

Flustered at another correction, Lilly sucked in a breath and began again. "As I have already said, there will be no sort of relations between Mr. Daniels and me." She snapped her fan closed and dropped it on her lap, scattering flower petals to the ground.

"No, no, Mama!" Frankie scolded, crumbs clinging to his lips. He hurried to pick up his offering and gently placed every petal back into her lap.

She ran her fingers through his silky curls. "Thank you, Frankie."

He beamed at her and then caught sight of a blue butterfly and leapt after it. Lilly watched him chase it a moment before turning her focus back to the three sets of eyes that watched her.

"Men are stubborn things, dear. Sometimes it takes them a good knock of sense before they come around to what's best for them."

The compassion on her employer's face only made Lilly love her more. Where would she have been without Mrs. Smith?

Grasping for a change in subject Lilly motioned to Violet. "Miss Wesson, have you found a new home for Miss Violet or is she staying here with you?"

Miss Wesson lowered the glass that was halfway to her pink lips. "You don't know?"

Lilly shot at glance at Mrs. Smith. "I don't know what?"

Mrs. Smith shooed a fly that dared to land on her black silk. "Violet is coming with us. That's the reason we've come."

Miss Wesson poked out her lower lip. "You mean you didn't come just to visit me?"

Mrs. Smith cast a glance to the heavens. "Goodness, Bulla, you sound like a petulant child."

Miss Wesson tossed a silver-streaked curl over her shoulder.

"I did come to see you, as you know I love to do. But you also sent word to have me come meet Violet, so that was another reason to stop by. Or don't you remember?"

Violet seemed as surprised by this as Lilly, but she said nothing. She was likely used to others deciding her fate.

Mrs. Smith turned to the girl. "What do you think, dear? Would you be interested in coming to New York with Lilly and me? You will receive a wage just as Lilly does."

The girl turned wide eyes on Mrs. Smith. "I's gonna get to be like Miss Lilly?"

"I'm going to get to be like Miss Lilly," Mrs. Smith corrected. Violet stared at her. "Come now, say it properly."

"I'm going to get to be likes Miss Lilly?" she squeaked out.

"Ah, well, that's progress, at least." Mrs. Smith took a sip and set the cup aside. "Yes, you will learn from Lilly all the things you need to know about how to run a house."

Lilly smiled at the girl, and Violet's face lit up.

"That way you'll have someone to help you when Lilly goes," Miss Wesson chirped.

Lilly's heart dropped to her slippers. "Go?" Mrs. Smith wanted to replace her?

Mrs. Smith cut a scathing look at Miss Wesson, who seemed not to notice. "Well, at the time, I thought perhaps you'd be starting a life of your own…" She trailed off, pain evident in her eyes.

Violet would have been her replacement had she wed George.

"Are you leaving, Miss Lilly?" Violet asked, the shimmer in her eyes prodding Lilly's tender heart.

"Oh, no, don't you worry. I'll be right there teaching you all about how to put up with Mrs. Smith correcting your words and stuffing you into stays and silks." She forced a laugh she didn't feel and was rewarded with the look of excitement on Violet's face.

Then the girl's face fell. "But, I's just a house slave. Ain't no house slave wearing silks."

"Ha! There are no slaves in my house," Mrs. Smith said. "I will teach you to be a lady. Just as I taught Lilly."

A lot of good it did.

The mean thought stabbed through her like a dagger.

Please, Lord, help me forget. I don't want to love him.

A plantation master—the last type man she ever wanted to be near—had inexplicably stolen her heart. He'd torn down all her notions of who he was supposed to be. He'd made her hope for a life she hadn't even known she wanted. And, oh, how she'd loved him.

Right up until the moment when all her fears had proven true and the color of her skin became more important to him than anything else. All along, he'd been no different. He was just another master who looked at her as something less than a person. All her life she'd been seen that way, yet it had never devastated her as it had when that same prejudice cut through the adoration in his eyes.

"Don't worry, sweet Lilly." Miss Wesson giggled. "George will open his eyes. He seemed a fine fellow." She winked. "And a right handsome one."

Frankie paused from where he'd been plucking grass from the dirt and beamed up at Lilly. "Orge? Where Orge?"

Lilly swallowed. "Mr. George isn't here. Miss Wesson only spoke his name."

Frankie tilted his head. "When Orge come?"

She fought past the constriction in her throat. "He's not, baby."

"Like Orge." Frankie grinned. "Ride." He plopped back down on the ground and resumed sticking his pudgy fingers into the dirt.

Lilly lifted a hand to her heart as though the motion could stop the fierce ache inside. Forcing back tears that threatened to spill, she stood. "I'm not feeling well. Would it be all right for me to take a rest before the evening meal?"

Mrs. Smith offered a sympathetic smile. "Of course, my dear. I'll keep an eye on the baby. You go rest."

Unraveling too quickly to protest that Frankie should stay with her, Lilly gave a grateful nod and escaped to the house where she could nurse her tattered heart in private.

Twenty-Four

"News has just been brought to me that President Davis
has been captured. If that be true, all our plans and
dangerous risks have been in vain."
John H. Surratt.

Rosswood Plantation
Lorman, Mississippi
May 24, 1865

The horses' hooves pounded out a steady trot past familiar
landscape. Rocks and mud clinging to the coach's wheels
periodically struck the side of the carriage to splatter the vehicle
with Mississippi clay. Annabelle drew a deep breath of the
earthy air, ripe with the scents of damp ground fresh from a
cleansing rain shower.

Fear churned in her gut. What if Uncle's papers from the
family solicitor weren't enough to oust Andrew? She glanced at
the two men bouncing across from her in the carriage and
dismissed the thought. She had two capable men at her side, and
another who would fight to see her lands restored to her.

Wouldn't he?

Oh, Lord. Please, help my Matthew.

The plea rolled through her mind for the thousandth time as the carriage made the final turn into the drive to Rosswood. Unable to contain herself, Annabelle poked her head out of the carriage window and ignored Peggy's startled yelp.

Rosswood's crippled lands gave way to the stately house on the hill, the white columns and welcoming porches waiting to greet Annabelle with comforting arms. She'd been afraid that they would return home only to find a few leaning columns and blistered chimneys. Like so many homes they'd passed.

Peggy tugged on her arm, and Annabelle reluctantly pulled her head back inside. They passed her little cemetery with the crudely shaped markers and heaviness tempered her joy. Would this nation ever recover from the wounds they'd wrought with their own hands?

The carriage came to a stop, and it took every ounce of Annabelle's self-control to remain seated until the coachman came to open the door. She hurried out of the carriage, barely placing her hand atop the coachman's for the briefest instant.

Once free of her confines, Annabelle paused and looked up at her home, emotions swirling within her. She'd feared she would never see Rosswood's mighty beauty again.

"This place looks as though it's been left to gypsies." Uncle peered at the house with disdain.

A retort lodged in her throat. Before she could pluck it free and sling it at her uncle, Peggy grabbed her arm and pulled her aside while the men unloaded their trunks onto the brick walk just inside the garden wall.

Uncle might notice Rosswood's chipping paint, crumbling stairs, and overgrown yard, but Annabelle saw only home.

As soon as the carriage rolled away, Uncle took her hand

and placed it on his arm. "My poor little Anna. What a burden to have been left here all alone." His nostrils flared. "Alone with that cur, anyway." He acted as though he would spit, but then remembered himself and sniffed instead. "Worthless fool."

They climbed the front steps, Peggy and an ever-pensive George on their heels. Leaves clung to the corners of the front door and debris scattered across the porch. The house appeared abandoned.

Perhaps Andrew had moved on once Uncle had threatened him with the legal papers. With him gone, there would be no reason for them to quarrel, and her time of peace could begin all the sooner.

Those thoughts were extinguished, however, when the front door swung open with a creak of ungreased hinges. In one quick movement, Uncle thrust Annabelle behind him, causing her to stumble. She had to snatch her skirt out from under her feet to keep from falling.

"Hold it!" someone shouted.

Gaining her balance, Annabelle poked her head out from behind Uncle's shoulder. A tall man with a hawkish nose, thinning hair, and hard eyes glared down at them over the top of a partially rusted rifle. "Not another step, Ross."

Her heart trembled. *Andrew.*

As though thinking his name drew his attention, Andrew's gaze narrowed in on her and he lowered the gun, flinging his arms wide. "My bride has finally returned to me!"

Disgust rolled through her at his predatory gaze.

A flash of black broadcloth swept past them and George stepped up onto the porch. Startled, Andrew leveled his weapon on George.

"Easy there, sir." George raised his hands. "No need for that."

Andrew grunted. "Who are you?"

George made a small mocking bow that made Annabelle cringe.

"I'm George Daniels, Master of Westerly and brother to your niece's betrothed."

Andrew sneered. "*I* am her betrothed. It was agreed upon months ago."

Bolstering her courage, Annabelle stepped forward. "I agreed to no such thing!"

Andrew's features tightened, but he flipped a nonchalant hand. "No matter." His gaze roamed over her. "Though I must say I'll regret not getting to enjoy you as wife, you're no longer needed."

Michael stiffened. "What are you talking about?"

Andrew grinned. "Belle Andrews Plantation belongs to me now, by way of Union law."

Annabelle sputtered. "Belle Andrews?"

He winked at her. "It was a surprise, you see, renaming it after me and you. Was supposed to be a wedding gift." He let the muzzle drift toward the ground again.

Michael snatched papers from his coat pocket. "I don't care what you plan on calling it, this land belongs to me. I have the papers from my brother's lawyer. It's all here in the will!" With each word Uncle pounded the folded papers into his palm.

Andrew just shrugged. "That means nothing now. This here place is crawling with Blues. They wanted to take it, you see, but when Pa told them that we were the remaining family, and not some squatters—they got that fool notion from some loose lips in town—they said it belonged to us."

Guilty for having forgotten him, Annabelle tried to smooth ruffled feathers. "Does Grandfather fare well?"

Andrew spat on Annabelle's porch. "Don't pretend you care, girl. Was you that brought the death of him."

She moved to take a step toward him, but Peggy clamped down on her arm.

Andrew swung the gun back up at them. "So now that that's all settled up, how about you people get off my land."

Michael reddened. "Why you—"

Before he could finish his sentence, George's fist caught Andrew right across the jaw. He crumpled to the ground, the gun tumbling to his feet.

No one moved.

George rubbed his knuckles. "I was getting tired of his mouth."

Michael smirked. "Nice swing, Daniels." He turned to the women. "Hurry now. Find something to bind him."

Annabelle scrambled into the house and to the dining room, only to find it empty. She stopped, her hand fluttering to her heart. Where was Father's table?

Peggy pushed past her. "I had some rope in the kitchen."

Annabelle swallowed the lump in her throat and scurried after her, passing down the empty hall and out onto the rear steps. What had happened to the last of their furniture?

Peggy flung open the door to the kitchen, and a foul smell smacked Annabelle in the face. She lifted her fingers to shield her nose from the intrusion, but bits of it seeped around her defense. "Ugh! What *is* that?"

Peggy grumbled something, then hurried back out with a

length of coarse rope. "Ain't nothing left in there but two of my pots and a rotting rabbit carcass!"

Annabelle cringed and followed Peggy back through the house, finding the men right where they'd left them. She clutched at the fabric at her waist. Oh, heavens. Rosswood stood, but it was as bare as a poorhouse cupboard.

Uncle bound Andrew's feet and wrists. Then with George's help, they propped him against the side of the house. They stood there for a few moments staring at him.

Annabelle rubbed her temples. "Now what do we do?"

The two men looked at each other. George opened his mouth, but before he could say anything, Michael puffed out his chest and held up a hand.

Annabelle put her hands on her hips, silencing the argument before it began. "Now is not the time for posturing like peacocks!"

George's mouth unhinged, and Uncle gaped at her.

"My father's will states that Rosswood belongs to me." She pointed a finger at them. "Now, what are you two going to do about this…" She gestured to Andrew. "This *unwelcome guest.*"

Her uncle began to protest, but she silenced him with a wag of her finger. "Rosswood will be under your name, but *only* until Matthew and I wed. At that point the property reverts to us. That was my father's wish, and *that* is what is going to happen."

George scratched at his chin and gave a nod. "That's all I've come here to do."

Michael sniffed and straightened his cravat. "We can settle the details of my niece's betrothal later. For now, we need to contact the Yanks and show them this paperwork."

"What for?" George grunted. "Just toss this lout off at the

end of the road and don't let him come back."

Though Annabelle wanted to agree with him, she knew that would only be a temporary solution. She shook her head. "No, Uncle is correct. He and I should go to Lorman and speak to someone. You stay here with Andrew and make sure Rosswood is safe."

George glanced at Andrew and dipped his chin. "Certainly, Miss Ross. I'm at your disposal."

"It is settled then." Michael smiled down warmly at her. "Everything will be fine, dear. You'll see. Don't fret your little head over it."

Too tired to be annoyed at his patronizing words, she offered him a tight smile. "I'll be peace once this is settled."

Uncle flipped out his pocket watch and checked the time. "It's much too late in the day to make the trip without the coachman."

She hadn't thought of that. If there wasn't any furniture in the house, then likely there wouldn't be a wagon. And she'd lost poor old Homer months ago.

"So we stay the night here and take on the Union first thing in the morning," George said.

The others agreed, and after a few moments they had Andrew locked in the dining room. Exhausted, Annabelle ran her hand along the smooth banister and ascended the steps to the upper floor to her room.

Peggy lumbered up behind her, Father's carpetbag in tow. "Lawd, but it's good to be back home."

Annabelle smiled and stepped into her room. Her bed! Even though it had been stripped of its feathered mattress, the frame remained.

Peggy huffed. "Someone done run off with the bedding!"

Annabelle lifted her shoulders, gliding her fingers over the deep mahogany wood. "At least Rosswood still stands. And look, I still have my bed."

Peggy patted her shoulder. "That's right." She dropped the bag on the bare floor. "I'm goin' to go look and see what's left of my room."

"If you find anything, bring it back up here and put it in the Rose Room."

Peggy paused in the doorway. "Why?"

Annabelle tugged pins from her hair. "The Rose Room belongs to you now. Anyone who says differently can deal with me."

Peggy's face broke into a wide smile, and she hurried off without another word.

Annabelle let her hair tumble down her back and then flung open her window, gazing at the brown fields. "Soon." she promised. "Soon you'll be green again, and new life will bloom at Rosswood."

Annabelle touched her fingers to her lips to feel the smile that refused to give up hope. So many uncertainties remained, but for now, it was enough simply to be home.

Twenty-Five

"I am safe here at any rate, under the protection of
those professing my own religion. I have sought a
sanctuary, and have found it. While here there is neither
fear of betrayal, nor risk of discovery."
John H. Surratt

Sweat beaded on George's brow and slid toward his eyes.
He wiped it away and looked up at the sun. A sweltering
day in late May. Summer came to Mississippi as it always did, air
already thick with moisture, yet it still wanted to draw water out
of a man. He grumbled to himself about having been told to
fetch the Feds since Michael's presence was needed at
Rosswood. How offensive would his odor be by the time he
reached Lorman?

Alone on this road with nothing but the chattering of squir-
rels and the squawk of blue jays to interrupt the quiet, George
was left alone with his thoughts. Something he didn't want.

Gravel crunched under his feet as he trudged along, pistol at
his side. Perhaps it was better he hadn't been the one to stay at
the plantation. From the way Annabelle kept looking at him, he
feared she'd find a way to corner him and make him listen to

words he didn't want to hear. That would be even worse than the torture of his own thoughts. He kicked a rock and sent it skittering across the road.

He'd made a muddle of his courtship with Lilly and, after the way he'd treated her, she'd never forgive him. George groaned. The ache that burned within him served to remind him that he deserved no better than the misery ahead of him.

Forgive me, Lord.

He'd ask forgiveness from the Almighty, even if he could never ask it from Lilly. How had it come to this? How had he found himself in such a crush of pain over the shades of skin?

George thought back to the war he'd fought and the issues of slavery, making himself truly examine it for the first time. He'd fought not necessarily to uphold the institution, but rather for the idea that the government shouldn't have such absolute power. States had joined the Union on their own vote, and the way George saw it, they should have been able to leave the Union under that same free will.

A government that mandated everything was a government the people could no longer control, and that was something dangerous. He plucked a leaf from an oak as he passed and rubbed it between his fingers.

Lord, we were fools.

Slavery had been around since the times in the Bible, God's own people having been captured and enslaved. To the victor of many a conquest, the defeated people were always enslaved. Guilt nagged at him. But this was different. They hadn't conquered a people. They'd purchased people stolen from their homes by enemy tribes or snatched from unsuspecting villages. Then they had kept them like animals, denying them basic rights. And why? Because it was a repercussion of war? No. Simply because they could.

They'd lied to themselves and said the Negro people were not really people. Said the colored man couldn't think and didn't feel. Lies they told themselves to make an atrocity feel all right. Westerly had cared for their slaves but only as one would a prized steed.

Why had he not seen? Worse, why had he never cared?

Lost in his thoughts, George didn't hear the horse approach until the crunch of hooves gained his side. He looked up to find a young Yankee soldier staring down at him.

Startled, George jerked to a halt, his fingers brushing the top of his pistol. The younger man regarded him from atop a gray horse, his mop of dark hair barely contained beneath his cap. He seemed entirely unconcerned that George could draw on him and fire before he ever got that rifle unsheathed from the saddle. That alone kept George from aiming at him. A man that relaxed couldn't be much of a threat. But George would keep at the ready, all the same. Yanks could never be trusted.

The fellow touched the brim of his kepi. "Afternoon, Mister. You heading to town?"

George glanced in both directions but saw no one else. That didn't mean Yankees wouldn't be hiding nearby. He shifted his weight and judged the distance between himself and the horse's bridle. Could he snatch it before the man could shoot him?

George stroked his chin. "Sure am."

"Where are you coming from?"

George rested his hand heavily on the stock of the pistol, a move the Yank didn't miss. "What's that to you?"

The fellow shrugged. "Nothing. Just not much out in these

parts."

George tipped his chin and turned to start forward. His senses screamed at him not to turn his back on a Blue Belly, but he somehow got the feeling that simply walking away would be the best course of action. He didn't owe anything to this man, and they were no longer at war.

The man made a clicking noise, and the horse plodded along beside him again. The fellow swiped sweat from his face. "It's hot down in these parts."

George grunted.

"You from around here?"

"Nope."

The Yankee fell silent again, content to ride alongside George and prod him to frustration with his nonchalance.

After about half an hour, George could stand it no longer. He stopped. "Who are you and why are you following me?"

The man lifted his shoulders. "I'm not following you. Just going the same place."

George ground his teeth. "Lot faster on horse than on foot."

"Yep. But horses aren't much by way of conversationalists."

George gaped at him, the easy humor in the fellow's face unraveling his ire. He chortled. "Looks like that gray and I have that in common."

"Nah." The man patted the horse's neck. "All I get out of him is a few snorts."

George snorted in mock irony to the statement and started walking again.

After about another half mile, the curious fellow said, "I'm Joshua."

"George." He rubbed the back of his neck. "How far is this town? Too much farther and I'm going to have to relieve you of that beast."

Joshua chuckled and pressed a leg into the horse, causing it to prance and then cross its legs in a sideways manner until came to the other side of the road. "Not far. Another mile, I think."

"What are you doing out here? Shouldn't you be with a unit?"

"I'm on personal time."

Something about him felt off. "Personal time? In war?"

"War's over."

George sucked his teeth. "You're occupation force, aren't you?"

"In a manner of speaking. We're just maintaining a presence. For peace reasons, you know."

"So, Mr. Joshua…?"

He straightened his spine. "Lieutenant."

"*Lieutenant…*"

He sighed. "Lieutenant Joshua Grierson."

George stumbled to a halt. "*Grierson?*"

The man nodded.

George's fists clenched. "Any relation to cavalry General Benjamin Grierson?"

"My uncle."

George gripped the pistol again. "The raider."

Grierson swung his horse around, cutting George off and coming to a standstill in the road. "The music teacher. Then Army man. A man who gave supplies to poor Southerners whom the rich seemed to have forgotten all about."

George's mouth fell open. "Supplies stolen from our army!"

"Better the civilians eat than the enemy."

George spat. "Grierson and his raiding parties destroyed wagons and machinery, leaving many of us to scrape up game from the woods to survive."

The man regarded him evenly but said nothing.

"You talk about handing out supplies. But what about stripping Southern civilians of their goods? I heard what he did on his way through Mississippi. The people of Bankston were defenseless, and Grierson let his men pillage them."

"They must have needed supplies."

George growled and lurched toward the horse, startling the creature and causing it to rear. Grierson made a grand effort of maintaining his saddle, but the more George screamed, the more the animal thrashed.

An instant later, the Yankee was on the ground. George lunged for him. He crashed into the enemy's chest, pinning the man down with his knees. "It was Grierson who sent me to Elmira!"

The man, not more than a youth really, stared up at him with big eyes. "But not I."

George snarled and lifted his fist to strike.

"Am I to pay for another's deeds because I share his name?"

The words, spoken so calmly they stilled George's hand, seeped into him.

"War is ugly, and both sides did things that civilized gentlemen would never do. Yet, in desperation to win, we do what we must."

George sat back, keeping his weight on the man who didn't

struggle beneath him. "I could take my revenge out on you, give your uncle a taste of my pain."

"You could." Grierson nodded. "You could add to his losses by attacking his favored nephew, but somehow I doubt that would cure what ails you."

He stood and eyed the boy warily. Grierson drew a deep breath and took his time coming back to his feet, then dusted his jacket and straightened his lapels. George watched him, waiting for an attack that didn't come.

"Much obliged to you for not knocking on my nose, Mr...."

"George Daniels."

"Mr. Daniels. But if it's all the same to you, I think I'll go on to town without the benefit of company."

George glared at him as he took a step back, tipped his hat, and then grabbed the reins of the horse that still stood nearby. He swung up into the saddle. "Do you happen to know a Miss Smith? She has a home somewhere around here."

George cocked his head. "No. Why do you ask?"

Grierson palmed the reins. "Just trying to make good on a promise, that's all." He tucked his chin. "Good day to you." He squeezed his legs and the horse broke into a canter, leaving George in a swirl of dust.

Never in his days had George encountered such an odd fellow. He restarted his trudge toward Lorman, rubbing at the fist he'd nearly unleashed on a friendly young man who'd done nothing more than try to engage him in conversation.

What has become of me?

George finally made his way into town, spotting what would be the best starting place for his mission. He thudded up the steps to the building marked "Black's General Store" and stepped inside.

One look at the portly man behind the counter and he broke into a grin. So this was the fellow who'd bested his brother? This rotund fellow with thinning hair and an apron? When Matthew had recounted the tale, he'd not said much about the shopkeeper who'd felled him. George would have never guessed it to be this fellow. Perhaps he was mistaken.

George stepped up to the counter. "Mr. Black?"

The fellow looked up from a stack of papers he'd been squinting over. "I am."

George chuckled. "Imagine that."

"What?"

George shook his head. "Never mind. I don't suppose you'd know who might handle a legal dispute over land these days, would you?"

The shopkeeper straightened his papers and placed them on the counter. "Far as I know, those things are handled by courts."

George leaned an arm on the polished counter. "Seems to me these Yanks are judge and jury now."

The man untied his apron, placed it on the counter, and regarded George thoughtfully. Then he gestured toward the rear of the building. "I got a crate in the back I'm having trouble with. Think you can help me with it?"

The man moved around the counter and started toward the back without waiting for George's answer. Reminding himself not to be taken in by this fellow's harmless appearance, George followed him.

They stepped into a sparse stockroom and the shopkeeper pointed to a crate on the floor. "Need two to get this one up."

George eyed the man as he bent over to lift one end, then he bent to put his fingers under the other end. They hefted the box, which felt filled with bricks, and lugged it into the front room where they deposited it behind the counter.

"Thanks, friend," Black said, rubbing the muscles in his lower back as he straightened.

George wiped his hands on his trousers. "Sure."

The shopkeeper tied his apron back on. "Don't recognize you."

No resemblance to his brother? George smiled, unable to help his amusement at Matthew's expense. "Never been here, but I think you'd recognize my brother. Big fellow you knocked in the head."

The portly man's eyes widened, and he took a step back. "Oh!" He scrubbed a hand down his face. "Look fellow, I don't want trouble."

George chuckled. "I still can't believe you dropped Matthew. Wait until he hears that I came in here, only to find *you* were the one to best him."

The man looked sheepish and put his hands in his pockets. "I was only trying to help Miss Ross."

George sobered. "I know. And my family is grateful. In fact, that's why I'm here. There is some trouble over the ownership of her lands."

His eyebrows rose. "You know about that?"

"My brother is her intended."

Mr. Black gawked. "He said he didn't know her!"

"Not at the time."

"But—"

George held up a hand. "It's a long story. Suffice it to say that Miss Ross and her uncle returned home only to discover that the Yankees gave her property to someone else."

"She found him." Mr. Black's features slackened with relief. "When we didn't hear from her again, I thought..." he shook his head. "Everyone here thought she wasn't coming back. I heard the second wife's family laid claim and since the Feds aren't redistributing land, they let it stand."

"Ross has legal papers that say otherwise, and we are capable of tossing the usurper out, but..."

"You don't want the Feds coming down on you," Mr. Black supplied.

"Indeed. We'd rather do this peaceful, if that's possible."

Mr. Black glanced around his sparse store, a look of resignation on his face. "It's what we're all doing these days." He rubbed the back of his thick neck. "Best one to talk to will be Lieutenant Grierson. He's in charge of keeping things civil around here. Though it's almost traitorous to say so, he's a decent fellow that seems to be trying to do right by folks."

George's jaw dropped. "Grierson?"

Black nodded.

Of all the luck. George groaned and turned toward the door.

"He's over at the old barber's shop," Mr. Black said, "across from the dressmaker's. It's to your left and over two streets. You should be able to find him there if he's not out wandering around again."

George reached for the door and looked back over his shoulder. "Much obliged."

He stepped back out into the afternoon sun. Good thing he hadn't pounded that fellow's face. He started in the direction the shopkeeper had given him. This would be an even more difficult discussion than he'd anticipated. Not only did he have to try to beg Yankees for Annabelle's land back, he'd have to beg it from a man who had every reason to make him pay for his temper.

Why do I get the feeling You are trying to teach me something?

George set his jaw, shoved his hands into his pockets, and hoped his stomach was big enough for all the humble pie he was about to have to swallow.

Twenty-Six

"The trial drags on its weary way, and they are trying to take evidence condemning me as well as the rest—for I feel convinced they are all doomed."

John H. Surratt

*A*nnabelle ran the comb through her hair, letting the warm air from the window send teasing strands around her face. The bare floors felt odd beneath her toes, but at least they were the floors she'd known all her life. Perhaps once they were able to get new crops planted and restart the brickmaking, she could afford to replace what had been stolen. After the wedding, of course.

If there is one.

Annabelle promptly ordered the disturbing thought away. Uncle would come around. Once he got to know Matthew, he'd see that his first meeting with Matthew didn't portray her betrothed accurately. She twisted the ring on her finger. He would be here soon. She could wait. The determined thought did little to ease the pang of impatience that often sank its fangs into her.

Annabelle eyed the crinoline cage that Peggy had dug up

from Lord only knew where and set it on a stand in her room. Struck by the absurdity of the fashion for the first time, Annabelle giggled. If she had tried to ride a horse with that bird cage strapped around her waist—she shook her head.

Petticoats had served her well thus far and she didn't need that wide contraption now.

There was a tap at the door and then Peggy bustled in, her arms full of garments. "Got everything clean for you, Miss Belle. I'm right pleased your grandma bought you all these things, else I woulda had me a time trying to make a lady out of you today."

Annabelle paused with the comb partway down her hair. "What do you mean 'make a lady out of me today'?"

Peggy rolled her eyes. "Don't you go gettin' your hackles up. Mr. Ross wants everyone looking proper before the officers come."

"What officers?"

Peggy spread the dresses out on the bed. "Which one you want?"

Annabelle grimaced. "Whichever is coolest."

Peggy dug around for a sheer muslin and an underskirt. "Them Federal officers is coming down today to listen to your cause."

Annabelle perked up. The men had been tight-lipped about the entire ordeal since George had come back from Lorman on a borrowed horse. Andrew, after waking to find himself bound, had been bellowing for nearly two days. She'd be glad to see this thing settled and him off her land for good.

"Mr. Ross said they's coming today to look at all the papers your uncle got and hear what you have to say."

Best look the part then. Annabelle stepped into the crinoline cage and tied the stays around her waist. "They'll side with us. Won't they, Peggy?"

Peggy wrapped Annabelle's corset around her waist and tugged on the ties. "Well, now, I can't speak for what men is thinkin', but I'd say they have no cause to give the land to Andrew when your uncle has your daddy's will and the loyalty papers from Washington."

Annabelle smiled. "I'll be glad to see him go. I just hope he doesn't put up too much of a fuss."

Peggy grunted. "He anything like your grandfather, he'll throw a hissy sure enough."

Annabelle slid the underskirt over her head and smoothed it over the cage. "I still feel guilty we left him here alone, Peggy. I should have said better goodbyes. I knew he wasn't in good health."

Peggy patted her arm. "Don't go doing that. That man gave you little choice. I'm sorry he left this life still being as mean as he was, but that ain't no reflection on you. You did better by him than he deserved."

He'd been a scoundrel, yes, but he'd also been here when she might have been left to the unrestrained actions of too many soldiers.

After Peggy finished buttoning the clasps down the back of her bodice, Annabelle turned to her. "Thank you."

"'course, child. It's what I'm here for."

"Peggy?"

Peggy tucked a loose end of her head wrap back into place and turned back to her. "Yes?"

"Now that the war is over and I'm safely home, what will you do?"

She cocked her head. "What?"

"Will you stay here?"

Peggy put her hands on her hips. "Where else am I going to go? You sendin' me away?"

Annabelle twisted her hair in her fingers. "Of course not. I only wanted to ask you. To be sure that I don't treat you like someone without a voice."

Peggy smiled. "Miss Belle, I'd like nothing more than to stay right here, cook fine meals for you and that big fellow, and play with little 'uns when they come around."

Annabelle swept Peggy into a hug. "I'd like nothing better myself." She released Peggy and wrinkled her nose. "Besides, I'm a terrible cook."

"Then it's about time you learn." Peggy swatted at her playfully. "Now let me see that hair. You're making a mess out of it."

Annabelle surrendered her head to the capable fingers that had braided and pinned her hair all her life. When Peggy finished, they descended the steps together. Annabelle glanced at Peggy's lavender dress, trimmed with strips of lace, and smiled. The dress was at odds with that ragged scarf Peggy still insisted on wrapping around her head, but Annabelle had given up trying to dissuade her from it.

Annabelle gave a nod to George, who stood watch over the door to the dining room where they kept Andrew, and continued out onto the front porch. Michael sat in a chair he'd mended with scraps of wood from the stable. He glanced up from the paper George had brought back from town.

"Ah, there you are, dear. Did you sleep well?"

"Yes, Uncle, thank you." She had, actually. Sleeping on

pallets on the floor had become somewhat familiar to her these last months.

He snapped the paper closed. "As soon as we get this settled, I'll go to Natchez and bring some furniture back here. At least the town home stayed intact, though that's a downright miracle."

Annabelle nodded her agreement. "Thank you. A few of the more necessary things would be very nice to tide us over. The rest Matthew and I can accumulate as we get Rosswood running again."

Michael frowned and waved Peggy away.

She gave a small grunt. "If you need me, Miss Belle, I'll be tryin' to put my kitchen back in order."

Annabelle offered her a warm smile as she took her time walking away, not in any hurry to jump at Uncle's commands. If he noticed Peggy's bit of defiance, he didn't comment.

He offered his arm. "A walk, perhaps? I have things I wish to discuss with you."

Trying to quell the worry gathering in her stomach, Annabelle slipped her fingers onto his shirtsleeve, and he guided her off the porch.

They slowly walked through Momma's rose garden, and Annabelle noted that they would need to repair the brick walk in several places. Uncle opened the iron gate at the end of the garden and led her to the shade of the towering oak just beyond the garden wall.

She reached up and patted her uncovered hair. "I hope you don't mind, Uncle. I didn't fetch my bonnet."

He looked at her as if truly noticing her for the first time. "Oh. No matter. We'll stay here in the shade so you won't freckle." He glanced back toward the house. "We won't be long."

Annabelle followed his gaze and wondered if he'd brought her here specifically to be out of earshot. "You wished to speak to me?"

He regarded her evenly, and she was suddenly washed in a memory of her father. He'd had much the same mannerism whenever he readied himself to deliver news she didn't want to hear. "I've decided you'll go to the town home in Natchez."

Her throat caught and it took her two tries to force out her words. "What? Why?"

His features softened. "Now, Anna, I know you love this place." He swept a hand back toward the house. "But look at it. It's in disrepair and nearly empty."

"Well, yes, but—"

"It's no place for a lady. We'll go to Natchez to The Roses and stay there until something can be done with Rosswood."

Annabelle fiddled with the folds of her skirt. "What will happen if we leave again? Andrew or someone else will try to take it."

"I've made inquiries into hiring an overseer. Give it some time, Anna. I'll have men out here to get the plantation going again."

He smiled. He meant well. Father's town home was cozy, comfortable, and if Uncle was correct, at least had mattresses on the beds. Resigned, she gave a nod. "Though I wish to return to Rosswood as soon as Matthew arrives. He and I can oversee everything after the wedding."

Uncle stiffened. "I've made it clear that I don't approve of that man. He's a drunkard and an unfit gentleman. I've heard tales of him before the war and…" He cleared his throat. "Besides that, no respectable gentleman would have dragged you across the country in the middle of a war." He puffed his cheeks out in frustration. "I simply cannot allow it."

Annabelle pressed her fingers into her palms. "I know you mean well, but I love Matthew. Please don't judge him too harshly on one mistake. He only indulged too much because he was trying to force away the dreams."

Uncle's eye twitched. "What dreams?"

"Horrible memories of battle. They are most intense."

Michael appeared thoughtful. "He's told you this?"

Feeling hope sprout, Annabelle nodded. "Yes. And he has apologized for making a fool of himself and sworn it'll never happen again."

Uncle stroked his chin. "Perhaps it's something I'll consider." She offered him a bright smile, and he frowned. "No promises. We'll revisit the issue later."

Sensing he'd give nothing more at the moment, her smile softened into one of tentative hope. She slipped her arm back into his. "Thank you. I'm grateful you'll consider my feelings."

He merely grunted and guided her back to the house.

Twenty-Seven

"Other presidents have died, though none have been
assassinated before President Lincoln—yet none were
ever so mourned."
Frederick Douglass

hen I get my hands on you," Andrew bellowed, his words
bouncing down the hall and skipping over Annabelle as
she followed Peggy with a tray from the kitchen. "I'm going to
skin you from your—"

Peggy screeched, nearly dropping her basket of biscuits in
her attempt to conceal Andrew's words from Annabelle's ears.
She heard them anyway and blushed. Peggy's cry, however, must
have alerted the men, because one of them growled out a series
of words she couldn't decipher, and Andrew fell silent.

"Lawd, I hope them men hurry up and put an end to this
mess! What's taking them so long?"

It had been days since George had gone to Lorman and
asked for help. The Union soldiers had been promised to arrive
the day before yesterday but had yet to appear. If she didn't
know any better, she'd think they were delaying on purpose.

She straightened her spine and sauntered into the dining

room with more cheer in her step than she had in her heart. "Look what I've brought, boys. Peggy's fried us up some sweet potatoes. Oh, my, but she does make a good hash."

George smiled. "I do fancy fried potatoes."

"Yes, suh, and I got biscuits, too," Peggy said, sweeping into the room without a speck of flour on her fine dress. How she'd managed it when Annabelle had needed to clean her own skirt even though she'd worn an apron, Annabelle couldn't fathom. It seemed she still had a lot to learn about cooking, and not all of her lessons had to do with making the most of scant ingredients.

Michael perked up from where he'd been resting against the wall near the hearth. "Splendid. Peggy, you're gifted in the kitchen."

"Thank you, Mr. Ross." Peggy dipped her chin, looking pleased with the attention.

George finished tying a knot around Andrew's ankles and turned to face them. "How about we take it out to the balcony?"

"What about me?" Andrew grumbled.

Uncle smirked. "As soon as you learn to behave like a gentleman, you might be allowed to dine with the civil folks. Until then,"—he plucked two of Peggy's biscuits from the pile in the basket—"you'll just have to stay here and think about how dimwitted it was to try to attack us when we gave you a measure of freedom." He dropped the biscuits unceremoniously into Andrew's lap. "Seems like you've chosen the ropes for the duration of your stay."

Annabelle frowned down at Andrew. He had the decency to glance away from her, mumbling something that might have been an apology. Dangerous as he might be, Annabelle still grew uncomfortable keeping him restrained for so long. What would they do if the Federals tarried much longer?

"Come on, child. Let's be gettin' outside," Peggy said when the others had gone and she still lingered, staring at the man who would have tried to make himself her husband.

She followed Peggy up the stairs and onto the upper hall. The doors at both ends had been opened to allow the breeze to pass through, cooling the space considerably. Out on the balcony, George had fashioned a bench for her and Peggy out of two stumps and a length of rough-hewn pine.

The men leaned against the rail as Peggy passed out plates heaped with fried potatoes and biscuits and Annabelle offered mismatched mugs of tepid water from the cistern. Then the women took their seat and the four began to eat in companionable silence.

Annabelle looked out over the front lands of Rosswood and wondered why she'd never taken a meal up here before. It was rather pleasant. She'd have to see about getting a small table and set of chairs. Perhaps it would be a good place for Matthew and her to dine once he returned.

Michael straightened. "What's that?"

Annabelle looked at where he pointed, down the lane and almost to the road. She squinted. "I don't see anything."

George leaned over the rail. "Someone's coming."

Uncle nodded. "We best head down."

Annabelle placed her barely touched plate on the bench. George shoveled in two more mouthfuls before handing his plate over to Peggy with a wink.

When they had gone down the stairs, Peggy looked at Annabelle and cocked her head. "What was that about?"

Annabelle shrugged. "I guess he's just glad the Feds have

finally arrived so we can get this mess resolved."

"Ha. Still don't explain him winkin' at me like we're some kind of friends."

"You're not?"

Peggy made a face. "He don't plan on being nothing with colored folks other than they master."

"Peggy!"

"What? You know it's true."

Lilly's face sprung to mind. If she didn't miss her guess, George loved Lilly. "I know you told me not to," Annabelle said, "but I have to talk to him about Lilly."

Peggy regarded her for a moment. "Man's been in a bad way since we left Washington. It's slung all over him like mud on the mule behind the wagon." She clicked her tongue. "Fool can't be both lovesick and prejudice over the same girl at the same time."

Annabelle smiled. "No, I don't suppose he can."

If George was the man she hoped he was, he'd choose love over prejudice. Happiness over the opinion of others.

She turned her attention back to the group of men coming down the drive. Michael and George waited for them at the garden wall. Something about the one in the front looked familiar.

Annabelle gasped.

"What?" Peggy chirped, her gaze swinging below.

"I think I know that man." Annabelle lifted her skirts and hurried down the stairs as quickly as dignity would allow, leaving Peggy sputtering behind her.

Twenty-Eight

"They have killed him, the Forgiver. The Avenger takes
his place."
Herman Melville

*A*nnabelle paused at the front door with her hand
resting on the frame. Her stomach felt like a jar
containing too many fireflies. It *was* him. Would he be angry at
her when he found out she'd lied to him? What would that
mean for Rosswood?

Peggy sidled up to her. "You all right? You look paler than
milk."

"I know him."

Peggy slipped past Annabelle and took a step onto the
porch. "Who?"

"That man. He's the Union Private I told you about."

"Which one?"

At the drive, George and Michael spoke to four men in blue
uniforms, one of whom was none other than Private Grierson.
As though feeling her gaze upon him, his eyes turned toward the
house. Surprise lit his face.

Annabelle sucked in a breath. "That one."

"That's the boy who helped you back to town and sent the doctor?"

Private Grierson stepped around Michael, who was still speaking to him, and started through the garden gate.

"Yes. That's the one," Annabelle said low. She pulled a smile onto her lips and stood at the end of the porch.

Private Grierson stopped at the bottom of the stairs and removed his cap. "Miss Smith! It seems I've found you at last."

Annabelle glanced over his head at Michael, whose red face had creased with an array of lines. She dropped her gaze back to the young Federal. "Um, yes, about that, Private Grierson...."

He puffed out his chest a bit. "It's lieutenant now."

"Oh." She offered a faltering smile. "I've something to tell you, Lieutenant."

"Remember, I asked you to call me Joshua."

Annabelle puffed out her cheeks. "I need to tell you—"

"What's the meaning of this?" Michael stalked up to them, his eyes flashing between Joshua and Annabelle. "Do you know these Yanks?"

Joshua stiffened, and Annabelle had to suppress a groan. "Yes, Uncle," Annabelle said in her sweetest tone. "I was once thrown from my horse on the way to town, and this gentleman was kind enough to take me into Lorman and fetch a doctor."

Michael eyed Joshua suspiciously.

"Why, if it weren't for his aid, who knows what troubles I might have found out there alone." She didn't even have to fabricate the shiver that shook her shoulders. God had been gracious in keeping her from many of the dangers she could have encountered.

"Why were you out without escort in the first place?"

She shifted in her stance.

"You know right well what kind of man was runnin' this here house," Peggy said quietly.

The statement startled Michael, and he cleared his throat. "Very well." He looked back at Joshua, who still unashamedly stared at Annabelle. "What's this about a Miss Smith?"

Humor danced in Joshua's eyes. "What? Oh. I'm sorry."

Annabelle's cheeks heated when he had the audacity to wink.

"Must have gotten the name confused. My apologies, Miss…?"

"Ross," Michael supplied.

Joshua chuckled. "Of course. How foolish of me." He made a small bow. "It's a pleasure to make your acquaintance again, Miss Ross. I'm glad you returned home safely after your incident."

Throat tight, Annabelle could only nod. She flicked her gaze to the other men making their way through the garden. Remembering herself, Annabelle straightened and clasped her hands in front of her as her mother had taught. "Good day, gentlemen, and thank you for coming. I would ask you inside, but as Rosswood no longer contains much by way of furnishings, perhaps it would be best to conduct our business here in the coolness of the porch?"

Joshua gave a nod and gestured for his men to take positions around on the wide front porch.

"Hey!"

Oh no. All eyes turned to the shout that came from the house.

"They've taken me prisoner!" Andrew bellowed. "Get me

out of here!"

Annabelle forced her features to remain serene. "That would be the man I told you about." She steadied her gaze on Joshua, and understanding sparked in his eyes. "He refused to leave my property peacefully. Since we couldn't trust him to remain civil, we thought it best to restrain him until the authorities arrived."

"I understand." He motioned to his men. "Bring him out."

After muffled words, some scraping sounds and a few grunts, Andrew was escorted out of the house by two stoic-looking men in blue and deposited by the dining room window.

"Now, this squatter refuses—" Michael began.

Joshua held up a hand to silence him. "One moment, please, Mr. Ross. I know who this man is. I'm the one who granted his request to this land."

A sinking feeling settled in Annabelle's stomach. Michael sputtered. George's face remained unreadable.

"However, that was before I realized that these lands belonged to this lady." He nodded at Annabelle.

"Well, now, they technically belong to me," Michael said. "Women don't own property." He looped his thumbs into the bracers under his jacket.

Joshua gave him a dismissive look and turned his attention back to Andrew. "You stated you had a claim to this land on the grounds that the rest of the remaining family had died." He gestured to Annabelle. "But as you can see, that's not the case."

Andrew sneered. "Miss Ross and I entered into a betrothal, and then she disappeared. I thought she was dead."

Shock registered on Joshua's face as both Annabelle and Michael spoke at the same time.

"I did not!"

"My niece would never marry my sister-in-law's brother!"

Joshua held up both hands. "One at a time."

They fell silent. Michael's eye twitched and Annabelle's fingers plucked her skirt.

Joshua scratched his chin. "When I left you at the inn," he said to Annabelle, "you mentioned your grandfather tried to marry you off to a man you despised."

"Yes, that's right."

"That him?" Joshua thrust his chin at Andrew.

"Yes. They planned to force a wedding in order to steal Rosswood from me."

Andrew snorted. "Now look here—"

"Silence!" Joshua barked. "You'll speak when I give you permission."

Andrew fell silent, and Annabelle stilled. Was this the same lighthearted young man she'd met a few months ago? This one spoke with assured authority.

He addressed Michael. "You're her uncle?"

"Her father's younger brother."

"And you?" Joshua asked Andrew. "Are you tied to the family in any way other than by a betrothal the lady states she didn't agree to?"

"My sister was the lady of Rosswood."

Joshua's face scrunched.

"Perhaps I can explain?" Annabelle offered.

Rubbing at his temples, Joshua nodded. "By all means."

"My mother died when I was young. My father remarried. His second wife also died. After my father and Michael both left for war, my stepmother's father came to stay at Rosswood. My father then died in battle. His will stated that Rosswood would be left to me upon my marriage. Grandfather and Andrew then decided that in order to fulfill the necessities of the will, I would marry Andrew and thereby give him control of Rosswood. Unfortunately for him, I had no desire to be wed to a scoundrel intent on using me for my land."

Joshua rubbed the back of his neck and gave Annabelle an apologetic smile. "It's no wonder you ran away."

"You what?" Michael took a step toward her.

"Perhaps it's a tale better left for later?" She'd given Michael few details about her journey since leaving Rosswood, certain the story would only get him wound tighter than bed ropes.

Michael huffed but thankfully let the matter drop.

Annabelle turned her attention back to Joshua. "I'd hoped to find Uncle Michael," she said, inclining her head in his direction. "Father wanted to keep Rosswood in his brother's trust until my wedding. I had tried several times to contact him after my father's death, but…" She turned out her palms, leaving Joshua to put together the pieces.

He nodded. "And you have documents for all of this?"

Michael plucked the papers from his jacket and handed them to the officer. "My brother's will, along with a letter from our solicitor stating that no one else has any legal claims to the property."

Joshua read through each paper while the others waited in anticipation. Annabelle glanced over to George, who offered her an encouraging smile.

"Well, this *does* seem to be in order," Joshua said, though something in his tone left a tendril of unease snaking around in Annabelle's gut.

"You going to tell them the rest?" Andrew asked, the smugness returning to his face.

Joshua shot Annabelle a pained look. "My orders are to give preference to Union loyalists in areas of property disputes."

"Yep, and seeing as how I repented of my rebellious ways and left the Confederate Army—"

Annabelle scowled at him, but he didn't seem to care.

"And I signed Union allegiance papers—along with my marital ties to the family and the grant on this land *already* in my name—I say my claim holds."

Annabelle's stomach clenched so tightly she feared she might lose what little she'd eaten.

"Papers like these?" George said, offering something to Joshua.

He turned to George, something that Annabelle couldn't identify flickering across his face, and held out his hand without a word.

"Those are my Union Allegiance papers," George stated as he placed the papers in the lieutenant's hand. "And they are identical to the ones my brother will have once he returns from Washington where he is currently serving with the New York cavalry detail that brought down Booth."

Joshua narrowed his eyes, not seeming impressed with the information. If anything, he seemed confused. "That's all well and good, sir. But I don't see how your family's supposed allegiances pertain to the current topic."

George glanced at Annabelle. She took a step forward. "His brother, Matthew, is my true intended and will become Master of Rosswood once he arrives."

Joshua lowered his voice. "How many men were you already

attached to when you offered for me to come call on you?"

Annabelle's face heated. "None. Matthew and I didn't become engaged until just a short time ago. Forgive me, I never meant to be deceitful."

He studied her a moment, then handed the papers back to George and cleared his throat. "In light of all these claims, I'm afraid I'm going to have to send for my commanding officer."

Annabelle's heart plummeted and she gripped his arm. "Please! Don't take my home from me. It is all I've ever known."

His eyes softened for an instant before he swung his gaze on to Andrew. "Until a final decision is made, you'll remove yourself from the property."

"But—"

"And if you set foot back on these lands before I have an official decision in hand, then you'll be in violation of the terms and all considerations for your claim will be forfeited."

Andrew's nostril's flared, but he nodded.

Joshua turned to Michael. "I'm leaving you over this place." He held up a hand to stop Michael's reply. "Which is a *temporary* position until my superiors reach a decision."

Michael flipped open his pocket watch. "You can contact me at our town home in Natchez, The Roses, once the official papers have been processed."

Joshua shook his head. "That wouldn't be wise. If you wish to stake claim, you need to be present."

Michael sputtered some kind of retort, but Joshua ignored him. He gestured to his men. "Release this man."

A flutter of hope bloomed in Annabelle's heart. She wouldn't have to leave Rosswood again after all. She tightened her jaw. Unless they granted it to Andrew. Why wouldn't the lieutenant simply turn Rosswood over to her now? He obviously had the authority to do so, since he'd given the property to Andrew. Surely he could overturn his own decision in her favor.

Joshua wiped his hands on his trousers. "Miss Ross, might I speak with you a moment?"

At her nod he offered his arm, and they walked off the porch and out to the shade tree.

"I'm terribly sorry for all the confusion." She wrung her hands. "And for not telling you the truth."

Joshua smiled. "That's not entirely true. You did tell me about your grandfather trying to force you to marry." The smile faded, and his features clouded. "You also said something about being thought a spy. I've been quite concerned for you since you disappeared."

"Again, I must offer my apology. It's quite a long story, but suffice it to say that I ended up in Washington trying to stop the abduction of Lincoln, only to witness him being murdered instead."

His eyes widened. "You were at the assassination?"

She tucked a stray lock behind her ear. "Unfortunately. I also testified at the trial. That's why I've been gone so long. I wasn't permitted to leave Washington until I stood before the Military Commission."

He rocked back on his heels. "That's good."

She cocked her head. "It is?"

"The story gives you good proof of Union allegiance, right?"

She nodded, hoping that all she'd been through would at least help solve the problem that had forced her to leave

Rosswood in the first place.

They were quiet a moment, and Annabelle's heart ached for the disappointment she saw cross Joshua Grierson's face. "I must admit something to you."

She waited as he searched for the right words.

"I requested this assignment just so I could take you up on your offer to come calling."

Annabelle twisted the ring on her finger and lowered her lashes. "I'm sorry."

They listened to the whisper of the wind through the leaves overhead.

"Do you love him?" Joshua asked, his voice tender.

The question startled her, and she glanced back up to see his eyes brimming with sincerity.

"I do. Most deeply," she replied, though she hated to cause him any hurt.

He smiled ruefully. "Ah, well. That's good then. But if you were only marrying him for Union ties and to save your land—"

Annabelle's heart lurched at the irony of how close that statement had actually been to the truth. At least at the start.

He looked at her hopefully, and she gave a gentle smile and shake of her head. "No, I will marry for love and that alone."

Joshua ran a hand through his hair. "I'm truly glad you found happiness, Miss Ross. You're a fine lady, and I wish you many years of a good life."

Her throat tightened. "Thank you." She ached to beg him to forgo the formalities and declare her owner of Rosswood. But she would not cheapen his fondness of her by taking advantage of him.

He straightened, and the commanding presence she'd glimpsed on the porch returned. "If you've chosen your husband, as your father's will states, then this land is yours."

Her heart leapt. "But you said…"

He winked. "I merely bought you some time. I wanted to be sure that Mr. Ross wasn't trying to lay his own claim."

Words stuck in her throat.

"Of course, I was also hoping that would leave a door open for me in the meantime."

She gave him a wry smile.

He chuckled. "Ah, well, I had to try." He sobered, lowering his voice, though Annabelle doubted the people on the porch could hear them. "This will get one zealous man off your land and keep the other in check until your betrothed arrives. Once he does, I'd suggest a quick wedding."

Tears welled in her eyes, and she placed her hand on his arm.

He looked down at her fingers and grinned. "Unless, of course, you change your mind."

She swatted at him playfully, then grew serious, giving his arm a squeeze. "Thank you, Joshua. You can't know what this means to me."

He took her hand and placed a featherlight kiss across her knuckles. "Be sure to bring me your intended's Union paperwork along with the marriage certificate and will. Having those things on record will staunch any future problems you may have, especially once I return north."

"I will. Thank you."

He dipped his chin and then turned on his heel, calling his men to return to him. They mounted their horses, Andrew in tow, and Annabelle offered one final wave. Joshua tipped his hat. Then he spurred his horse, leading his men as they galloped away.

Twenty-Nine

"It is said the trial is over, and the evidence so strong
that none will escape. What a narrow escape I have had.
If taken in the States, my fate would have been settled
long before this."
John H. Surratt

Washington, D.C.
June 30, 1865

*M*atthew placed his palm against Mr. Fitch's and pumped
the man's hand.

"Are you sure we can't get you to stay? I'm sure I could find
a place for you here at the station."

Matthew shook his head. "I'm flattered, but I've had my fill
of Washington."

Two lawmen dressed in sharp suits parted around them,
scurrying off to whatever business kept the police building
buzzing with activity. The smell of coffee hung on the air. The
men had kept the strong brew flowing all through the night as
they debated about what the Military Commission would decide.

"Will you at least stay and see the verdict?" Fitch asked.

Matthew had a feeling Fitch knew as well as Matthew that

all the accused would be found guilty. "I'm afraid not. I have a lady waiting for me, whom I've been away from for far too long."

Fitch's eyes glimmered. "Ah, yes. The lovely Miss Ross."

Matthew winked. "Soon to be Mrs. Daniels, quick as I can get back south."

Fitch chuckled. "You best be on your way then." He sobered. "If you ever find your way back to Washington, though, do stop by."

Matthew patted his shoulder. "You have my word."

After shaking a few more hands and finally making his way back out into the sunlight, Matthew checked the watch he'd purchased with some of his Union pay and determined he had plenty of time to find a gift for Annabelle before he boarded the train.

He'd sent a letter to Rosswood a fortnight ago with his most heartfelt apology and a plea for her forgiveness. He'd written about the changes the Lord had brought about in his heart and how the nightmares came much less frequently now. He'd told her how deeply he missed her and could not wait to begin their new life together.

So far, he'd not received word back.

Trying not to let that worry him, Matthew stepped onto the now familiar busyness of the Washington streets and tried to think about what to get an unconventional woman for her wedding day. Each bauble that came to mind was soundly dismissed, knowing that while she would find them pretty, such things would mean little.

By the time he had wandered over Washington for an hour without coming up with an idea, Matthew turned back to gather his things from the National Hotel.

He'd been surprised the Union would pay for this room for the duration of the trial. He'd expected a demoted private to have been given much humbler accommodations.

Turned out he'd been right. When he'd asked his commanding officer if he needed to change rooms to something cheaper, the man had been baffled. The army hadn't paid for anything—Matthew was responsible for his own boarding.

Mrs. Smith had told the National to keep his room open for as long as he remained in Washington and had put the charges to her account.

He nodded at the man at the front desk before ascending the main staircase. For all her bluster, Mrs. Smith was one of the most generous people he'd ever encountered. He'd penned her a short letter last night, giving her his thanks and urging her to make haste to Rosswood. He planned to wed her granddaughter as soon as he arrived.

Matthew stuffed his few belongings into his Union haversack and slung the strap over his shoulder. He gave one final glance around the room before locking the door behind him. Down below, Matthew returned his key at the desk and then took a hired coach to the train station.

Once he stepped onto the platform, memories of the last time he was here flooded him. Memories of O'Malley's deranged eyes the night he'd tried to murder the Grants.

He'd not seen the man since that night in the alleyway and hoped never to again. Still, he knew O'Malley well enough to know that if he'd set his mind on Matthew, nothing would sway him from his course. Matthew had been on edge ever since, only going where the army required and never out at night.

How O'Malley had managed to escape being arrested and tried, Matthew couldn't fathom. He'd given account of O'Malley's involvement, as had Annabelle, yet somehow things pertaining to O'Malley's certificate of arrest kept slipping through someone's notice.

If Matthew didn't know better, he would think that someone worked to keep O'Malley from his due. Because, if Dr. Mudd hadn't escaped arrest for such a minor thing as giving medical aid to a man in need, then how had O'Malley not been sought after with more gusto?

The train whistle blew, and Matthew shrugged off the questions. All he wanted now was to get back to Mississippi. Let O'Malley live out his days in hiding. What did it matter to him?

Matthew handed over his ticket and stepped into the train car, selecting a seat near the back by the window. Not many others joined the car, and the smattering of travelers congregated more toward the front. He'd be able to travel in relative solitude.

He settled back in his seat and watched as Washington gave way to open lands. He thanked the Lord he'd been granted his freedom. What would become of those accused? Execution? Imprisonment?

Had it not been for Annabelle, they might very well have been successful in capturing Lincoln back in March. Then Matthew might have been sitting in the Old Capitol Prison with the others, waiting to see if the noose would find his neck.

His sweet Annabelle. How he longed to see her once more and become the man she deserved. It would take a lot of prayer, but Lord willing, he'd become the man worthy of such a precious woman.

Matthew closed his eyes and tried to figure out a wedding gift. New furnishings perhaps? Rosswood had been a bit bare the last time he'd been there and—

Something snaked around his neck and bit into his skin. Matthew lurched, but he was held firm against the back of the chair by the intense pressure cutting off his air. Flailing his arms, Matthew tried to scream, but nothing escaped the noose choking him. He clawed his fingers into his neck, his nails scraping at the thin cord that held him.

"Relax, my friend. The more you struggle the longer you'll suffer."

Matthew's chest heaved, desperate for the breath he couldn't catch. O'Malley? His vision darkened around the edges, but Matthew resisted unconsciousness. He couldn't let O'Malley kill him now.

The cord dug deeper, and Matthew feared it would slice his throat open. He stilled.

"There now…" O'Malley's voice tickled his ears as Matthew's vision went black. "It's time to play our game."

Plink

Plink

Matthew groaned and his throat exploded with pain. He rolled to his side, coughing up phlegm and sucking in burning breaths. Dirt clung to his skin and smeared his face. Why was he on the ground?

Plink

Plink

Matthew stilled, breathing slowly and listening to the unfamiliar sound in the utter darkness. Where was he? He slowly lifted his fingers to gently probe at the raw skin on his neck.

Something shifted, and Matthew realized he wasn't alone. He jerked upright and was rewarded for the sudden movement with a burst of pain in his head and a tide of nausea in his stomach.

He tried to touch his face, only to find his wrists chained. He tugged, but the short length gave him little room. Feeling sick, he struggled to get his feet under him but couldn't rise any higher than to his knees.

"Wouldn't move too much at first, if I were you."

Matthew strained his eyes but couldn't see the man in the inky room. "O'Malley?"

Plink

Plink

"Yes, it took several hours for my headache to subside. Nasty, that one."

Matthew swallowed, his dry throat aching for moisture.

"Do you like the game?"

Matthew closed his eyes. *Lord, help me.* He'd thought O'Malley mad before, but that had been nothing compared to this. "What game is that?"

"You don't know?" The disappointment in O'Malley's tone dissolved into a chuckle. "Ah, well, I should have expected. A shame, though. I'd hoped you'd see it."

Plink

Plink

Matthew remained silent. What was that noise? It wasn't rhythmic enough to be dripping water. It was almost…metallic.

O'Malley sighed. "It's no fun if you won't even try."

The hairs on the nape of Matthew's neck stood on end. A faint smell drifted on the stale air. The scent of a body soured from lack of bathing. Matthew shifted on the dirt, musty air swirling around him and making him cough.

Plink.

The sound came again, followed by a rattle. A sound he recognized. Something heavy…metallic. The answer erupted through his foggy mind.

Chains.

Breathing hard, he tried to make out anything in front of him, but he might as well be trying to see with his eyes closed for all the good it did him.

The shadows shifted, an odd thing he couldn't explain. In utter darkness, how could something be even blacker than everything around it? Matthew shivered, though the musty room overflowed with sultry heat.

"A hint, then?"

Plink

Plink

"Very well, I'll give you a morsel to get your brain working. Let's see, what about your ride on the train feels familiar?"

Realization cut through the fog and the throbbing in Matthew's head. He tried once again to swallow. "Retaliation. You're recreating what I did to you."

The chains clinked, and Matthew tensed.

Plink

Plink

O'Malley's dark chuckle grated across his ears. "Ah, so you understand. Good. I wanted to be certain you didn't think this mindless."

Matthew tried to force himself to remain calm. "O'Malley. I couldn't let you murder Grant and his wife. Surely you understand."

He twisted his hands and felt his right one slip a little. He tugged as discreetly as he could.

A scraping sound, and then a small flame burst into life. Matthew blinked against the tiny light that cast O'Malley's features into planes of dancing shadows. O'Malley put the flame to a lantern. The light illuminated the small place Matthew shared with a man he no longer recognized.

Dirt floor. Stone walls. No windows. Only one door.

Plink.

Matthew's gaze darted back to his captor. O'Malley swung a small chain around in oscillating circles, the end of which occasionally clicked against the heavy chains filling his lap. He sat in a chair a few paces away, directly in front of the door. O'Malley's face split with a wicked smile.

The windowless walls gave no evidence of the time of day or night. "Where am I?"

Plink

Plink

A metal loop protruded from the dirt floor with a length of chain threaded through the center. Manacles attached to both ends pinched his wrists. He lowered his left hand down far enough to swipe the sweat from his forehead with his right.

"Disconcerting, isn't it? To wake up with a pounding headache without knowing where you are, only to find yourself trapped."

Matthew kept his tone even. "I took you to a tavern and paid for a comfortable room. One which you were free to leave the next day. This is not the same."

Plink

Plink

O'Malley swung the little chain around again, and Matthew's fingers involuntarily found the raw skin on his throat where the chain had cut him.

"Robbed, I recall, by the *honorable* Mr. Daniels. When I couldn't pay, the idiot running the place left me to sleep on the kitchen floor and then sent me away without food." O'Malley clicked his tongue. "Everything I had to do after that was entirely your fault, you see. You gave me no other options."

"I never meant to cause you any hardships."

"Then I suppose that's where we'll differ in this little game. I intend quite a few hardships for you, you see."

Panic clawed at him. "David!" Matthew pleaded. "What happened to you?"

O'Malley rose and the chains in his lap tumbled to the floor, scattering dust. He stepped closer and held the lantern up to his face. The eyes that stared at Matthew swam with fury.

"Lord, help me," Matthew whispered, trying to put as much distance between him and the other man as possible.

For just an instant, O'Malley's eyes cleared, and Matthew caught a glimpse of the man he'd known before. Matthew spoke slowly. "David. Tell me what happened to you. Perhaps I can help."

The flash of humanity in his eyes disappeared, and O'Malley laughed. "I don't need your help!"

Matthew pulled against the chains. The loop in the ground wiggled. "Something is very wrong with you. Can't you see that?"

O'Malley's face twisted, and Matthew wondered about the war that flickered over his features. Maybe there was a bit of sanity left in him somewhere. "Let me help you, David."

O'Malley straightened. The conflict in his eyes dimmed, replaced by a cold edge that made Matthew shiver. He lifted the chain in his hands. "We're going to play our game now."

O'Malley lunged for him. Matthew ducked.

Pray!

The thought slammed into him like a war hammer. He wasn't sure if it was from his mind or somewhere else.

O'Malley lunged for him again, a feral screech tearing from his lips. Matthew scrambled as far as the restraint would let him. He gave a mighty yank and the loop loosened a little more in the dirt. He yanked again but lost his balance and his shoulder smashed into the ground.

Lord, I need You!

David O'Malley stood over him and growled. Rough as splintered wood, O'Malley's voice scraped across him. "You're weak!" He lifted the chain again, eyes dancing.

"David! This isn't you!"

O'Malley snarled and snatched the heavy chain from the ground. He swung it around his head and aimed for Matthew's face. Matthew ducked. The thick end looped back around and smacked against the side of David's face. His eyes glazed over as a thick gash on the side of his head opened and blood poured down his cheek and onto his shirt collar.

He blinked, dazed. Would the blow knock him out? Allow Matthew to escape?

O'Malley sank to the floor but held onto consciousness. He glared at Matthew. "You're nothing. A failure. What makes you think you'll succeed? Haven't you failed everyone you ever cared for? You are worthless. A coward. A deserter. A liar." Pain and hatred twisted O'Malley's lips into a snarl.

Matthew forced his breathing to slow. "I was those things. But no longer."

O'Malley fingered the gash in his face, his eyes never leaving Matthew.

If he could show O'Malley hope for a new future, maybe he could change. By the grace of God, Matthew had. "I'm something new now. Redeemed. A soldier in a different army."

O'Malley's eyes rolled back in his head and he dropped to the dirt floor. His body shook violently.

Matthew pulled his feet under him and with every ounce of his strength, snatched the metal loop in the ground. It gave an inch. Then another. With a roar, Matthew pulled again. The loop jerked free.

Matthew dropped to his knees and grabbed O'Malley's lurching form, trying to contain the spasms. O'Malley stilled, his eyelids fluttering. Matthew cradled the man's bleeding head. David's chest heaved.

Then with a final shudder, O'Malley lay still in Matthew's arms.

Thirty

"I believe the people of the South would have been spared very much of the hard feeling that was engendered by Mr. Johnson's course towards them during the first few months of his administration. Be this as it may, Mr. Lincoln's assassination was particularly unfortunate for the entire nation."

General Ulysses S. Grant

*M*atthew pulled on the door again. Maybe the fifth try would somehow make the lock spring free. He lifted the lantern and tried to judge the thickness of the door. Could he break through it? A groan stirred the stillness and Matthew whirled around, his nerves set on edge.

O'Malley drew slow breaths from where Matthew had left him on the floor. He took a step closer and lifted the lantern. Blood soaked through the shirt Matthew had wrapped around O'Malley's head. If he didn't find a way out of here, he didn't think the man would make it.

O'Malley's eyes fluttered open and he looked up at Matthew. "Daniels?" His eyes darted around their confinement. "Where am I?"

Matthew grunted. "I was hoping you could tell *me* that."

O'Malley touched Matthew's shirt wrapped around his head. "Did you hit me?"

Matthew crossed the two strides between them and crouched at his side. "No, you did that yourself."

"But, I…" He moaned again. "What happened?"

Matthew stroked his chin. "You don't remember?"

O'Malley started to shake his head and then paused. "I remember very little." He eyed Matthew with suspicion. "Why are you keeping me here?"

Matthew forced his jaw to unclench. "I'm not. You brought me here after you choked me on the train."

Confusion flittered over O'Malley's face, but then he grunted. "How fitting."

Matthew rocked back on his haunches and said nothing.

"I can't move my legs."

Startled, Matthew's gaze swept down O'Malley's outstretched body. "What do you mean?"

O'Malley wheezed, and it seemed a struggle for him to take a breath. "I mean what I said. I can't feel my legs, nor can I move them.

"David, I—"

"Stop. I know I'm not long for this life." His chest lifted with a heavy breath. "I've come to the end, and I failed them."

"Failed who?"

O'Malley closed his eyes, a tear squeezing from the corner and sliding down his face. "My Liza. Our boy. I failed to bring them justice."

Matthew placed a hand on O'Malley's shoulder. "Killing Lincoln or anyone else wouldn't have brought them back, nor would it have changed what happened."

"They deserved justice. Vengeance."

Matthew pulled up words he'd heard army chaplains say. "Vengeance belongs to God, O'Malley. Not you."

"I gained…nothing." He struggled for another breath.

Urgency flooded Matthew. "Make your peace with God and you'll see them again."

"No…He won't give me that. The Almighty knows…I'd speak words of loyalty to Him only because I want my family. Not because…" He labored for another breath. "…I wished to serve Him."

Matthew's fingers tightened on O'Malley's shoulder. "Call to Him, and He will help you."

O'Malley opened his eyes and looked at Matthew with more clarity than he'd seen in him since before George had been taken to Elmira. "You truly believe that? Is there hope for me?"

Matthew nodded. "Confess and be forgiven, then take the peace offered. I did."

O'Malley studied him, as though judging the truth in his words. His breathing wheezed as he grunted. "Would you forgive me, knowing all I have done?"

"I do forgive you," Matthew said, surprised he meant the words.

His eyelids fluttered. "If that's true…then maybe…" O'Malley closed his eyes. "God, forgive me." His breath caught. "Don't let me slip into the endless night. I beg You, have mercy."

A smile tilted the corners of O'Malley's mouth. A gentle smile, one so different from the others Matthew had seen on those lips. Matthew offered up a silent prayer of thanks.

O'Malley's hand dropped to the ground. Lifeless eyes stared ahead, and David O'Malley parted from the world that had so wounded him.

Matthew sat there in silence a moment, saying a prayer of thanks for the Lord's incomprehensible mercy. O'Malley's tortured soul had finally found rest.

Matthew ran his hand over O'Malley's face, closing his eyes. "Find your peace now. The war is done."

Two hours later, with trembling, bloody fingers, Matthew pried the casing back from the doorframe with a snap. He studied the gap in between. If only he had something to use as a pry bar.

He stepped around O'Malley's body and snapped off one of the chair legs. It was thin, but it might do. Matthew shoved it into the crack and pushed on the lever he'd created. The wood groaned. "Come on, just a bit more."

The gap widened and Matthew shoved the tapered leg in farther, then pulled again. "Come on…"

It snapped and the wood splintered. Shards cut into his hand as he lost his balance. With a groan, Matthew dropped the broken chair leg and looked back at the door. At least he'd made enough room that he could get his fingers in.

Matthew put both hands into the space between the splintered frame and the door, and then braced one leg against the stone wall. He pulled, struggling with all his might and ignoring the blood that flowed from his palms and dripped down his forearms.

Matthew screamed and gave a mighty yank, and something popped free, sending him sprawling backward and onto O'Malley's body. Matthew quickly rolled back up to his feet and snatched the lantern up from the floor. Cautiously, he stepped through the doorway that now stood open.

On the other side, a set of narrow stairs led up to yet another thick door. Light seeped under the crack in the bottom, giving him hope. What would he find on the other side?

Matthew glanced down at his bare chest, his coat and shirt having been sacrificed to O'Malley's bleeding. He held the lantern up to survey the room he now guessed to be some kind of unused cellar. He shook his head and turned back to the stairs. Better to emerge into the unknown bare-chested than soaked in another's blood.

Matthew eased up the stairs and placed his bloody hand on the knob, praying that he wouldn't have to break through another door. Holding his breath, he twisted.

The knob turned easily, and Matthew swung the door open to a room flooded with light. He braced himself against the frame and blinked until his eyes adjusted. He stood on the threshold of a cabin. He took in the small space in one sweeping glance.

A stone hearth lay cold, and a layer of dust settled on humble furnishings. Matthew stood there for a moment, wondering who the abandoned place belonged to and what had happened to them.

He put his back to the wall and crossed to a glassless window, pushing aside a tattered curtain. Birdsong filtered through from a quiet meadow beyond. Matthew let the curtain fall back and walked over to a cupboard by the hearth. He opened drawers, leaving bloody fingerprints.

Finally, in the bottom drawer he found something of use. Two tattered rags would serve well enough for his sore hands, at least until he had the opportunity to properly clean and wrap them. He glanced back toward the cellar door. What to do about O'Malley?

There was only one thing that could be done.

He crossed the plank floor and stepped out onto a porch that sagged on one side. The cabin was nestled in an open field surrounded on all sides by towering trees. He looked up to find the sun. Late afternoon. Not much time, but perhaps enough.

He circled around to the back of the cabin and found a rusted pick and an axe. A spade would have been better, but this would do. Hefting the pick over his shoulder, Matthew chose a place at the edge of the woods, under the shade of an ancient oak.

By the time the sun dipped behind the trees, Matthew shouldered O'Malley's body and carried him to the grave. He hoped he'd dug deep enough to keep animals at bay. He placed the body in the ground and then grabbed a pinch of dirt. He sprinkled it on the man below. "Dust we were, and to dust we return. Rest well now, your soul is at peace."

It seemed too little by way of funeral rites, but it was all Matthew could muster. With numb hands and tired feet, Matthew shoved dirt back into the hole and then patted it down.

When he finished, sweat, dirt, and dried blood caked his trembling muscles. He found a pump and worked the rusted handle, but it produced no water for either his filth or his thirst.

Matthew returned the tools to where he'd found them, and then stepped back into the cabin. He'd seen a buckskin coat on a peg by the door that would serve as covering. Once he found somewhere to wash himself. He shook it out, then slung it over his shoulder and stepped back outside.

Then, choosing the only direction that he hoped would eventually lead him home, Matthew squared his shoulders and started south.

Thirty-One

"Today every loyal heart must suffer the terrible shock, and swell with overburdening grief at the calamity which has been permitted to befall us in the assassination of the Chief Magistrate."

New York World

Rosswood Plantation
July 3, 1865

"Annabelle, I think perhaps it's time I go." George wiped the sweat from his brow. "I don't think you need me here any longer." He set his latest offering—a small bench Peggy had requested for the kitchen—on the porch. He wasn't much in the way of a carpenter, but the makeshift table and wobbly chairs he'd managed to construct would at least keep his future sister-in-law from having to sit on the floor.

Annabelle looked up at him from her perch, a width of log turned on its side and smoothed enough so as not to snag the lady's skirts. "I suspected you'd say that." She dropped a pea hull into the wooden bowl at her feet then grabbed another handful to put in the basket in her lap. Her deft fingers worked quickly, the skin around her nails stained purple.

Peggy grunted an agreement, and his eyes drifted over to her. She wore the same style cotton day dress as Annabelle, and her fingers worked on the peas even more efficiently than the lady's. He took in the two of them, struck by just how much four years of war had changed their lives.

"Where will you go?"

Annabelle's question was ripe with insinuation, and he looked at his feet. "To try to right a wrong. Then home to my mother at Westerly, where I'm long overdue. The news sheets say the trial is over. It shouldn't be much longer before Matthew returns."

Worry skittered over her eyes. So far, no word had arrived from his brother. He softened his tone. "You know the post service has been dreadfully behind."

She plucked more purple hulled peas from their shells and offered him a contrived smile. "Of course." Then she brightened. "I wish you the best of luck on your quest."

He smirked. "No doubt. You haven't exactly withheld your opinion on the matter."

Annabelle ducked her chin to try to hide the upturn of her lips.

"You goin' to New York?" Peggy asked, her brown eyes boring into him. "That where this *wrong-that-needs-to-be-righted* is?"

George studied the woman he'd grown rather fond of these past weeks at Rosswood. She was brashly honest in a way most people weren't, though her words were tempered with kindness. He'd seen the affection between her and Annabelle. The more he'd spent time around Rosswood—and the more nights he spent on his knees in prayer—the more his mindset had changed.

He put his hands in his pockets and gave her a sheepish grin. "I was thinking of riding that way, yes."

"You know it ain't gonna be no easy thing."

Annabelle dropped a half-shelled pea hull. "Peggy! Don't you go trying to discourage him!"

Peggy huffed. "That poor girl done been through enough. She's got a fence around her heart, sure enough. And even if she didn't, after…" Peggy looked up at George, embarrassed, and trailed off.

Annabelle wrinkled her nose. "I still think he should try."

George watched a silent argument go on between the two women by way of flashing eyes. He cleared his throat. They both turned to him as though they had forgotten he stood there. How many times had they discussed him?

"My actions were unacceptable." George pushed past emotions that tried to gather in his throat. "But the Lord has done a work in me that I hope she'll see. I must tell her my regrets, and, in time, I pray she'll be able to forgive me."

Annabelle put aside her basket and rose to place a hand on George's arm. "Oh, George. Please don't give up on the feelings I know you have for her."

He'd always been more controlled with his emotions, not flinging them around for the world to see as Matthew did. How had he become a man so easily read? Somehow, the beautiful woman that both his Southern rearing and the law said he shouldn't love had undone him. How cruel to have finally found the one he yearned for only to realize she'd never stand by his side.

As though reading his thoughts, Annabelle squeezed his arm, her gaze bright as she studied him. "Lilly is a fine lady.

Where she was born means so little, especially now." She gestured toward the stump she'd vacated. "Why, just look at me. Born into a wealthy family, and yet here I am staining my calloused hands with pea hulls."

George swallowed, unable to give the chuckle that the levity in her voice tried to tease out.

She gave a small shake of her head, and bits of golden hair stirred around her face. "Our world's not what it once was."

He glanced again at Peggy, who watched him openly, then looked back to his future sister-in-law. "Indeed. Much has changed. Though not enough."

Annabelle crossed her arms and looked past George across the barren fields of Rosswood. "Many fought for changes, and many fought for things to stay the same. Nothing will come easy. Whatever we want out of the days ahead, we'll have to work for it." She swung her gaze back to George. "What future are *you* willing to fight for?"

Peggy gave a soft chuckle. "That's my Miss Belle. Never did give no mind to what color package a soul comes in."

Unbidden images from his dream on the train flashed through George's mind and he clenched his hands, a million reasons against the idea pounding against one relentless truth— he loved Lilly. He shook his head. "It isn't possible."

Annabelle opened her mouth to protest, but George continued before she had the chance to pelt him with foolish hopes. "Even if Lilly could forgive me, and if she cared enough for me to accept me, it still isn't possible."

Annabelle looked annoyed. "Why not?"

"The anti-miscegenation laws."

Surprise bloomed on her face, and she twisted her hands at

her waist. "Oh."

George had thought through all of the possibilities left to him. Even if Lilly forgave and accepted him, she could never be his bride. He thought he'd come to accept that fate, but the tightening in his chest said otherwise.

Annabelle wagged a finger at him. "Surely those things will no longer be upheld. Not since slavery's been abolished."

George gave her a dubious look, and she faltered. He admired her determined hopefulness, but he knew better. Things hadn't changed as much as she thought. If anything, he believed resentment between the races would only increase. "Even if that were the case, there would always be those that would hate my family. What kind of life would that be for her and Frankie?"

"A right sad thing, that," Peggy said.

George agreed, but said nothing more as Annabelle floundered for an argument that would hold water.

"But if some folks don't start trying to *make* things change," Peggy continued, her eyes not leaving her peas, "and aren't brave enough to fight through the hate, then how's things ever going to be different?"

Unable to refute the simple logic, George couldn't help but smile. "Wise words. For a cook."

Peggy turned up the corner of her mouth. "Funny how that works, ain't it?" Her deep brown eyes held both worry and compassion.

He'd discovered that Peggy was a quick-witted woman with a keen insight into the thoughts and motivations of those around her. She tore down every notion that her people lacked the mental capacity their masters possessed.

Sensing his discomfort, she flashed him a smile. "I say, Mr.

Daniels, that you're a changed man."

He opened his mouth to speak, but she pointed a finger at him. "But even so, if you want that girl, you're goin' to have to fight for her. Maybe even fight against the whole world to do it. But if you've decided that she's worth it, then you need to be man enough to win her and keep her."

George gaped at Peggy, never before having his manhood challenged by a woman of color.

Annabelle laughed. "Indeed." She brushed her hands on the apron hanging in front of her skirt. "So, when do you plan to go?"

George found his composure again and tugged on his broadcloth jacket. "At first light tomorrow. Your uncle has been kind enough to lend me a horse."

A smile played on her mouth. "How generous of him."

"That's only because he's ready to see you go," Peggy quipped.

Annabelle turned her eyes to the heavens. "Peggy, you still have a great deal to learn about propriety. There are some things you simply don't speak aloud."

George chuckled. "She speaks truth, and we all know it."

"I don't think my uncle dislikes you. He simply has concerns about—" Annabelle's voice wavered.

"I understand." George gripped her shoulder. "Matthew will be here soon, and you'll be my sister in no time."

She gave a tight nod, and George wondered if she doubted that was true. Then the light returned to her eyes and she smirked at him. "I hope you'll manage to provide *me* a sister as well."

He knew she meant the words in hopeful humor, but they

still stung. Had he followed his heart, and even the Lord's own will, weeks ago, such a thing might have been possible. Now…well, he had little optimism for anything beyond begging forgiveness. "I'll go to her," he finally said with a glance at Peggy, "and try to fight an impossible battle, but I wouldn't put too much hope in it."

Annabelle cocked her head. "On the contrary, I believe that's exactly what we should do. If we don't hope and pray for better, then we're resigned to things as they are." She looked up at him with blue eyes that brimmed with sincerity. "A woman knows when you hope for her, George. Show her that."

George nodded, feeling too many emotions to risk embarrassing himself further with wavering words.

Annabelle returned to the stool he'd made for her and replaced the basket in her lap. "Now, I need to get back to these peas. Peggy's going to show me how to cook them, and if we want them to be ready by supper, I'd better hurry."

How the two of them had managed to revive an abandoned garden and coax food from the earth was a miracle George's stomach revered.

A few hours later he took his place at the rough-hewn table at the end opposite of Michael. The women came in and placed bowls of peas, okra, and potatoes on the table, and the smell awakened the hunger that hours spent at hard labor had produced.

"Sorry there still ain't no meat," Peggy said as she took her seat between the men and opposite Annabelle at the small dining space.

Michael glanced at Peggy, but his discomfort with her sitting by his side at the four-person table seemed to lessen with each meal. George tapped a finger on the base of his fork, nearly bemused at the situation. Changes, indeed.

They helped themselves to the vegetables, passing the bowls around with an easy familiarity George hadn't often experienced, especially among the genteel. After Michael asked grace over the food, George took a bite of his peas and looked at Annabelle. "They turned out quite well. I'd say your cooking skills are coming along wonderfully."

Michael grunted. "I still don't see why a lady needs to learn such things."

Annabelle looked to the ceiling as though petitioning the Almighty for patience. Then she turned a sweet smile to her uncle. "It is a useful skill, Uncle Michael. One of many I have learned these past years."

Michael's brow furrowed. "I must get this place restored before my niece is nothing more than a field hand. What would your father think?"

Annabelle straightened. "I should hope that he'd be proud to see that I've found the strength necessary to persevere through hardships."

Michael's eyes softened. "Of course, Anna. I meant no offense. Only that it would pain him to see the changes this war as wrought."

She lowered her eyes. "Not all of the changes are bad, Uncle."

She didn't look at him, but George knew that Annabelle's words were directed at him. He glanced at Peggy, but the other woman kept her focus on her plate.

They continued the meal in silence, and when all had been consumed, Michael sat back and regarded George. "I should thank you for all you've done here. I didn't expect you to work that hard while you tarried."

George dipped his chin, choosing to focus more on the gratitude than the slight. "No thanks required. I wish I could do more for my future sister-in-law."

Michael's eyes darkened, but he simply nodded. George glanced again at Annabelle, who seemed quite uncomfortable. Her disquiet and the obvious dislike Michael harbored for Matthew made George think that perhaps he should stay until Matthew arrived.

"You'll be leaving us at first light?" Michael asked, the satisfaction in his voice evident.

Though Michael's words were a question, they felt more like a command, and George regretted sharing his thoughts of leaving with the man. He'd needed the horse, though. "Actually, upon giving it further thought, I may wait a few days more, so as not to miss my brother in passing."

Michael's face reddened.

"Surely you haven't changed your mind?" Annabelle asked, her meaning about his intentions with Lilly clear.

Leaving such things unspoken, he shook his head. "I'll still make the planned journey."

She frowned. "Then why wait?"

His jaw tightened. How to explain his concerns without riling her uncle? He determinedly kept his gaze from flicking the man's direction. "As I said, since we haven't heard from my brother, I think it better I stay until he arrives."

Annabelle stiffened.

Michael narrowed his eyes. "And what if he doesn't?"

George gave Annabelle a reassuring look that seemed to do

nothing to ease her distress. Annoyed the man couldn't see—or worse, didn't care—what effect his callous words had on his niece, George glared at Michael. "Now that the trial is over, I'm sure he's on his way. And since I gave my word to watch over his intended until his return, it'd be wrong of me to leave before that promise is fulfilled."

Michael spread his hands wide. "Yet, this very morning you stated you were ready to be on your way."

He had, but now he saw his mistake. Though he longed to go after his own ambitions, his selfishness had blinded him to his brother's needs in Washington. He wouldn't let that happen again. "I shouldn't have."

Michael's color deepened. "I'm capable of caring for my niece."

"I'm not saying anything to the contrary. Forgive me if I've implied otherwise. I mean only to wait for my brother's arrival and, thus, fulfill my promise to him. I should have never thought about leaving early."

Annabelle spoke up, her soft voice an attempt to soothe the tension gathering in the room. "I thank you both for your concern for me. Though I am content to be home under Uncle's care, I understand the promise made between two brothers who are very close." She looked at Michael. "As my dear uncle was close with my father, I'm sure he knows well the duty felt toward one's brother."

Michael softened. George inwardly smiled. Here was a woman who knew how to prod a man in just the right way. Poor Matthew. He might very well have his hands full with this one.

Michael rose from his chair. "Of course." He looked at

George flatly. "You're welcome here as long as you need." He tipped his chin to Annabelle. "I think I'll retire to the study."

She inclined her head. "Good evening, Uncle."

When he had gone, George rose. "I beg your leave as well."

Annabelle came to her feet, and Peggy started clearing the empty, mismatched dishes from the table.

"You needn't linger for my sake, George. I know you promised him, but I'll be fine."

George sighed. "That's likely true." No sense in telling her he didn't want to leave her to whatever schemes he thought Michael might cook up. "But since Matthew asked that I stay until he comes, and I gave my word to do so, that's what I should do. I should have never let my own desires make me think to cut that promise short. I'd thought that since the trial has ended, it was close enough. That was selfish of me. What I need to do can wait a few days longer."

Peggy stepped quietly out of the room with her load, leaving George and Annabelle alone. Annabelle clasped her hands tightly, and the voice that barely reached his ears was strained. "What if he doesn't come?"

George frowned. "What do you mean?"

She glanced away, but not before he saw the glimmer of tears in her eyes. "When I left, Matthew said he had things to work on...and...well, I haven't heard from him, and—" Her voice caught and compassion stirred in George's chest.

He took her elbow. "He'll come. I know my brother well, and he loves you."

She bit her lip and gave a nod, but her eyes didn't look convinced. She steadied herself with a determined strength that George had come to admire and set her shoulders back. "Then we'll pray he doesn't continue to dally."

The corner of George's mouth turned up. "The trial has only just concluded. There's no need to worry."

She inclined her head, not offering further comment. She bade George a good night, and then slipped through the door and out to the kitchen where he knew she would work side by side with the woman who had once been her slave. A mightily changed world indeed.

After the last of the day's light retreated from the sky and robbed George of the ability to read a book he couldn't focus on, he settled on his pallet in the guest chamber and once again struggled with the notion of sleep.

His mind swirled with thoughts of his future and robbed his body of the rest it craved. For long hours George sorted through every possible outcome of what his heart demanded he do. Regardless of what might happen, he couldn't live this way. He'd thought that once he was away from her, Lilly wouldn't occupy his mind so often. Then when the Lord had given him mercy and the nightmares had subsided, he thought he'd no longer crave the calm her presence offered. But if anything, those thoughts and feelings had only increased, overwhelming him with misery.

George moaned and rolled to his side, trying to force his mind to still. But when first light finally arrived, he'd only managed to grasp at sleep a few scant moments, leaving him tired and ill-equipped for another long day of waiting.

Thirty-Two

"…saddened as the country was by the terrible calamity
brought upon it by the [...] deeds of these deep-dyed
villains, astounded as it has been by the daily revelations
of the trial of the criminals, it was doubtless unprepared,
as were all here, for the quick flash of the sword of
power, whose blade to-day fell upon the guilty heads of
the assassins of our lamented President."

Special dispatch to *The New-York Times*

*M*atthew's feet ached terribly. Without money and
dressed like a beggar, people avoided him as though
he'd brought them the plague. They scurried away, turned up
their noses, and passed him on the opposite side of the street.
At first, he'd tried to get someone to listen to his tale, find
anyone who might lend an ear of sympathy. Everyone seemed
too laden with their own troubles to care.

And so he had trudged on, mile after mile, adding to the
blisters on his feet but bringing him closer to Annabelle. He'd
been unable to send a telegraph or even acquire a horse to speed
his journey. What would she think when he didn't return as
promised, now that the trial had ended?

He stopped at the edge of the road to sit on a fallen log and swiped the sweat from his brow. Another town left behind. How long had it been since he'd left Washington?

He scratched the scruff on his chin. According to the snatches of conversations he'd heard, it had been about a week since the trial had ended and he'd boarded the train in Washington. He rubbed his still sore neck. O'Malley had then taken him farther south. He'd emerged from the woods in the foothills somewhere in the southern part of Virginia.

Yet, for all his long days of walking, he'd not made progress much farther than Charlotte. Would Annabelle think he'd abandoned her? Groaning, he gained his feet once more. He must continue. Every moment he dallied would be another she would spend in worry.

The dust stirred under his boots, coating them with another layer of earth. Dust from the states he'd trudged through—lands devoured by the beast of war, touched by atrocities that men committed. At every place he'd passed he'd heard tales. Stories of terrible things men had done in the fever of war. Battle had caused them to shed their morals and humanity. Had he been any different?

Matthew breathed in the Carolina air and let it out with a prayer for peace. Then he asked for the safety of those he loved. He'd slipped through towns where Union forces handed out food to people desperate enough to endure the taunts and abuse in order to fill their stomachs. Twice he'd had to swallow his pride and stand in one of those lines when he couldn't coax enough sustenance from nature. What he'd been given made hardtack and old jerky seem a lost luxury. And with every town he passed, despite his prayers to ward off his hatred for the Blue Bellies, it only grew.

Wind stirred his hair around his shoulders, and he had to push it out of his face. If he ever made it back to Mississippi, he would shed these locks he'd grown throughout the war. A symbol of cutting off the war itself. If only he could shed the memories just as easily.

A noise caught his attention. The crunch of wagon wheels. Many travelers had eyed him warily and pointedly ignored his plea for a few moments off his feet.

He looked over his shoulder, briefly wondering if he should duck into the woods and avoid the scorn of another battered soul who now looked at every stranger with suspicion. But he ached from crown to heel. The slightest possibility of obtaining a ride made him shake some of the dust from his sleeves and straighten his sweat-stained coat.

The wagon topped the rise, and Matthew caught sight of a man with a gray beard that grazed his open-collar shirt. Matthew lifted his hand in a friendly wave. Seeing him, the man pulled up on the reins and brought two nags to a halt.

Guarded hope stirred and Matthew closed the remaining distance. He offered a friendly, though weary, smile.

The man rose in his seat and pulled out a pistol, leveling it on Matthew. "Hold it there, fellow. What do you want?"

Surprised he hadn't been prepared for such a response, Matthew lifted his hands. "I mean no harm, sir."

The man lowered the weapon a fraction. "What do you want?"

"Only the kindness of a ride to rest my worn feet.

He grunted. "You aren't getting any of my grain. I'll shoot you if you so much as brush your dirty fingers across it. I swear I will."

Matthew slowly lowered his hands. "I don't want anything besides a chance to ride."

The man lowered the pistol. "Where're you headed?"

"Mississippi."

The man cocked his head. "That's a long trip, fellow. You trying to make it on foot?"

"I was disabled, robbed, and left only with clothing I could scavenge. Walking's been my only option for getting back home."

He stared at Matthew so long that Matthew thought he might shoot him and leave his body to rot on the road. "That what gave you that nasty bruise?"

Matthew reached up to touch the still-tender flesh. "He tried to strangle me."

The man watched him, no doubt thinking Matthew had just as likely escaped a lawman's noose. Finally, the fellow lifted his shoulders. "All right. Climb up. But one suspicious move and I'll put a bullet through you."

Matthew smiled. "Yes, sir. I understand."

He climbed up into the buckboard. The springs underneath the seat compressed with his weight. The man eyed him from beneath the wide brim of his hat but snapped the reins and they started to roll forward.

Matthew's shoulders slumped with fatigue. "I'm most grateful for your kindness. Many have taken one look at me and gone the other way."

The man's mustache twitched with a smile, and he seemed to relax as the nags picked up pace. "I can see as how that would happen. Name's Carter."

Not sure if that was his first name or his last, Matthew replied, "Matthew Daniels. A pleasure, sir."

Carter glanced at him from the corner of his eye. "You talk like one of those silver-spoon types. But you look like a haggard trapper from the hills."

"I was robbed."

The man chuckled. "What do you have left in Mississippi that war didn't take from you?"

A rather direct question, though probably a common one these days. "Just the lady I pray still waits for me."

Carter gave him a knowing look. "I figure many a man is doing the same as you, lad. What part of Mississippi are you headed for?"

"South of Vicksburg before you reach Natchez."

The man nodded. "I can't take you that far, but if you help me load and unload my cargo, I'll take you as far as Atlanta."

He'd not expected anything more than the next town. "I'll lift whatever you need me to."

Carter bobbed his head. "Good man. We'll make a trade then. I'll save your feet, and you'll save this old back."

Matthew rested his elbows on the back of the bench. "A good trade."

Annabelle stared at the disgruntled man at her door. "I'm sorry, what did you say?"

The man looked down his nose at her. "I said, you are to allow accommodations for ten of my men."

She'd heard the words but hadn't wanted to believe them.

"I'm sorry, sir. We aren't able to host guests at this time."

The space between his eyebrows shortened. "It's not a request. This house is being commandeered."

Annabelle's fingers tightened on the doorframe. "The war's over. You cannot force yourselves into my home." She glanced behind him and glared at the men standing in her mother's garden. One noticed her regard and removed his polished boot from a daylily sprout.

"We have orders to be a peace-keeping presence," the man said, drawing her regard back to him.

"We are already peaceful here, sir." Annabelle lifted her chin. "And we certainly don't need the oversight of so many men."

He took a step closer, his frame towering over her.

Annabelle refused to let her unrest show.

"The town has no more accommodations available for men on service to this area. Therefore, they will reside in outlying residences while not on duty." He removed a paper from his coat and waved it at her. "While under martial law, citizens are to comply with our authority."

Refusing to be cowed by his demands, Annabelle crossed her arms. "I wish to speak with Lieutenant Grierson prior to these arrangements."

The man narrowed his eyes. "For what reason? The orders remain."

"Still, as this property has fallen under his temporary authority, I believe he should be consulted."

The man glowered at her. Annabelle forced her gaze to remain calm but firm. Finally, he released a breath that was more growl than sigh and shoved the papers back inside his coat. "Very well. We'll remain outside while you prepare the lodging and one of my men goes after the lieutenant."

Knowing she wouldn't get a better offer, she inclined her head. "My uncle should be in from the fields soon. He will speak with you further."

He opened his mouth to respond, but she closed the door before he had the opportunity. She slid the lock into place, knowing it wouldn't keep them out. Breathing hard, she put her back against the door.

Peggy wrung her hands. "What they wanting to do, Miss Belle?"

Annabelle wrinkled her nose. "Take over the house."

"Can they do that?"

She grabbed Peggy's hand and pulled her away from the door. "I don't know. I've gained us some time, I think. Hopefully Joshua will help us."

Annabelle had taken only two steps up the stairs when shouts from outside sent her running back for the front door. She pulled it open to find Michael standing nose to nose with the Federal soldier who'd knocked on her door.

"You'll leave immediately!" Michael shouted, his face red.

The Federal set his jaw, and his hand went for the firearm at his side. Fearing the worst, Annabelle ran from the house, nearly tripping on her skirts in her hurry from the porch. "Uncle! They've already sent for Lieutenant Grierson. He'll be here soon."

The two men turned to look at her, then took a step back from one another. The Union man rested his hand on his pistol. "I did as the lady requested, though it won't make much difference. This region is under occupation."

Michael stiffened, and Annabelle hurried to take his arm before he deepened their predicament. "Uncle, would you come inside with me, please?"

He turned fiery eyes on her. "Anna, now is not the time. Can't you see that I must deal with this—"

Annabelle placed a hand to her forehead and swayed. As she predicted, Michael leapt to steady her. "Come, Anna. I'll take you indoors."

He glared at the soldier. "Then you and I will continue this conversation."

She tugged on her uncle's arm and hurried toward the house. Once inside, she latched the door and swung around. "What are you thinking?"

His eyes widened. "You aren't experiencing flutters."

She crossed her arms. "I am not."

"Then why did you…?" His words trailed off, and he pinched the bridge of his nose. "I've no time for your games. These men must be removed from Rosswood."

"Forgive the deception, but it was the only way I knew to stop you from saying something foolish."

Michael clenched his hands. "Take care how you speak, niece."

"I mean no disrespect. But heated words will only cause more trouble for us. They outnumber you, and if it comes to a fight, then what? They'd arrest you for fighting a soldier while we're under martial law. What would become of me then?"

He clenched his fists, but she could see he understood her logic.

"They'd *still* take the house, and I'd have no one here to protect me." *Except George*, she thought, but thought it wise to keep that comment to herself.

The fury cleared in Michael's eyes and his shoulders drooped. "How foolish of me not to think—" He shook his head. "Those Yanks. They abide by no law. They take whatever they wish." She nodded in understanding and he sighed. "Forgive me."

Annabelle placed a hand on his arm. "I no more want them here than you. But I fear this is a dangerous game where we must outmaneuver them rather than threaten or overpower them."

Michael regarded her for a moment. "You're quite a capable woman. The man who claims you will have a treasure indeed."

Annabelle smiled. "Thank you, Uncle."

He frowned back at the door. "I'm begrudgingly glad Mr. Daniels refused to leave. I may need him."

Annabelle inclined her head in consent, having already thought the same.

"Wait here." Michael strode past Peggy and up the stairs, returning a few moments later with a pistol in hand.

He extended the cold metal object to Annabelle. It settled in the heat of her palm and her arm drooped. She'd never held a pistol before, and it was heavier than she'd anticipated.

"There's no time for a lesson, but it's fairly simple." Michael gestured toward the door. "It's already loaded. If one of them breaks through, all you need do is pull the hammer—" he pulled back on a bit of metal that gave a click, "—and then point it."

Annabelle placed both hands on the stock and lifted the weapon to point it at the door. The tip of the gun wavered, and she took a deep breath to try to steady her hands. "Like this?"

"Very good. Then you pull the trigger. Try to aim for his

chest, if you can."

Annabelle turned wide eyes on him. "That will kill him."

"That's the intention."

Annabelle lowered the muzzle. "I cannot."

He rested a hand on her shoulder. "You must."

"Surely that won't be necessary."

Michael's fingers tightened. "Unfortunately, my dear, it may be. You don't know the things I've seen men do."

The sincerity and concern in his eyes made Annabelle shiver.

"I must find George. You and Peggy stay here in the hall. If anyone breaks through that door, he has no good intentions in mind. Shoot him, Anna, before he can reach you."

Annabelle swallowed hard, only able to give a small dip of her chin. She'd aim for his leg.

Michael strode to the rear door. It closed behind him with a soft click, and then Peggy slid the lock into place.

She looked at Annabelle with a somber expression. "Your uncle's right, you know. If that man forces his way in here, you pull that trigger."

Annabelle turned back toward the door, a single tear sliding down her face. Peggy had given her a weapon once, a dagger the Confederate Army had taken from her. She'd never had cause to use it. Her throat constricted, and she hoped she wouldn't have a reason to use the pistol either.

Please, Lord, don't let them come through the door, she prayed. Then she set her feet and steadied the weight of steel and death in her hands.

Thirty-Three

"Tried, convicted and sentenced, they stood this
morning upon the threshold of the house of death, all
covered with the great sin whose pall fell darkly on
the land."
Special dispatch to *The New-York Times*

Georgia
July 7, 1865

"Should be in Atlanta, or what's left of it, by nightfall,"
Carter said, stretching his shoulders.

Matthew smiled at the man who'd not only given him a
place in his buckboard but had also provided him with a decent
shirt and food enough to suppress his ravenous hunger. "I'll
miss your good company, but I'm pleased to be that much
closer to home."

Carter pushed back the brim of his hat. "What will you do
then?"

Matthew shrugged. "Start walking again, I presume."

Carter tugged on his beard. "No promises, but I know a
fellow in Atlanta. He's making runs same as me, though his
route is Atlanta to Jackson. He might be willing to take on a

strong back as well."

"I'm most indebted to you, Carter. You've saved me weeks of travel." He winked. "And the ire of my beloved."

Carter chuckled. "Think nothing of it, boy. You earned your keep, far as I'm concerned. I didn't have to lift a single sack. Wish I could take you on the return trip."

"Then you'd risk my lady's wrath as well." Matthew laughed.

They reached the outskirts of what had been Atlanta just as the sky turned from pristine sapphire to deep violet.

"Eight months, and the ash still stirs in the air." Carter shook his head. "He was insane, you know. He left his post in Kentucky in '61 because of emotional tumult."

Matthew shifted in his seat and looked out of the corner of his eye at the man whose wartime loyalties he'd not inquired about. "Sherman?"

Carter nodded grimly. "What he did when he left here…what he allowed his men to do." He glanced at Matthew. "What side did you serve, boy?"

The truth? "Both."

Carter frowned.

"I served for Mississippi to protect our homes and families from invasion. Then, after the war ended, I was…persuaded to lend aid to the efforts to capture the assassin and was thus turned from a Confederate Captain to a Union Private."

Carter considered him a moment. "Interesting tale you got there, if you'd be inclined to tell it."

A tale, indeed, though not one Matthew wished to dig up.

"They hung them all," Carter pointed out. "Even the woman. Can you imagine such a thing? What have we come to?"

Matthew had heard of the swift sentencing of the people

who'd stood trial but didn't want to think on it. He turned the subject. "Did you serve, Carter?"

The man barked a laugh. "Not hardly. I'm too old for such things. Used to have a nice shipping company, though. Did pretty well until this war up and ruined all I had worked my entire life to build. Now I'm starting over so I don't leave my girls destitute when they put me in the ground."

Matthew nodded, though Carter hadn't truly answered his question.

"But to answer what you really want to know," Carter said, "I pledged loyalty to neither side. Didn't agree with the South on slavery and didn't agree with the North on forcing states to stay in the Union." He puffed out his cheeks and let a long breath stir his mustache. "Living in Virginia, declaring for neither side turned out to be a good way to be hated by both."

Not knowing what to say, Matthew could only offer a nod. Serving on both had earned him much of the same loathing.

The buckboard rolled past homes with nothing left but charred chimneys and a few crumbling bricks. When they reached the town, the sense of despair hung so thickly in the air that Matthew thought he might choke on it.

"Sad, it is. What war makes of men," Carter said.

They passed a man in a ragged Confederate uniform slumped alongside a crumbling wall. He regarded them with vacant eyes.

Matthew remained silent, watching little children as they poked dirty faces out of ruined buildings to assess the load of sacks in the wagon.

"My friend has a block house on the other side of town that mostly survived the fire. We'll stay with him for the night and see if he'll take you with him to Jackson."

"Thank you," Matthew managed to say. His heart felt weighted with a cannon ball. He'd be glad to get away from this place as soon as possible.

George watched the men setting tents in the front grasslands beyond the garden wall and felt a new wave of appreciation for his brother's intended. Strange how Matthew had once thought the woman a match for George. The men below stilled as the Lady of Rosswood came into their view, and George wondered what those Blue Bellies thought of her. A woman whom George had come to think of as a tiny, golden-haired dragon—nice to look at, dangerous to provoke.

She confidently strode through the garden with her shoulders back. Annabelle had always been Matthew's perfect complement. Matthew needed one not easily tamed yet with a gentle soul. God in His wisdom knew that no other would both challenge and temper Matthew as this woman could. And Lord help him, he'd be certain his brother would return to find his intended had been well protected. Thus, he'd risk taking aim at the Yankees.

Thankful he hadn't allowed his own desires make him depart early, George readied his rifle and poked it through the balcony railing. Lying on his stomach, he hoped they wouldn't be able to see him. If any should forget their manners, he'd be able to pick a few of them off. In the end it would mean his life. If they even so much as caught a glimpse of his barrel, he'd be shot without question.

Annabelle reached the men and spoke with the sergeant. He frowned, looking displeased with whatever she had to tell him. Grierson, who seemed to have an inappropriately soft spot for Annabelle, had been away. Annabelle refused entrance to any man until he arrived.

George grinned. She'd insisted she be the one to talk to the Yanks. Suited him fine, since that gave George and Michael the opportunity to set vantage points. Should any of those men give them adequate reason, they'd find themselves buried in Annabelle's graveyard.

She finished her say and turned back toward the house. George took aim at the man who watched her walk away, but he merely puckered his face and then turned aside. George kept his weapon on the man until he heard the front door close, then he relaxed and scooted back away from the rail.

He propped the weapon against the wall by the house and then turned to watch the squatters below. George reached into his pocket and fingered the slip of paper he'd withheld from Annabelle.

The day before the Yankees had arrived, he'd gone to Lorman to send word to Washington. The telegram had cost him more than he could spare, but since he hadn't heard from Matthew—and given his brother's strange behavior prior to George's departure—worry had pushed him to seek reassurance.

The reply had come from the office of Mr. Fitch, the lawman Matthew had worked with. He'd said that Matthew had left Washington on June 29.

Having experienced the deplorable conditions of the railways, George knew that travel could be delayed, but Matthew still should have arrived by now.

What had kept him so long? Each day that passed seemed to weigh more on Annabelle, and the worry that haunted her eyes pained George. Whatever had happened between her and Matthew before they'd left Washington, it caused her to fear Matthew wouldn't return.

George had dismissed the notion at first, knowing that Matthew cared greatly for Annabelle. He rubbed the muscles on the back of his neck and watched the intruders. Had Matthew changed his mind? Before the war he'd been known to dally with many young ladies. He'd never seemed to keep interest in one for very long. Now that the adventurous part of their relationship had come to an end, did Matthew fear the responsibility of marriage and the daunting task of rebuilding a life in the South?

Already there were tales of people fleeing the Union occupation in droves. Some went west, some to Mexico territory, and some, he'd heard, were even going as far as to try to make new Southern utopian colonies in South America.

George swiped a bit of hair that had fallen into his eyes, obscuring the Blues below. He could see the appeal of starting life anew somewhere where they wouldn't be held under the Union's thumb. At the sound of rustling fabric, he turned to glance back at the house.

Annabelle stepped through the open door and onto the balcony, coming to join him at the rail.

She jutted her chin at the men. "They won't stay there much longer."

"You managed to convince them to leave Rosswood?"

She swung a startled gaze back at him. "What? No. I mean that they won't stay in those tents much longer. Soon they'll force their way into the house, and I can't stop them."

The despair in her voice raked across him. "I won't let them to do that. The first man who tries to force his way into your house will gain my lead in his gut."

Her features tightened, and she hesitated only a moment before giving a small shake of her head. "I wish for there to be no more death at Rosswood."

George gripped the railing. "Yet neither can you let them take advantage of you. I won't allow it."

She wrapped her arms around her waist and continued to stare at the men below. "Joshua will be here soon."

George's jaw tightened at the familiar use of Grierson's name. Worse than that, she looked to a Yankee for deliverance! Not him, not her uncle, and not even the one to whom she should be longing to come to her side.

"What of Matthew?" George snapped.

Still she stared ahead, a distant look in her eyes. "If he ever comes, what could he do? There's nothing you and Uncle can do about it. Our only hope is Joshua."

George spun away and scooped up his rifle, swinging it toward the men below. "I can send them all below the earth, *that's* what I can do."

Fear replaced the vacancy in her eyes. "George, no!" Annabelle gripped his arm, tilting his rifle away from the leader of the band below.

The commotion drew the men's attention and they looked up. Noticing the glint of the weapon, the head Yankee grabbed for his pistol, took aim, and fired.

The crack of gunfire sounded a half-second before a chunk of the column next to George exploded. He dropped to the floor, pulling Annabelle down with him in a heap.

"Those are the scoundrels you would protect?" George said, his words coming out in a near growl.

Annabelle scrambled away, struggling against all the fabric and petticoats that entangled her legs. She put her back against the house and stared at him with eyes that flashed more with anger than with fear. "We're no longer at war. What you propose is nothing more than murder!"

Her words hit him like a bucket of cold water. He jumped to his feet and raised his hands, stepping over to the railing in submission. *Fool!* He'd lost his wits and endangered them all.

The Yanks below had gathered and all knelt behind the cover of the brick garden wall. The one who'd fired propped his elbows upon the wall and kept his pistol trained on George but, surprisingly, didn't kill him.

George kept his hands raised and shouted to those below. "A misunderstanding, gentleman! We mean no harm!"

The Blue Belly looked to his men, then after a moment stood from behind the cover. "You will surrender all weapons immediately!"

George's shoulders stiffened. He'd caused a predicament. He groped for an excuse. "I need the rifle to hunt."

"Gather them all and deposit them on the front porch." When George hesitated, he shouted, "Now! Aim that weapon again, Reb and it'll be the end of you." The man kept his pistol trained on George, and George had no doubt the sergeant meant the words.

Annabelle gained her feet and stood in the doorway, studying him. She closed her eyes and drew a long breath. When she opened them, her frustration manifested in a glimmer of tears. "That was a reckless thing to do!"

George ran a hand through his hair, unable to deny it. What had come over him? "Forgive me," he said through clenched teeth. "Though I must admit, it infuriates and pains me deeply to know you look to a *Yank* with a longing that should be reserved only for my brother."

Her mouth gaped open, but he merely pushed past her to collect the weapons—an action that would not only add further coals to the anger of Michael Ross but also feed the wolves salivating at their door.

Thirty-Four

"The conspirators have gone to their long home, the swift hand of justice has smitten them, and they stand before the judgment seat."

The New-York Times

$\mathcal{A}$nnabelle leaned over the pot and drew in another whiff of the apples simmering inside their bath of honey and cinnamon.

"Shoulda let them men in sooner," Peggy said, her fingers pressing the pie crust against the edges of the tin.

Annabelle dropped her spoon. "Peggy! Why would you say such a thing?"

Peggy cocked her head. "'Cause. As soon as they made their beds inside, they stocked my kitchen." She breathed deep. "Yes, ma'am, it sure is nice to be able to make a real meal again!"

Only hours after George had surrendered all of their weapons—well, most of them, anyway—the Federals had taken her home. Two days later, and she was still furious at George's foolishness. She plucked the spoon from the edge of the pot and stirred the apples again. Despite that, she begrudgingly had to admit that she agreed with Peggy. It was certainly nice to have food in the kitchen again.

And truth be told, the Union soldiers had been nothing but gentlemen since entering the house. She and Peggy shared her room, George and Michael shared Father's room, and the men had taken the other two rooms and the parlor, with the sergeant having his own space in the library. Most of the men would leave during the days, and other than asking her to cook the evening meals with the supplies they provided, they hadn't required anything from her.

Annabelle scraped the apples into the crust Peggy had ready, then wiped a hand across her face. Plopping down on the bench George had fashioned, she watched Peggy place strips of dough in a basket weave across the top of the pie.

"Why don't you go ahead and spill out what's festering in your heart, Miss Belle," Peggy said, not looking up from her work.

Annabelle briefly considered using her often practiced fake smile and forced insistence that everything was fine, but it was only a lie Peggy already saw through. She pushed a loose pin back into the twist of her hair. "I don't want them in my house. They've brought supplies we need, yes, but I'd rather eat nothing but peas and be left in peace."

"Hmm. That all?"

Tears immediately threatened, and Annabelle had to swallow back a burning in her throat. "I fear for Matthew."

Peggy finished the crust and opened the oven to check the coals. Satisfied with the heat, she slid the pie inside. She wiped her hands on her apron and took a seat next to Annabelle. "I know that, baby girl. And I'm gettin' a mite worried about him myself. But I just heard them men this morning talking about the sentencing after the trial. Maybe he stayed for that."

Annabelle's face puckered. "They've come to a sentencing so soon?"

Peggy nodded. "Seems it's already been carried out, according to what the soldiers say. Couple of them went to prison, but most of them they hung at the same prison that they took you to."

She shuddered. "Then it's finished."

Peggy patted her hand. "Don't you be worrying too much. I'm sure he'll be comin' along now that it's all done."

"But he said he'd leave as soon as the trial concluded."

Peggy shrugged. "Maybe they didn't let him. You know how close they was to keeping him."

Annabelle nodded, though she wasn't so sure. She'd feared in Washington that Matthew had stayed away from her on purpose. And then when he'd told her to go home and that he had things he had to think through... Tears welled again. "Peggy, what if he doesn't want to come?"

"He loves you. Put a ring on your hand before you even wed. Trust in that, Miss Belle."

Annabelle wanted to, she truly did, but fear and anger still stirred in her. How could he do this to her? Proclaim his love and promise to be by her side no matter what their future held, and then so easily dismiss that promise merely because of a single incident that wounded his pride?

Annabelle rose and plucked an ear of corn from the basket and shucked it. Peggy remained silent and did the same. Annabelle's frustration festered while they cleaned half the bushel. By the time they tossed the corn into boiling water, Annabelle felt as though that same bubbling heat coursed through her veins.

Men and their foolish pride! When she saw him again… Pain gripped her. *If* she saw him again. The thought constricted her chest so tightly she ached.

Annabelle ducked away from Peggy's motherly gaze, begging a moment of fresh air. She stumbled out into the hot afternoon but found no relief in the breezeless day beyond the kitchen. She steadied herself and took a long draw of air thick with moisture.

The aching caused by the thought that he would reject her now squeezed so hard that she nearly lost her breath. She couldn't take the pain. She groped for hope but found her stores depleted. A sob rose in her throat. She couldn't drown in this sea of remorse, frustration, and agony. If she did, she might never recover. Flailing, she gripped onto the only other emotion that remained.

He'd lied, tricked and deceived her, and toyed with her heart. The irritation over his foolishness blossomed and she grabbed onto it because anger was the only thing that could overpower the sorrow.

Annabelle reached into the pocket of her skirt and withdrew the silver horse Matthew had given her for her twentieth birthday and gripped it tight. Then she turned toward the house and stalked away.

"You're a good worker, Daniels, and strong as an ox. Sure I can't convince you to stay on?"

Matthew smiled at Jim Barlow, Carter's partner from Jackson. "No, sir, I'm afraid not."

The man shrugged his narrow shoulders. "Well, can't blame me for trying," he said around the wad of tobacco in his cheek.

Matthew hefted the last bag of flour from the cart and placed it beside the stacks of grain, cornmeal, and rice that had already been added to the storeroom. They'd been delayed for longer than he would like already, but an extra day of delivering goods around the city was worth the time he would have lost traveling on foot.

Matthew brushed his hands on his trousers. "That's the last of it."

Jim spat a stream of tobacco. "Now we'll see what we can get loaded for my trip back."

Matthew withheld a groan. Hadn't he paid for his ride? He'd already loaded and distributed a wagon so heavy it'd taken four good horses to pull it. He rubbed the back of his neck. "I didn't know that was part of it. I need to be on my way."

Jim laughed. "That lady that's waitin' on you, huh?"

Matthew smiled. "One I've left waiting far too long."

"Understand that." He spat again. "Still, if you stay one more day and help me load, I'll give you a good wage. Enough, say, to get you the rest of the way to Jefferson County?"

Knowing the day spent in labor would save him several more if he didn't happen across anyone else headed south willing to give him a ride, Matthew gave a nod.

Jim slapped him on the shoulder. "Good. It's getting dark. I'll get us some rooms and then we'll get back to it in the morning." He stretched his shoulders, though it had been Matthew who'd done all the work. "Get us some drink, too. I'd say you've earned a few cups."

Matthew shook his head. "A hearty supper is all I require."

Jim cocked his head. "Suit yourself."

Matthew climbed back onto the driver's bench and handed Jim the reins. They rode through the streets of Jackson, past the capitol building, and to a place that looked more tavern than inn. Too tired to care much, Matthew looked forward to a full stomach and a place to rest his head.

A little while later, after seeing the horses tended, Matthew trudged into the small building that looked close to falling in and spotted Jim at a card table. Content to be left on his own, he chose a seat and told the serving girl to add his supper charge onto Jim's.

The plink of an out-of-tune piano grated on his senses, so he tried to focus on the men around him while he waited for his meal.

Smoke spiraled around grinning faces tempered by vacant eyes. He recognized the look of men who sought to hide from life outside this squalid den of smoke and drink. Matthew tried not to breathe too deeply the smells of stale ale, cigar ash, and unwashed bodies.

Where once he'd thought a place like this full of life and revelry, now he saw that it was only an illusion. A shallow theatre where people tried to disguise their sorrows.

The rotund woman returned with his platter of chicken and okra, and after finishing off two plates worth, half of a basket of rolls, and a bowl of peach cobbler, Matthew wiped his mouth and left the napkin on the table.

As he turned to go, Jim caught his eye. "Join us in the game?"

"Thank you, but I think I'll find my bed. It'll be an early morning."

Jim laughed and waved him away.

The comment made him wonder when the man might rise from the effects of a drunken stupor. "A word before I go?"

Jim gestured to the table. "After this hand."

Matthew waited and watched Jim lose all he'd wagered, and then waited further until Jim's cursing subsided and he finally rose from his chair. Irritated, Jim scowled at Matthew. "What is it?"

"Could I get a bit of that pay early? I'd like to send a telegram." It felt odd, having never asked for a wage in his life, but Matthew no longer cared about such things. Bit by bit, the prideful man he'd been mellowed into one much less concerned with his status.

"Sure. First thing tomorrow. Can't send it tonight."

Matthew looked past him to the card table. "Perhaps now would be best, so I don't need to trouble you with it early in the morning. I'll send the telegram before breakfast."

Some of Jim's good humor slid off his face and his dark eyes turned to slits. "You'll get your pay when the work's done."

Matthew's hands clenched at his sides. He gave a jerk of his chin, not trusting his words to remain polite.

Jim smiled and patted Matthew's tightened shoulder. "Good then. Off with you."

Withholding his building anger, Matthew turned his back on the men and their laughter.

Annabelle. Please don't give up on me. Matthew entered his room and washed the sweat from his face and neck with the water from the basin, then removed his shoes and fell onto the bed.

He stared up at the ceiling, listening to the boisterous noises below.

He pushed the sounds aside and turned his thoughts to how her face would light up when he returned. He imagined the warmth of her arms slipping around his neck and the sweetness of her kisses.

Contented, Matthew closed his eyes and began to dream of Annabelle.

Thirty-Five

"They have hung my mother. Curse them! In every way curse them! …they are all hung, and the rest have been sent to the Dry Tortugas. But, my mother! Curse them! I curse them all!"

John H. Surratt

Rosswood Plantation
July 14, 1865

*M*atthew quickened his pace. Did he recognize this bend? If he was correct, then the plantation road into Rosswood would be just beyond this turn. After spending an extra two days stuck in Jackson working for Jim before he'd finally received his pay, Matthew found he'd reached the end of his patience.

Jim must have recognized it as well. He'd been rather pale when he'd handed over Matthew's pay. Probably because Matthew had calmly refused to release the man's collar until he did so.

Thankfully, the telegram he'd sent to Mrs. Smith in New York would already be two days received. He'd thought himself only a day's ride from Rosswood, so he had chosen not to send word to Lorman. A mistake, it seemed, since not only had he labored longer for Jim than anticipated but he had also encountered numerous delays on the ride here. After the wheel spoke broke on the rickety wagon belonging to the haggard man he'd paid to bring him here, Matthew had leapt from the cart and left the man to his own mending. If he hurried, he could make it to Rosswood on foot before the day's light dissipated and the fireflies took flight.

There! The bend in the road revealed the tree-lined passage into Rosswood and to his beloved's arms. Matthew broke into a trot and churned up red dust underneath his feet. After weeks of frustration and waiting, he'd finally be reunited with the woman he prayed never to be parted from again.

He jogged past the markers that would forever remind them that the war had not left Rosswood untouched. The grand columns of the house beckoned him home.

As his eyes dropped from the columns to the expanse of the front porch, his smile faltered and his feet slowed.

By the front door stood his bride with a soft smile on her lips and her hand on a Yankee's sleeve. A soldier whose embrace she'd already known.

Annabelle offered Joshua a tempered smile, hoping that he would soon be on his way. She was once again indebted to him. He'd sent the soldiers away despite their claims that all homes were opened to them. If it hadn't been for Joshua Grierson, she feared poor George would have lost all of his senses and

Michael would have exploded from the pressures building inside of him.

"I received word from Washington stating that this land belongs to you, by way of thanks for the services rendered to the Union, no matter what you decide on…other matters."

Granted not to any man, but hers alone? She placed a hand at her heart. "Oh, Joshua! That's wonderful news!"

"I'm glad to be of service again," Joshua said with a grin. His eyes bored into hers. "I'll be near for as long as you need me."

She shifted. "Weren't you going to another post?"

He thrust his hands into his pockets and looked down at his boots. "I requested the transfer wait until I was certain things were settled for you here."

Annabelle stepped closer and placed a hand on his arm, trying to choose gentle words. "I'm grateful for all you've done. You have been a good friend, Joshua."

His features saddened, as though knowing what the rest of her words would hold.

"But you do know that's all that will ever exist between us, don't you?"

His eyes twinkled. "But we aren't yet certain that your situation will change…" His words trailed off and he turned to look toward the garden.

Annabelle followed his gaze and her heart nearly came to a halt. There at the wrought iron gate stood the man she'd waited on—the one who'd taken weeks in coming. Her world came to a halt. Matthew's sharp eyes leveled on Joshua.

Annabelle dropped her hand off Joshua's arm and crossed to the stairs. She had to stop and place her hand on the column to support knees that threatened to buckle. Matthew shifted his gaze and stared at her. Weeks of beard grew on his cheeks. She frowned. Below his tightened jaw, the skin seemed yellowed, as though from a fading bruise.

Then the vein in his neck bulged, warning Annabelle of the anger that simmered just below the surface. Understanding dawned, and she feared the jealousy that had caused him to lash out at her uncle would be unleashed on Joshua.

Matthew breathed deeply and released the tension in his face. Then he opened the gate and followed the brick path through the small garden and to the bottom of the stairs. He looked up at her with hope and longing, tearing at her armored heart.

Her pulse pounded in her ears. She longed to fling herself into his arms, but the anger she'd allowed to take a bit more of her each day glued her feet to the floor.

"Where have you been?" Her words leapt out with the fierceness of a viper, and she regretted the pained expression they caused on his face.

"I left the day after the trial ended, as soon as the council went to discussions."

Annabelle wrapped her arms around herself. "That was weeks ago! The trains are poor, but not so much as that. Why did you dally?"

"It was because—"

She took two steps closer to him and cut off his words. "Because you had things to think about, Matthew? Because you think you're the only one who suffered great wounds and you thought you'd lick them in solitude?"

He opened his mouth, but she forged on. Pent-up frustration pouring from her tattered heart.

"How quickly you forgot your commitment. One stab at your pride and you withdraw." She flung a hand back toward Joshua. "Even now you stand there with accusation in your eyes, thinking things of me that I've never given you cause to believe."

Regret flashed in his eyes and he lowered his head. "I don't think such things of you. I admit it's hard for me to see you look at any man with affection, but I believe your heart belongs to me."

At her silence, he snatched his head up.

"Does it still belong to me, Annabelle? Or have I ruined what is most precious to me?"

Joshua cleared his throat and Matthew turned darkened eyes on him. Annabelle's words lodged in her throat.

"Perhaps I should leave you two in privacy." Joshua nodded toward Matthew. "Your betrothed, I assume?"

"He is."

"I'll honor what I told you, should you still wish it."

"Thank you. I'll send word tomorrow."

Joshua tipped his hat and then skirted around Matthew without bothering with the pretense of unwelcome pleasantries. Annabelle watched him stride through the garden, then retrieve his horse from the chinaberry tree and mount it.

Matthew took her hand, and only then did she notice it trembled. "I have much to ask forgiveness for. I was so caught up in the emotions that fought within me that I abandoned what I hold most dear."

The gentle way he ran his fingers across the back of her hand threatened to undo her. She forced strength into her words. "I don't know how we'll build a marriage that way."

More of her anger melted underneath the love that radiated from his eyes. "I've found peace, my love. The Lord has changed me. I pray that you'll give me a lifetime to prove my love to you and show you that I'll strive to never again leave your side."

The tears she'd tried to withhold slipped down her cheeks. She threw herself into his arms, and he enveloped her in his strength.

"I missed you."

He buried his face into her neck, whispering endearments and promises of a lifetime of love. After a time, she pulled her face away. "Is that what took you so long, the time spent discovering the peace of the Creator?"

His forehead creased. "No. Didn't you receive my letter? I sent it not long after you returned to Rosswood, telling you of how I met my Savior in truth and found reprieve from the dreams that haunted me."

Her breath caught. "I haven't heard anything from you since that day outside the trial, when you told me to go home."

He pulled her tighter, and a thrill at how well their bodies fit against one another pulsed through her. "I'm truly sorry for all that I made you endure."

She snaked a hand around his neck and loosed the hair from its tie, running her fingers through its lengths.

Matthew grimaced. "I'll cut it into a more fashionable style before we wed."

A smile tugged on her lips. "Actually," she said as she slipped her fingers into the hair at his nape, "I rather prefer it this way."

Matthew chuckled, a husky sound that warmed places deep within her. "Then if pleases you, my lady, so it shall remain."

He placed his forehead on hers, and she knew he meant to kiss her. Still, there was one thing she had to know. If only to put to rest all the wayward thoughts her mind had conjured in Matthew's absence. She pulled back. "If not for that, then why have you been so long in coming to me?"

Something flashed in his eyes she did not understand. "David O'Malley attacked me on the train ride from Washington. He strangled me, and then he held me prisoner in a cellar of a deserted cabin."

Annabelle gasped. "Oh, Matthew! Forgive me. I thought..." She shook her head. Why had she thought the worst of him? Here she'd been growing in her anger and blaming him for the pain that swelled within her. She'd thought he'd dallied for pleasure's sake or because he sought a way to break his betrothal. Shame washed over her. Instead, he'd been trying to get to her and had been in danger. Tears welled anew.

Matthew wiped a hot tear from her cheek. "There's nothing to forgive. You had every cause to be fearful and angry."

"What happened? How did you break free?"

He ran his fingers up the nape of her neck, releasing pins. His eyes held sadness. "He tried to attack me but wound up injuring himself instead. I tried to save him, but—" He shook his head.

Annabelle blinked at him, not knowing what to say. He tugged his hand until the last of her pins gave way and he was able to pull his fingers through the hair that now tumbled down past her waist. "At least in the end he found peace and died with the hope of seeing his family in heaven."

There were more questions she wanted to ask, but they could wait. The way he was looking at her…

Matthew pressed his lips to hers, and all Annabelle's questions drifted away. Matthew was home, and she was in his arms. The concerns of life melted beneath the heat rising in her chest. She sighed against his lips, and with a little groan he deepened the kiss.

Something stirred within her, and when he finally pulled away, they were both breathing heavily. Matthew rested his head on hers. "I think the wedding needs to come soon." The huskiness in his voice reminded her that she still needed to press Peggy about what all transpired on a bride's wedding night. She gave a nervous laugh. "Well, we need only—"

Her words were interrupted by an excited shout, and then George was nearly upon them. She stepped away from Matthew, pleased by the longing that lingered in his eyes.

Reluctantly, he turned to embrace his brother, and Annabelle smiled at the affection between them.

"Anna!" Michael bustled out of the house.

Just then she remembered that Matthew had loosed her hair from its confines. Heat seared into her cheeks.

Michael gripped her arm, his seething voice slithering into her ear. "What's the meaning of this? I'll not allow you to make yourself a harlot."

Her mouth fell open, but before she could respond, Peggy appeared behind him. "Don't you go saying that to my girl! She ain't no harlot."

Michael's eyes widened so far that they seemed to bulge. Matthew stiffened, but George laid a hand on his arm and shook his head. Matthew glanced at Annabelle, but then humor twinkled in his eyes and he looked back at Peggy.

Peggy pointed a finger at Michael, who had not yet recovered from his shock. "She's going to marry the captain."

Michael's face reddened. "I haven't given permission for her to wed that drunkard."

Matthew made a low sound in his throat, but once again his brother's pressure on his arm stayed him.

Peggy cocked her head. "She don't need your permission."

"You…you forget your place!"

Peggy put her hands on her hips. "Nope. I know my place. Do you know yours?"

Michael reddened further, though Annabelle hadn't thought it possible. She placed her hand on Michael's arm. "Though I appreciate all you've done for me and I know your concern is only out of your care for me, I've made my choice. Matthew is a good man, and he'll be a good husband for me."

Michael cast a derisive look at Matthew. "Look at him. Not only a drunkard, but hardly a gentleman."

The muscle in Matthew's jaw ticked, and he pulled out of George's grasp. Annabelle's breath caught. Would he display a temper that would only further antagonize her uncle?

Dressed in a coarse shirt without vest or cravat, he did indeed look more like a laborer than a gentleman. Though when he straightened himself and regarded her uncle with the calm assurance of one used to being in command of others, his attire couldn't have seemed more out of place. "Mr. Ross. My current appearance aside, and with my apologies for the unfortunate circumstances that caused my delay in coming, I assure you that your assessment of me is incorrect."

"Is it? I remember tales of you before the war. My niece

isn't the first to garner your attentions. How long before you tire of her as well?"

Matthew shook his head. "I'll never tire of her. I'll make her my wife and spend every day of my life in devotion to her and her alone."

"And what of your fondness for the drink?"

"I've learned to avoid what tempts me. I ask your forgiveness for my unacceptable behavior in Washington." Matthew stepped over to Annabelle and took her hand. "Just as I'm no longer the wayward youth I was before the war, neither am I the heavily burdened man I was in the days following it."

Annabelle smiled up at him, and he looked down on her with eyes that brimmed with sincerity.

Michael turned to Annabelle. "You believe this to be true?"

She eased closer into Matthew's side. "I do. Father did well all those years ago when he chose Matthew as a suitor for me. My heart will never belong to another."

Michael looked around at those gathered against him and pinched the bridge of his nose. "I won't be able to stop you, will I?"

Peggy harrumphed, but Michael ignored her.

Annabelle beamed up at Matthew. "No, Uncle. You shall not."

Matthew's brows puckered. "Though I do wish to have your blessing, sir. Family is of utmost importance, and Annabelle and I would want you to visit often from Natchez."

Something lit in Michael's eyes. Annabelle couldn't tell if it came from respect, gratitude, or relief. Regardless, Michael finally smiled and then clapped Matthew on the shoulder. "You seem to have developed into a man of character. So I'll give my blessing upon this union—"

"Oh, Uncle Michael, thank you!" Annabelle interrupted.

He ignored her and continued. "But if I ever suspect you don't treat my niece with the utmost devotion, or if you allow my family's lands to fall to squalor…"

"You have my word. I'll love Annabelle well and throw all of my strength into restoring her home for her."

Annabelle glanced around at the people she loved, and joy bubbled within her.

Matthew slipped his arm around her waist. "I've already sent word to your grandmother to come with the utmost haste, and to my mother at Westerly. As soon as they arrive, I shall make you my bride."

She pushed up on her toes and pressed her lips to his, ignoring the gasps and grumbles of those around her. All that mattered was this wonderful man, whom she loved more with each day that dawned.

Thirty-Six

"All has been prepared for me to go to Europe, and I shall therefore bid a long farewell to that country for which I have risked so much—and in vain. I do not wish to die yet—I desire to live if only to make some parties suffer for having murdered my mother."

John H. Surratt

Rosswood Plantation
July 30, 1865

George paced the perimeter of his room yet again, but passing the window once more, he found that the carriage had still not arrived. He wiped the sweat from his palms. Over and again he'd played out what he would say, and over and again he'd sought a better way.

He turned from the window. Better to find his knees than to keep up this infernal, useless pacing. But though George tried to pray, his thoughts wouldn't stay on a single trajectory. Try as he might to form his anxiety into eloquent words worthy of the Almighty's ear, they crumbled into sputtering pleas for the impossible. Once he stopped trying to be formal, however, he found that the simple outpouring of his heart proved the most productive. Finally, his jumbled thoughts slowed and the anxious words on his lips subsided.

The crunch of wheels drew his head up, and George finished his "amen" as he scrambled back to the window. There! Just beyond the garden wall, at the end of the brick walk, a fine black carriage waited.

George gripped the windowsill and stared below as the driver opened the door and helped Mrs. Smith down the step. She fluttered about, waving her hands and no doubt giving orders.

People emerged from the house, and in a flash of yellow fabric Annabelle embraced her grandmother. George's eyes lingered on the carriage. What if she hadn't come?

For two weeks he'd remained at Rosswood anticipating that she would come south with Mrs. Smith. Matthew, having known George's mind, had sent word to New York before he'd even made it to Rosswood. He'd requested that Mrs. Smith come at once and that she be sure to bring Lilly along.

Movement stirred at the carriage door, and his pulse quickened. A man poked his head from the carriage and stepped down. He shielded his eyes from the sun and looked up at the house. George frowned. The man removed a bowler hat and ran his hand through sandy hair, then replaced the cap and turned back toward the carriage and extended his hand.

A delicate set of fingers slipped into the man's waiting hand, followed by the emerging of the radiant beauty George had ached to see. She stepped out in a blue and green gown and gave a polite nod to the man as she removed her hand from his. George slumped against the window frame.

She'd come. Had she wanted to or had she come only at the

insistence of her employer? George glanced back at Mrs. Smith, who chattered to Matthew. George smiled, despite the tightness in his chest. He'd never seen his brother this happy.

Would he ever have what his brother had found? Lilly turned back to the carriage as a little boy scrambled down, his cherub face alight with excitement. Unable to stay away any longer, George hurried from his room and down the stairs to the front hall.

George stepped outside into the heat of another July day, but the fire within him had nothing to do with the sweltering weather. He came down the steps and through the garden, watching Lilly while she had yet to notice him. She wore her hair swept back from her face, pinned in an elaborate style that left a spiral of ebony hanging down the curve of her neck.

Suddenly an excited squeal pierced the chatter of the adults, and George looked down to see little Frankie running for him with outstretched hands. George dropped to one knee, and Frankie leapt into his arms.

"Orge!"

George laughed at the way the boy said his name and hefted the little one up.

"Toss!"

Unable to resist the sweet moment, George gripped the boy beneath the arms and threw him in the air. Frankie laughed, and George tossed him a second time, catching the boy and then situating him in his arms.

"Why, Frankie, I believe you've grown since last I saw you! You're as big as a horse."

The little boy grinned, but then his face puckered. "Long time, Orge. Where you go?"

George looked up to see everyone had turned to watch them. His gaze slid over the others and landed on Lilly. Her hand was pressed to her throat, and the tension on her face sent a pang through him.

Frankie patted his cheek with chubby hands. "Like Orge."

George smiled. "I like you as well, Frankie. I've missed you."

Frankie's cheeks dimpled and his dark curls stirred in the breeze. "Like Momma, too, Orge?"

George glanced up at Lilly and saw her eyes widen. He held her gaze. "Yes, Frankie. I like your mother a great deal."

He placed the boy back on his feet and watched him scurry off to pluck one of Annabelle's struggling roses. He presented it to Lilly. She turned away from George and focused on the boy, and the quiet that had hung over the group as they watched George and Lilly's exchange transformed into awkwardness.

George tore his eyes away from Lilly to find Mrs. Smith watching him intently, the lines around her mouth tight. He dipped his chin to her, but she didn't return the acknowledgment.

Matthew spoke up, cutting through the tension. "George! Come and meet Mr. Jenkins. He's performing the ceremony for us."

George had forgotten all about the man who had come with Lilly and Mrs. Smith. He stepped forward to shake the man's hand. "A pleasure, preacher. My brother's most eager to be wed."

Annabelle laughed, and Matthew smiled at her. Laughter came more easily to them both these days.

"Pleased to meet you, sir," the preacher said, giving

George's hand a firm pump. "Yes, I find most grooms to be of the eager sort." A grin played under the man's moustache, and George found him an easy fellow to like.

"Did you come all the way from New York?"

Jenkins shook his head. "No, I came from Natchez. My father and Mr. Smith were good friends, and when Mrs. Smith requested I come, I made plans to meet her in Lorman and ride out with her."

Matthew clapped the man on the shoulder, and he stumbled slightly. Matthew gripped him to keep the spindly man from falling forward. "We're most grateful, Mr. Jenkins. I'm afraid Rosswood has little left to offer by way of comforts, but you're welcome to stay for as long as you like."

After enduring a few more moments of necessary pleasantries and the disgruntled stares of Annabelle's grandmother, George and Matthew carried the trunks and baggage upstairs. On the third trip, George began to wonder if Mrs. Smith planned on moving into Rosswood. By the time he and Matthew had hefted the final trunk to the upper hall, George heard Michael's voice down below.

Downstairs, a very stiff looking Mrs. Smith addressed an even more uncomfortable looking Mr. Ross.

Michael glanced at Annabelle, who looked up at him imploringly. His eyes narrowed, but a polite smile tempered his expression. "Welcome to Rosswood, Mrs. Smith. I trust you'll find your stay tolerable. I fear we cannot offer anything up to your standards."

Mrs. Smith regarded him evenly. "Come now, Michael. Let's find common ground on our affections for Annabelle and not continue to add to animosities better left in the past."

Michael blanched. "My niece speaks most highly of you." Then with an unexpected smile, he turned up a palm. "Let's begin anew."

Mrs. Smith grinned. "That would please me greatly."

They turned away with Annabelle, Mrs. Smith clicking her tongue over the state of the house.

Matthew leaned close to George's ear. "I'll see to the others and the little one with a tour around Rosswood. Perhaps you and Lilly might find a moment alone on the porch?"

He and Matthew had spoken at length about a great many things these past days, Lilly chiefly among them. Bolstering more courage than he'd needed for battle, he gave Matthew a grateful look. Lilly stood awkwardly by the front door, seeming to be in deep thought about what to do with a stack of crates that Mrs. Smith had made them leave in the hall.

"Lilly?"

She looked up at him, a spark of pain in her eyes. She shook her head and tried to step around him, but George grabbed her arm.

She looked down at his hand. "Please release me, Mr. Daniels. I didn't wish to come here, and it'd be easier to endure if you wouldn't presume to touch me."

George slid his fingers off the smooth fabric of her dress and hung his head. She wanted nothing to do with him. "Please, I must beg your forgiveness. Shock rendered me a fool. I know you may always look at me with disdain, but I need you to know the depth of my regrets. If nothing else, you must know that the man before you isn't the same one who was too much of a coward to stop you from leaving that night."

She drew a shuddering breath, and he nodded toward the

door. "Could you give me only a few moments? And then if you wish it, I'll never impose on you again."

The cool, impassive expression that had ruled her features when they'd first met slid onto her face once more, but her eyes spoke of turmoil. Finally, after a tiny dip of her chin that he might not have noticed had he not been watching her closely, he took her elbow and guided her through the door and onto the front porch.

"Would you like to sit?" George asked, gesturing toward the crude furniture.

Her delicate eyebrows dipped. "Not the furnishings I would expect at a plantation."

George rubbed the back of his neck. "I'm not much of a carpenter. These makeshift seats are the best I could manage."

She tilted her head. "*You* made these?"

"Yes, though I'm not sure if I should claim credit or blame for them."

Lilly stared at him a moment. "A plantation master roughing up his hands on pitiful log seating."

Her words held a bite he knew he deserved. He looked at his hands. "These hands haven't been the ones of a privileged plantation son for some time. They've seen war and the long days of labor in prison, constructing coffins to lay my friends inside."

Her face had softened. She seemed as though she might reach a hand to him but thought better of it. "I'm sorry for the hardships you faced."

He clasped his hands behind his back. "They are nothing compared to the life you must have endured. I can understand fully why you would distrust men such as me."

She began to shake her head but then stopped. "Yes, indeed."

George swallowed. "Lilly, I want so much to tell you that things have changed—that this world is different now—but it hasn't changed in so many ways that matter."

"I know." Her words were soft, laced with regret and pain that George desperately wanted to erase.

He stepped closer, causing her to have to tilt her chin to look up at him. Her lashes fluttered, but she didn't look away. "I'm glad of your heritage, Lilly."

Her mouth fell open. "But…but…you…"

He took her shoulders in his hands. "I was wrong. I was brought up in a world where we were taught that some people were less than others simply because of the tone of their skin." A smile tugged at his lips. "The Almighty had a way of showing me just how wrong I was about that."

Her lips parted. He longed to know what their softness would feel like beneath his. He forced his eyes back up to hers. "I wanted to come to you but gave my word to my brother that I'd stay with Annabelle until he arrived at Rosswood. Once he did, he promised me that Mrs. Smith would bring you down with her."

She turned her face away, but not before he caught the shine of tears in her eyes. George reached up and cupped her chin, gently turning her to face him once more.

"Had you not, I would have come to you. Had you refused to see me, I would have waited outside your door until you did. You are beautiful, Lilly. And not only because of the tones of your skin, a golden glow I've admired since first I laid eyes on you. But you're beautiful because you are strong and kind. I love you, Lilly, both inside and out."

She lifted her lashes and turned her deep brown eyes on him, her breath quick.

"I'd give most anything to have reacted differently. I lie awake every night wishing I had gone after you. Though I would have understood if you refused to see me again, I knew I must beg you for forgiveness for my foolishness or I'd live forever in regret."

"I…" her voice wavered. "I forgive you."

Peace swelled through him. "Thank you, my love."

Her breath caught, and he offered a sad smile. "My battered heart has never loved any but you, Lilly. Nor shall it ever."

"But…"

He placed a finger on her lips. "I know you cannot return my affections, not after what I did to you. I ask only that you allow me to let you know how I feel."

She reached up and brushed away his hand. "May I speak now, George?"

The use of his name upon her lips constricted his chest so that all he could do was nod.

She drew a long breath and let it out slowly. "I've tried relentlessly to forget you. To hate you even. But even as I prayed my love for you would go away, it seemed those prayers only made the feelings grow. And Frankie…" She gave a small shrug. "Oh, but that boy. He once even asked me if you were his papa."

George stared, hardly able to believe her. "I'd love nothing more than to be his papa. To be a husband to you, and a father to him."

Tears welled and slid down her cheeks. "Even knowing that

we're both of mixed descent?"

"I'm thankful for the people who brought you into this world, and for the man who gave you Frankie. Without them, neither of you would be who you are."

The tears surged again, and George wrapped his arms around her. Lilly allowed him to pull her close and stroke her back as her shoulders shook. Regretting all the pain he'd caused, he buried his face into her soft scent and spoke against the tickle of her hair. "Ah, love, I don't want you to cry."

She sniffled against him and then pulled back. "I, too, must ask your forgiveness."

He stroked her cheek, unable to believe she'd done anything that required forgiveness. "Whatever for?"

She looked away. "I should have told you the truth from the start. I allowed myself to watch your affections grow, knowing I hadn't been honest with you."

He gazed down at her. "There's nothing to forgive. I know why you did it."

She pressed her cheek into his hand. "I didn't tell you because I thought if you didn't know, if no one ever knew, then I might have a chance with you."

His chest constricted. "It doesn't matter who knows."

She shook her head. "We both know that isn't true."

George let emotions he'd tried to bury burn in his eyes. "No, it is true. I never thought I'd be able to ask again." He took a deep breath. "Lilly, if you'd have me, if you'd give me a lifetime to show you that I can be a good man for you and Frankie, I'd like to ask you to be my wife. No matter what anyone might have to say against us."

She sucked in a breath, more tears welling in her eyes. "It's not possible."

He'd expected her response, but the words still pierced.

"I love you, but we'll never be accepted."

George pulled away and clenched his hands. "I don't care what others think of us. Heaven help any man who dares to try to stand between me and my family."

"But...but..."

George knew she sorted through the same reasons against their union that had threatened to bury him. He took her face in his hands, wiping away her tears with his thumbs. "I'll fight for us, Lilly. Let them say what they will."

She parted her lips, and he lowered his forehead to hers. "I vow to protect you, honor you, and love you until the last breath leaves my body. I'll love your son as my son, and I'll make him the heir to Westerly. Forget every reason that's against us. Our love matters more. Be my wife, Lilly, and make my life whole."

She closed her eyes, her feather-like lashes splaying against her cheeks, and then in one startling, breathtaking moment, she lifted her chin and pressed her lips to his.

Thirty-Seven

"In the end, it is not the years in your life that count. It's
the life in your years."
Abraham Lincoln

Rosswood Plantation
August 9, 1865

Annabelle wrapped her arms around Molly's neck. "Oh,
how I have missed you!"

Her friend patted her shoulder and pulled back. "I've missed
you as well." She frowned. "Though I'd always thought I would
have been able to make you the most stunning gown in the
South for your wedding day."

Annabelle looked down at her rose red dress with a paisley
print that covered every inch of the fabric from the hem to the
pagoda sleeves. "Yes, but this one does match Matthew's
cravat."

"Ha! But it's not a wedding gown."

"I agree," Eudora said, tugging at the black silk around her
neck. "But since my granddaughter simply wouldn't wait to have
one made, it'll have to do." She fanned her face and huffed.
"How you survive this heat I'll never know."

"Worst of the heat done passed, Mrs. Smith," Peggy said. "Evening be comin' soon."

Annabelle twisted the ring on her finger. An evening wedding, a feast with the abundance of supplies Eudora had brought, and then she and Matthew would retire back to this room, the room her father had shared with her mother.

Eudora laughed and guided Annabelle to sit at the dressing chair. "Breathe, girl. You look as white as winter snow."

Annabelle looked at her reflection in the polished mirror and once again marveled at the furnishings Grandmother had bought and had delivered to Rosswood. The house was still sparse, but the new dining room set had been put into place and stocked with wares. The master's chamber boasted a blue rug, a finely crafted armoire and bureau, a dressing table and screen, and a massive canopy bed to replace the one that had been stolen. Annabelle eyed the thick covering across it and wondered if she'd need a stool to climb up.

She'd thus far stayed in her own chamber, not being allowed inside this one until Eudora had declared it presentable yesterday. She'd said that the new couple would need both a personal sanctuary and a place to host, and so her wedding gift to them would be the bedroom and dining furnishings.

Matthew, knowing her as he did, had given her seeds as a wedding present. A wagon stacked with sacks of them so they could replant the fields.

The door opened and Lilly came in, her nervous fingers playing with the ruffles on her bright yellow gown. Annabelle jumped to her feet, ignoring Peggy's yelp. She'd been about to start fussing with Annabelle's hair just as Lilly entered.

"Lilly! You look stunning." Annabelle took the woman's

hands and guided her deeper into the room. "Peggy was about to do my hair. Then she'll work on yours."

Lilly shifted. "Are you sure about this?"

Annabelle offered a reassuring smile, her tone playful. "How many times must I answer that question before you'll stop asking it?"

Lilly glanced at Eudora. "But this is your wedding day."

Annabelle squeezed her hand. "And nothing would please Matthew and me more than to have you and George speak vows next to us."

Worry tightened Lilly's mouth, and Annabelle wondered if it had something to do with the letter that had arrived by courier from Westerly. Matthew and George's mother hadn't approved of George's choice to marry Lilly—since he had been honest about her heritage—or Matthew's support of it. Thus, she declared she wouldn't attend the wedding. She'd also said that if George defied her and returned to Westerly with Lilly, she'd go live with her sister in Tupelo. Annabelle didn't know what reply George sent back with Eudora's messenger, but she knew it hadn't deterred his course.

"Besides," Eudora quipped, "we're all already here. And I doubt we'll be able to pry Annabelle and Matthew from Rosswood anytime soon. Best go on and get married while everyone's gathered and the preacher's on hand."

Lilly gaped at her, then snapped her mouth closed. She offered no further argument and waited quietly for her turn under Peggy's care.

In another hour, they were ready—Annabelle having honored Matthew's request to pin up only half of her hair, leaving the remaining length to fall down her back in a cascade of curls.

Who cared if it was a little improper?

The group of excited women emerged from the house. Out front, the slightly cooler breeze of evening swept across the garden, carrying with it the scent of roses.

Michael took Annabelle's arm, and together they walked down the front steps. Behind them, Eudora followed with Lilly, trailed by Molly, then Peggy with Frankie on her hip.

Near the wrought iron gate, the preacher stood with Matthew on his right and George on his left. Annabelle took in the sight of the man who would soon be her husband. Dressed in a fine broadcloth suit—a gift from Eudora that fit him splendidly—with a deep red cravat, he stood with his feet set apart and his hands behind his back like a man who'd forgotten he was no longer a soldier.

His face free from stubble, his broad mouth turned up at the sight of her, sending her heart fluttering. His long hair had been pulled back and secured.

Annabelle flashed him a brilliant smile and relished the look of appreciation in his eyes.

The witnesses took their seats on mismatched chairs and benches by Momma's roses. As they came to a stop, Annabelle gave Michael's arm a squeeze. "I thank you, dearest Uncle, for all you've done for me."

He patted her hand, and when he spoke, the emotion in his voice surprised her. "I'm glad you'll be happy. Don't forget about your old bachelor uncle, eh?"

She smiled. "We'll expect you to stay with us often."

He patted her fingers again and then took his seat. Annabelle stepped to Matthew's side and watched Eudora embrace Lilly, whispering something in her ear. Lilly's lips turned up and she gave a nod. Lilly took George's hand.

Matthew took both of Annabelle's hands, rubbing his fingers over her knuckles. Her heart swelled as she stared into eyes that spoke promises that made her knees quiver.

Mr. Jenkins addressed the gathering. "We come here today to bear witness to the joining of souls before our Holy God. Whereas a man shall leave his father and mother and be cleaved to his wife." He shifted his feet to face Annabelle and Matthew.

"Mr. Matthew Daniels, do you take Miss Annabelle Ross to be your own, to be ever satisfied with the wife of your youth, the only woman to whom you'll give yourself for as long as she shall live? Do you promise to protect her, provide for her, and love her as Christ loved the church, giving Himself up for her?"

Matthew squeezed her hands. "Yes, I do."

Mr. Jenkins turned to Annabelle, "Miss Ross, do you pledge to take this man as your husband—to respect him, follow him as he leads you in love, and to be his and his alone for all the days of his life? Do you promise to keep his home and tend his children, should God bless you with them?"

Annabelle squeezed Matthew's hands and spoke from the love overflowing from her heart. "Yes, this I vow."

Mr. Jenkins smiled at them and then turned to George and Lilly, repeating the same words and garnering the same promises from them. George's voice was thick with emotion, and Lilly paid no heed to the tears that flowed down her cheeks and into her radiant smile.

Annabelle pressed close into Matthew's side, saying a prayer of thanks for the love that filled Rosswood on this day.

When George and Lilly completed their vows, Mr. Jenkins lifted his hands. "Then with the covenant of the vows you have spoken and by the authority granted to me by the Father, Son, and Holy Ghost," he said, gesturing to Annabelle and Matthew, "I declare you Mr. and Mrs. Daniels." He swung his gaze to George and Lilly. "And Mr. and Mrs. Daniels. Gentlemen, you may kiss your brides!"

Before the final word had even escaped the preacher's lips, Matthew wrapped his arms around Annabelle's waist. He tipped her back, and she gasped as his face hovered over hers. "Our first kiss, Mrs. Daniels," he said with a husky voice, the warmth of his breath upon her lips.

"One of many, Captain."

His eyes glimmered and his lips met hers, spreading heat through her chest and all the way to her toes. When he set her right again, her cheeks flushed. She looked at Peggy, who had both hands clasped at her chin, her tears of joy mingling with her smile.

The loved ones who were gathered clapped their hands, sending sounds of celebration into the day's fading light.

"One more thing, preacher, if I may," George called out, causing everyone to turn. When they quieted, he gestured to Peggy.

"Oh!" She lurched to her feet. "Hang on."

Annabelle looked at Lilly for explanation, but the other woman seemed confused.

Peggy bustled over to the house and plucked something from the porch. She scurried back toward the couples. Annabelle frowned. What on earth did Peggy need with a broom? This was hardly the time to be cleaning.

Peggy hurried forward and extended the offering to George, who accepted it with a slight bow. "Thank you, Peggy."

She beamed at him, flashed a smile at Annabelle, and then returned to her place next to Eudora, who seemed to know what was going on.

George looked at his bride. "In order to honor *all* the traditions and customs of our families, I asked Peggy to provide us with a broom."

Lilly placed a hand to her throat. "Oh, George…"

He tossed it down in front of them, took her hand, and together they jumped over it. Peggy and Eudora clapped, and Frankie—who could be contained no longer—ran forward to latch onto his mother's legs.

He turned his cherub cheeks up to Lilly. "Mama, do I have a papa now?"

Lilly's eyes shimmered. "Yes, baby. Yes, you do."

The three of them embraced, and Annabelle turned to look at the happiness on the face of the man she loved. Sensing her gaze, Matthew turned his eyes back to Annabelle, the joy there deepening into something much more.

He leaned close to her ear. "I've waited what feels like years. I'm most eager to finish our marital rights."

Heat flooded Annabelle's face. "I'm afraid you'll have to wait until after we've eaten what Peggy has prepared." She laughed. "Or we'll never hear the end of it."

Matthew groaned, and she slowly slid her hand up his sleeve, offering a smile that hinted that she looked forward to the time as well.

Matthew took her arm and led the way back inside to the dining room. The rose-scented breeze drifted through the dining room windows and mingled with the smells of the food that nearly overflowed their table.

Annabelle took her place next to her husband at one end of the finely polished table. George and Lilly sat at the other end, and the rest of the group filled in around the sides. She ran her hand across the inlaid wood. A different pattern from what Father's had been, but every bit as beautiful. At least, as much as she could see of it underneath the platters of food clustered in the center.

Annabelle had insisted that Peggy not serve them, but rather they all passed around the platters so that they could serve themselves. Though it all smelled heavenly, Annabelle found her stomach danced too much for her to enjoy more than a few bites. Even Matthew picked at his plate, his usual robust appetite absent.

When the meal came to an end and they had passed around Peggy's chocolate pie, Matthew rose and extended his hand to Annabelle. She placed her hand in his, noticing how warm it felt beneath her fingers.

He inclined his head to their guests. "I thank you all for this time of fellowship, laughter, and good food, but it's time I carry my bride to our chamber."

Annabelle looked to Lilly, who gave her a knowing smile and then rose as well, gesturing for George to follow. The look on his face might have been comical if not for the fact that Annabelle now had an idea about the meaning of the look that passed between George and his bride. Having both been wed before, they knew the secrets of what went on between husband and wife.

Something she was soon to discover. Matthew took her hand, gently tugged her away from the table, and scooped her into his arms. She laughed as her feet were swept off the floor, accompanied by the laughs of those in attendance. Matthew nodded to the others, and then his long strides whisked her from the room. In a matter of heartbeats, he sat her down in their new chamber.

Flustered, Annabelle sought a match to light the lantern—something for her nervous hands to do. Behind her, Matthew made a low noise in his throat, and then his arms were around her waist. She tilted her head to the side, the match falling from her fingers.

He trailed soft kisses up her neck and to the soft spot behind her ear, and she trembled.

The next morning Annabelle awoke in a tangle of sheets, her head resting on the hard muscles of Matthew's chest. He breathed evenly, the golden hair she'd asked him not to cut splayed out across the pillow. She let her gaze wander over him.

"Good morning."

Annabelle startled, tearing her gaze back to his face.

Amused, he lifted his hand to tangle his fingers in her loose hair. "Like what you see?"

Heat flushed through her, but she gave him a coy smile. "Quite."

His eyes glinted and he drew her closer.

An hour later they emerged from their room to greet a day that had already grown hot. They opened the door at the end of the upper hall and stepped out onto the balcony to catch the breeze. Matthew wrapped his arm around Annabelle's shoulders and drew her close, gesturing to the land below. "Soon, we will see these fields green once more, sprouting with new crops."

She wrapped her arms around his waist and looked out over

the land she loved, dreaming of seeing it restored. Heavy footsteps in the hall made them turn.

Peggy puffed out her cheeks, her hands on her hips. She stepped through the door and pointed a finger at them. "You two know what time it is?"

Annabelle glanced at Matthew. "No... I don't believe we do."

"It's past nine in the morning, that's what."

Annabelle stared at Peggy, confused.

Peggy huffed. "Y'all know you gonna *make* me serve you cold breakfast! Get on down them stairs before my biscuits go to waste!"

Matthew laughed. "Forgive us, Peggy. We'll be down in a moment."

They watched Peggy turn to go, mumbling something about them having no regard for good food.

Alone again, Matthew slipped his hand around Annabelle's waist. "Much as I'd like to skip breakfast and return you to our room, I think we best not risk her ire."

Annabelle laughed as they stepped inside the house. "No, best not do that." She looked up at him with a sly smile. "But perhaps after..."

Matthew pulled her close, his love for her gleaming in his eyes. "Yes, Mrs. Daniels, after."

Epilogue

Christmas, 1867

*A*nnabelle admired the decorations on the hearth as she placed a tray of candied yams on the table.

"Looks nice, don't it?" Peggy asked, stepping up beside her to deposit a basket of steaming rolls and a platter of smoked venison.

Annabelle placed a finger to her nose, hoping the mingling smells of such an array of food wouldn't turn her stomach.

Peggy lifted her eyebrows and gave Annabelle a look that made her wonder if she guessed Annabelle's secret. The corners of Peggy's mouth turned up. "I think some more of your guests arrived. Why don't you go on out to the hall and greet them?"

Grateful, Annabelle slipped from the room just as there was a knock at the front door. Matthew emerged from the parlor and in two strides reached the door before her. After a hearty laugh and manly shoulder slapping, Matthew stepped back from the door and ushered in a distinguished looking man with dark hair. The beautiful woman on his arm smiled brightly, her green gown the perfect complement to her peachy lips and mahogany hair.

Matthew gestured to his waiting wife. "Annabelle! Come meet my favorite cousin Charles Harper and his wife, Lydia!"

Annabelle stepped closer and welcomed the couple she'd heard a great deal about. "It's a pleasure to finally meet you both!"

A small figure suddenly burst through the door, ducking between the adults' legs and rushing headlong down the hall without pause.

"Robert!" Lydia scolded, lifting her skirts and hurrying to chase after the boy who turned and darted into the parlor.

"Hands full there, Charles?" Matthew asked.

His cousin chuckled. "More than you know." He grinned. "And I've just learned our family will grow once more."

Matthew slapped his cousin on the shoulder again, conveying his congratulations. By that time, Lydia emerged from the parlor with the pouting boy in tow. Warm air still much too temperate for December drifted through the open door. To think, Christmas Eve, and for the last week they'd only needed to stoke the hearths at night.

A large man filled the doorway, his height and width as imposing as Matthew's. He twisted a hat in his large hands, standing there awkwardly as a willowy woman several shades lighter than the man's ebony tones pushed past him.

"Don't just stand there gawkin', Noah," the woman scolded. "Help me get Lucas to come inside the house. He won't stop playin' with the carriage horses."

The big man nodded at her and scrambled back outside, looking relieved. Lydia, having deposited her energetic boy into Peggy's care in the dining room, took the woman's hand and pulled her closer, gesturing to Annabelle. "Ruth, this is

Annabelle, the bride of Charles's cousin Matthew."

The woman offered her a pretty smile. "Thank you for welcoming me and Noah into your home, ma'am."

Annabelle smiled. "I'm most pleased. George and Lilly should be here soon with their boy Frankie and baby Anna. I'm sure the children would love to play together." She lifted her eyebrows. "Perhaps that will help tempt your boy indoors?"

Ruth gave Lydia an appreciative look before speaking to Annabelle. "I reckon it would. Thank you, Mrs. Daniels."

"Please, Annabelle is fine." She nodded toward the stairs. "Come, let me show you to your rooms so your husbands will know where to bring your things."

Later that evening, once all their guests had arrived and settled, they gathered in the dining room and around the table Eudora had gifted them on their wedding day. Matthew took his place at the head of the table, and Annabelle sat to his right.

"We thank you all for joining us to celebrate the birth of the Savior. It's a great honor to have you all in our home," Matthew said, smiling at the guests.

Annabelle let her gaze drift over the faces seated at their table—George and Lilly, who smiled down at the sweet baby girl in her arms; Eudora and her new companion Violet; Peggy; Uncle Michael and the charming Miss Nettles—whom Annabelle suspected he might soon ask to be his bride; Charles and Lydia with their friends and plantation managers Noah and Ruth; and then finally the little boys, Frankie, Robert, and Lucas, who all seemed keen on finding mischief.

The meal was shared in a warmth of laughter and love, and Annabelle's heart swelled with the sounds of the family around her. The times of reconstruction had been hard on them all, and

Rosswood had experienced quite a few hardships. But in spite of all that war had brought, here in the love and warmth of family, Annabelle knew that the future held joy. Underneath the table, she slid her fingers across the velvet at her waist. The time had come to present Matthew with her gift.

As her husband called for an end to the meal, she placed a hand on his arm. "I'd like to give you a present."

The table quieted, and Matthew cocked his head. "I thought we'd exchange gifts in the morning."

She gave a sly smile. "I'd like to tell you about this one now."

In response to his curious expression, she patted his arm and rose to retrieve the small bundle she'd hidden in the china cabinet drawer. She'd wrapped it in a plain cotton cloth and secured it with a ribbon. She smiled at those gathered at the table, noting the way the women smiled knowingly and the men looked confused.

Annabelle placed the bundle in Matthew's waiting hands, and then stood by his side as he tugged the ribbon free. He pulled the cloth aside, and then slowly his fingers grasped what was folded inside. His shoulders lifted with a sudden intake of breath.

He unfolded the tiny gown and raised it up for the others to see.

"Oh!" Eudora clapped her hands.

As the others began to cheer, Matthew turned wide eyes on her. "A baby, Annabelle?"

She smiled, her heart swelling to the point she feared it would burst. After two years, it seemed the Lord had finally blessed them with new life. She nodded, her throat too tight for words.

"How long have you known?" he asked, looking at the tiny garment in his hands.

"A few weeks now. I wanted to wait to tell you until we were surrounded by family. I thought Christmas would be a good time."

Matthew stared at her, then gave a mighty shout and pulled her down into his lap. She laughed as he pressed his face against her hair. "It's the best of gifts, my love."

Before she could melt from embarrassment, he set her on her feet, and soon they were surrounded with the well wishes and congratulations of the others, wrapping them in a cocoon of happiness.

Matthew held tight to her hand, and she placed her fingers on the life within. A new little one to grow up at Rosswood.

Here they would build a new future for their child, free from the pains of war. And Annabelle prayed that in the generations that came after, ever would there be love and joy echoing within the halls of Rosswood.

If you enjoyed A Daring Pursuit, please take a moment to leave a quick online review. It helps me keep putting books in your hands!

If you would like to read more about Matthew's cousin Charles Harper, read his and Lydia's story in The Whistle Walk.

Historical Note

After the assassination of Abraham Lincoln, hundreds of people were taken in by the Washington City Police and held for questioning in the Old Capitol Prison—which citizens did attempt to burn. While the descriptions of the prison itself were by my own design, the events that happened within it are recorded in history.

The events that unfolded at the Surratt house, including the odd dress and the words spoken by Lewis Payne, are recorded in the testimony given by the detectives during the trial. I adjusted some of the dialogue of the historical figures in order to make the sentences easier for modern readers, but the statements are all in keeping with the trial transcripts. All of Payne's interactions with Mrs. Surratt as well as Mrs. Surratt's words with the detectives, are as they are recorded in the trial records.

The trial records also provided a valuable insight into the manhunt and capture of John Wilkes Booth. All of the manhunt events I used in this book are recorded there, including the interview with Jett and the scene of finding Booth in the barn. All the words by Conger and Baker, except some direct words to Matthew, are taken from their testimony at the trial. Words from the soldiers, the Garrett family, and Booth and Harold in this scene are as they are recorded in the trial records, as given on multiple accounts from those present. I found it fascinating that at one point Booth calls out to a Captain, declaring he knew him to be "an honorable man." Though I don't know the actual person he addressed, it seemed Matthew would be a perfect fit in this scene. The trial records with the people's exact wording are available through the National Archives.

The details given about the White House and Lincoln's funeral, including those in attendance, the tickets needed to enter, and all the words spoken by the officiators are as described in various newspapers from the time.

Though the term "post-traumatic stress disorder" had not yet been realized, soldiers from the Civil War nonetheless suffered from its effects. The use of alcohol and the nightmares and panic attacks George and Matthew face are things soldiers dealt with.

As with the other books, the quotes at the top of each chapter are direct quotes taken from various historical accounts.

I sincerely hope you enjoyed this trip back in time with me, and that my characters' involvement in this tumultuous time in history brought it to life for you.

Acknowledgments

Primarily, I'd like to thank my husband. The year spent writing this series was filled with various trials for our family. He was always there to support me, often by way of dishes I'd forgot to wash and laundry I never managed to fold. He's supported me in every way imaginable, and I don't think this series would have come out without him.

To Linda. What would I do without you? Your sweet spirit and willingness to help me with the rewrite of this series mean more than you know.

One final shout out to all the awesome people involved in the photo shoots and design of the cover. Melissa Harper for costume work and photography and Katie Beth and Mark for a long day in stifling period attire. All of you were a pleasure to work with. Evelyne, thank you for reimagining this series and providing me with beautiful covers.

I'd also like to thank Rich Stevens for his help with the military aspects of this novel. He helped me have a deeper understanding of the post-traumatic stress disorder that plagued soldiers as well as the technicalities of weapons and mannerisms of soldiers during that time. Any inaccuracies or errors are on me.

To the wonderful real family of Rosswood. Mr. Hylander, I would like to thank you for your enthusiasm about this project and for allowing me to feature your beautiful home in my stories.

Books by Stephenia H. McGee

Ironwood Plantation
The Whistle Walk
Heir of Hope
Missing Mercy
*Ironwood Series Set
*Get the entire series at a discounted price

The Accidental Spy Series
*Previously published as The Liberator Series
An Accidental Spy
A Dangerous Performance
A Daring Pursuit
*Accidental Spy Series Set
*Get the entire series at a discounted price

Stand Alone Titles
In His Eyes
Eternity Between Us

Time Travel
Her Place in Time
(Stand alone, but ties to Rosswood from The Accidental Spy Series)
The Hope of Christmas Past
(Stand alone, but ties to Belmont from In His Eyes)

Novellas
The Heart of Home
The Hope of Christmas Past

www.StepheniaMcGee.com
Sign up for my newsletter to be the first to see new cover reveals
and be notified of release dates
New newsletter subscribers receive a free book!
Get yours here
bookhip.com/QCZVKZ

About the Author

Award winning author of Christian historical novels, Stephenia H. McGee writes stories of faith, hope, and healing set in the Deep South. When she's not twirling around in hoop skirts, reading, or sipping sweet tea on the front porch, she's a homeschool mom of two boys, writer, dreamer, and husband spoiler. Visit her at www.StepheniaMcGee.com for books and updates.

Visit her website at www.StepheniaMcGee.com and be sure to sign up for the newsletter to get sneak peeks, behind-the-scenes fun, the occasional recipe, and special giveaways.
Facebook: Stephenia H. McGee, Christian Fiction Author
Twitter: @StepheniaHMcGee
Pinterest: Stephenia H. McGee

Made in the USA
Monee, IL
08 August 2023

40638146R00218